Contents

Prologue

Alan ran through the dark, damp forest. He was tired, cold, and most of all, scared. He had no idea how he had gotten here, nor why he was running. The last thing he remembered was being at home with his mother, safe and warm. Now, he was racing through an unknown woodland as if his life depended on it.

But from what?

His feet pounded against the uneven ground as he wove through the trees. His heartbeat roared in his ears, drowning out everything else. Then, as he slowed to catch his breath, the sounds around him became clearer—the deep, rhythmic pounding of hooves.

The noise sent a fresh wave of panic through him. He remembered now—he was being chased.

Alan had seen the rider before, though only briefly. The figure was large and imposing, clad in dark gray armor that had a dull shine in places. A heavy cloak had concealed most of their face, making it impossible for Alan to tell who—or what—they were. But he knew one thing for certain: they were relentless.

He had made a mistake in slowing down. The delay had allowed his pursuer to gain on him. With renewed urgency, he forced his legs to move faster, even though exhaustion clawed at his body. He knew he couldn't keep this up much longer. The fear was pushing him beyond his limits, but his body wasn't built for this kind of abuse.

Then, his body gave out.

Pain shot through his legs as his feet cramped, and before he could correct himself, he tripped over a root sticking out of the forest floor. He barely had time to gasp before he hit the ground, landing hard on his front. The impact knocked the air from his lungs, leaving him momentarily stunned.

Move! his mind screamed. Get up!

But his body wouldn't cooperate. He struggled to push himself upright, but it was too late.

The rider had caught up.

The massive horse skidded to a stop just inches from him, steam pouring from its nostrils as it let out a deep, menacing grunt. Alan had always liked horses, but this one was different—towering, powerful, and intimidating. A chanfron covered its head, the beaked design giving it an almost bird-like appearance.

Alan's breath came in quick, shallow gasps as he looked up at the rider.

Slowly, the figure raised a hand and threw back their hood. A fierce-looking helmet was revealed, its jagged edges forming something akin to a twisted crown. Alan couldn't see their eyes—the slits in the dark metal visor were too narrow—but in the shadows of the forest, he could have sworn he saw them glowing red.

But it wasn't the helmet that terrified him the most.

It was the sword.

Jagged and broad, the blade gleamed menacingly in the dim light. Fresh crimson blood dripped from the metal, sliding down toward the tip. Alan instinctively tried to scoot backward, but the rider moved the sword downward, blocking his attempt to flee.

The silence between them was heavy, suffocating.

Then, the rider spoke.

Their voice was smooth, almost pleasant to the ear, but their words were filled with a cold, sharp malice.

"I will come for you again in the Red Pine Forest. Be ready to join me, or die."

Alan's breath hitched.

Then, with a swift, fluid motion, the rider raised their sword—and swung.

Chapter One

Rude Awakening

Alan jolted up in bed, his heart pounding wildly as his eyes scanned the room, struggling to adjust. He wiped the sweat from his face with the tangled sheet wrapped around his limbs, but the more he wiped, the more his pores produced. As he calmed down, exhaustion and soreness settled over him. Instinctively, he ran his hands over his body, searching for wounds. He was sure he had been stabbed, yet as his fingers brushed over his skin, he found nothing. Letting out a deep sigh, he allowed his head to fall back onto the pillow.

After taking several deep, calming breaths, Alan turned onto his side and glanced at the clock. The familiar glow of the alarm clock he had owned since childhood stared back at him—4:45 AM. He still had an hour before he needed to get up for school. Knowing he wouldn't fall back asleep, he simply lay there, staring at the ceiling. This had become his routine for the past week.

It had all started Sunday night, after he had gone to bed. At first, his dream had been pleasant—memories of the Renaissance fair from the weekend. This year had been special; for the first time, he, his twin sister Abigail, and his best friend Mei were allowed to compete in several sword-fighting competitions. Naturally, his dreams placed him in a medieval world, a knight in shining armor. But then, the dream shifted. Darkness fell, and suddenly, he was running through a barren forest and swamp, stripped of his armor, wearing only the pajamas he had gone to bed in. When he woke Monday morning, it felt as though he had truly been running all night.

That day at school, he had fallen asleep in study hall—something he never did. After school, he and Abigail had met up with Mei and her younger brother, Tadashi, at The Academy of Historical Martial Arts. Tadashi was a first-year student, but Alan, Abigail, and Mei were in their third. Having grown up in a town known for its Renaissance Festival, most kids took these classes in the hopes of working there when the festival was active. That night, exhausted, Alan had gone straight to bed after dinner and homework.

His second dream had started innocently enough—he and his mom shopping at the grocery store. He had reached for a box of cereal when, suddenly, he was no longer in the store but standing in a cold, dark forest. This time, curiosity took over. He began walking along a narrow path. Ahead, he spotted a rider on horseback. Just as he tried to make out their face, his alarm went off.

Each night since, the dreams had continued. Each time, the forest seemed more real, and each time, he got closer to the mysterious rider. Now, after last night's dream, he wished he had never caught up to them. The experience had felt too real—his body ached as if he had truly been there. Were these just dreams? Or was something else happening?

Reluctantly, Alan swung his legs over the side of the bed. His muscles protested, and his head pounded. Maybe he should convince his mom to let him stay home. But no—today was important. Every year, the school took seniors on a camping trip to Red Pine Forest. He had been looking forward to this trip for months. A hot shower and some pain relievers would have to be enough. He could catch up on sleep during the two-hour bus ride.

He walked to his closet and pulled out a black long-sleeved shirt and blue jeans, tossing them over his shoulder before grabbing fresh socks. As he turned to leave, he hesitated in the doorway, scanning his room. His sanctuary. His walls, painted cobalt blue, were decorated with black-framed movie posters of his favorite fantasy and sci-fi films. Above them, an oak shelf held collectibles from his favorite books and movies. Wooden swords and hand-carved masks adorned the other walls. But his gaze landed on a small shelf near the light switch—his mother's fantasy story. She had written it for him and Abigail when they were little. Abigail had lost interest, but Alan never had. His mother had placed it there so he could always find it. Maybe that was what had been influencing his dreams. Yet, that thought didn't put him at ease.

Shaking off the unease, Alan entered the bathroom he shared with Abigail. They were close—not like most siblings who argued constantly. He grabbed his face wash and toothpaste from the cabinet and fell into his usual morning routine. His body moved on autopilot, scrubbing, brushing, rinsing. As he looked in the mirror, he flashed a toothy grin and muttered, "Good enough."

His damp pajamas reminded him of the night's restlessness. He set them aside and stepped into the shower, letting the hot water soothe his aching muscles. Once dressed, he cleaned up after himself and headed downstairs, knowing Abigail would be waiting for the bathroom.

In the kitchen, he greeted his mother with a hug and a kiss.

"You look exhausted," she noted, concern in her voice. "Even more so than yesterday. Are you feeling okay?"

Alan plopped into a chair, stifling a yawn. "Didn't sleep well again. I must've been tossing and turning all night because I woke up sore, and I have a pounding headache. Can I take something for it?"

His mother retrieved a bottle of pain relievers and a multivitamin. "Take these after you eat. Breakfast is almost ready."

Alan smiled. "What's on the menu?"

"Two eggs over hard, crispy bacon, hash browns, and a big glass of chocolate milk."

His grin widened. "Sounds perfect! Just don't forget my banana."

His mom chuckled. "Of course."

As he ate, he asked, "Is Dad still coming home this weekend? I was hoping he'd be here when we got back."

His mom hesitated before answering. "I spoke to him last night. His project had some setbacks, so he'll be delayed by at least a month."

Alan tried to mask his disappointment. "I don't think Dad wants to be here anymore."

His mother sighed. "Alan, your father loves you and Abigail very much. His job has been hard on him, too. But... he's planning to return to his old job after this project."

Alan's eyes lit up. "Really?"

"Shh," she warned. "It's not official yet. Don't tell your sister."

At that moment, Abigail rushed in. "Good morning, Mom!" She kissed her on the cheek before sitting at the table. "This looks great! I've heard horror stories about camp food."

Their mom smiled. "I packed you both extra goodies, including peanut butter and pita bread, just in case."

After breakfast, they grabbed their backpacks. As they walked outside, they saw Mei and Tadashi saying goodbye to their grandmother.

Mei grinned. "Ready for the camping trip?"

Abigail, eager to claim the best seat on the bus, replied, "Let's go!"

As they walked, Alan's eyes lingered on the house next door. A moving van was parked out front. "I wonder what our new neighbors will be like," he mused.

Then, something else crossed his mind—Avery, their old neighbor, who had vanished without a goodbye.

Mei noticed Alan's sudden silence. "What's wrong?"

Alan hesitated, then quietly told her about his dreams. As he finished, he stopped walking, his face pale. The trees in his dreams whispered... just like the ones at Red Pine Forest.

Chapter Two

The Final Warning

Alan and Mei got in line to be checked off for attendance before a teacher directed them to their assigned bus. The principal had decided to send students directly to the waiting buses rather than to their homerooms, as the drive would take some time.

As Alan stepped onto the bus, Mei finally spoke. "I think you should try to take a nap during the drive. You'll feel better by the time we get there."

Just then, Alan spotted his sister, Abigail, sitting in the front seat, grinning triumphantly. She was clearly pleased with herself for securing her favorite spot.

Abigail moved her backpack, which she had been using to save a seat for her brother, allowing him to sit beside her. Alan sank into the seat with a muttered, "Thanks. At least someone is having a good day."

One of the chaperones for the trip was Mrs. Monk, the school's so-called living fossil. She had been teaching American literature since the school first opened forty years ago. Set in her ways, she could be cranky and abrupt with students, but she made learning enjoyable, which was important.

Standing at the front of the bus, Mrs. Monk attempted to get the students' attention. After three failed attempts to quiet the rowdy crowd, the bus driver reached under his seat and blasted an air horn.

Mrs. Monk jumped nearly three feet in the air before turning to glare at the driver. In her commanding voice, she snapped, "Really, young man? Were you trying to give me a heart attack?"

Without waiting for a response, she turned back to the students, who now sat in stunned silence.

"All right, everyone, now that I have your attention, I need to go over a few things before we head out. First, I would appreciate it if we kept the noise level down. This will be about a two-hour drive. Secondly, I will be your head chaperone for this trip. Other adults will be assisting, and each has been assigned a group of four students. You were each handed an envelope upon boarding. In a moment, you may open it to see your group members for the next three days.

"I expect you to be on your best behavior and follow all the State Park's rules. If anyone is caught breaking rules or causing any kind of disruption, you will be sent home immediately and suspended for three months. You may now open your packets. If you have any questions, raise your hand, and I will come around once we are on the road."

Just then, the bus driver announced over the speaker that they were pulling out and reminded everyone to remain seated, with only Mrs. Monk permitted to move around.

Alan opened his packet, and the first thing he saw made him smile. He had been grouped with his sister, Mei, and Tadashi. This was going to be an awesome field trip. He had other friends, of course, but none he felt comfortable sharing a cabin with.

Abigail elbowed him excitedly, shoving her paper in his face. "Ow! What is it?" he asked.

"Look at who our chaperone is! It's Avery A. Do you think the 'A' stands for Ambrose?"

Alan read the paper over and over. He couldn't believe it. He had just been thinking about Avery Ambrose that morning—was this really just a coincidence? Somehow, it didn't feel like one. He raised his hand to ask Mrs. Monk about it.

After answering an endless stream of questions from Helga Lindspot, Mrs. Monk finally turned to Alan. "Yes, Alan? What can I help you with?"

"Our chaperone is listed as Avery A. Is that Avery Ambrose? The Avery Ambrose who was my neighbor? The one who teaches American History at the college?"

Mrs. Monk scowled. "I don't have time for this. I have never taught at the college, nor do I live in your neighborhood. Yes, his name is Avery Ambrose. He's filling in for Mr. Isaac while he's on medical leave. Apparently, he claims he was attacked by smoke. Personally, I think he was on drugs and fell down a hill."

Muttering to herself, she moved on to another student.

Alan turned to Abigail. "Hey, I'm exhausted. Do you mind switching seats so I can rest against the window?"

Abigail was happy to swap, as it meant she could chat with her friends across the aisle.

After twenty minutes of staring at nothing but trees, Alan succumbed to exhaustion and fell into a deep sleep.

Once again, he found himself in the strange, dead world from his nightmares. The air turned cold, and a familiar presence lingered nearby. Suddenly, a voice echoed through the darkness. "You are almost here. I hope you are ready to join me. Do not take my warning lightly."

Alan turned toward the voice and saw the same helmed figure as before. This time, his sword was clean, and his cloak was gone, revealing segmented metal armor with jagged shoulder pauldrons.

Alan felt his knees tremble as sweat formed on his brow. With a dry, shaky voice, he asked, "Who are you?"

A chilling silence filled the air. Alan felt something twisted lurking behind the man's mask, something soulless.

Finally, the man replied, "Who am I? Oh, deep down past all that fear you feel in my presence... I am simply... a friend. A friend to you, Abigail, Mei, and Tadashi. A friend who seeks to protect you from a terrible, terrible burden."

Alan's breath caught as the man continued. "I warned you not to come to Red Pine for your own good, yet here you are. So, once more, I say: be ready to join me."

Alan gulped. "What's your name?"

The man chuckled darkly. "My name isn't important. But for now, you may call me a name I detest—a name given to me by those who misunderstand me. You may call me... the Shadow-Lord."

Alan took a step back, then turned and ran through the dead forest.

"Oh, not this again," the Shadow-Lord muttered before calling out, "Don't go that way!"

Alan glanced back. The Shadow-Lord wasn't chasing him, just standing still. But as Alan looked ahead, a black cloud of smoke moved toward him. His eyes widened in horror as a mouth formed within the cloud, opening to devour him.

Alan's body jolted violently, slamming his head against the bus window. Gasping, he frantically patted himself down. No bite marks. No wounds. It wasn't real... was it?

Abigail, startled, shot him an annoyed look. "Dude, what is wrong with you?"

Alan scanned the bus, ensuring everything was normal before shakily replying, "Yeah, just woke up too quick."

As the bus came to a stop, Abigail eagerly called for Mei and Tadashi to stick together. Alan remained seated until Mei yelled in his ear, snapping him out of his daze.

"It's those dreams again," he muttered as they exited the bus. "This time, he called himself the Shadow-Lord. He told me to be ready to join him."

Mei raised an eyebrow. "You mean like what Mrs. Monk said about Mr. Isaac?"

Alan nodded. "Maybe it's just my imagination... or maybe it's something else. Something crazier."

Mei was about to ask what he meant by that but had to refrain from doing so, as Mrs. Monk was starting to speak to their group.

Chapter Three

Avery Ambrose

Alan and Mei went to stand next to Tadashi and Abigail. As Alan looked around, he took in his surroundings—a dense forest filled with a variety of coniferous trees rising high above them.

Off to the side of the gravel parking lot stood a large sign reading "Red Pine Forest." Next to it was a smaller sign that appeared to show a map, though from this distance, he couldn't make it out. What gave Alan some comfort was the fact that nothing resembled the forest from his nightmare.

Alan didn't remember the times his parents had brought his sister and him here—it had been before either of them could walk. They had talked about coming back now that they were older, but with Dad being away so much, they had never gotten around to it. His mom had been right, though—this place was beautiful. The trees displayed a stunning array of fall colors. Only the evergreens remained green, contrasting against the oranges, reds, and yellows. The clear blue sky, dotted with a few fluffy white clouds, added to the scenery's charm.

Abigail nudged Alan's arm. "Hey, have you seen Avery anywhere yet?

"Maybe it isn't the Avery Ambrose we know. If it was, I'd have thought he'd come to find us by now. He was always punctual. And seeing how the other chaperones are already pairing off with their groups, this Avery Ambrose seems to be taking his good old time."

"No, I haven't seen him yet... If I had, I would've walked over to him. But I'm getting the sinking feeling you might be right—this may not be the Avery we knew." Alan glanced toward Mrs. Monk, who was once again trying to get everyone's attention. However, the thought of finding out whether their chaperone was the Avery he knew consumed him, and he chose to ignore her, scanning the area instead.

After a few minutes of searching, he finally spotted their chaperone. It was indeed Avery Ambrose, emerging from what appeared to be the park ranger's office. As Avery approached them, Alan realized it was as if he had never left. He still wore the same utilitarian style of clothing. His hair remained short in a military-esque style, accompanied by a neatly trimmed uniform beard. However, there was more white than gray in his hair now, and deep wrinkles lined his eyes—signs of aging, perhaps, but more likely a result of the stress Avery had endured.

Mei noticed Alan wasn't listening to Mrs. Monk, who had called his name several times. She was clearly getting irritated by his lack of attention. Mei punched Alan in the arm, causing him to turn toward her. That was when she noticed the big grin spreading across his face.

Mei shook her head. "I don't know what's up with you. One minute you're freaked out by a dream, and the next you're grinning like a kid who just got a puppy. Whatever it is, you'd better answer Mrs. Monk, or else you're going to be sent home before this trip even begins."

Alan quickly turned to Mrs. Monk. "I'm sorry, Mrs. Monk. I was just taking in the view. You have my undivided attention."

The other kids snickered at his apology, and Mrs. Monk simply shook her head before continuing to call out the rest of the students' names.

Once Alan was sure Mrs. Monk was no longer paying him any attention, he grabbed Mei's head and turned it toward Avery. "Look! Avery is over there!" he said excitedly.

Before he could say another word, Abigail took off running toward Avery. She didn't seem to care whether Mrs. Monk got mad or not. Alan quickly followed her lead.

As he got closer, he pushed past his sister and hugged Mr. Ambrose. "Hi, Avery! We were so excited to hear you were going to be our chaperone this week!"

Avery smiled and pulled away from the hug. "Wait a minute now—let me have a good look at you all." He studied them carefully. "Alan, you've gotten so tall. And Abigail, you too. Mei, you're the spitting image of your grandma. And Tadashi, I see you're still excelling in school. You were always a bright kid, skipping kindergarten and first grade."

Tadashi grinned. "Yeah, it feels good knowing I'll be the class valedictorian—even though I'm two years younger than everyone else in the class. They never stood a chance. I almost feel bad for them."

Avery chuckled. "I was happy when Principal Adler asked me to chaperone this field trip. I just recently moved back to the area and heard they needed a substitute history teacher. I saw this as a great opportunity to get to know some of the students. Of course, when I saw your names on the sign-up sheet, I jumped at the chance."

His smile faltered slightly. "To be honest, I'm surprised by how happy you all are to see me. I thought you might still be upset with me after all these years. I hope you can accept my apology. I've truly missed you all."

Alan spoke for the group. "To be honest, we were all disappointed when you up and vanished. But as we got older, we realized how hard it must have been for you. We never believed you hit that kid, but we were surprised you never stuck around to clear your name. I'm glad the school board finally did. And I think we all agree—having you back in Rumford is the best thing to happen this year."

Avery smiled. "I was very emotional at the time. They fired me first, then decided to investigate. That's one reason why I chose to teach at Rumford High instead of going back to the college." He shook his head. "That's old news, though. Let's focus on the field trip now."

Alan grinned. "It's just good to see you again."

Avery cleared his throat and straightened his posture. "We'll be assigned to Oak Moose Cabin. So grab your packs, and we'll head out. It's a bit of a hike to get there, but after that long bus ride, I'm sure stretching your legs will feel nice."

As the rest of the group chattered excitedly, Alan just shook his head. He wasn't looking forward to the hike, not after his restless night. But he'd do his best to ignore his exhaustion and enjoy the time with his friends.

Once the teens settled down, Avery gestured toward the sign Alan had noticed earlier. It was a map of the forest. "We won't need to worry about following the map. The route we're taking is an old one, not pictured here—we'll be in uncharted territory."

He laughed as he said that, then quickly added, "Don't worry, I know my way around these woods."

Alan noticed that the path Avery led them down seemed darker than the others. As they walked, the shadows only deepened. A nagging sense of unease crept in. "Aren't all the cabins near one another? Why are the other kids heading in the opposite direction?"

Avery put an arm around Alan's shoulder. "Don't worry, Alan. I just know a shortcut. And while it took some convincing, Mrs. Monk and I have a little bet going on—who can get their group to the cabins first. This route may be more adventurous, but it's quicker."

Alan wasn't sure he liked the sound of that.

Chapter Four

The Quest Begins

Alan and the others followed Avery deeper into the forest. As they walked, Alan let himself fall back so he was walking with Abigail. He wanted to ask her if she thought something was off. When he felt they were far enough from Avery that he wouldn't overhear, he asked, "Hey, don't you think something feels wrong about all this? It seems a bit strange to me. I mean, Mrs. Monk was very specific about staying close to the group. She even said we'd get detention for not following the rules. And now, she's making bets with Avery—who she herself said doesn't know. That seems so out of character for her."

Abigail laughed and shook her head. "You're overthinking things. What you need is to get some sleep tonight."

Alan shoved his sister. "Whatever. I may not have slept well, but I do know when something feels off, and this is definitely off."

Irritated, Alan moved past Tadashi and joined Mei, hoping she might agree with him and sense that something was wrong with what Avery was doing.

Now that he was closer to Avery, Alan leaned toward Mei's ear so he could whisper his question. "Hey, Mei, does any of this feel off to you?"

Mei didn't answer right away. She continued walking for a few paces before stepping closer to Alan. Then, she whispered back, "I have to admit, it seems like we're heading farther and farther away from everyone else. If we didn't know Mr. Ambrose, I'd be terrified. But we can trust him, right?"

Before Alan had a chance to respond, Avery, who had noticed their hushed whispers, called out, "Hey Alan, come up here and walk with me. We have so much to catch up on."

Alan glanced at his friends, a strange feeling crawling up his spine like something awful was about to happen. He pushed the thought aside and moved to join Avery.

Avery matched Alan's pace and asked, "So, Alan, tell me, how have you been?"

Alan decided that maybe it was just his subconscious trying to protect him from getting too close to Avery again. If he were truly honest, Avery's departure had hurt him deeply.

"I've been doing well," Alan replied. "Keeping busy with my friends, and of course, working hard at school."

Avery smiled. "That's the simple answer. But tell me, what have you been up to since I left? You and the others were interested in astronomy. Do you still stargaze?"

Alan thought back to their nightly adventures watching the stars. A smile tugged at his lips. "Not really. We still like to watch the sky at night and go camping over summer breaks—when we're not working at the Renaissance fair. But mostly, the four of us are involved in our HEMA club. Ten years is a lot of time to fill you in on—we've done a lot of different things."

Avery nodded. "So, do you have a love for archaeology? Are you planning on following in your father's footsteps?"

Alan thought it over. "I haven't decided yet. I figure I still have a few months to think about that stuff. For now, I just want to keep my options open. I want to make sure I enjoy whatever I choose. One thing I do know is that I don't want a job that keeps me away from my family. Writing is my true love, so I'm leaning toward using that in my career."

Avery frowned. "Has something changed with your father's occupation? Does he no longer teach at the college?"

Alan didn't want to talk about that. Yes, he was proud of his dad for doing well in his career, but he also felt his father had given too much of himself and his time to his current job. But all that would hopefully change soon, so he answered politely and steered the conversation back to Avery. "No, he chose to put his archaeology knowledge to work instead of teaching. He's currently working on a project somewhere far away. I can't even remember the name of the town. But if I may ask, what happened to you? Where did you go when you left here?"

Avery seemed to want to pursue his line of questioning but paused and answered anyway. "I hope you'll never experience humiliation like I did. The fact that I was accused of something completely out of character was devastating. What made it worse... what made me leave... was being fired on the spot. They didn't even listen to my side of the story. They just took the word of that young man because his father donated a lot of money to the athletic program each year. Months later, I learned that your father and a few other professors had proven that I didn't touch that student, and they had cleared the way for me to be reinstated. But it was too late. I had already moved on, and I believe it all happened the way it should have. You see, it gave me time to look at my life more closely. I saw why my daughter hated me so much. I was ashamed of how I treated her, and I went to repair that relationship."

Alan remembered his mom telling him about Agnes. His father had gone to school with her. They had been good friends until high school, when Agnes went to a vocational school and lost touch. "So, did you fix your relationship with her?"

Avery stopped and turned to face Alan. "Yes, for the most part, I did. The underlying hurt I caused her is still there. She's always waiting for me to disappoint her again. But enough about that. I want you to know that I thought about the four of you often. I missed our talks and adventures. But moving on is part of life."

Alan cocked his head to the side. "If you moved on, then why did you come back?"

"Well, Alan, the answer is simple now. Now that my relationship with my daughter is in a better place, I felt it was time to return to the life I once enjoyed here. I missed being able to visit this forest and see all the people I used to be friends with. Not to mention, I wanted to taste Ms. Cornwall's homemade apple pie again. And... well... I truly missed all of you."

Avery waited for the rest of the group to catch up. "We'll stop here and rest for a couple of minutes. We're halfway to the cabin, only two more miles to go. I think we've been making great time—it's only 10:30, and I'm sure the other groups aren't as far along as we are."

Abigail pulled out her cell phone and shouted at it. "Really? In this modern age of cell towers, and no reception? This stinks!"

Avery walked over to her. "Abigail, you're surrounded by nature. You should be enjoying that, not distracted by electronics. Put the phone away—there's no service here anyway. Nothing's that important that it can't wait until we return in a few days."

Avery walked over to a rock and sat down, leaving the rest of the group to talk in private. Abigail nudged Alan in the arm, a habit she had. "So, the three of us think you might be onto something. Tadashi studied a map of the area before we left this morning. He says the main cabin area is miles in the other direction. This path is taking us further toward the mountain range."

Alan thought it over. Tadashi had an impressive ability to memorize information, and if he said they were headed the wrong way, Alan believed him. But the more he talked with Avery, the more he convinced himself that everything was fine and he'd been wrong to suspect anything. "Why would he lead us all the way out here then?

Maybe this place has changed since the map you read was made. I guess we'll know for sure in two miles. Let's keep moving, and we'll find out."

The group grabbed their things and approached Avery, ready to continue. Alan fell into pace alongside him. As they walked, he noticed a sign that read, "No Hiking Beyond This Point." Alan quickly glanced back at Mei, wanting to get her attention, but Avery noticed the change in Alan and interrupted.

"Is everything okay, Alan? You seem worried all of a sudden."

Alan hesitated. Panic wasn't something that came naturally to him, but the combination of the strange dreams he'd been having and the sign about no hiking had him on edge. They were far away from the rest of the group now, and that made him uneasy. He pushed the thought aside. It was just Avery—not a serial killer.

Avery, sensing Alan's hesitation, grinned. "Let me guess—it's girl trouble, and the girl is Mei."

That snapped Alan out of his stupor. "What? Oh, no, no, no. Mei and I are just close friends. Dating her would be as weird as dating a blood relative. Besides, I'm too young to be dealing with all that relationship stuff."

Avery chuckled. "Good for you. Not rushing into relationships. Not that I regret marrying Marion just a few months after we turned eighteen, but I'm saying... caution should be exercised when it comes to romance."

Alan nodded. "Yeah, it's a mix of caution and disinterest. Just haven't met the right girl yet. Plus, I'm stressed out enough without adding that to the mix."

Avery glanced at him. "Tell me, Alan, what's weighing on your shoulders that stresses you so much?"

Alan debated whether to tell Avery about the dreams. He didn't want his old teacher and friend to think he was crazy. Years ago, Avery had been their neighbor and often babysat them while their parents went out, which is how the kids had become so close to him. For Alan, Avery had been like the grandfather he never had.

After a few seconds, Alan decided to share. He didn't want to make a big deal of it, though. "It's not that big of a deal, really. But I've been having some bizarre dreams—almost too real—and they've got me on edge. No, that's not exactly true. They've got me completely terrified. And then you take us away from the rest of the kids and Mrs. Monk, and I see this 'No Hiking' sign... I guess you can see how that has me freaked out."

Avery smiled. "Oh, that old sign? Don't worry about it. It's been there for years. Nobody ever pays attention to it. But what does concern me are these dreams of yours. Tell me more."

Alan still wasn't sure about the direction they were headed in, but he brushed it off. It was probably just his imagination. He explained, "There's this cloaked figure that chases me, threatens me, and at one point it felt like he killed me. Then there's this black cloud of smoke that... eats me."

Alan saw what looked like a smirk on Avery's face, and he quickly added, "No, really. I woke up feeling like I had been eaten. That's why I'm so tired and not myself. I can't stop thinking about it, and it scares me to even think about falling asleep again. It's not like it happened only once—these dreams started a few days ago, and they only get worse."

Avery paused. "Let me think about this for a minute. Start climbing over these rocks while I do."

Alan hadn't noticed the rocks at first and wanted to wait to help Abigail and Mei, but Avery didn't give him a chance. He gave Alan a boost up the small incline.

Avery quickly joined him and put his arm around Alan's shoulders, blocking his view from the rest of the group. Alan tried to look back, but Avery's grip was tight, and soon he was distracted by Avery's questions.

"So, this dream—nightmare, I guess you could call it—had a cloaked man. Did you see his face at all? What kind of threats did he make?"

Alan explained the nightmare in detail, knowing if Avery could help, he needed to know everything. As he spoke, he was on autopilot, not paying attention to his surroundings. When he finished, he was surprised to see they had reached a dead-end. Upon closer inspection, he realized there was a small entrance to a dark cave.

Avery finally released Alan and turned to look behind him. Alan's heart sank. The others were gone. Panic surged through him. Everything he had been questioning earlier came rushing back—his gut instinct had been right: Avery couldn't be trusted.

He quickly turned back to Avery and yelled, "What happened to the others? What did you do? I knew something was off the moment I first saw you! Where are Mrs. Monk and the rest of the class?"

Avery tried to place his hand on Alan's shoulder to calm him, but Alan jerked away, his anger flaring.

"Tell me, tell me now!" Alan demanded.

Avery gave a sinister smile as he finally replied, "I am hurt that you feel you cannot trust me. Know that your friends are safe. I just needed to speak to you in private. I need your help with something, and the others may not understand. Once you hear what this is about, I'll need you to convince them..."

Alan's eyes went wide, but he couldn't grasp anything Avery was saying. All he needed was one answer. With anger and fear building in his chest, he demanded, "What did you do to them, Avery?!"

Avery didn't respond to his question. Instead, he ordered, "Listen to me, Alan. I need you and the others to help me prevent the destruction of not just this world, but another. There are things at play here that are too complex for you to fully comprehend, but trust me when I say, you and your friends are my only hope."

Alan closed his eyes, shaking his head, trying to make sense of what he had just heard. Avery was completely out of his mind. "What in the world are you talking about?"

Avery's patience was running thin. He didn't have much time left. "Look, Alan, I need you to trust me! You may not agree with my methods, but the fate of two worlds is at stake. I'm trying to be civil here, trying to avoid threats of torture to force your obedience. But for your sake and the sake of the others, please, listen to me. If you can't, then I will have to harm you and the others."

Alan stared in shock, his voice shaking as he replied, "It sure sounds like you're threatening us. Bring them to me, and we'll decide together what happens. You won't bully me into doing what you want."

Avery's face twisted with fury. He reached out, grabbing Alan and turning him to shove him forward. "Welcome to your dreams," he sneered.

Alan stumbled, struggling to regain his footing. When he righted himself, he realized the surroundings had changed. Everything was pitch black. "Where are we?" he called out, panic rising in his chest. "You didn't have to do this to us. Why couldn't you have just talked to us?"

Avery's voice came from the darkness, but he was nowhere to be seen. "I would have... but the fact that he has been communicating with you made me realize I must move up my timetable. That's why the Mist attacked you— to sever the connection between you and the Shadow-Lord, so I could have a chance to speak with you."

Suddenly, Avery appeared, a torch in hand. Alan could now see they were in a short tunnel that led to a large, rocky room. Avery used the flame to light more torches. As he did, Alan looked across the room and saw his friends—hanging from the walls by what appeared to be tree roots, their heads drooping and motionless. Alan's heart stopped. "Abigail! Abigail, answer me!"

When no response came, he ran forward, pulling on the roots that held Abigail in place. Nothing budged. He yelled in a panic, "Why won't you break apart? Let go of my sister! Avery, what did you do to them?!"

Before he could get an answer, a loud explosion rocked the air nearby, followed by a thick wall of smoke. Alan coughed, eyes stinging, his chest burning. He squeezed his eyes shut, trying to stop the pain. Then, just as quickly as it had appeared, the smoke cleared, and Alan took a clean breath of air. When he opened his eyes again, he was alone with Abigail and the others. "Avery? Where did you go?"

"Looking for someone?" A deep, loud voice filled the air, and Alan froze. He knew that voice—Shadow-Lord. Fear surged through him.

He slowly turned to his right, dreading the confrontation. And there, standing in front of him, was the same menacing figure, now wearing the mask Alan had first seen him with. Alan had to be strong; any weakness would only give Shadow-Lord an advantage. But there was no fooling him.

Shadow-Lord slowly walked toward Abigail and the others. Alan found his voice and shouted, "Don't touch them!"

Shadow-Lord turned, his gaze piercing Alan. "You don't want me to help get them down?"

Alan was beyond confused. Avery had betrayed them, but now Shadow-Lord, the very being who had threatened him in his dreams, was offering help. How could this be happening?

Alan slapped himself in the face, trying to wake up. This had to be a dream. He hit himself over and over, but nothing changed. This was real.

Shadow-Lord's calm voice broke through his frustration. "You really must stop hitting yourself. This is not a dream like the others. You are standing before me in the flesh."

Alan's confusion deepened. "Why would you help me now? The last time you appeared to me, you threatened me... you had that Mist eat me."

Shadow-Lord replied coolly, "I told you before, I am your friend. And as for the Mist, I believe Ambrose is the one who used it against you, but I understand in your panic you missed that detail. As for why I'm here, it's because I need your help to defeat Avery Ambrose."

Alan blinked in disbelief. "Avery wants our help, and you want ours? No one's telling us what's going on. And let me be clear—the way you both have approached us makes no sense. People don't threaten others when they ask for help! All the fear, the stress, the threats—it's too much. And now I'm supposed to forget all that and just help you?"

Shadow-Lord paused, as if considering his words. "I overheard Avery's explanation to you. You resisted him out of fear for your friends. So, I intervened, using a spell to send him away."

Alan shook his head, trying to make sense of it. "Spell? Magic? If you want to defeat him, why not just attack him here? Why send him away?"

Shadow-Lord sighed. "My magic is strong, but Avery's is far greater. If I hadn't caught him off guard, he'd have countered my attack with something far more painful. But now is not the time for that discussion. Let me get the others down first."

Alan hesitated but eventually relented. If Shadow-Lord was going to release them, who was he to interfere?

"Alright... Fine. But that doesn't mean I trust you."

Shadow-Lord raised his hand. With a flick of his wrist, Abigail, Mei, and Tadashi fell slowly to the ground. They groaned and moaned as they recovered. Alan rushed to Abigail's side, rubbing her back. "You're all alright now. At least I think we're alright. Avery lied to us and led us here, but that's the least of our problems. Shadow-Lord, the guy from my dreams, is here. He claims to need our help, and I guess I better let him explain because I don't know any more than that."

Tadashi, still shocked, stared at Shadow-Lord. "A guy from your dreams? Why am I just hearing about this?"

Shadow-Lord's deep voice startled him. He jumped back as the man began to speak.

"Alan can explain later. That's unimportant now. What matters is that you help me stop Avery Ambrose from destroying this world... and possibly your own."

Tadashi looked at the others, panic creeping into his voice. "This world? Our world? What do you mean? Where are we?"

"When you passed through the cave entrance, you were transported to a different world. Ten billion lightyears away from your home. There's no way to return without Avery. But once we succeed, I can help you return home."

Alan stepped forward, his voice firm. "No. You and Avery don't get to bully us into this. Before we do anything else, you need to explain how you know Avery, why he's trying to destroy your world, and how all of this is possible. You need to explain why you've been terrorizing me in my dreams."

Shadow-Lord's mask flared with a deep red glow, his temper rising. He took a slow breath, forcing himself to calm. He needed them to cooperate.

"Appearing in your dreams was the only way I could get your attention," he said quietly. "The spell caused me great strain and pain... so I wasn't at my best. I apologize. But I knew Avery's plan involved finding you at Red Pine Forest, and I had to intercept it, to have a chance to speak with you."

He paused, continuing after a moment. "I've been following Avery for some time. I didn't expect him to bring you here so forcefully. I thought he had more humanity than that. But when I saw you resist him, I knew I had to step in to protect you. Now, if you help me, you can return to your world unharmed."

The teens exchanged confused glances.

"This is all so unbelievable," Alan muttered. "Maybe I'm in a coma, and this is some twisted dream."

Shadow-Lord sighed. "You're not in a coma. This is real. Avery believes two of you possess something he needs, not an object, but a power. I need to know if that's true, so I must test you."

Abigail frowned. "Why not just tell us what you need? We can tell you if we have the ability or not. That would save you time."

Shadow-Lord gave her a stern look. "Your world has a broken connection to magic. You won't be aware of the abilities... you must be tested."

Abigail tilted her head. "You still haven't explained anything."

Shadow-Lord nodded slowly. "Yes, there's much to explain. But first, understand this: Avery and I are both powerful magic users. The difference is, he's using his to destroy both our world and yours. I stand against him, and he wants to destroy me in return."

He paused again. "Meet me at the Grotto of Life. There's a Great Cherry Blossom Tree inside. That's where I'll explain further."

Alan nodded. "Are you going to give us a map?"

Shadow-Lord exhaled. "No, I won't give you a map. You must navigate on your own. That's part of the test. I need to see how well you work together and how well you make decisions. Only then will I know if you have the skills—and the magic—needed to stop Avery."

He turned toward the rubble in the back of the cave, scanning the shadows. After a moment, he returned to the teens. "Choosing the wrong path will only delay you. The horrors you'll face along the way will test you. But you need to experience it to understand what I need."

Alan looked at the others. This was no longer the adventure they thought it was. They were in this for real now.

Before Shadow-Lord disappeared, he called out, "Head North to reach the Grotto. Don't stray. It will be a long journey, but you need to experience it to learn what's at stake."

Chapter Five

The Forest

The teens stood in stunned silence, still processing what they had just heard from Shadow-Lord.

After a few moments, Alan broke the silence. "I guess we'd better get moving. We can't just stand here, hoping this problem will go away. We need to figure out what's required of us so this nightmare can end. Let's spread out and search for an exit. Everyone, grab a torch from the wall."

But Abigail didn't move. "Seriously? You're just going to accept this? We've not only been kidnapped, but now we're in some other world? How can you be so calm, Alan?!"

Alan let out a low, humorless chuckle. "Calm? Do you really think I'm calm? No, I'm anything but calm, Abigail. This situation is unbelievable, but I know this isn't a dream. Not anymore. This is real, so... we have to keep moving. We can't stop and think about it—if we do, we might not survive whatever comes next. We need to focus and work together."

With that, they each grabbed their backpacks and began searching in different directions.

A few minutes later, Mei called out, "Hey, I found something. It looks like a crumbling archway. It doesn't seem like a natural formation... It's got tree roots around it, and they look dead. Beyond it, I can see sunlight—or maybe it's another torch. Either way, it might be the way out."

As they crossed through the archway, they emerged into a forest, but it was nothing like the Red Pine Forest they'd left behind. The reality that Shadow-Lord had been telling the truth—that they were no longer on Earth—became unmistakable.

Alan looked up at the bright blue sky and noticed something that made his heart skip: two moons. That alone should've been a clear sign, but it wasn't until Abigail called out to him, "Alan, look to your left!" that he realized for sure they were in an entirely different world. The trees no longer resembled the ones from Red Pine Forest. They were gray and leafless, with empty, brittle branches. Some had looked charred before they entered the cave, but now every tree seemed dead. The ground was rocky and black, and there were pools of bubbling red liquid scattered around. Alan had never seen anything like it. The liquid wasn't thick like lava—it was thin and translucent. Curious, he took a step toward one of the pools, but Abigail pulled him back. "Don't, Alan. We don't know what that is."

Tadashi, ever the pragmatist, voiced the obvious question: "How is this even possible? How did we travel all those billions of light years using magic?"

Alan turned to him and replied, "I don't know the answer to that, but it seems we're really in Shadow-Lord's world now. The cave must have acted as a portal. If we find this Grotto and do what he asks, we should be able to go home."

He could see the unease in his friends' eyes; it mirrored his own. Taking a deep breath, he added, "We can do this. I know you're all scared—I am too—but I also know we have the strength and courage to get through this."

Abigail, trying to be as convincing as possible, nodded. "I agree with Alan. We can do this."

Tadashi and Mei exchanged glances, and then Tadashi spoke. "Alright, we're in."

Alan took a step forward. "Okay, the first decision we need to make is how to find this cherry tree. Does anyone know which way is north?"

Tadashi spoke up. "Actually, we're looking for a cherry blossom tree. They're ornamental and have beautiful pink flowers. A regular cherry tree produces edible fruit, has white flowers, and isn't very decorative. Also, the cherry blossom is a symbol of many things in my culture."

Alan facepalmed. "Really? You just had to get technical, didn't you? Can we please just refer to it as a cherry tree from now on, for simplicity?"

Tadashi smiled. "Simple it is."

Everyone laughed, but Mei then chimed in. "If we look hard enough, we might find clues in the nature around us. Remember, Shadow-Lord said there could be clues to help along the way. Let's start looking. I'll take the left, Abigail, you take the right, and you two—" she pointed at Alan and Tadashi, "—can check the opposite sides."

Alan was relieved to be heading toward the bubbling red liquid. He still wanted a closer look. He found a stick on the ground and poked it into one of the pools.

When he tried to pull the stick back out, the part that had been submerged was gone. It had disintegrated. He called out, "Uh, guys, just so you know, this red stuff is corrosive. We need to be careful around it."

Abigail shook her head, exasperated. "What made you think a strange, red, bubbling liquid would be safe anyway? Come on, we need to find moss or spider webs to figure out which way is north. That's the only way I know how to do it without a compass. Actually... wait, I can use the compass app on my phone. It doesn't need the internet."

Tadashi quickly squashed that idea. "You can try, but I wouldn't bet on it. I'm pretty sure the portal fried our phones. There was probably some kind of electrical interference when we passed through."

Abigail tried turning her phone on and frowned when nothing happened. "I was hoping Mr. Brainiac was wrong... but it looks like our phones are useless now. Ugh! Does this mean we've lost all our pictures? I never backed them up."

Tadashi patted her on the back. "Don't you save them to the cloud?"

Abigail sighed. "No, I used up all the space my provider gave me."

Mei rolled her eyes. "Seriously? We're on a completely different planet, and all you can think about are your pictures?"

Abigail nodded. "Yeah, you're right. We've got bigger problems right now than worrying about cat and dog memes."

The group refocused on their task, each searching for anything that could help them. After a few more minutes, Abigail called out, "I don't see any moss or spider webs here—just some strange amber-colored sap that seems to harden as it seeps from the trees."

Alan replied, "I've seen the same thing over here. It's strange, but I haven't noticed any insects. Normally, we'd see tons of bugs by now."

Tadashi called out, "Does black, furry fungus count as moss on this planet? There's a lot of it on these trees, but if you look closely, it's only on the right sides. So, using Earth logic, we should go right."

Mei agreed. "That sounds good to me."

Abigail and Alan nodded, and the group headed to the right, carefully avoiding the red liquid. Soon, they found themselves in an area with several large rocks and what appeared to be a dried-up creek bed. The stones were worn smooth, as if they had once been part of a river.

"Look," Alan pointed ahead, "Do you see that rock pillar? Does anyone else think it looks like Shadow-Lord's helmet?"

Mei squinted at the rock formation. "Now that you mention it... I guess it does. Maybe we should take a closer look."

As they neared the formation, they saw that it wasn't just a single rock, but many stacked together to form what could only be a statue of Shadow-Lord.

Tadashi asked, "So, is this one of the clues he was talking about?"

They decided to take a break. They'd been moving nonstop since leaving the cave, and while they'd made some progress, it was best to think things through before moving on.

As they rested, Abigail surveyed the surroundings. "Look over there," she said, pointing. "It looks like more of that amber liquid. I wonder what it is, or what it does."

Mei laughed. "Now you sound like Alan. I think we should avoid all strange substances as best we can. But it is in the direction we think is north, so maybe we should just keep heading that way."

The others agreed, and they continued walking. It wasn't long before Tadashi's voice rang out, frantic. "Mei, don't move! There's a giant, hairy, blue caterpillar thing on your back. And when I say giant, I mean giant!"

Alan and Abigail ran over to help, but Mei just clamped her lips shut. "Tadashi, can you just grab a stick and flick it off me?"

Tadashi didn't move. "I don't think a stick is going to work. It looks like a caterpillar, but it's the size of your backpack! I didn't notice it at first because I thought it was your backpack, but then I remembered your backpack is orange."

Once Alan and Abigail reached Mei, they both gasped in shock. Abigail tried her best not to scream, squeezing her lips together in an attempt to control her fear for her friend.

Alan observed the giant insect with a level of fascination that most would reserve for something awe-inspiring. He wasn't afraid or shocked—he was curious. He always had been, especially when it came to unfamiliar creatures. To him, it was amazing to see something so different.

He approached Mei's back cautiously, squatting down for a closer look. The more he examined the bug, the more he realized it wasn't just one large insect, but a whole family huddling together.

Mei's patience was clearly wearing thin, and her voice trembled with irritation. "Alan, will you please do something already? I need to move."

Alan pondered the safest way to remove her backpack without disturbing the creatures. He didn't know whether they'd bite or not. "The good news is, it's not a giant caterpillar," he said, "but rather an army of strange blue insects. When you're ready, shrug off your backpack quickly and run forward. Tadashi and I will use sticks to keep them focused on the pack."

Mei didn't hesitate to act. She did as Alan suggested, freeing herself from her backpack. The insects stayed clumped on the pack, oblivious to being tossed aside.

The other three examined the situation as Alan moved back toward their starting point.

"I figured it out," Alan said, turning to the group. "The insects were attracted to your backpack because of the color. If you look closely, the amber liquid we saw earlier—that's where they're feeding."

Mei shivered from head to toe, making sure none of the insects remained on her. "Okay, I know you're fascinated by them, but can you please get my backpack away from those things? I'll need my stuff later, especially the food."

Abigail grabbed a stick and, with the boys, began knocking the insects away. It was tough work, since the insects kept returning to the backpack. Tadashi came up with a new idea. "Alan, help me move that big log over there. If we place it near the pack, maybe they'll leave it alone."

They managed to get the insects off the backpack and moved on, heading in what they believed to be the northern direction.

As they walked, Tadashi kept his eyes focused on the ground. He wasn't sure what he was looking for, but it made him feel safer to concentrate on the terrain. He didn't enjoy bugs or anything that crawled, and certainly didn't want to encounter more.

It was this focus that led him to spot their next clue. A collection of sticks scattered on the forest floor looked strangely like a stick figure, one that seemed to be pointing in a direction. He called everyone over to take a look.

"Nice catch, Tadashi," Mei said, impressed. Alan kneeled to examine it further. As he studied the arrangement, he frowned. "Wait—these aren't sticks. These are bones... It's a skeleton of some kind."

Abigail moved some black vines to get a better look and uncovered a skull. Like the rest of the bones, it was much larger than that of any human or gorilla.

Mei followed the shape of the skeleton and noted that the hand was pointing across the clearing.

Alan and Abigail exchanged a glance, silently acknowledging the gravity of their situation. Neither of them wanted to voice it aloud, as if doing so might somehow make it more real.

Mei's voice trembled as she tried to steady her nerves. "We need to find that cherry tree, and we need to do it fast."

Everyone agreed, and they continued on their way. It wasn't long before they reached the edge of the forest. Ahead of them was a clearing of about twenty feet. On the other side, a thin grey fog shrouded some dark green bushes and trees. Alan noticed a gravel path cutting across the clearing and leading into the mist. That's where he led the others.

As they entered the fog, they realized they had entered a swamp. Instead of the red, bubbling pools from earlier, there was thick, stagnant green water surrounding the path. Dead trees rose out of the water in various shapes and sizes.

Alan paused, and everyone else had to stop behind him. "We need to be careful here," he warned. "We don't know what's in the water, and we have no idea how deep it is, so watch your step."

They all nodded, and Alan could see the same fear in their eyes that he felt inside. "I'll lead the way. Tadashi, you stay behind me. Mei, watch his back. And Abigail, you take up the rear."

He met his sister's gaze. Without saying a word, she understood. They shared that silent bond, a communication only they could understand. His look told her that he trusted her and needed her to stay safe, and she responded with a brief nod, silently telling him to stay careful, too.

As they moved deeper into the swamp, the sounds of nature grew louder. Unlike the silent forest, here they could hear more activity around them, though it was still unsettling.

Tadashi slapped his arm and then his face. "Ow!"

Mei's voice came next. "Ow!"

Abigail reached into her backpack and pulled out a can of bug spray. "Everyone, gather around and hold still!" The swarm of insects that had suddenly appeared dispersed as the spray took effect.

Alan nodded in approval. "Nice thinking, Abs. Are you guys okay? We might need to respray every hour if we're stuck in this swamp too long."

Tadashi and Mei groaned. "These bites itch like crazy," Tadashi muttered. "I took an allergy pill this morning, but it's not helping. You know how allergic I am to bites, but this swelling is worse than usual."

Mei dug into her backpack and pulled out some cream. "Here, Tadashi. Sobo made me pack this just in case." She started rubbing cortisone on his arm. "Did either of you get bit?"

Abigail rubbed her neck. "I got a small bite, but it's nothing too bad."

Alan smirked. "Guess I'm not as sweet as the rest of you. They left me alone." He chuckled.

Abigail rolled her eyes. "Very funny, Alan."

The swamp seemed endless. Massive trees towered on either side of the path, creating an oppressive feeling.

"It's like these trees go on forever," Alan said.

Tadashi marveled at them. "Even the branches are as wide as tree trunks. This place is amazing."

The stagnant water seemed to clear up ahead, and piles of large branches created natural dams, separating the clean water from the murky green.

"They must have beavers here," Abigail said. "Look at how the branches are blocking the water from mixing with the fresh stream."

Alan nodded. "This is a good sign. It's the first evidence we've seen that not everything on this planet is bleak."

The stream led them to a large river, bringing them to a sudden halt.

Tadashi looked at the river and mused, "How are we supposed to get across? I don't think we should try wading through the water—who knows what's living in there."

Mei looked up, then across to the other side. Alan followed her gaze and realized what she was thinking. "You're onto something, Mei. If we can get up to that branch, we could slide across to the other side."

Tadashi and Abigail also looked up, scanning the trees for something that would help them climb.

Alan spotted something. "Look over there. That tree root is wide and flat. If we get up there, I can reach the branch. Once I'm up, I'll pull the rest of you up."

"That could work," Mei agreed. "But how do we get down once we're across?"

Alan squinted at the other side. "I think the branch is lower over there. We might be able to hang from it and drop down safely."

The group discussed it briefly and agreed it was their best option—no one wanted to risk swimming across.

Once they all made it up to the branch, Alan took the lead, slowly scooting across. "Make sure to keep your hands pressed firmly to the limb. It'll help you balance. Move slowly, and stay close to one another in case someone needs help."

The distance across seemed even longer now. "It's about the length of our basement," Alan muttered. "This could take a while."

Mei laughed. "Yep, about fifty feet. I always wished our basement was that big."

Abigail sighed. "At least you two get full access to your basement. Half of ours is Dad's 'territory.' It's a long room, but not wide enough for a pool table."

"Hey, Abigail, remember the time we tried to sneak into Dad's work area? It was the first time he raised his voice at us. Makes you wonder what he's doing in there."

Before Abigail could respond, a sudden shout from Tadashi cut through the air. "Ah!" He slipped off the branch, yelling as he fell into the water below.

"Did he say 'snake'?" Alan asked, his voice tense.

Abigail's face twisted in panic. "Alan, what do I do? There's a giant snake heading toward me!"

Alan quickly moved toward her. "Hang on, Abs, I'm right here."

As he approached, he recognized the type of snake—it looked like one common in their area.

"Hold still, Abs."

Tadashi called up from the other side. "Made it across without a problem, in case anyone was wondering."

Alan had completely forgotten about his friend, but hearing his response gave him the answer to his sister's question. "Alright, slowly back up to where the trunk and branch meet. You should be able to drop down into the water safely from there. It looks like you'll have to swim across."

Abigail wasn't thrilled by the idea but agreed it was their only option. "Fine, but from now on, someone else is taking up the rear."

Once Abigail had successfully descended from the tree, Alan quickly turned around, scooted across, and dropped down to join Mei and Tadashi, who was just finishing his story about how he fell off the branch.

"So here I was, thinking I was reaching for a vine to steady myself, but instead, I pulled that snake down from above."

The three of them turned to watch Abigail swim across the river. It wasn't exactly swimming—more like a panicked crawl—which surprised them, as Abigail was an excellent swimmer.

When she reached the shore, Alan asked, "What was with the flailing?"

"I didn't want to get my hair wet," she replied.

Alan just shook his head. "Come on, everyone. We better get moving."

They walked on in silence. All of them were extremely tired, but no one wanted to be the one to suggest stopping—not here, anyway.

Then, all of a sudden, Alan stopped abruptly. He had just heard a loud clicking noise, and it seemed to be getting louder the further they walked.

Tadashi was the first to voice what was on everyone's mind. "What do you think is making that sound? I was okay with the hoots, tweets, and occasional howls—it made things feel more normal—but whatever's making this noise sounds awfully big."

Mei added, "And we seem to be getting closer and closer to it."

Abigail spotted a large rock. "Hey, Alan, why don't we let Mei and Tadashi sit this one out, and you and I can go investigate this sound?"

Alan thought it over before replying, "No, I think we should stick together. But maybe they should lag a little behind, just in case we need to turn tail and run."

Everyone covered their ears as they made their way deeper into the swamp. The clicking had become that piercing. Within moments, the noise was replaced by a high-pitched, hysterical scream—not from the girls, but from Alan, who had spotted the grossest thing he had ever seen.

Tadashi moved further back with Mei, while Abigail joined Alan in trying to figure out what they had just come across.

With a gag, she asked, "Oh... jeez... what do you think that thing was?"

Alan's heart was still pounding in his chest and ears as he replied, "I—I don't know. Can't be sure with all those insects swarming it... The skin looks like it might've been green... like an orc or goblin, maybe. Think those exist here?"

Abigail looked a bit closer. "Maybe. I mean, if magic exists, there's a chance other things we know from fairy tales could exist—or at least the things that inspired those stories. You know, those insects are acting like scavengers, eating away what's left of the flesh."

Alan felt like vomiting. Between the scene in front of them, the noise the insects were making, and the putrid smell, he couldn't take much more. He wasn't sure how Abigail could stand looking at it, but then again, she had taken both Honors Biology I and II, so she was accustomed to looking at pictures of gross things.

Abigail led Alan away from the rotting body and quickly moved back to where Mei and Tadashi were waiting. "Insects are feeding on a dead body over there. It was pretty large, and the skin that hadn't been eaten looked green. Might be the same species as that skeleton we saw... I'd guess it's been dead for a few days."

Alan was still shaken by the sight, his voice betraying his unease as he said, "With how large the skeleton and that body were, I wonder how big the thing was that killed it..."

Mei, who hadn't seen it and didn't want to, replied in a shaky voice, "Let's just hope it dropped dead of natural causes."

Alan's anxiety grew, and Abigail could see it not just in his movements but in his entire demeanor. She knew they needed to get moving. "We need to get out of here. There has to be an end to this swamp at some point."

Mei, having been thinking along similar lines, spoke up. "While we were waiting for you two, I spotted a way to get through the swamp without passing the dead thing and still stay on course."

Alan's tension eased a little as he asked, "Where do we need to go?"

Mei led them to an area denser with fog. "You see those logs lying on the ground? They'll take us to that island mass over there. When we first came this way, the fog wasn't as thick, and I remember seeing more logs further up that crossed to this side. I didn't say anything before because the logs are narrow and slippery, and I wasn't sure if we could cross them without falling into the murky water."

Tadashi moved next to his sister, then picked up a small rock and threw it into the swamp at the point where they would have to cross the logs. Alan called out, "What are you doing?"

Tadashi gave a timid laugh. "Just wanted to see if anything popped up out of the water. You know, like a swamp creature."

Alan shook his head. "I doubt there are any swamp creatures around here. In fact, we haven't seen any sign of movement in these waters so far. Let's give this a shot. We'll all feel better once we're out of here."

Mei, ever the cautious one, replied, "Let's just hope there's a way out of here. Who's to say Shadow-Lord was telling us the truth?"

The first log they crossed was at least thirty feet long and barely wide enough for one of their shoes, let alone both. Alan figured out it was best to move their feet from side to side, like a crab, to maintain balance.

Once they reached the other side, they saw visible light breaking through the fog to the east. Now came the decision: they could head that way and turn north later, or continue through the fog and murky waters of the swamp.

Alan called for a vote. "So, who thinks we should go off-course a bit and head that way?"

Mei and Tadashi spoke in unison. "I do."

They laughed at their synchronized response.

Abigail was still weighing the options. "Who knows if we're even on the right path to begin with? I mean, we don't have a map or someone guiding us. It's all been guesswork up until now. I guess it wouldn't hurt to head toward what seems like safer surroundings."

Alan nodded. "Alright then, it's unanimous. We get out of the swamp. And once we do, we need to find a place to sit and rest. I, for one, would like something to eat."

Before they could exit the swamp, they still had to cross one last section of murky water. This time, the only way was by stepping on rocks of various sizes and angles. Alan chose to take up the rear, letting Abigail lead the way.

They had about sixty feet to traverse, but Alan noticed that the further they got from the swamp, the clearer the water became. He spoke loudly so everyone could hear. "The water's getting clearer."

Abigail replied, "That means it has more oxygen in it, which means the chances for aquatic life are higher now than when we were deeper in the swamp."

Just as she finished speaking, the rock under Alan's right foot began to shift, causing him to slip and fall into the water. The loud splash caught everyone's attention. Mei and Tadashi had just joined Abigail on the shore, and Alan had been about twenty feet away, but now he was clearly in trouble.

Alan stood up in the waist-deep water and waved to his friends, laughing off his embarrassment. "I'm okay, the rock just slipped out from under me."

Abigail saw something else first and yelled, "That's not a rock, Alan! Get out of the water now!"

Alan didn't hesitate. He abandoned the rocks and ran through the water, creating small waves around him. Once he reached dry land, he turned around to see what he'd thought was a rock.

Tadashi laughed. "Aww, that thing's so cute! It's like a giant gecko—look at those big eyes!"

Mei yanked him back just in time as the creature opened its mouth, revealing rows of tiny sharp teeth—like a piranha's.

Tadashi quickly scrambled away as Mei called out, "You can stop. They can't come onto dry land. He probably has no feet."

Though the creature could have posed a threat had they still been near the water, the kids couldn't help but laugh at Tadashi's scramble. It was a much-needed moment of humor that helped ease the tension.

They walked further until they found a clearing bordered on three sides by rocky cliffs that rose about thirty feet. The kids took a much-needed break near a few downed trees.

Alan dug through his backpack and pulled out a crunchy peanut butter and chocolate brownie energy bar, saving the corned beef sandwich for later.

Abigail, sitting next to him, ate a blueberry crisp energy bar and sipped from her thermos, which contained a blueberry smoothie. After a moment of silence, she asked, "Do you think anyone is looking for us? Mom's going to go crazy with worry." She offered Alan her thermos.

Alan took a sip of the smoothie. "I promised to text Mom once a night, so she may not think anything's wrong yet, unless Mrs. Monk called her. But yeah, Mom's going to be a handful. I can already see her walloping Mrs. Monk first, then asking questions later."

This made the twins smile. They both loved their dad, but it was their mom they relied on the most since their dad's work kept him away so much. Honestly, the kids wished he would go back to teaching.

Alan was having an internal debate but finally said, "Mom told me something this morning to calm me down about Dad. She said it isn't definite, but Dad's trying to take steps to go back to teaching."

Abigail smiled. "Thanks for telling me. After the day we've had, it gives me hope. Now let's just pray we make it back so we can see them again."

Mei and Tadashi had been having a similar conversation as they ate lunch, which their Sobo had packed. Even though she was their grandma, she'd raised them their whole lives after both of their parents were killed in a house fire when they were very young.

Tadashi said, "I know Sobo is strong-willed, but she'll be worried about us. Not to mention, she relies on us for help too."

Mei wrapped her arm around her brother and gave him a side hug. "Sobo will be fine. I'm sure Alan and Abigail's mom will look in on her."

That made Tadashi smile. He was wrapped around his Sobo's finger, and she was wrapped around his.

Alan yawned and stretched as he stood up, calling out, "If I sit any longer, I'm going to fall asleep. I'm going to climb up the rock face and see what's on the other side. Why don't you guys see if there's an opening in the rocks?"

The hike up the rock face was easy and didn't take long. As Alan walked across the plateau to see the other side, he realized this would not be an easy trek. The other side dropped straight down again, but instead of just rocks, it was interspersed with river-like channels of corrosive red liquid—something they'd encountered earlier in the day.

Staring at the new challenge, Alan headed back down to inform the others. But when he reached the clearing, they were no longer there. A few moments later, he heard Mei's voice calling for him.

"Alan, come over here. We found an entrance to a cave."

It took Alan a moment to spot Mei near some vines. He ran over to her and the others. "Wow, can this place get any more foreboding?"

Abigail replied, "That's what we thought when we first saw this. What does it even mean?"

There was a sign hanging above the narrow cave entrance with unusual symbols carved into it. Alan studied the carving. There were three symbols, none of which seemed to match the others.

Alan shook his head. "I have no clue what it means, but one of the symbols resembles a tree. Maybe it's a signpost. Shadow-Lord did say the symbols would be obscured. The bipedal lizard holding a spear is... just plain weird. I can't tell what meaning that holds. And the spiral, maybe it represents water?"

Tadashi added, "In some cultures, the spiral represents life and death. The tree might represent life too, but as for the lizard with the spear... no clue. Unless he's an ancient hunter. Whatever it means, I agree the tree must be a sign that this is the way to go."

The boys looked to the girls for their opinion, but Abigail scoffed. "Yeah, some choice. We've only got two options: go into the cave or head back into the swamp. Unless, of course, Alan found a way over the rock wall."

"About that," Alan said, "I think, given the three choices, this is the safest bet. The rock wall's not hard to get up, but what I saw on the other side makes me think we should go into the cave."

"I'll go back and grab our backpacks," Tadashi said, not even wanting to know what Alan had seen.

Chapter Six

The Cave

When they first walked through the cave entrance, there was barely enough room for them to fit.

Alan frowned. "I thought you said this was a cave? It seems more like a rocky alcove with very little light."

Tadashi reached into his backpack, pulled out a glow stick, and cracked it. He aimed the light at a hole in the floor near where they were standing. "Look, that's the entrance to the cave. Just stick your head through, and you'll see."

Alan smiled. "You're always so prepared. I never thought to pack one of those."

Mei laughed. "Oh, don't worry. He brought a dozen of them, and they're the long-lasting kind—at least 12 hours of light."

Alan went into the hole first. Once through, Abigail handed him the three back-packs, and soon the rest of them followed.

The cave turned out to have more light than they had first thought. The walls and ceiling, about twenty feet above them, were embedded with crystal-like rocks that helped illuminate their immediate surroundings. They would still need the glow stick to see farther distances, but they were not in total darkness.

Mei noticed two paths they needed to choose from. The path on the right gradually inclined, while the one on the left seemed to lead further underground. Alan didn't stop to ask for anyone's opinion; it just made sense to head up rather than down.

He motioned for Tadashi to hand him the glow stick and led the group through the cave. As they progressed, the path became narrower, and soon they were walking single file.

Alan stopped abruptly, causing Tadashi to bump into him. "Sorry, Tadashi," Alan muttered. "Does anyone else think it's weird how quiet it is?"

Abigail chimed in, "Now that you mention it, we should be hearing an echo when we talk. That's what happens in caves, right? Maybe it just means there's an opening up ahead. Let's take it slow."

Alan continued walking, shining the light toward the ground to see where he was going. After another forty feet, he stopped again, this time holding out his arm to keep anyone from moving forward. "End of the line, guys. We need to turn back. The reason we haven't heard echoes is that the sounds are being absorbed by this massive pool of water. It looks like it goes on forever."

Mei gasped. "This doesn't make any sense. We've been traveling upward. How is there water above where we were? If we turn back and take the other path, won't we just run into the water?"

"I agree, it's strange," Abigail replied. "But I think it has to do with the rocks. If that were the case, the tunnels would be flooded. Maybe it's just an illusion, or maybe this chamber is cut off from the others?"

Alan moved past the others to take the lead again as they headed back to where they started. "There's only one way to find out. Let's just be careful and stay observant."

The trip back went much quicker since it was downhill. Soon, they were continuing their descent down the second path. This one wasn't as narrow as the first, but the ceiling gradually became lower.

"Look, guys," Alan said. "This area's got a lot of stalactites and stalagmites."

"Yeah," Mei replied, "but it's getting darker in here. The crystals are fewer and farther between."

Tadashi stopped and pulled out three more glow sticks. "Here, take one each. It's better if we all have our own."

Alan tripped slightly. "Watch your footing. The floor's becoming uneven."

Abigail, relieved to have her own light, used it to examine the wall they were passing. "There are symbols and pictures carved into this wall. They remind me of Egyptian hieroglyphs."

The others stopped to take a closer look.

The first set of symbols depicted a bipedal lizard extending its hand toward a human kneeling before it. The images progressed to show lizards and humans standing together around a castle-like structure, and later working in harmony—growing crops and raising cattle on a farm.

The second set of symbols, however, told a different story. Instead of cooperation, they depicted chaos—silhouettes huddled together, red lines slashing through them, symbolizing a bloody conflict. Many of the other symbols had faded, suggesting war had torn apart the once peaceful relationship between the lizards and humans.

"Abs..." Alan said quietly, "ever since I saw the carving of the lizard holding a spear, I've been thinking... do you remember the book Mom wrote us?"

Abigail stopped to think, trying to recall the details. "Kinda, what about it?"

Alan pointed to one of the carvings of a bipedal lizard-man. "Remember the race she wrote about?"

Abigail stared blankly, then nodded. "You mean the tribes of the Ark-Narikan?"

Alan smiled, rolling his eyes. "No, Arkarnians. That's what they were called."

Abigail looked back at the symbols. "What are you trying to say? You think these carvings are about them?"

Alan shrugged. "I don't know, Abigail. All I know is, they look very similar to what she drew—just without her usual fine detail."

As Mei moved to the right, studying the images, she found a small two-foot opening at knee height. She knelt to peer inside. "Check this out, Alan."

When Alan turned to see, she was gone. "Mei? Where did you go?"

She popped her head back out. "In here. Come on, everyone, you need to see this."

Just as the others began crawling through the opening, Mei let out a scream.

Once they stood up, they saw Mei pinned against a wall, a mummy lying on top of her. "Well, don't just stand there—get this thing off me!"

Tadashi and Abigail rushed to lift the mummy off of Mei, while Alan stood still, absorbed in the small room, seemingly oblivious to Mei's frustration.

"Don't worry, Alan, I'm fine. No need to help. Keep doing whatever you're doing."

Alan turned to look at Mei for the first time since entering. "Huh? Oh, yeah, sorry. I think you stumbled upon a tomb."

Behind them, Tadashi and Abigail struggled to return the mummy to its alcove. But when they finally thought it was secure, the mummy fell again—and this time, it wasn't the only thing to fall. Several more mummies, along with part of the ceiling, came crashing down.

Alan acted quickly, ensuring everyone was safe from the falling debris.

Once the dust settled, they realized they were trapped. The only way out was blocked.

"Is everyone okay?" Alan asked.

"If being trapped with all these dead bodies is considered okay, then yeah, I'm great."

Alan shook his head. His sister's sarcasm could be grating.

Mei, already lifting rocks out of the way, didn't like being in enclosed spaces for long. The small ones were manageable, but the large ones, filled with glowing gems, were a struggle.

Alan moved to help her but found the bigger rocks a challenge. "If we had a lever, it would make this easier. Distribute the weight."

Abigail's voice dripped with sarcasm. "Let me just pull out my phone and order one."

The tension was rising as exhaustion took its toll on everyone's emotions.

Tadashi, who had been sitting on the ground, stood up. "Look, we're all in this together. Can we stop with the sarcasm and focus on getting out of here? This room's small, and if we don't unblock the exit, this will be our tomb."

Everyone looked at Tadashi in shock. He shrugged. "What? I'm not being pessimistic. The oxygen in here won't last long, especially with four people."

Abigail slumped to the ground. "You're right. I'm sorry. I'm just tired. It's been a trying day for all of us. We've probably been walking for nine hours. We've rested, but come on—let's get out of here and find a place to sleep. I'd really love something more substantial than an energy bar."

Alan smiled at his sister. "Yeah, I've been thinking about the sandwiches Mom made for us too. Mei, Tadashi, did you guys pack any food?"

Mei replied, "Sobo packed us each a bento box, plus we have a lot of protein bars. I think she was thinking the same way your mom was."

Alan and Tadashi tried again to lift the larger rocks. The first few came free easily, but others were stubborn, lodged in place.

Abigail stared at the rocks, thinking. "Alan, you were right. We need a lever."

Alan gave her a look of exasperation. "Oh, let me guess—your phone's got one on the way, right? In a gazillion lightyears?"

"No, silly. Now who's being sarcastic? Look around. There are several right here with us." She pointed to the bodies. "We just need to get to them."

Tadashi quickly moved to the fallen mummy. "Hey, Mei, grab my pocket knife from my backpack. Let's cut this open."

Mei glanced at him. "Really? You seem overly excited about this."

Tadashi shrugged. "What? You've never wondered what's wrapped up in them?"

Alan laughed, glad for the lighter moment, though he felt bad about bursting Tadashi's bubble. "Tadashi, you can save the mummy autopsy for another time. I think you missed the pile of bones that fell earlier. We need to get out of here, sooner rather than later."

"Aww, man. Fine. It would've been cool to see what the people of this planet looked like. I mean, all we saw of the Shadow-Lord were his eyes—and, oh, we did see those lizard men."

Abigail and Mei each picked up a large bone and used them to lever one of the heavy rocks blocking their way. "Here we go. Let's get this stuff moved."

Once they got one of the big rocks unstuck, the others seemed to come loose more easily. Mei was the first to crawl through the opening. "Now, let's find our way out of here."

Once the others joined her, they continued along the path in the direction they had been heading before being distracted.

As they walked, the path widened, and soon they could see light ahead. After about another twenty minutes, they reached an opening to the outside.

Abigail was the first to step out, halting as she looked ahead. "Now what?" she asked.

Alan, following her, replied, "This is what I saw when I climbed the rock face before we found the cave. This is why I said it wouldn't be a good direction to go. Looks like we'll have to cross the liquid-filled channels, or whatever they are. It'll be slow going, but I don't see another way unless we head back into the swamp. However, we can deal with that tomorrow. It's getting dark, and I don't think any of us has the energy to go any further. Why don't we head back into the cave and call it a day? We can eat and rest properly."

CHAPTER SEVEN

Climbing Down

Tadashi had been the first to wake up, so he decided to let the others sleep while he stepped outside to come up with a plan for traversing the area.

As he emerged from the cave, Tadashi was struck by how beautiful the sunrise was. The moons faded into the sky as the first light of day spread across the landscape. For such a desolate world, it was a sight to behold. Tadashi took out his binoculars and began scanning the area. The decline from the summit was covered in rocks, boulders, and stones, interspersed with the red, bubbly liquid they had encountered when they first entered the Forgotten Lands. The rocks were jagged, and the slope was steep, making the journey ahead seem extremely difficult.

Tadashi returned to the cave and sat down next to Alan, who was still asleep. As the minutes ticked by, his impatience grew, and he leaned closer to Alan's face to see if he was waking up soon.

Alan, who had been dreaming of eating the world's largest hot dog, suddenly felt a hot breath on his face. He jolted awake in a panic, knocking Tadashi backwards.

"What the heck, Tadashi? Are you trying to give me a heart attack?" Alan exclaimed.

Soon, the others began to stir, rubbing their eyes. Abigail groggily called out, "What time is it?"

Tadashi, despite feeling guilty for waking them, couldn't help but reply sarcastically, "Oh, it's 7:00 a.m., and you're late for school."

Abigail shook her head as Alan laughed, putting Tadashi at ease. "Good one, Tadashi. Anyway, it's about time we were up. Let's have breakfast, then we can head out and see what we can do."

Tadashi smiled and replied, "No need. I've already taken a look, and I think I've figured something out."

As they packed their bags and headed out of the cave, Tadashi said, "I know why you didn't think this was the way to go, Alan. At first glance, it doesn't seem safe or smart. But—well, take a look for yourself and see if you notice what I did."

Alan took the binoculars from Tadashi and peered down at the slope. He pointed to the decline. "Is that what you were looking at? I think I have a good idea of your plan, but maybe you should write it down in your notebook so we're all on the same page."

Tadashi grabbed his notebook from his backpack and took the binoculars back from Alan, sketching quickly to mark the rocks and where the red liquid flowed. Every so often, he'd glance through the binoculars before returning to his drawing. Meanwhile, the others made sure the bottoms of their shoes were dry, knowing they'd need good traction to avoid slipping.

A few minutes later, Tadashi spoke again, "Well, I think we need to stick to the center and veer left when we get to the channels of red liquid. The first one looks narrow enough to step over, but the second one is further away, and I'm not sure we'll be able to step over that one. We'll figure it out once we're down there."

The others picked up on Tadashi's lack of confidence as he spoke. "You don't seem too sure about this plan," Mei pointed out.

Tadashi scratched his head and handed Alan the binoculars. "It's not the plan itself—it's what's waiting for us at the bottom. All this red stuff is draining out of the mountain into a trench that looks about three feet wide. The other side of the trench seems to be solid ground. It's reasonable to think we could jump across, especially since the far side is lower than where we are."

Alan handed the binoculars to Mei, who took a quick look before handing them back.

Alan turned to Mei. "I know this isn't rock climbing, but you're the one with the most experience, since you joined that gym with the rock wall. You know more about footholds and such. Why don't you take the lead and guide us down?"

Mei stared at Alan for a moment, clearly skeptical. If her looks could speak, she was thinking he was nuts for expecting her to lead them safely down.

"You do know we use gear when we climb, right? Ropes are pretty important for ascending and descending a wall."

Alan ran a hand through his hair, stressed. "Humor me, okay? I just thought maybe they taught you what to look for when placing your feet on rocks. I know we don't have safety equipment. You know what? Never mind. We'll just have to trust our own judgment and hope we make it."

Mei shook her head, but there was sympathy in her eyes. "Fine. I'll do my best to help. But I'm not an expert. And there aren't any footholds—it's mostly flat-faced boulders. I suggest we stay close and talk it through as we go."

Abigail had been silent up to this point, but now she spoke up. "You know, we have another option."

The others looked at her, waiting for her to elaborate.

"We could just stay here, sit on the rocks, eat our food, and let Shadow-Lord come find us. He said he'd be watching, so maybe he can see us right now. Maybe he has some crystal ball that shows him we're done."

Abigail sat down on a small boulder, crossing her legs as if she had already made up her mind not to budge any further.

The others exchanged glances, unsure of how to react. Alan and Tadashi just shrugged. Mei shook her head and moved to sit next to Abigail, pinching her arm as she did.

"Ow! What was that for?" Abigail yelled.

"Just wanted to make sure you realized this isn't a dream," Mei said, her voice firm but kind. "Yes, we're all stressed. Yes, we'd give anything to be back on Earth with our families. But we're not. And we need to suck it up and do whatever it takes to get back there—even if it means doing things we're afraid of."

Abigail knew she was on the verge of tears, but she didn't want to break down in front of them. Instead, she threw her head back and screamed at the top of her lungs. "GAAH!!!"

Mei jumped, startled by the outburst. Alan and Tadashi, unable to hold back, burst into laughter. Soon, both Abigail and Mei were laughing too.

Once the laughter died down, Alan pulled Abigail into a hug. "Do you feel better now? I know I do. What do you say? Ready to move and put an end to this nightmare?"

Abigail nodded, wiping her eyes. "Thanks, guys. I do feel better."

Mei and Abigail approached the first boulder they needed to descend. "Alright, we'll sit on the boulder and scooch down," Mei said. "Just leave enough room for the boys to sit behind us."

"Grab our waists as we move," Abigail added. "Use your feet to brace against the rock so we don't slide too fast. Once we're halfway down, we should be able to drop the last two feet easily."

They moved down the boulders in a steady rhythm, getting closer to the first red river. The first channel was easy to cross—they simply stepped over the foot-wide liquid.

They resumed their boulder routine until the second channel appeared before them.

"Uh, guys, what do we do now?" Mei asked. "This one's much wider, and there's no place to stand at the edge. The boulder's right up against the channel."

"I don't know," Tadashi said. "We can't jump either, since the other side is all boulders too."

Tadashi, who had been thinking about this moment ever since he saw it through the binoculars, had an idea.

"I think if we position ourselves on that boulder next to us, and sit side by side, we could use our legs to push the boulder in front of us. Hopefully, we'll cause a small rockslide."

The others stared at him as if he were crazy, but he didn't back down. "No, seriously. Look at the smaller rocks in front of the boulder. It doesn't seem as stable as the others we've been on. Can we at least give it a try? If it works, great. If not, I'm all ears for other ideas."

Alan thought it over. "Who can argue with that? But let's make sure we apply a lot of pressure with our hands and wrists for support. I don't want anyone to get caught in the rockslide."

At first, it seemed like Tadashi's plan wouldn't work, but after the fifth try, they felt the boulder start to shift.

"Yes! I knew it would work!" Tadashi grinned. "Let's push hard on the next try, and I'm sure it'll go."

Mei glared at him, sweat pouring down her face. "Really? 'Give it our all'? What do you think we've been doing?"

Tadashi grimaced but tried to lighten the mood. "Good, use that frustration on the boulder. On the count of three, we push."

The plan worked. The boulder shifted, and Abigail's hand began to slip. "Alan!" she cried.

"I've got you!" Alan reached out and pulled her back next to him. "Thanks, that was close."

After the boulder and rocks settled into place, they crossed the channel and took a snack break. The last leg of the descent was twice as long as what they had just done. They simply had to scoot and drop until they reached the trench, and once they crossed it, they'd be in the clear.

When they began moving again, there was little talking—just intense focus to keep pressure on the rocks to avoid slipping. It took a while, but they eventually reached the last boulder, which sat on the edge of the trench.

"Well, I guess I'll go first." Alan steadied himself, moving his left foot forward. He bounced a few times to gain momentum, then pushed off.

Abigail and the others felt more at ease when they saw Alan land on the other side with ease.

"That wasn't too bad," Alan said. "Just make sure you feel like you can do it before you jump. If it doesn't feel right, wait until it does."

Abigail nodded without saying a word and took position to leap across. Mei went next, followed by Tadashi.

Once on the other side, Alan gave everyone a quick side hug. "See? I told you we could do it."

"Yep," Abigail agreed. "And this side seems like the most normal place we've been so far."

Mei shook her head. "I really hope you didn't just jinx us."

CHAPTER EIGHT

The Cave

"Which way do you think we should head?" Tadashi asked, sitting on the soft but very black grass.

Alan looked at Abigail and Mei, then, with an unspoken agreement, they sat down as well. Alan responded, "Let's take a quick break and eat something. I'm already famished— that energy bar from breakfast didn't do much. Then we can look around for clues that might point us in the right direction."

Abigail finished her snack first, did a few stretches, and said, "I'm going to head over that way. I'll shout if I find anything. You guys do the same."

Abigail soon came upon a grove of dead trees. Along the outer edge of the grove, she spotted a wooden sign sticking out of the ground. Carved into the wood was a map showing the areas they had passed through, as well as other locations they had yet to see.

"I found it!" Abigail called out. At the center of the map was the image of a large tree set within a circle, and beneath it, the words: The Grotto of Life.

Everyone rushed over to see what Abigail had found.

"This is the best thing that's happened to us since we got here," Mei said.

Alan tried to pull the sign out of the ground, but it wouldn't budge. He turned to Tadashi. "Can you take out your notebook and sketch this map? It might come in handy later."

Tadashi grinned. "Sure thing. Now we know how to find this tree and end this nightmare once and for all."

Mei wrapped her arm around Tadashi and gave him a side hug. "We can't get too excited. Even though we know the way, we still don't know what awaits us when we get there, or what other obstacles we might face."

Mei's words dampened the group's spirits, but it was a wise reminder—one they all knew to be true.

Alan nodded. "Mei's right. We still need to stay cautious. This could be the calm before the storm. Let's get moving."

The group packed up their gear and began following Alan. No one spoke for a while as they all pondered what might be ahead. As they walked, the landscape continually shifted, and one thing was clear—this world was something none of them would ever forget.

Abigail, relieved not to be in a swamp, cave, or forest, was at least glad to be in open fields. Yes, the area was still colorless, but it felt safer to her. The one thing that bothered her was the eerie silence. No songbirds, no crickets, no bees. Just the sound of their footsteps and a few grunts from the others. The place was too quiet.

Just as she thought this, a loud, unfamiliar sound cut through the silence.

"LERP, LERP, LERP!" The noise echoed every few seconds, growing louder with each passing moment.

Alan, who had been walking ahead, called back, "Whatever it is, it seems to be getting closer."

He spotted a bush large enough for them all to hide behind. "Hey, everyone, let's hide over there."

"LERP, LERP, LERP!"

The group crouched behind the bush, waiting in silence. Mei suddenly started to laugh, followed by Abigail shrieking in delight. The boys just shook their heads. Mei and Abigail popped out from behind the bush and began calling to the creature making the noise.

"LERP, LERP, LERP!"

"Come here, you little cutie. I won't hurt you," Mei said, grinning.

Abigail knelt to get on eye level with the cute orange-and-red furry creature. It was about the size of a dog and seemed very gentle. "Hi there, little Lerpy. It's okay, come to me."

Alan shook his head and whispered to Tadashi, "We're in trouble now. She named it."

The creature slowly approached Abigail and stood before her. Just as Alan was about to warn her not to touch it, Abigail picked it up.

"LERP, LERP, LERP!!!" the creature shrieked violently.

Abigail, frightened by the sudden outburst, jumped back, dropping the creature onto the ground. The earth began to shake as a much larger creature, the size of an elephant, charged toward them from behind a pile of fallen trees. Mei and Abigail slowly backed away as the giant Lerpy nuzzled its baby. The creature then lifted its head and let out a loud, bellowing, "LLEERRP!!"

Frozen in place, Abigail and Mei watched as the mama Lerp scooped up her baby by the scruff of its neck and began to walk away, content that her baby was unharmed. She seemed to decide they weren't a threat and let them be.

"Really? You had to pick it up?" Alan was upset, his mind racing with what could've happened.

Mei sighed. "It was cute. Besides, if Mama had gotten to know us, she would have liked us. And you would've picked it up eventually."

Alan gave her a look of surprise. "Me? I don't know what you're talking about. I don't pick up stray animals."

He flashed a knowing smile that spoke volumes.

They continued their journey for another hour, and every so often, Alan glanced over his shoulder, feeling the eerie sensation of being watched. It wasn't the first time, and he didn't believe Shadow-Lord was the cause of it. No, this felt different, like the unsettling feeling one gets when gazing into a deep pool of water—knowing something could be lurking inside.

Alan's thoughts were interrupted when Tadashi suddenly stopped. "Wait, I think I see something moving ahead. It could be a person."

Mei pulled out her binoculars, trying to see what was ahead. Tadashi grabbed them away before she could get a good look. "Remember those etchings in the cave of what looked like bipedal lizards? Well, they're not extinct. There are three of them, and they have horses. If I had to guess, they're about seven feet tall... the lizardmen, not the horses. The horses are tall, too, but—hey!"

Mei and Abigail scrambled to take the binoculars back from Tadashi, but Alan was quicker.

"What the hell are those things?" Alan muttered.

Abigail swatted him. "Language."

She took a look for herself, then passed them to Mei.

Tadashi broke the silence. "We need to keep heading in that direction, so changing course isn't an option. But what if we 'bush-hop' our way to the river?"

Mei punched her brother's arm. "What's a 'bush-hop'?"

"OW! We move from bush to bush across the field, trying to avoid being seen. We need to stay as quiet as possible. Once we get closer, we'll figure out what to do."

Abigail, always the optimist, spoke up. "Who knows? Maybe they're a friendly lizard race."

"I don't know about friendly lizards," Tadashi said. "Back on Earth, our lizards have a heightened sense of smell. If they're not friendly, they'll pick up on us in no time."

Alan shook his head. "Do you ever have any positive news for us? I guess one good thing is they haven't noticed us yet. Does your big brain have any ideas on how to handle this?"

Tadashi thought for a moment. "Does anyone have eggs or garlic in their packs? Those are the only scents I know that lizards don't like. They'd still detect it, but maybe they'd leave."

Abigail shook her head. "The obvious plan is to stay quiet, stay low, and hope they mistake us for the wind."

As they got closer to the creatures, the number of bushes to hide behind grew fewer. When they were about twenty feet away, they could hear voices.

"I wish I could make out what they're saying," Alan whispered. "Maybe if I move a little closer, I can hear better."

Abigail disagreed. "We're pushing our luck. We should wait it out, and once they move on, we can continue."

But Alan was already moving toward a small bush. He had to lie down to hide. As he lay there, the lizardmen stopped talking. Alan wasn't aware they were now looking directly at him. After a brief pause, they resumed speaking.

The first lizard, smaller and skinnier than the others, complained in a heavy accent. "I'm starving. Those human scouts barely had any meat on them. It was all tough grizzle…"

A tall, muscular lizard with red scales and black war paint glared at the smaller one. Alan guessed he was the leader.

"Pitiful," the leader growled. "How are you the most talented trainee in your village? The pain of your hunger is nothing compared to the pain you'll feel if you don't silence yourself."

The skinny lizard didn't back down. "Please, Chief Korvas, let me and Xevarus grab one of those newborn Lerps. They're juicy and tender when you roast them over a fire…"

Xevarus, the third lizard, remained silent as Korvas berated the smaller one.

"You're the most pitiful warrior I've ever had to evaluate," Korvas snapped. "Your teacher and village recommended you highly, yet you're always complaining about the cold, whining about your belly, second-guessing my orders…" Korvas paused, sniffing the air. He stared in Alan's direction for a moment, then looked away.

"We will discuss this later," Korvas muttered. "Something is watching us."

The skinny lizard, undeterred, suggested, "Then let's hunt it down and eat it."

Korvas growled. "Enough. The scent is strong, but too clean to be human. It must be a morgudite, one of the Shadow-Lord's servants. We've come too close to his territory… His creatures have proved more capable than some of the finest warriors I know. These lands aren't worth a war with him. They are near death. Now, leave. Be silent, and fall in line."

With that, the lizardmen left with their horses.

The others quickly joined Alan at the bush. "They've gone," Mei whispered. "Let's move."

Alan slowly rose, his expression grim. "Korvas seems to fear the Shadow-Lord. He mentioned something about 'morgudites'—creatures that serve him. Korvas thought my scent was too clean for a human, which is why they left. But don't get me wrong, we don't want to mess with them. One of them said something about eating human scouts…"

The gravity of the situation sank in, but Alan pressed on. "We can't worry about this now. Let's keep our focus on the shrine. Maybe we can pick up the pace. At least we know there are humans here..."

Abigail nodded. "Just like Mom's story... Humans and lizard people sharing a world—just not so peacefully. Maybe you're on to something, Alan."

After crossing a narrow river, they came to a dead end—a wall of thick black bramble, devoid of fruit or flowers.

Mei studied the bramble. "Look at those branches. They're as wide as tree trunks, and the thorns are bigger than my hand."

Alan frowned. "That's not even the worst part. Look at the gray mist just beyond. I don't like this. It feels... evil."

"I think we should find a different path," Mei said. "I don't want to go in there. Do you guys want to go right or left? Either way, we should keep moving."

Abigail replied, "We should go left. The grotto is to the northwest."

The others agreed, and they began to walk along the edge of the bramble.

Tadashi, walking ahead, suddenly stopped. "Guys, this bramble seems endless. Our best bet might be to go through this small opening. It's too small for any of those Lerps or lizardmen to fit inside. Maybe the inside of the bramble isn't as bad as we think."

Alan sighed, looking at Abigail and Mei. Their eyes met, and there was a silent agreement that this was their best option, but they were hesitant.

Tadashi took the lead, stepping into the unknown. The others followed, their progress slow. Every now and then, they heard painful sounds as the thorns tore at their skin.

"Ouch! Ahh!!" Tadashi cried. "These thorns are ripping me apart!"

Mei quipped, "If you'd just use some finesse, you wouldn't be getting scratched up like that. Look at me—no cuts."

Just then, Abigail accidentally allowed a bramble to swing back and hit Mei in the shoulder.

"AH CRAP!" Mei yelled. "Abigail, watch what you're doing! That hurt!"

Tadashi snickered. "Language, sister."

Alan was the last to make it through. He moved slowly, not just to be careful, but because the apprehension about continuing was making him feel sick.

As they stood in the mist, the air around them began to change. They could only hope their journey through it would be a quick one.

Chapter Nine

Stalker in the Mist

The further the group walked, the thicker the mist became. The humidity was stifling, and breathing was growing more difficult.

Mei was the first to notice the change in air quality. "This is bad, guys... I think we should turn back..."

Abigail shook her head. "We shouldn't give up yet. Everyone grab your water bottles and stay hydrated; it'll help. Don't overthink it either—if you get too anxious, you might pass out. We still have enough oxygen to breathe, so don't worry about it running out."

"I agree," Alan said firmly. "We have to keep going. No question. We're probably keeping Shadow-Lord waiting, and I sure don't want to find out what happens if we fail his test. We need to reach the Cherry Tree."

Tadashi interrupted with a smile. "Remember, Alan—Cherry Blossom Tree."

Alan shot him a glare but continued. "If Shadow-Lord wanted us to reach the Cherry Blossom Tree, why would he send us on a route that might kill us?"

Mei countered Alan's optimism. "Alan, there's a chance that the bones we saw—the symbols we thought were a sign—weren't the ones Shadow-Lord intended for us to find."

Just then, Tadashi interrupted them with a shout. "Look! There's light! Come on!"

The light at the end of the passage was breaking through another thick section of bramble.

"The thorny patches aren't as tightly woven as when we entered. I think we should go through here," Tadashi said.

As Alan stepped through, he called out, "Wow, the air's not even humid on this side. How is that possible?"

Mei and Abigail pushed through, eager to feel the relief Alan and Tadashi had already experienced.

"Oh my, I never thought I'd feel a breeze again. I could probably wring out my clothes," Mei remarked.

"Let's take a quick five-minute break. That short time in the mist wiped me out," Abigail suggested.

Tadashi flopped onto the ground. "Look, guys, I know the Cherry Tree is important, but I'm exhausted. My body's had it."

Alan laughed. "Don't you mean the Cherry Blossom Tree?"

Tadashi, now lying down and staring at the sky, responded, "Ha ha, real funny. But have you looked up yet? We didn't find an exit to the bramble; we're inside it. It's like we're in a bramble bubble," he said with a laugh.

As the others looked up, Mei observed a dark spot on the ceiling of the structure. "Is that mold on the ceiling?"

Alan squinted, trying to make it out. "Hm... no, I don't think it's mold. It looks like smoke."

Abigail spoke up. "It looks like it's coming toward us. If it were smoke, shouldn't it be escaping through the bramble gaps into the air?"

Alan studied it. As it got closer, he muttered, "If it's not smoke, then it could be... mist?"

They sat in silence, observing the mist as it slowly descended.

All at once, they sprang to their feet, scrambling to find a place to hide—but there was none.

They began to panic, shouting over each other. Out of the dark, shadowy mist, two glowing eyes appeared.

"RED EYES! RED EYES! OH MY GOD, RED EYES!" Alan shouted, his voice filled with terror.

Abigail, trying to remain calm, yelled, "EVERYONE CALM DOWN. THERE COULD BE MANY EXPLANATIONS—RED-EYED FROGS, LIZARDS, WHO KNOWS."

Mei, who had been ranting "THIS IS ALL A BAD DREAM, THIS IS ALL A BAD DREAM," suddenly cut off Abigail. "FROGS AND LIZARDS DON'T FLY!"

Sure enough, the red, glowing eyes were followed by a mouthful of razor-sharp teeth.

Alan screamed, "WE NEED TO RUN!"

Tadashi was the first to react. "Let's go this way! I see more light coming through. There must be another exit in the bramble!"

The group ran as fast as they could. Alan made sure to stay at the rear, watching over the others. As he broke through, he looked around at the new passage they'd entered.

"Wow, this area's more open, and the bramble looks more like individual tree trunks," Alan said, glancing upward. "Wait... is that a ceiling made of rock? Are we back in a cave?"

Abigail replied, "It would be a strange cave, but yeah, this area's more like a bramble forest. At least the air here is still fresh and breathable."

Alan was about to agree when a howling wind from behind him made him turn. "RUN! THAT MISTY-TOOTHED CREATURE IS STILL AFTER US!"

They sprinted, each focused on putting distance between themselves and the danger. The bramble trunks, which were at least two or three feet wide, offered perfect hiding spots, but the further they could get, the better.

Alan hadn't taken up the rear this time, so when he stopped to regroup, he was surprised to see that he was alone. He turned, peering around a bramble for the others. That's when he was hit with a blast of bitterly cold air. The others were nowhere in sight. Slowly, he turned back to his hiding spot.

He took a few deep breaths, trying to calm his racing heart, but the relief would be short-lived.

"GRRRRRR."

The deep growl was coming from somewhere behind him. Alan ran forward, hiding behind a large rock jutting out of the ground. Peeking around it, he could see the mist, but he hoped it couldn't see him.

From his hiding spot, Alan watched as the creature spread its misty form outward, covering the ground in different directions. It seemed to be searching for him, so he stayed as still as possible, praying it couldn't smell him.

The growling stopped, replaced by words that Alan couldn't understand. How was this creature, which appeared to have no physical body, speaking incoherent words?

The creature repeated the unknown phrase several times. Alan was convinced it was a different language. Even if he wanted to communicate, he couldn't.

As Alan watched, the dark mist dissipated slightly, revealing that the creature wasn't mist itself. It had a body—but as soon as it was exposed, the mist covered it again.

Alan didn't know what to do. He couldn't run without being spotted. One thing was certain, though: this creature was evil, and the mist was creeping closer.

Alan squeezed his mouth and eyes shut, mentally repeating to himself, "It's fine, you'll be okay. This thing doesn't know you're here."

Suddenly, there was silence—no growling, no strange words. Alan cautiously opened his eyes, wondering if the creature had moved on. He sighed in relief, but the moment he let his guard down, a clawed hand reached over the rock and swiped at him.

Alan was quicker. The claws scraped the rock where he had been resting.

He ran, yelling over his shoulder, "I don't know where you guys are, but I suggest you run and find a way out!"

His words were mixed with heavy breaths. He didn't dare look back—he knew it would slow him down. But he kept yelling, hoping the others were still somewhere nearby, and praying they were safe.

"This thing sounds like it runs on four legs. Four very large legs. If you're feeling the ground shaking, that's it. And it feels like it's gaining on me... Oomph!"

Suddenly, Alan was shoved from behind and slammed into the ground, the wind knocked out of him. As he gasped for air, the creature had him pinned with one claw on his back. Alan's ears rang, but he could make out some of the creature's words—though it seemed like broken English, the meaning was clear.

"Too... easy... no sport... it... weak... I... hunt it... later... when is... a... challenge..."

Just as quickly as Alan was knocked down, the creature turned and left him there. Alan turned, watching as it returned to the previous chamber in the center of the bramble.

Relieved, Alan struggled to catch his breath. His ribs ached, but he didn't think they were broken.

"Alan! Alan, where are you?" Mei called, followed by the voices of the others.

"Over here," Alan grunted, trying to stand. The movement still hurt, but it was getting easier to breathe.

Abigail immediately noticed that Alan appeared injured. If his expression wasn't enough, the torn knee of his pants gave it away.

The others bombarded him with questions. "What happened? Where's the Mist Creature? Why didn't you follow us? The way out's not far."

Abigail, however, was the first to focus on Alan's well-being. She glared at the others, then asked, "Alan, are you okay? Is anything broken or bleeding?"

Alan looked at his sister, ignoring the others for a moment. "I'm pretty sure nothing's broken. Just skinned my knee. It hurt to breathe at first, but it's getting better. I'm bruised, but it shouldn't slow me down."

He turned to the others, shaking his head at their apologetic looks. "Now, to answer your questions: I couldn't see where you all were, and I didn't have time to figure it out with that creature chasing me. I hid, hoping it would leave, but it found me. Eventually, it caught up and pinned me to the ground."

Tadashi, always blunt, asked, "So, what did it want? It didn't eat you."

Mei smacked her brother's arm. "Really, Tadashi?" she scolded.

Tadashi quickly added, "Sorry."

Alan didn't feel sorry for Tadashi. "Sorry to disappoint you, but it seems I wasn't worth eating."

The others were confused. "What?"

Alan repeated the cryptic dialogue. "I don't know what it means, but from the sound of it, it's not done with me... with all of us. I guess it's a good thing I ran. If I'd tried to stand up to it, I might not have been so lucky."

After their curiosity was satisfied, the group gave Alan a quick hug, relieved that he was okay.

Alan shook his head. "Yeah, yeah, so what's this about finding a way out?"

Once Alan was led out of the bramble, he groaned. "Oh my God, not another forest."

The others agreed, and Tadashi once again pleaded for a break.

Alan looked ahead. "Look, I'm just as exhausted as all of you. We should keep moving. I promise, once it starts getting dark, we'll stop. Plus, we need to put some distance between us and that mist."

Mei, Abigail, and Tadashi knew Alan was making the right call, so they secured their packs and slowly began walking into the forest.

The forest turned out to be uneventful, and by the time the sky turned a light grey, they had reached an area with more of the soft black grass. Alan stopped and turned to the others. "Alright, this is where we'll camp for the night. But first, let me make us some peanut butter sandwiches."

***

The next day, after a quick breakfast, Tadashi offered some encouraging news. "If my map sketch is accurate, the distance we have left is about the same as what we covered yesterday—since we left the cave and entered the bramble."

They gathered their things and set out for the day, hoping the hike would be less taxing. However, it didn't take long before they encountered another obstacle: a red lava river, about twenty feet across.

Mei spotted a solution. "Look over there! That fallen tree stretches all the way across. It should be easy."

She was right. They crossed without difficulty and were soon back on solid ground.

The day continued without incident. No lizardmen, no Lerps, no mist—just the strange flora and fauna. That is, until they reached a dead-end: a rock face, at least fifty feet tall.

"Not again," groaned Abigail.

Tadashi, who had been ahead, called out, "Hey, everyone, come look at this!"

The group walked over to him and saw a white stone arch carved into the rock. Beyond it stood a massive Cherry Blossom Tree—the Grotto of Life.

Before stepping through, Alan smiled at the others. "This is it. We finally made it. Now, let's see what our fate holds."

Chapter Ten

The Grotto of Life

As they stepped through, they were all shocked. The dead world they had been in was gone, replaced by beautiful plants, a cascading waterfall emptying into a small pond filled with an abundance of fish. Some of the fauna were exotic and unfamiliar, while others, like tulips, lilies, and roses, were plants from Earth. However, their attention was drawn to the center of the Grotto, where a Giant Cherry Blossom Tree stood in full bloom. A soft yellow light, emanating from an unknown gaseous substance, made it seem as though the sun itself was shining down upon the tree.

Alan approached a smaller cherry blossom tree and gently caressed the flowers, lost in his thoughts. Why would someone like the Shadow-Lord have any connection to such a beautiful place? Alan could understand how the dark figure might belong to the world beyond the Grotto, but here, everything was beautiful and calm, untouched by evil or destruction.

He glanced over his shoulder to see Abigail kneeling next to a patch of blue tulips, her brow furrowed as she sniffed them. Alan knew she was thinking the same thing he was. He was about to speak, but instead, he decided to let her wrestle with her own thoughts while he continued to take in the peaceful environment, which brought a sense of quiet reflection.

Moving on, Alan came across a pair of stone statues. They depicted two bipedal reptilian figures, standing with their clawed hands outstretched as though they were meant to hold something. The statues were surrounded by shallow, crystal-clear water. Alan reached in to touch it and was surprised by how cold it felt. Just as he was thinking about wading through the water to get a closer look at the statues, Abigail came up to him and tugged at his arm, stopping him.

"What do you think you're doing?" she asked, her voice sharp. "Haven't you learned anything yet in this place?"

Before Alan could respond, a deep voice echoed across the Grotto. "There is no harm in what Alan is doing, Abigail. His curiosity is fair and refreshing. There are few humans in this world who regard ancient places such as these with innocent curiosity. These statues are called the Statues of Eternity. They once shielded the purity of this world from the dark forces that now ravage it."

Abigail could no longer contain herself. She wanted nothing more than to return to Earth, a world she knew and understood. She had no patience for Shadow-Lord's words. "Why have you brought us here? Where is Avery? And why won't you let us go home?" she blurted out.

The Shadow-Lord gestured for them to sit. "We shall sit, and I will explain all that I can. But first, allow me to apologize for the harsh methods I used to bring you here."

"Harsh methods?!" Abigail retorted. "You invaded Alan's dreams, terrorized him, and somehow transported all of us to this awful place. And now you expect us to listen to you? Trust you? We want to go home, now!"

Alan reached out, touching Abigail's shoulder, silently urging her to relax. He then turned to the Shadow-Lord. "As you can see, we're all a bit on edge after everything that's happened. While I would like to go home, I don't want to leave without understanding why all of this is happening. So go ahead, explain yourself. But after that, we want to return to our own home. I think you can understand that."

The fear that had driven the teens thus far had shifted into determination. They had attitude and nerve now, something the Shadow-Lord had been waiting for.

He remained silent for a moment, considering their request. He knew that to convince them to stay and help, he had to give them answers—answers that could shape their futures.

"I will do my best to explain the past and present state of this world. I know what I'm about to reveal will be hard for you to believe, especially since it involves someone you know and trust. But I ask that you keep an open mind. Things in life are not always as they appear. Not everyone can be trusted."

The Shadow-Lord hoped his words would allow the teens to stay open-minded, for what he was about to say would be difficult for them, especially Alan.

Taking a deep breath, he began. "I'll start with a brief geography lesson. As I mentioned earlier, this world is known to some as the Forgotten Lands, but most people here call it Whenua."

Alan and Abigail exchanged a glance. Could their mother's book, which they'd assumed was fiction, actually contain more truth than they'd realized? They decided to stay silent and listen, offering no interruptions.

"The known world consists of two continents surrounded by one ocean, with a tall, impassable wall surrounding it. No one knows what lies beyond this great barrier, but that's not important. We're currently on the Western Continent, in an area that no longer has a ruler. The people here fend for themselves, but life has become increasingly difficult due to a forest of magically created brambles that has taken root. This bramble appeared five years ago."

Tadashi spoke up. "You mean that thorny stuff we had to navigate through, where that mist chased us?"

"Yes, that's what I mean," the Shadow-Lord replied quickly, trying not to be annoyed by the interruption. "Now, if I may continue. This corruption threatens to spread throughout the two continents. In the West, there are three major regions: Wethen, ruled by a King; Kardica, governed by a council of Kings and Queens; and New Arkarnia, a warrior society."

"The region that most concerns you right now is the Kingdom of Wethen, governed by King Alfonse Belmont and Queen Eshe Belmont. They are greatly influenced by someone you may know... Avery Ambrose..."

Before Alan could speak, the Shadow-Lord held up his hand, silencing him. "Let me explain what Avery is doing. It was my intent for you to witness firsthand the loss and destruction he has brought to this world. That is why I wanted you to make your way through the Shadow-Lands on your own..."

Tadashi snickered. "Shadow-Lands, huh? Did you name it?"

"I did not name it," the Shadow-Lord replied, his tone cold. "Nor did I name myself 'Shadow-Lord.' People gave me that name because of this accursed place."

"So what is your real name?" Mei asked.

The Shadow-Lord ignored her question and continued. "As I was saying, the destruction I wanted you to witness is Avery's doing. He created the bramble, and the mist you encountered, but these were not powerful enough to destroy the world quickly enough for him. So, he altered his plan, and it now involves all of you."

"The reason people believe him instead of me is because he holds power as the Court Wizard to the King and Queen of Wethen. His actions are hidden behind his position."

"He's draining the life from this world, and if we don't stop him, both Whenua and Earth will cease to exist as you know them. They may not be destroyed, but they will be irrevocably changed."

Everyone gasped in shock, except for Alan. The others exchanged looks of disbelief, but Alan remained undeterred, his eyes narrowing at the Shadow-Lord.

The Shadow-Lord raised his hand, knowing the teens would have questions, but he needed to finish explaining everything first. Before he could speak, Alan reached out and swatted the Shadow-Lord's hand aside. The gesture made the Shadow-Lord smile inwardly, though he remained outwardly calm. "I still don't believe a word you're saying, but humor me—tell me, why would Avery do this?"

The Shadow-Lord nodded. "I understand your disbelief. Avery is draining the life from this world in an attempt to revive his wife. She was killed many years ago by raiders from New Arkarnia, a group of humanoid reptilians known as the Arkarnians..."

Alan interrupted. "Arkarnians... there are three major tribes: the Rau-Trava, who lost their homeland to a magical disaster and started a war with Wethen; the Kalko, who are peaceful and live in Kardica; and the Dinalo, who once belonged to the Rau-Trava but now live in Wethen... right?"

The Shadow-Lord paused. "More or less... Yes. But how do you know all of this?"

Abigail answered. "Our mother wrote us a book... a fantasy book about a world called Whenua. It mentioned the Arkarnians and went into detail about them. I don't remember all of it, but Alan remembers more. In fact, he loved that book."

Alan closed his eyes, unwilling to accept that Avery could be behind the destruction of this world. But the story in his mother's book had mentioned a dark wizard who nearly destroyed everything.

Ignoring the interruption, the Shadow-Lord continued, "Yes, the Arkarnians once dominated these lands long before humans settled here."

Alan interjected. "Yes, the book mentioned how the Rau-Trava and the tribes broke away from the Arkanian Empire, and how the Arkarnians subjugated other species. They didn't enslave them, but they wouldn't allow them to hold titles or marry into prominent Arkanian families, am I right?"

The Shadow-Lord nodded, looking concerned beneath his helmet. "Indeed. The empire collapsed when the Arkarnians grew too greedy for power. They colonized the East, and sought to take the West. A war nearly destroyed them, and they brought humans from another world to be their slave soldiers. Eventually, the humans turned against the empire, with help from some Arkarnians who became known as the Kalko tribe."

After the humans escaped, they sought the help of a long-forgotten species, who gifted them with magic. Civil war broke out within the Arkanian Empire, and it fragmented. From its ashes came the Kingdom of Rau-Trava, in their ancestral homeland, now called Old Arkarnia. Other Arkanian tribes left, and many assimilated into the other kingdoms. As you mentioned, a magical disaster devastated Old Arkarnia, leading to the Rau-Travan invasion of Astursis, the kingdom that once existed here, and the current cold war between the Rau-Trava and Wethen."

Alan scratched his chin. "I didn't know humans were brought from Earth..."

The Shadow-Lord reached out and patted Alan on the shoulder, making Alan stiffen in surprise. "Your mother didn't want to make things too obvious. You and Abigail are smart. If she had included too many details about Earth's connection to Whenua, you would have figured it out."

He paused, then looked at Alan and Abigail. "Your parents—and your grandmother—were born here, in Whenua. And so were all of you."

The teens were stunned. They didn't want to believe it, but too many things suddenly made sense. For now, they stayed silent and allowed the Shadow-Lord to continue.

"The reason Avery is doing this is because the Rau-Travans killed his wife when she was trying to broker a peace agreement between Wethen and the Rau-Travans. Avery's wife was a Consul, appointed by the King. It was her job to protect the citizens. But the Rau-Travans, poisoned by their leader Korvas, rejected peace and brutally killed her as Avery watched, helpless. It broke him. He had sworn not to interfere if things went wrong. And I think you can understand why Avery's daughter is upset with him."

The Shadow-Lord looked at them, gauging their reactions. Alan seemed the most doubtful, but the others appeared to be absorbing the information.

"I brought you here to show you these statues because if we are going to stop Avery, we must reach the Shrine of Morimor and Livimor. One is on this continent, the other is missing. When the Orbs are reunited at the Statues of Eternity, whoever holds both will have the power to heal or destroy the Forgotten Lands."

Shadow-Lord's story didn't sit right with Alan. If the Orbs had such power, why would Avery risk damaging not just Whenua, but Earth as well? If they were as powerful as Shadow-Lord claimed, they could likely restore Avery's wife. This led Alan to conclude that Shadow-Lord was either lying to himself and them about the orbs' ability to restore the Forgotten Lands to keep a single flame of hope alive, or he was lying about Avery. Alan chose to believe the latter. Abigail, Mei, and Tadashi shared similar doubts, but they didn't feel the need to assume Shadow-Lord was lying. After all, he had been patient with their interruptions and seemed less intimidating than before. To Abigail, he seemed like someone desperately trying to hide his own fear.

When Shadow-Lord saw their skeptical expressions, he sighed and spoke again. "I think I know what you must be wondering. What could someone like me possibly need you for? Why can't a man with magical abilities stop Avery himself? Well, there are two reasons for that. First, the location of the Shrine of Livimor has yet to be revealed to me. Second, while I know where the Shrine of Morimor is, a curse was placed on the Orb there, and it can only be removed by a descendant of a man named Alan Elwyn. That's why Avery couldn't use the Orbs in his plot and why he sought to force you to help him. Don't think ill of him. It isn't his fault—grief can change people. I've heard his wife was his soulmate, that they were destined to be. Such love is rare. I can only shudder to think of what it feels like when it's torn away."

Shadow-Lord paused. The next part of his explanation would be difficult for the kids to accept. "Now, to explain why I said that Mei and Tadashi wouldn't have the abilities I need from either Alan or Abigail..."

Alan interrupted. "How can you be sure? Maybe my mother heard the story from the person you really want, and this is all a mistake on your and Avery's part."

He glanced at the others, seeking support. Mei was the only one who spoke up. "I'm kind of leaning toward what Alan just said. Where's your proof that you really need Alan and Abigail?"

Shadow-Lord nodded in understanding. "I wish it were possible that this was a mistake, that I could just send you all home. But consider a few things. Only those born in this world can travel back here after going to Earth. It's a defense mechanism to prevent invaders from entering this world. They can't even see the portals that connect Earth and Whenua. And then there's the matter of how your parents died, Mei. Don't you find it strange that there are no pictures of them? That's because photography doesn't exist here. The truth is, Avery accidentally caused their deaths. That's why he came to Earth, to see his children grow and atone for his guilt. As for you, Alan and Abigail, have you ever wondered about all the time your father's been away? Or did you believe the stories that he's been running around Earth, digging holes and finding vases and other ancient curiosities?"

The weight of Shadow-Lord's words stunned them into silence. Alan's resistance to the idea that they might have been born in Whenua began to crumble.

"Now, let me explain my family tree. Listen closely. My triple-great-grandfather, Alban Elwyn, had a son and a daughter. The son, Terrance Elwyn, and the daughter, Gwendolyn Elwyn. Gwendolyn married a man named Materall Ambrose I. Do you see where I'm going with this? We now have two branches of the tree: Elwyn and Ambrose. One of those names should be familiar to you, the other should be if your parents told you the truth. Alan and Abigail, your true last name is Elwyn, which makes us... fourth cousins, I believe?"

Alan and Abigail shook their heads in disbelief. Shadow-Lord continued, "By now, I hope you've realized why I need you. You are the great-grandchildren of Alan Elwyn I. One of you, or perhaps both, was born with untapped magical abilities. It is that ability that is needed to obtain the Orbs..."

Tadashi and Mei were visibly upset by what they had just heard. Once Shadow-Lord finished speaking, Tadashi blurted out, "What about us? Why are we even here if you only need them?"

Shadow-Lord turned to them. "Because, if I've learned anything about you, it's that you are a team. Would you be willing to go home and leave Alan and Abigail behind?"

Mei exchanged a glance with her brother. They didn't respond, but the weight of Shadow-Lord's words settled in. Despite the shocking revelations about Avery and their parents, they silently agreed they wouldn't leave their friends behind.

Alan huffed, "So, that would make Avery your uncle? I don't know what to believe, especially with you being my distant cousin, but... either you've given this scheme a lot of thought, or this really is true. I can't imagine someone making up this whole family tree from nothing."

Shadow-Lord smiled, feeling he was making progress with Alan. "I've given you a lot to consider. I know you'll need rest before we depart for my castle, Darkspire. I still have some preparations to make, so I'll return in the morning. Have you eaten? If not, I think I have some fruit and bread in my saddlebag."

Abigail sighed. "No, thank you. We'll be fine."

Once Shadow-Lord was gone, everyone turned to Alan, who was still shaking his head.

Finally, Abigail, who had been sitting in the circle with the others, stood and stepped over to him, shaking his shoulder. "Stop!" she exclaimed.

Alan buried his face in his hands, continuing to shake his head. Abigail sat down beside him, never taking her hand off his shoulder.

"I know this is a lot for all of us," she said quietly. "What Shadow-Lord has told us seems plausible. Avery did leave years ago without saying goodbye, and he showed up just before this nightmare began. That alone makes me question his role in all of this. I think it should make you question it too. As for us being from this world, I have no answers—just a lot of questions for Mom and Dad."

Mei muttered, "Yeah, I think Tadashi and I have some questions too. This feels so surreal..."

Tadashi, who had regained control of his emotions, spoke. "Even though I'm not very hungry right now, I think we should eat something and then turn in. I don't want to talk anymore—I just want to rest. But there's one more thing to consider. Do you see Avery here? No. He was teleported away at the cave. Why was that? Shadow-Lord saved us from Avery. Yes, he freaked you out at first with those living dreams, but as he said, he needed to get your attention. And I think it worked. He's got mine. I want the truth. What if we don't help him, and it turns out he wasn't lying? How would we feel if we lost everyone we love? If we agree to help him, we can control what happens. If we learn we've been deceived, we can act accordingly."

The group sat in silence, looking at one another, waiting to see if Alan would respond.

After a long pause, Alan finally looked up. He touched his sister's knee and said, "Tadashi, you make a good point. I agree, we need to proceed cautiously. I do think Shadow-Lord isn't being completely truthful—parts of his story don't add up. But for now, I'll go along with him and see what he plans."

Abigail didn't want to sway her brother's decision, feeling it was his to make. But deep down, she had a sense that Shadow-Lord was telling the truth, and Avery was up to no good.

Mei stretched her legs out. "Good, now that we've decided on our next move, let's eat and relax before bed."

Everyone followed Mei's suggestion. The four teens set aside their worries about tomorrow, settling into a quiet moment of rest.

Chapter Eleven

The Journey to Darkspire

The Shadow-Lord returned the next morning, as promised. "Here, I've brought you some bread, fruit, and water for breakfast. Eat up—we have a long journey ahead."

Alan and the others didn't want to seem rude, so they took the food, though they added peanut butter to the bread.

As they ate, Shadow-Lord filled them in on their journey.

"Once you've eaten, you can change into the clothes I've brought you. The people of this world do not dress the way you do. The journey to my castle will take us about ten hours. Some of that will be walking, but for the most part, we'll be riding horses."

Tadashi muttered between bites, "Thank God. I'm sick of all this walking."

Shadow-Lord ignored him and continued, "The first part of the journey will be a three-hour walk. When we reach the Village of Fordenbar, you'll purchase horses for the rest of the journey."

Alan took the pouch of coins Shadow-Lord handed him, but before he could ask why, Shadow-Lord added, "We'll be traveling on the outskirts of Shadow-Lands. When we reach Fordenbar, you'll go farm to farm until you find someone willing to sell you the horses. If anyone asks where you're from, tell them Kardica."

Alan opened his mouth to ask why the people wouldn't be willing to sell, but Shadow-Lord cut him off. "Let's get moving."

The beauty of the Grotto stretched beyond its walls. The sky was blue, and the landscape was colorful, though the hues were more subdued compared to those inside the Grotto.

This was more proof of what the Shadow-Lord had told them. Half the world was dead, and here life was slowly fading. If they didn't stop Avery, it would die as well.

For the first few miles, they traveled in silence, each lost in their own thoughts. Abigail broke the silence with a sigh. "I think Mom is probably a wreck, and has everyone looking for us. I wonder if Dad will be allowed to come home to be with her?"

Alan chimed in, "Yeah, for a while I thought the same. But I think Dad is somewhere here, in this world... that's the only part of what Shadow-Lord said I believe. It just... makes sense. HEMA... the book... we were being prepared for the truth... but why, Abigail? Why weren't we raised here? It wasn't to keep us from Avery. What if we were hidden from Shadow-Lord—or whoever taught him? I imagine the knowledge to wield magic doesn't just appear. Maybe we were raised on Earth because his father was the evil wizard the book talked about."

Abigail nodded. "That's a distinct possibility, Alan. But for now, as Tadashi said, we'll play along. If something doesn't feel right, we'll go against his plans. It's obvious he needs our cooperation, so we can figure out how to use that against him if it turns out he lied, and Avery was just having a rough day when he forced us here."

Alan smirked humorlessly. "Yeah, if that was even Avery... how much do you want to bet there's some magic spell that lets someone take on another's appearance?"

Abigail shrugged. "Maybe. Personally, though, I think it was Avery."

Alan went back to replaying the conversations with both Avery and Shadow-Lord in his head. He was trying to decide what was believable and what wasn't—trying to think with his head, not his heart. His thoughts came to a sudden halt when Tadashi tapped him on the arm. "Hey, daydreamer, check it out. We're entering a populated area. This place is like something out of our history books. The farms ahead look almost medieval."

Alan glanced in the direction Tadashi was pointing. Sure enough, he could see several farms ahead, with stone fences surrounding the homes and gardens.

The Shadow-Lord stopped and called out to them. "It would be best for me to meet you on the other side of the village. Do your best to be quick. Hopefully, you won't have any issues with the farmers. Don't tell them you're traveling with me—the less you say, the better."

Alan immediately jumped in. "Why? What happens if we do?"

Shadow-Lord huffed. "Simple. You'd be walking the whole way to my castle."

Shadow-Lord studied Alan's reaction and added, "And if you're thinking of asking them about me, think again. That, too, could result in you not getting any horses."

Without waiting for a reply, Shadow-Lord mounted his horse and rode off, presumably to wait for them on the other side.

As they walked past the first farm, which appeared to be growing endless rows of corn, they noticed several people staring at them. Abigail felt uncomfortable. "Do any of you get the feeling they know we don't belong here?"

Tadashi and Mei laughed uneasily. "I guess they don't get many strangers here. They're probably wondering why we're walking toward them from such a desolate area. Maybe if we wave politely, they'll see we're friendly."

Alan pushed past them. He wasn't intimidated by the farmers; in fact, he saw them as a potential solution to his questions. The others watched as he approached.

Alan said, "Hello. My name is Alan. My friends and I are travelers. We find ourselves in need of horses. Can you help us?"

The man and woman exchanged a long, silent glance. Finally, the man spoke. "You'd best keep walking. We don't help the likes of you."

Alan wasn't deterred. "The likes of me? You don't even know me."

The man looked at his wife, who went inside the house. Turning back to Alan, he growled, "You were in the presence of the dark one, the Shadow-Lord. Any friend of his is our enemy. Now, you'd best leave... or you won't be leaving at all."

Alan's frustration boiled over. "We're not friends with him, sir. We were forced to come here. All we want is to go home to our families. Please..."

The man wasn't convinced. "I'll not listen to these false tales. That foul man is responsible for destroying most of our crops. You see these fields? They used to stretch for miles, but now all that remains are these pitiful patches of corn. We've heard rumors—Shadow-Lord wants us to depend on him. But we won't let him win. He sends his Morgudites into our villages at night to destroy and pillage, then offers us protection. But we won't trust him. He just wants to control us."

Alan shook his head. "I'm sorry for what he's done to you, but you must believe me, we are not his allies. We're just trying to get home. Yes, we're traveling to his castle, but only so we can figure out how to make him send us back. What do we have to gain by lying?"

Abigail knew this was a lost cause. They needed to move on, just as Shadow-Lord had warned them. She grabbed Alan's arm and pulled him along. "Good day, sir. We won't bother you further." She whispered under her breath, "We don't have time for this. We'll go to the next farm, and I'll ask about horses. You need to keep quiet. No one is above suspicion."

They visited several more farms, but none of the farmers had any horses to spare. The last farmer, however, was the most helpful. He told them there was a livery to the west, about a half-hour walk, but the horses there would cost a hefty sum of coin. Abigail thanked him, and they quickened their pace.

On the way, they noticed several posters hanging on a fence. One advertised a reward for a lost ox, offering five pounds of butter for any information that led to his return. The one that caught Alan's attention, however, was a warning about the Shadow-Lord, with a caricature of him.

Alan pointed at the poster. "Look, these people don't like or trust the guy. Why don't you believe me when I say we can't trust him?"

Abigail sighed. "It's not that we don't believe you. We're just keeping an open mind. To be honest, the three of us don't trust either of them, and neither should you."

Alan huffed. "I'd think you'd be more willing to trust the man we know, instead of the one we don't."

Abigail was exasperated. "Did you not hear a word I said? We don't trust either of them. And I, for one, no longer know Avery. He left years ago. You should be wary, too. Shadow-Lord seems sincere, but we'll see what happens. You need to keep an open mind. What if Avery wasn't part of the equation? What if it was Tom the Butcher? Would you still be so willing to follow him?"

Alan relented, though not before pushing past Abigail. "It sure as hell seems like you trust Shadow-Lord, so don't act like I'm the one going against what we're supposed to do."

Abigail shook her head but let Alan go. She didn't want an argument.

They continued on their way. Alan was frustrated that his friends were at odds with him over something so important—the fate of the world. He mulled over what Abigail had said and, before entering the livery, he stopped and spoke without looking at her. "I'm sorry. But I'm not going to give up on Avery. He may have left years ago, but that doesn't erase all the good memories we have of him. I don't want Shadow-Lord to drive a wedge between us. So for now, I'll try to keep an open mind."

Abigail smiled, relieved to ease the tension. "I think we can all agree on that."

The man in the livery turned out to be welcoming, especially when he saw the gold coins Alan offered. Soon, they were saddled up and ready to go.

About a hundred yards further, they met back up with the Shadow-Lord. "I take it you had trouble getting horses. No matter, you have them now. Let's not waste any more time. The journey from here will take us five hours, but we'll travel at a slow trot. I don't want to wear out the horses, and I doubt you're very skilled at riding."

As they trotted, Alan began formulating questions he felt the Shadow-Lord needed to answer. He wanted to better understand who they were dealing with. Once he felt ready, he asked, "Back in the village, they had posters of you, warnings about you. What have you done to provoke such an attitude? If this world is being destroyed, and you truly want to see it recover, why not show them your true intentions?"

Shadow-Lord looked irritated. Mei, riding next to Alan, didn't think he was going to reply. But instead of striking Alan, Shadow-Lord pointed at the sky and said, "These imbeciles would rather listen to that senile excuse of a wizard than to me. They fear my appearance rather than see the truth."

Alan huffed. "I don't think they fear a helmet. What they fear is the man behind it. So tell me, what awful things have you done to generate such an attitude?"

Shadow-Lord sighed in defeat. "Fine. You win. I misjudged these peasants at first. They worshipped Avery and his magic. I thought the best way to win them over was to show them I was more powerful than he, that I knew better how to lead them. It backfired because Avery set me up from the beginning. He knew I would react that way. I didn't know he had warned the villagers that I could destroy them and their world. So when I used my powers, they saw it as the beginning of their destruction."

Alan and the others shook their heads. Before Alan could ask more questions, Shadow-Lord continued, "What I did with my powers isn't what you think. I used a spell that turned their water from blue to red. It didn't taste any different, but Avery counteracted it with his own spell, making it undrinkable, contaminated. Soon, the villagers were sick, and their livestock died. Since they were devoted to Avery, I couldn't defend myself. So, I embraced the evil they chose to believe I was, hoping one day I could prove Avery's deceit."

It seemed the others were beginning to believe Shadow-Lord's story, but Alan wasn't convinced. He was more certain than ever of his treachery. However, he decided it was best not to agitate him further. He picked up his pace and rode away, leading the others toward what he believed to be a fate worse than death.

A little while later, Abigail cantered up to Alan's side. "Do you smell that?" she asked.

Alan slowed his horse to a walk, sniffing the air. "Yeah, I smell that. I don't think it's a simple campfire; that smells like something bigger."

Just then, Mei and Tadashi, who had been riding further back, galloped toward them, shouting, "Look over there! Black smoke is billowing toward the sky!"

They all stopped their horses and turned to look. The sky was darkening quickly. The Shadow-Lord observed, "It appears to be a fire. The Village of Halworth lies in that direction..."

Before the Shadow-Lord could finish speaking, Alan kicked his horse into motion, racing toward the village. He ignored the Shadow-Lord's calls to stop. With Alan not listening, the Shadow-Lord addressed the others. "We don't have time to waste, but I understand his concern. We should go help. I'll stay here, so I don't impede you. They may be more willing to accept your help. Go ahead and assist Alan."

As Alan reached the village gate, he was met with chaos and destruction. He asked a villager if he could help. Just then, the others arrived and dismounted. The villager eyed them warily but, seeing their sincerity, told them to grab buckets and fetch water from the well. Soon, a human chain was formed, passing buckets from person to person. It took over an hour, but eventually, the fires were extinguished.

A few villagers thanked them for their help. Alan asked, "What started the fire?" The villager's response left him even more confused.

"The Shadow-Lord sent creatures to set fire to our town—his servants, the morgudites. They're tall, muscular, vicious creatures, part man, part arkarnian. Black scales, glowing eyes like flame. All because we wouldn't pledge allegiance to him."

The villager suddenly stopped, then asked, "Who are you, anyway? Where do you come from?"

Mei replied, "Kardica."

One of the older men looked at them suspiciously. "If that's the case, why are you traveling from the South? I doubt four youngsters could have survived the journey. So tell me, who are you really?"

Abigail and Tadashi grabbed Alan's and Mei's hands. "Time to go, guys," Abigail said. "I believe we've worn out our welcome." The group quickly mounted their horses and raced back to the Shadow-Lord.

"So, are the villagers safe?" the Shadow-Lord asked.

Mei nodded. "Yes, but we're just as unwelcome as you are now. Telling them we were from Kardica only fueled their suspicions. I'm curious, though, about the morgudites—the creatures that work for you. What do they look like?"

The Shadow-Lord seemed put off by her question but answered, "They are large, with green, mossy skin. To humans, they might appear overweight, but that's normal. They prefer to be called 'morgs'; 'morgudite' is more of a slur the Rau-Travans use."

Abigail spoke up, "The villagers said you sent those creatures to burn down their town. But their description is different. They said the attackers looked like human-arkarnian hybrids, with black scales and glowing eyes."

The Shadow-Lord's tone darkened. "Those are not morgs. They are hybrids, created by Korvas using ancient arkarnian alchemy. Korvas intended them to be powerful warriors for war, made from arkarnian rejects and human prisoners. They were meant to have insatiable bloodlust... but they were too wild to follow orders. They escaped New Arkarnia and have become a blight I have to deal with. Do not listen to the villagers—they are far too suspicious and assume I am behind everything bad that happens."

He turned and began trotting off, adding, "I'm sure you're all hungry. There are ruins up ahead. We can stop there for lunch."

After another hour of travel, the group stopped for lunch. When they saw the ruins, they wanted to explore. The structures were in various states of decay—some had only single walls standing, while others had collapsed into rubble. Abigail asked, "What happened here?"

The Shadow-Lord replied, "It was destroyed during the Arkarnian Invasion of Wethen and the kingdom that once existed in the Shadow-Lands."

Suddenly, a gruff voice startled them. "This was Fort Duncrest. I was one of the knights loyal to the crown during the civil war before the Arkarnian invasion. My comrades died here, and I decided long ago I would remain. Most villagers treat me like a mad hermit. You see those mountains in the distance? The three waterfalls to the east, and the grasslands you traveled through—that's what the Shadow-Lands were like until about forty years ago. It will all be gone soon. Some say the Shadow-Lord caused this, but they are wrong. The war caused this sickness... some sort of black magic used by either the Arkarnian invaders or my people."

The Shadow-Lord looked at the man with a puzzled expression and commented, "Curious. Why have our paths not crossed before? I would welcome you to my castle. You seem more knowledgeable than most of the inhabitants here."

The hermit laughed. "The humans who live here are too young to understand what they've lived through. They teach their children their own ignorant version of history. Some don't even remember the name Astursis. As for your offer... there was a time I would have accepted such kindness. But no... I stay here, in these ruins, because I seek to wither away and die here. That way, I can pass on knowing my fallen brothers and sisters are near."

The Shadow-Lord bowed his head respectfully. "A shame... I would have liked to know you better, to hear about Astursis's final days from someone who lived through it. I wish you peace."

As they left the ruins, the kids glanced back at the hermit. They felt sympathy for him but believed that, if he had survived this long alone, he would likely find peace as he wished.

When they reached the base of the mountain, Alan spoke to the Shadow-Lord. "I don't understand. Why don't you talk to people the way you spoke to that man? If you had spoken to me like that instead of acting like a psychopath when we first met, I might have trusted you."

The Shadow-Lord glared at him. "You know nothing of what I've been through or how I've tried to help these people. Yes, I could have been nicer, but niceness doesn't help when the survival of the world is at stake."

Alan wasn't buying it. Something felt off about the hermit's appearance, too convenient. But he decided to stay quiet for now. His sister and friends seemed to believe every word, so he would wait to speak with them in private.

As they neared the foothills, Tadashi asked, "How are we getting the horses up that mountain?"

The Shadow-Lord called out, "There's a pass to the right. It's narrow, but manageable. Just keep the horses slow and in single file. I'll lead; my horse knows the way."

Alan shook his head, pushing past the others and entering the pass. He just wanted this journey to be over—he wanted to find Avery and go home.

The mountain pass proved to be a struggle. Shadow-Lord's horse had no trouble, but the others, unfamiliar with the rocky terrain, hesitated and nearly stopped moving. Mei understood why no one had attacked the Shadow-Lord—though people could traverse to the other side, bringing weapons or supplies through would be impossible. Eventually, they coaxed the horses through and made it out of the pass.

Alan and Abigail were the first to emerge, and they felt an eerie resemblance to the desolate feeling when they first entered the Forgotten Lands. The air was thick with a gray, lifeless atmosphere. Abigail said, "The villagers were wrong. The Shadow-Lord isn't living it up here."

Alan shrugged. He'd been mostly quiet during the journey through the pass. Abigail had assumed it was because he was focused on not slipping, but now she wondered. "What's wrong, Alan? You seem distant."

Alan glanced at the Shadow-Lord, then turned to Abigail. "I'll explain later."

The castle came into view from a distance. The closer they got, the harder it became to see the full extent of the structure. Unlike the ruins they'd seen earlier, these walls were intact—at least forty feet high.

Just outside the castle, before the drawbridge, Tadashi called to Alan, "Hey, are those Morgs? They look just like how the Shadow-Lord described them. Guess he wasn't lying about the hybrids."

The Shadow-Lord ordered them to dismount and called, "Gorb, come here. Our visitors have arrived."

Alan's eyes widened as the creature bounded toward them. He tried to step away, but it quickly grabbed him. He struggled to break free, but once he stopped, he realized the creature was hugging him.

"I'm sorry for scaring you, Alan Foster. I mean you no harm. My name is Gorb. Will you be my friend?" The creature spoke slowly, its speech pattern odd.

The Shadow-Lord looked at Gorb and ordered, "Take the children into the castle. Show them to their rooms. I need to speak with our cook about dinner arrangements."

To the kids, the Shadow-Lord said, "Follow Gorb. You may rest until I send for you. We will discuss everything after dinner."

Once alone, Alan shared his feelings. "I've given him the benefit of the doubt, but after seeing the villagers' reaction, listening to the hermit, and observing him, I still don't trust the Shadow-Lord. We need to find Avery. There's no reason to go any further with him."

Abigail glanced at the others, who seemed to indicate she needed to play devil's advocate. "I've been thinking too, and I don't think we have enough information to decide who we can trust. We need to hear the Shadow-Lord out, and from there, we can decide what to do."

Alan wasn't surprised by his sister's answer, but it didn't make him feel any better. "Fine. I'll listen to him, but that's it. I'm finding Avery, with or without your help."

Just then, Gorb appeared, announcing dinner was ready. The conversation was cut short as the kids followed him to the dining hall.

The hall was vast, the table at least twenty feet long, with high-backed chairs on either side. At one end, pewter dinnerware and goblets were set. Gorb instructed them to take a seat. Soon, several smaller Morgs arrived, bringing platters of food. Gorb served them drinks, which Mei believed to be apple juice—or something that tasted like it.

The Shadow-Lord soon joined them, removing his helmet for the first time. Alan stared at his face, and Abigail whispered, "He looks a lot younger than I thought, and look at those scars. No wonder he wears a helmet."

Alan didn't respond. He grabbed a turkey leg and took a large bite. Abigail didn't push him further. She knew he was disappointed with her decision and respected his space as they ate in silence.

After the meal, Shadow-Lord cleared his throat. "Now that you've eaten, let me explain what I require. Once this is done, I'll keep my promise and return you to Earth."

He went to a bookshelf, rifling through scrolls, muttering about how disorganized they were. After several minutes, he found one, a large scroll, and returned to the table. Spreading it out, he revealed a map of Whenua's eastern continent. "We are near the northernmost part of the Shadow-Lands. We need to travel to the place marked on the map, in the Polar Region, where the Shrine of Morimor is located."

The Sirine of Moravel
The Polar Region
The Reservations
New Arkarnia
Wethan
Overgate and Undergate
The Shadow Lands
Erkar Peninsula
New Arkarnia
Kardica

"As you can see, it's quite a distance," Shadow-Lord continued, "so the journey will take us about two weeks. Once we obtain the orb, we will travel by boat to the Eastern Continent. In my search for the location of the second orb—the one belonging to the Shrine of Livimor—I was informed by reliable sources that it is somewhere over there. I must admit, I haven't been to that area in quite some time, so we'll have our work cut out for us once we arrive. As for the present journey, I must warn you that there is still an ongoing war, so I will be arming you for your protection."

Tadashi interrupted, "Why not just zap us there?"

Shadow-Lord shook his head. "Magic doesn't work like that. I wish it did."

Alan scoffed. "How did you zap Avery away, then?"

Shadow-Lord sighed. "Oh, sure, magic can work that way when you teleport without any clue where you're going to end up."

He glanced around to see if there were more questions before continuing. "As I was saying, it's a long journey. I'll provide you with the necessary gear, including warm clothing and food. We'll ride horses for part of the journey, but once we reach the outskirts of the forest, we'll have to leave them behind. For some reason, horses get skittish whenever I try to ride into those woods. We'll have to walk for several days, and once we're out of the forest, we'll acquire more horses. As we approach the Polar Region, we'll need to switch again, as the temperatures will be too cold for the horses to continue. After that, we'll need to walk until we can obtain Durbos. They're larger than horses and can survive the frigid cold."

Shadow-Lord's gaze lingered on Alan. He sensed something—was it deception, or just apprehension about the task ahead? He wasn't sure, but he knew he would need to keep an eye on him. He couldn't afford to let Alan undermine his plans.

"We'll be leaving at first light," Shadow-Lord declared. "So, return to your rooms and get some rest."

Without waiting for any more questions, he left the dining hall, his footsteps echoing in the silence.

Once in their room, Mei and Tadashi immediately went to their beds, eager to lie down. But Abigail stood still, watching her brother. She could sense that Alan wasn't ready to sleep. "Alan, I know you don't agree with following Shadow-Lord, but I think we need to do so—for now. I have a feeling Avery will show up at some point. Just lay down and sleep. We're in this together."

Alan didn't want to argue. He had too much on his mind. "Fine, I'll lay down. You should get some rest too." He called out to the others, "Goodnight."

Chapter Twelve

Dark Discoveries

Alan found it difficult to sleep, even more so than when they were at the Grotto. The weather outside was cold and rainy, and the room felt damp. A draft seemed to blow straight down on him. One of the Morgs had made sure that he and the others had extra blankets, but they weren't doing much to help. As he lay there, he glanced over at his sister, then to Mei and Tadashi—they were sound asleep. This surprised Alan. How were they able to let their minds rest after everything they had endured, everything they'd been told? Exhaustion, that must be the answer. But if that was the case, why couldn't he shut everything off? The questions kept spinning in his mind—doubt, confusion, frustration.

"If Shadow-Lord is the good guy, why doesn't he try to convince the villagers of his heroism, rather than let them fear, hate, and blame him because of what Avery supposedly told them?"

"And if Avery is the villain that Shadow-Lord makes him out to be, why did he spend so many years as my neighbor and friend? Why didn't Avery terrorize me in my dreams, but Shadow-Lord did? I don't buy what Shadow-Lord told us... I just don't understand why the others want to believe him so badly. It's like they're actively searching for a reason to hate Avery... And then there's the whole business of being from here, possibly having magical abilities. If that's true, I can see why Mom and Dad wanted to protect us, but it's still hard for me to wrap my head around."

Alan got out of bed. He knew sleep wouldn't come to him. What he needed was answers, and the only person he trusted to give them was Avery. Alan opened his backpack and pulled out his sweatshirt. He knew he still had to blend in, but no one said he couldn't wear his own clothing underneath the tunic. After slinging the pack over his shoulder, he took one last look around the room. The others were still asleep. In his heart, he knew this was the best way to figure things out—the others were already set in their beliefs. They'd get in his way. Alan walked over to his sister's bed and grabbed the notebook and pen sitting on her nightstand.

Before Alan wrote anything, he glanced over what Abigail had last written. It pained him to read. Here he was, focused on himself, and most twins had a sense of each other's emotions, but Alan had closed himself off from what his sister was dealing with. He'd been selfish, as usual, but it still wasn't enough to make him change his mind. Still, he couldn't help but keep reading her private thoughts.

This whole ordeal has been taking unspoken and subtle tolls on my best friends. In Tadashi, I've noticed his optimism fade ever since Shadow-Lord told us these things about Avery and our parents... I think he's confused and hurt like the rest of us, not sure what to believe. But even more affected are Mei and Alan...Mei has been quiet this entire evening here at Shadow-Lord's castle. I think she's silently torn up, wondering why her grandma never told the truth about her parents' deaths. And then there's Alan...I think I'm most worried about him. I know he loves Avery, but it's been so many years. As much as I want to believe Shadow-Lord is lying, I don't feel that he's trying to deceive us. I mean, we obviously don't know Shadow-Lord or Avery very well, but Avery was the one who brought us here in such a brute-like manner. Honestly, I think Alan will continue to challenge Shadow-Lord at every turn in our journey. I can't stop him every single time. I just don't want to see him get hurt if it turns out Avery is the villain. I truly hope we come across Avery on our journey to hear his side of the story. But for now, everything is shrouded in lies, hearsay, and what we desperately want to believe. That's how life is sometimes. The one thing I know for sure is that we can get through this together, whether it's Avery or Shadow-Lord who turns out to be our enemy.

Alan set the notebook back down and ran his hand through his hair. He felt even more weight on his shoulders. His sister was the optimistic one, and what he was about to do would cause her pain and worry, though that wasn't his intention. He hoped that his words would somehow ease their minds before he left.

Guys, I can't wrap my head around all of this. I know you're worried about me, Abigail—don't be. I know you all are probably wrestling with the same questions I have, but you know me. I'm not one to just sit idly by when I don't agree with something. I need to take action, and under Shadow-Lord's control, I don't feel like I'll get the answers I need. That's why I'm going to look for Avery alone. I just need to see for myself that Avery is what Shadow-Lord says he is. One thing I do believe is that Shadow-Lord will not hurt any of you. I do think he is sincere in that he feels we are his only hope, but to what end? Is he using us for good, or are we pawns in a greater scheme? I hope to find answers by heading to the Castle in Wethan that Shadow-Lord spoke of. If anything, maybe I can send back help. I'm sorry if you feel like I'm abandoning you, but we'll see each other again, I promise. Love, Alan.

Alan placed the note on his bed and walked quietly toward the staircase. He could hear voices downstairs, so he pressed his back flat against the cold brick wall, straining to listen. That's when he realized it was Shadow-Lord speaking with a Morg at the bottom of the stairs. A few feet ahead, there was a small alcove. Alan moved quietly toward it to eavesdrop.

"Boss, scouts you sent to Bramble... they watch Mist... have reported back. Mist have left Bramble... have gone abroad..."

Shadow-Lord sighed, looking weary. Alan felt a twinge of sympathy for him, but his conviction that Shadow-Lord was lying remained.

"Did you ensure we have guards on every wall? Have you locked down the gate?" Shadow-Lord asked.

"Yes, Boss, all done."

Shadow-Lord turned to look up the stairs, sensing something wasn't right. But after seeing nothing, he walked away with the Morg.

Alan's plan to walk out the front door was now hindered. He would head up instead of down. He couldn't allow Shadow-Lord to catch him. Alan made sure to walk softly up each step, keeping close to the outside wall. He had no idea how he'd get out, especially with the gate locked. Maybe if he reached the top of the castle, he could get a better view of the grounds.

At the next landing, Alan turned a corner and bumped into something—a Morg.

The Morg looked down at Alan, speaking gruffly. "What small hoo-mun doing?"

Alan gulped. "Um... looking for the highest point in the castle."

He expected the Morg to beat him senseless, but instead, the Morg replied.

"Oh, the Spire? Stairwell down the hall, on the left... first right. Can't miss it."

Alan looked down the hall where the Morg gestured. "Thanks!"

"No problem, small hoo-man. You have good night now."

Alan smiled, "Thanks! You too!"

As he followed the Morg's directions, Alan was still amazed by the help. Shadow-Lord definitely took good care of them.

As he climbed the stairs to the tower, Alan noticed that this part of the castle was less well-kept than the lower floors. The walls were cracked and falling apart. Just then, stone particles began falling from above.

The climb to the top seemed endless. After fifty steps, Alan stopped counting and began questioning himself.

What would happen to his friends when he left? Was it worth the risk to find Avery? Was everything he knew about Avery a lie? Why hadn't his parents told him and Abigail about the Forgotten Lands? Did Avery cause Mei and Tadashi's parents' deaths? Could the Mist attacking the castle be his fault? Was the Mist making good on its promise to hunt him?

When Alan reached the top, he collapsed—not from physical exhaustion, but mental overload. He needed his mind to shut off. He began hitting his palms against his head to refocus. First, he tried thinking about food, but that only brought him back to the last meal with his friends. He then replayed the last movie he watched, but it only reminded him of laughing with Mei and Abigail. Guilt started to creep in, but he shut it down. He promised himself he was doing this for them—he needed to see it through to get them home safely.

As Alan stood up, he almost lost his balance, his right foot caught in a wide crack in the floor. Once steady, he looked around the spire, which was almost completely destroyed. The floor looked as if a jackhammer had been used on it. He took a deep breath and cautiously stepped toward what might have once been a balcony.

Alan's heart raced as he feared the floor might collapse beneath him, but the panic faded when he reached the balcony. Looking out toward the grounds, he saw Morgs gathered at the South, East, and West walls. That meant the North wall was his best bet for escaping.

After planning his next steps, Alan made his way carefully to the stairs. When he reached the top, a loud voice from below stopped him—Shadow-Lord.

"HE DID WHAAAT?!"

Then, in the distance, Alan heard an earth-shattering roar. He turned, hoping the spire hadn't collapsed, but quickly realized it was the Mist.

Alan hurried down the stairs, avoiding the Morgs rushing to fortify the castle. He ignored Shadow-Lord, who was trying to calm Abigail, who demanded he find Alan before he got too far. Alan heard her shout, "Alan! Stop!" but he kept running, focused on escape.

Finally, Alan reached the courtyard, but the Morgs had blocked the end of the bridge. He stopped, assessing his options. The way back was blocked, but the only choice left was insane—jump over the bridge and into the moat twenty feet below.

Alan took a deep breath, climbed onto the bridge's wall, and jumped. The momentum sent him deep into the water. He swam several feet underwater before surfacing. Realizing the Morgs were about to jump in after him, he dove again, swimming as fast and far as he could to get a better head start.

When Alan finally reached the bank, there was no sign of the Morgs. It was pitch dark, but he remained light on his feet as he moved toward the forest.

As Alan jogged deeper into the woods, he realized the Mist's roar was still lingering in the air. He hoped it hadn't picked up his trail yet, at least long enough for him to put some distance between himself and the castle.

The stars above were blocked by the trees, and Alan couldn't run at full speed, so he kept a steady pace. Occasionally, he stopped to catch his breath, running on adrenaline and very little sleep. He soon heard movement behind him. The Mist had picked up his trail. Alan began running faster, desperate to outrun the creature that had hunted him for so long.

Suddenly, Alan missed his footing and fell, tumbling down through branches, rocks, and debris. Then, everything went black as he hit the ground.

He slowly sat up, struggling to breathe, feeling the weight of the fall on his body. But when he realized the roar was gone, he finally relaxed, and the exhaustion overtook him. He fell into a deep sleep, knowing that, for now, he had escaped.

CHAPTER THIRTEEN

Another Perspective

Abigail lay quietly in bed, her eyes closed, but sleep eluded her. She could feel that Alan wasn't sleeping either, though she knew any attempt to talk to him would likely lead to an argument about Avery.

Abigail understood his feelings but couldn't grasp how, after all the evidence Shadow-Lord had presented, Alan still refused to believe him. After all, it had been Avery who brought them to this strange world, not Shadow-Lord.

Her swirling thoughts eventually lulled her to sleep. When she awoke a short time later, she was surprised to feel somewhat rested, but there was an unease deep in her gut. Something wasn't right. She turned to look at the others. Mei and Tadashi were sleeping soundly, but Alan's bed was empty.

Abigail quietly got up and approached his bed, only to find it unoccupied. As she tried to gather her thoughts, she noticed a piece of paper on the nightstand.

The first time she read his words, her brain couldn't process what Alan had written. With all the chaotic thoughts swirling around her mind, it was hard to focus. She shook her head, trying to clear the whirlwind of emotions, and began calmly rereading the note.

This time, she absorbed every word. When she finished, she realized tears were streaming down her face. She cried out frantically, "Mei! Tadashi! Wake up! Wake up!"

Not getting any reply, Abigail ran to Mei's bedside and shook her friend awake. In her deep sleep, Mei accidentally backhanded Abigail across the face.

"Ow!" Abigail yelped, rubbing her reddened cheek.

Mei, now alert but still groggy, realized what she had done. Her eyes widened. "OH MY GOD! Abigail! I'm so sorry! I was dreaming I was about to slap that witch Sheila Towley!"

Abigail, still in shock from her friend's slap and frazzled by Alan's note, paused for a moment. "Wait... who?"

"She's this mean girl from school. She's blonde, has a fake spray tan, dresses like a—"

Abigail shook her head. "Oh, yeah, that jerk. Anyway, sorry to cut you off, but I need your help! Alan is gone!"

Mei, still trying to shake off sleep, asked, "What do you mean, he's gone?" She glanced over at his bed.

Abigail sat down next to Mei, handing her the note. "He left this. He's gone to look for Avery. We have to stop him! We can't let him go out there alone!"

Just then, Tadashi stirred, having been dreaming of fuzzy baby lerps licking his face. He wanted to get back to his dream, but he couldn't ignore Mei and Abigail's voices. "What's the big idea? Can't a guy get any sleep around here?"

Abigail shouted, "We have no time for sleep! Alan is gone! He left to find Avery! I need you both to get our packs ready and meet me downstairs. I'm going to see if I can find him."

As Abigail ran through the castle, she bumped into Shadow-Lord, who was shouting orders to his Morgs. "Seal the castle! I'll do my best to repel the mist!"

He turned and noticed Abigail. "Get back to your room! It's not safe down here..."

Abigail shook her head, screaming, "NO! Alan's missing! He left a note. He went to search for Avery. We need to find him!"

Just then, Alan ran past. "Alan?! Stop!" Abigail yelled, but Alan kept running. As she tried to follow, Shadow-Lord grabbed her arm.

"No, I'll deal with Alan," he said.

Abigail fought against his grip, determined to be the one to go after her brother.

Outside, she saw Alan leap off the bridge and into the moat. She rushed to the edge, looking desperately for him in the water. When she couldn't see him, she cried out, "Alan! Where are you? If you didn't drown, I'm going to kill you!" Several Morgs advanced toward her, so she had no choice. With determination, she jumped into the water after him.

It was dark, and the water was murky, making it hard to see. Abigail climbed up an embankment, hoping Alan had done the same. She spotted him running from the Mist, which seemed to be herding him back toward the castle. But Alan wasn't letting it stop him. He was heading for the woods, and Abigail kept chasing the Mist. Once she crossed into the woods, the Mist turned and began chasing her, forcing her to flee.

"Oh crap! Alan! If you can hear me, help!" she yelled. She ran as fast as she could back toward Darkspire.

Just before reaching the main gate, Abigail saw Shadow-Lord. He stood with his arms raised. As she neared, he shouted, "Hurry! Get behind me!"

Abigail turned to see the Mist no longer following her, instead hovering a few yards from Shadow-Lord. After a few tense minutes, the Mist began to retreat.

Shadow-Lord called to Gorb and Glum, "Take the supplies we've readied. Get the kids onto the horses and head north. I'll catch up with you as soon as I can."

Abigail stood there, not moving, which only angered Shadow-Lord. His concentration wavered, and the Mist began to creep toward her again. He bellowed, "GO! GO NOW!"

Reluctantly, Abigail followed Gorb to the horses. Mei and Tadashi were already in their saddles.

"Hurry up, Abigail. I know you're worried about Alan, we all are, but we won't be able to help him if we're dead," Mei said.

Abigail mounted the horse that Glum had brought over to her, but before they rode away, she took one last glance at Shadow-Lord, pushing the Mist back into the forest. Her thoughts were only of Alan. Please be okay.

Gorb led the group of horses, holding a lantern to light their path. Abigail rode behind him, marveling at the size of his horse compared to hers.

Mei rode up beside her. "I have to say, if it weren't for the fact that we're living in a nightmare and have no idea where Alan is, this would feel like the most normal situation we've had in a while."

Abigail shot her a sharp look. "What? You think this is normal?"

Mei realized how callous her comment might have sounded. "Um, no, not really. I just meant, you know, riding horses like we did at your Uncle Travis's ranch over the summer. It just feels familiar and calming. I didn't mean to downplay the fact that Alan's missing."

Abigail took a deep breath. "I'm sorry. I didn't mean to snap. I'm just worried. Alan shouldn't have left us. I'm worried about him, but I've come to terms with the fact that it was his choice to go. As it's my choice to help Marik fix things."

Mei didn't reply right away. After a few minutes, Abigail added, "And yeah, this does remind me of last summer, but it also makes me question things."

Mei didn't understand. "What do you mean?"

Abigail laughed softly, "I don't know, like, is my Uncle Travis really my uncle? Is my name even Abigail? I just don't like the sound of Abigail Elwyn. Abigail Foster has a better ring to it."

Mei nodded. "Yeah, I get it. But think about it—remember how kids at school made fun of Tadashi and me, calling us fish and asking where our scales were? I kind of like the name Mei Mikan, but honestly, I still need to get to know that person."

Abigail smiled. "Well, I can tell you one thing. Whether you're Mei Koi or Mei Mikan, you're a great friend, and that's all that matters."

Tadashi, who had been riding next to Mei, called out, "If you get any sappier, you're going to make me cry." He laughed to lighten the mood.

After riding in silence for a while, Tadashi broke the quiet. "Are you guys as exhausted as I am?"

Mei and Abigail responded in unison, "Yes."

Gorb, overhearing, spoke for the first time, "Still four hours away."

The three friends groaned and continued riding in silence behind the Morgs.

As they rode, Mei found herself debating everything that had happened since they arrived in the Forgotten Lands. She wasn't sure which side was telling the truth. She didn't understand why Abigail had so quickly come to trust Shadow-Lord, especially after everything that had happened. And she couldn't shake the feeling that Abigail was dismissing Alan's feelings too easily.

At the same time, Tadashi was worried about Alan. He looked up to him and felt that Alan had been their guide through the worst. Tadashi trusted Abigail and Mei, but he also knew that Alan's conflict ran deep. He just prayed they would all be reunited and see Sobo again.

Abigail wasn't thinking about Avery or Shadow-Lord. She was lost in thoughts of her parents, wondering if they had prepared her for something like this. Had everything, from martial arts to family camping trips, been part of some larger plan? She also wondered about her friends—who among them might be from this place, and if she'd ever make it back to Earth.

The group eventually arrived at camp, and Gorb called out, "We here at camp. Once Glum puts up tents, you sleep."

The kids dismounted from their horses and waited for the Morgs to set up their camp. Once they did, the three friends shared a tent. Abigail pulled out the jar of peanut butter her mother had packed for her. "Tadashi, do you still have that loaf of bread you swiped at dinner?"

Tadashi smiled. "I and my stomach thank you."

They ate, and after, they closed their eyes, dreaming of home.

Chapter Fourteen

The Prison

"Ahhh... uhhh?... What the... where... tu! Ptuh! Bleh! What the hell?" Alan groaned as small rocks and dirt pelted his face, spitting and sputtering as the soil particles found their way into his open mouth.

After slowly sitting up and spitting a few more times, he realized that for the first time since arriving in Whenua, he felt rested. His stomach, however, was growling, reminding him he should have eaten more at dinner the night before. His body was sore all over, but nothing seemed broken, so he was thankful for that.

Though no one was around, he said aloud, "Guess it's time for a protein bar. Glad Shadow-Lord supplied us with water flasks, at least I can stay hydrated. The way to Wethan has a large river, and he said the water's drinkable."

Alan slowly made his way to his feet and surveyed his surroundings. A faint natural light seemed to be emanating from a tunnel ahead. The place he had fallen into appeared to be an old mineshaft. He glanced upward to the spot where he had fallen and began thinking aloud, "Climbing out of here seems unlikely... I'd just slide down the muddy walls. There's nothing to grab onto. I guess the only option is to follow this tunnel and see where it leads."

As he walked through the mineshaft, he noticed the wooden support beams, old and cracked in several places. This place felt as dangerous as the spire had been. The last thing he needed was a cave-in. That would be the end of him, and he doubted anyone would ever find his body.

The ground gradually sloped downward. A few feet later, his footing gave way, and he slid down a steep incline. When he reached the bottom, the ground leveled out, and he realized the light ahead was growing brighter.

Despite being unsure of his surroundings, one thing was certain: the Mist was no longer chasing him. That fact alone made this path feel less foreboding.

The tunnel eventually opened into a vast chamber with a ceiling that seemed to stretch for miles. At the center of the room stood a massive, bright blue crystalline structure that rose to the top. Alan spoke aloud, feeling a mix of awe and loneliness, "Wow, it's like a pillar of sapphires. Abigail and Mei would love to see this." His words echoed back to him.

Turning to take in the beauty around him, Alan marveled not only at the central structure but at the walls, embedded with smaller glowing crystals of all colors. The chamber's vastness created a distinct reverb, so he started saying things just to hear his own voice. He recited lines from books and movies, his thoughts swirling.

"Hello there," he said with a half-hearted British accent. Though he tried to stay upbeat, the weight of solitude was crushing, and doubt crept into his mind.

"Too bad I don't have a camera. This is beautiful."

He wandered the chamber, taking in his surroundings.

"I might as well pick up a souvenir for Abigail and Mei. Maybe it'll help them forgive me... though I'm not sure I'll ever forgive myself."

The crystals embedded in the walls were too deep to take, but he found smaller, pebble-sized ones scattered on the floor.

"This is better anyway. With all these colors, they can each get something different. Mom would love these too. I can't forget about her."

He paused, lost in thought. "Mom, I wish you were here. I have so many questions. Were the characters in the story real, since the world and history themselves are? Did you and Dad have adventures like in the story?" He sighed. "But you're not here, and neither is Dad. I guess questioning this out loud is pointless... No one's here... no one but me. I'm alone. And what's worse, it was my choice... Oh, God, Abigail... Mom, please don't be mad at me. I left Abigail for what I believe were the right reasons. She's safer where she is... maybe I'm wrong about Avery, but I need to find that out on my own. I couldn't risk her, Mei, or Tadashi..." Alan shook his head, pushing the darker thoughts away. "You'd be proud of Abigail, Mom. She's been amazing, considering everything that's happened. I know Abigail and I have you to thank for surviving all we've faced. Maybe this is what you were preparing us for all our lives..."

The tunnel twisted and turned, and Alan felt a breeze coming from ahead. Maybe there was a way out. He was getting tired of caves. He longed to see home again... but where was home?

"I don't doubt I was born here... but do I have family here that I never knew? Aunts? Uncles? Cousins? Maybe even grandparents? But this world... it's different. Living here would mean no creature comforts. Then again, I'm sure they have books. You had to have learned how to read and write somewhere, since this isn't Earth. Maybe living in Whenua wouldn't be so bad... I need to see more before I make a decision, if I even have a choice. So far, I'm not impressed... but according to Shadow-Lord, not everything is as dead as I've seen. There must be places of unreal beauty, like the Grotto of Life... mountains... places I only dreamed of seeing back on Earth. Maybe I'm crazy... but maybe this is where we're meant to be. Home... can't figure it out by—"

He suddenly stopped. Wrapped up in his thoughts, he almost didn't notice the wide gully ahead that separated him from the other side of the cave. "That was close," he muttered. "I'd better focus."

Turning around, Alan retraced his steps. He remembered seeing a corridor not far back and decided to try that route.

It didn't take long to find the passageway, which was three times as wide as the tunnel he'd been following, with a higher ceiling. The only problem? It wasn't lit by the gemstones. He paused and cracked a glowstick, immediately seeing the path more clearly.

Halfway down, Alan noticed something protruding from both sides of the walls. Upon closer inspection with his glowstick, he realized they were pulsating silk sacs. Panic set in as he heard a loud chirping sound. "Oh shit!"

He quickly moved down the passage, careful not to bump into the sacs. From science class, he knew that chirping spiders were agitated.

The corridor opened into a larger room, lit by torches spaced every few feet. As Alan ran into the room, he muttered, "I hate spiders... I hate spiders... I hate spiders!"

Out of nowhere, a voice interrupted, "Still yourself, and do not speak. The creatures are blind. They sense vibrations from your voice and movements. Carefully and slowly walk over to one of the torches on the wall. If they are lit, hold it out towards them. They are warm-blooded and will retreat from the heat of the flame."

Alan froze. Could someone be down here with him, or was he hallucinating? Either way, grabbing a torch was a good idea, so that's what he did.

With the torch in hand, Alan gently waved it in front of him, and the spiders retreated. He breathed a sigh of relief, but it was short-lived.

A cracked voice spoke again, "Who are you? How did you find this place?"

Alan carefully walked toward the voice, unsure if it was real or just in his head. Soon, he saw large iron doors lined with thick metal bars. Behind one of them stood an old man, battered and bruised.

Alan's first instinct was to help. "I wasn't sure if you were real. I'll try to get you out. What is this place? Wait... before I open the door, you're not a mass murderer or anything, are you?"

The older man eyed Alan warily. He seemed familiar, but it was more likely this was a trick of Shadow-Lord's. Cautiously, he asked, "Who are you? How did you come to be here?"

Alan chuckled nervously, realizing he was still stunned to hear another voice. "I fell down a hole while being chased by something called the Mist. I couldn't climb back up, so I've been wandering these tunnels, looking for a way out."

The man studied him but didn't respond right away. Alan continued, "Don't worry, I'm not a threat. I won't hurt you or anyone. I'm just a normal teenager. I wouldn't hurt a fly... well, maybe a fly if it's annoying, but never a person. I promise."

The old man stood up and approached the iron door. Alan's awkward mannerisms made him think this boy wasn't a servant of his captor. He decided to trust him, for now. "You still haven't told me your name..."

Alan slapped his forehead. "Right, forgot. My name's Alan... Alan Foster, or maybe Alan Elwyn. Not sure which surname I should go by. Anyway, who are you?"

The man's eyes widened in shock. "Alan? No... why are you here?" He shook his head. "It's hard to believe, but I'm your old neighbor and friend, Avery Ambrose."

Alan's jaw dropped. He couldn't find words at first. Finally, he stammered, "Avery? You... You're real?"

Avery laughed, though it was a bittersweet sound. "Oh, boy, it's good to see you, even if it's under horrible circumstances." He paused, then added, "That spider, by the way? It was harmless. Just a fishing spider."

Alan laughed too, but the laughter quickly turned to tears. "I can't explain how happy I am to see you. Wait until Abigail, Mei, and Tadashi find out you're here."

Avery cut him off. "Wait, they're here too? Where are they? Why aren't they with you?"

Alan wiped his face. "I'll explain everything. Just let me grab a rock to break this lock and get you out of here."

Several hard hits later, the lock fell to the ground. Alan embraced Avery in a bear hug, but quickly pulled away when Avery winced in pain.

"I'm so sorry. Did I hurt you?"

Avery smiled faintly. "It's nothing. My captor wasn't gentle, but the wounds are healing. Now, where are the others?"

"Do we have time for that right now? Is your captor coming back? Is it Shadow-Lord?" Alan asked.

Avery nodded. "I was worried he was behind you being here. We'll talk as we go. But first, I need to know where the others are."

"I left them at Shadow-Lord's fortress. We weren't sure who to trust. Shadow-Lord convinced them that you're evil, but I wasn't convinced. I wanted to prove he wasn't telling the truth about you... or the other Avery. Maybe I've figured it out."

Avery frowned. "Slow down. I don't understand. Let's talk as we walk. It's been months since I was brought here, but I know the way out."

By the time they reached the exit, Alan had told Avery everything—about Shadow-Lord, his dreams, and what led him to this point.

Avery looked at Alan, his expression somber. "You've been through a lot. I wish none of this had happened, especially without knowing your past, your family's past. Let's rest for a bit. You need to understand something. There's only one Avery Ambrose, and the man who brought you here—he's an ally of Shadow-Lord."

Alan shook his head, "I thought he was you. I should have seen through it."

Avery gave him a reassuring pat on the back. "Don't beat yourself up. In the end, you saw the truth. As for the other Avery... well, I need to tell you the real story of who I am... and why your family left Whenua. It starts with my history. My true history."

CHAPTER FIFTEEN

The History

Alan reached into his backpack and pulled out some bread and grapes he had taken from the castle. "Here, we should eat something while you tell me everything I need to know. I'm not sure when you last ate, but I'm sure it's been a while."

Avery smiled. "Thank you, my boy. It has been a few days, but Shadow-Lord has sent his Morgs on occasion to feed me. He didn't need me dead just yet—he still had questions, and I didn't give him any answers."

Alan interjected, "From what I understand, the Morgs seem... innocent, and my mother's book didn't mention them."

Avery nodded. "They are innocent. Despite serving Shadow-Lord, I've come to realize that they're being tricked by him. He takes advantage of their innocent nature. The Arkarnian Empire created them by accident during a series of failed alchemy experiments long ago, before most of the kingdoms of the world existed. The Arkarnians labeled them 'morgudite,' which roughly translates to 'one who is foolish' in our language. Eventually, the Morgs escaped and found sanctuary in the manor of an Arkarnian alchemist who despised how his empire was abusing his craft. He cast a spell around his manor to protect it throughout the ages. But after the alchemist died, the manor fell into disrepair—he never could teach the Morgs how to repair what he couldn't. Eventually, I suspect Shadow-Lord stumbled upon the ruins and renamed it Darkspire."

Avery paused to chew a few grapes, savoring their sweetness. After swallowing, he continued, "I am a wizard. I've served as an Advisor to the King and Queen of Wethen for the past thirty years. My wife, Marion, served as a special consul to the King and Queen. One of her duties was to broker a peace agreement with the Arkarnians. Unfortunately, it was unsuccessful, and she was killed..."

Alan nodded. "Shadow-Lord said you weren't allowed to intervene. Did you really not put up a fight?"

Avery shook his head. "No, that's not true. I did everything in my power to stop Korvas from killing her. I wasn't strong enough. I failed her. I had another matter I was attending to at the time... I barely remember what it was now. By the time I learned she was in danger and that Korvas had no intention of making peace, I arrived too late."

Alan watched Avery's face, seeing the lingering pain from that time. He felt guilty for making him relive it. He moved to sit beside him, placing a hand on his shoulder. "I... I'm sorry about your wife. I saw Korvas the other day. He was evaluating two young Arkarnians, and he was angry at one of them. Korvas smelled me, but he assumed I was Shadow-Lord, so he left with the others. They talked about killing and eating human scouts. I presume they were from Wethen. Is that the kingdom my parents are from?"

Avery nodded. "Indeed, your father was born and raised in Wethen. Your mother is from elsewhere in Whenua, but she came to live here later. Both of them serve the King and Queen of Wethen—Alfonse and Eshe Belmont. They are all good friends. Your father, James, is the Grandmaster of Wethen's military. He oversees the defense of the kingdom during this cold war with the Rau-Trava."

"When I look at him," Alan said, "I can see how much being away from you and Abigail weighs him down... but his job is important."

Avery raised an eyebrow. "I think it's not just being away from you and Abigail, though. You see, the basement of your home has a portal to a place in Whenua... Wethen specifically. Your mother, Madeline, is Wethen's most experienced diplomatic advisor and councilor. She apprenticed under my wife. She's responsible for many important treaties and alliances."

Alan asked, "Why were the four of us—myself, Abigail, Mei, and Tadashi—all raised on Earth?"

Avery smiled. "I think we should get moving now. I'll explain as we walk."

Alan grabbed his backpack and helped Avery to his feet. "How far do you think we are from the castle?"

Avery thought for a moment. "About two hours away."

Alan ran his hand through his hair. "Crap... we'll be too late."

Avery looked at him with concern. "What do you mean by that?"

"Shadow-Lord's plan... we were supposed to leave first thing this morning for the Polar Regions. I doubt my leaving will make him rethink that, especially if he knows I went toward where he was keeping you."

Avery pulled Alan's arm to urge him to move. "Time is of the essence. We must travel faster. There's a chance he's sent Morgs to find you. He doesn't know if he still needs you, but I presume he's told you about the Orbs of Livimor and Morimor?"

Alan nodded. "Yes, he said either Abigail or I can obtain Morimor's orb because of an enchantment. He said the orbs once gave life to Whenua, and that you want to use them to take life from Whenua and Earth to revive your wife. I know that isn't true, of course, but... is it Shadow-Lord who's destroying the world?"

As they moved quickly through the forest, Avery began to speak. "First of all, I'll answer your question about why you and the others were raised on Earth..."

"There was a group—followers of a dark wizard who died long ago—that sought the Orbs. The night you and Abigail were born, they snuck into the castle of Overgate, which I believe your mother would have mentioned in her book. The attackers tried to kidnap you both, knowing about the enchantment on the Orb of Morimor. They wanted to use you to further their own agenda. Of course, the attackers were apprehended or killed."

"Afterward, your parents came to me. Few know that Whenua is still connected to the worlds that the Ancient Arkarnian Empire touched. Your parents, along with the King and Queen of Wethen, were among the few I trusted with that secret. They asked me to help keep you both safe. I found as many archaic tomes as I could and did something I thought only the Orbs could do. I opened an ancient gateway between Whenua and Earth—a portal that ran from your father's chambers in Overgate to the basement of the home where you and Abigail would be raised. The previous owner of that house was doing laundry when I arrived through the portal. He was quite cooperative once I gave him a heavy bar of gold. As for how Mei and Tadashi came to be raised on Earth, well, their father is a good friend of your father. He asked your parents to take his children and mother-in-law with them. He and his wife hold important roles in Wethen—roles they couldn't perform with a double life, unlike your parents."

Alan choked on his own saliva. "Wait—do you mean they're alive?!"

Avery nodded. "Yes, Alan. Mei and Tadashi's parents are alive. One day, I hope to see them reunited. There's no reason for them not to be, though I hope in time they can forgive their parents for not being there."

Alan didn't ask any further. He'd learn more later. For now, he needed to understand what was happening. "So how did all of this lead to what's happening now? What's destroying the Forgotten Lands? Why are the Orbs so important?"

Avery didn't respond right away, gathering his thoughts. "We'll get to that, but first, there are things I need to tell you that will make it all clearer."

"Long ago... I had a brother. His name was Materall."

Alan could sense the emotional pain Avery was still carrying. He asked the obvious. "This isn't a happy story, is it?"

Avery shook his head. "No, it's not."

"First, while I'm sure your mother detailed what she knew in the book she wrote about the world, I'll give a brief rundown in case she missed anything important. Ah, here..." Avery picked up a scrap of blank parchment from the ground and waved his fingers across it, creating a map.

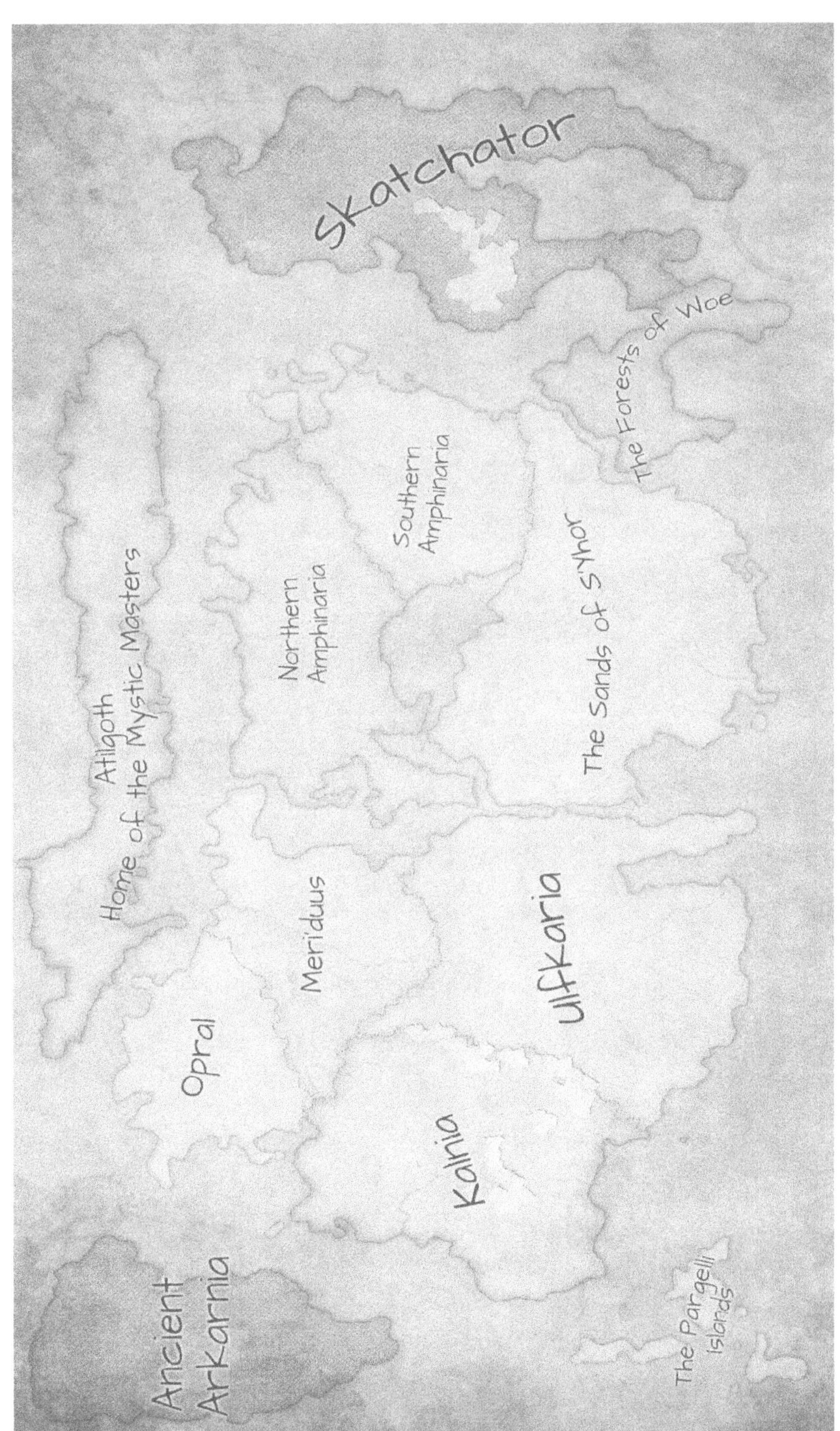
Skatchator
The Forests of Woe
Southern Amphinaria
Northern Amphinaria
The Sands of S'Yhor
Atilgoth
Home of the Mystic Masters
Meriduus
Ulfkaria
Opral
Kalnia
Ancient Arkarnia
The Pargelli Islands

"Now, this map shows the Eastern Continent. There are seven kingdoms. The first two are the Swamplands of the Amphinarians, a race of frogmen who were split into two factions: the North and the South. The third kingdom is Ulfkaria, home to the Dwargs, a race of bipedal dog people. The fourth kingdom is the beautiful Republic of Opral, a mixed-race kingdom with no definitive majority. The fifth kingdom is the Commonwealth of Kalnia, which democratically elects its King and Queen. Like Opral, Kalnia is mostly mixed-race, though humans are less common there. The sixth kingdom is Meri'duus, an aristocratic society mostly made up of humans. Finally, the seventh kingdom isn't really a kingdom at all, but a society divided into separate regions. This area is known as the Sands of S'yhor, inhabited by a species of lizardmen who are not Arkarnian."

"Surrounding the seven kingdoms on three sides are several large islands, so massive that one might think they should be considered continents themselves. Think of Greenland on Earth, which, despite its size, is still considered an island. These islands are Skatchator, Atilgoth, and Ancient Arkarnia. Atilgoth is home to the Mystic Masters, a quasi-religious order of wizards to which I have belonged my entire life."

"Ancient Arkarnia was once home to the majority of the Arkarnian race, but now it is devoid of all life. Over here is Skatchator, a land of many mountain kingdoms and various forms of government. You'd need someone more familiar with them for an in-depth analysis of their way of life—I don't know much about them myself. Finally, this is the island of Pargellia, where a species of fish people, the Pargellians, live."

Avery then turned the map over. "This is the Western Continent, where we currently are. I've made two separate maps on this side—one shows the land as it once was, and the other shows it as it is now. The reason I've done this for the West and not the East is because the East hasn't changed much in the past sixty years, while the West has." Avery held up both maps.

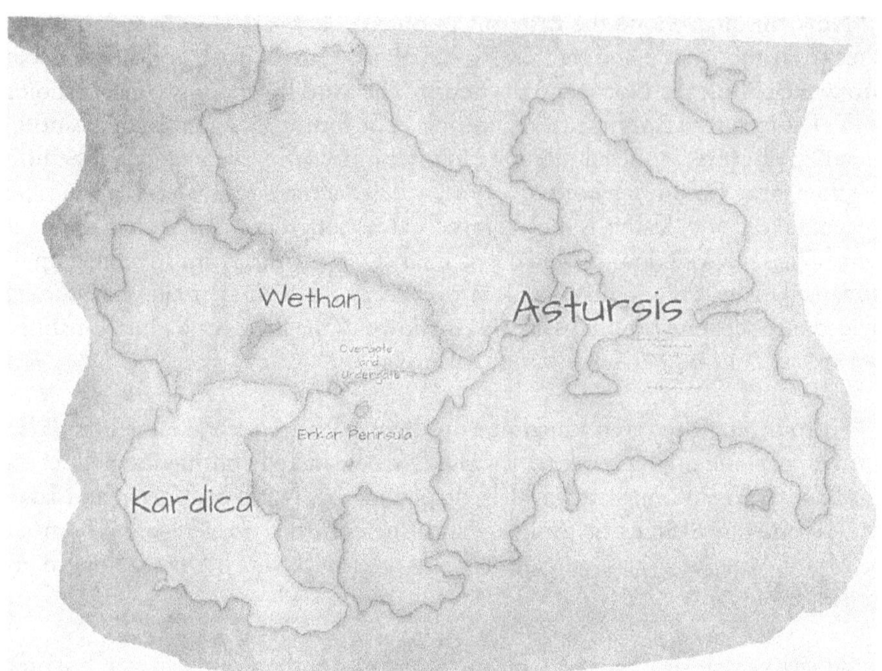

Wethan
Astursis
Overgate
and
Undergate
Erkar Peninsula
Kardica

The Polar Region
The Sirrid of Mirania
The Reservations
New Arkarnia
Wethan
Overgate and Undergate
The Shadow Lands
Erkar Peninsua
New Arkarnia
Kardica

"In the present, the West is home to three kingdoms, Kardica, Wethan, and New Arkarnia. As you can see, some of these territories were once part of the now-fallen human kingdom of Astursis. These kingdoms once prospered greatly. However, as the fall of Astursis and the total destruction of Ancient Arkarnia imply, that prosperity no longer holds true today."

"Now, it's time to tell you the story of my family..."

"My brother and our parents, Aiden and Morgana Ambrose, were also members of the Mystic Masters. My father held the position of Wethen's resident Mystic Master, while my mother was content overseeing the training of me and Materall, without the burdens of political tasks. Because of my father's high rank, my brother and I had a very happy childhood. We lived in a tower near Overgate, which I still call home today, though my duties to Wethen rarely allow me to stay there long."

"For a while, things stayed the same. But around my brother's tenth birthday, when I was seven, I noticed he was changing. One night, when our parents were asleep, he came to me and entrusted me with a secret..."

"He told me, and his best friend Tannis, that he was learning forbidden forms of magic. He wanted me and Tannis to join him. I'm ashamed to admit it, but I allowed him to control me. I wanted him to respect me because I looked up to him..."

"Tannis was a bright boy—older than me but younger than Materall. While Materall quickly realized that Tannis lacked the potential for magic, he decided that Tannis could be a loyal ally. Tannis, like me, looked up to Materall. The only difference was that I eventually couldn't stomach what it took to gain Materall's trust and admiration. When I was sixteen, and Materall was nineteen, he began speaking to Tannis about gathering followers... amassing an army of disgruntled people to form a great empire. I realized things had escalated too far and that he was out of control. I told my father, but he didn't listen... he accused me of lying."

"That's when I exploded. You see, Alan... I always felt that my mother and father preferred Materall. He was the best at magic, the best at learning... I screamed at the top of my lungs that he was a fool, blinded by his love for his favored son, and that his blindness could lead to the deaths of millions... My father was furious, but my mother, who had been listening nearby, intervened. She told him that she believed me. I was shocked. I always assumed she favored Materall over me, just as my father did. But the fact that she was willing to believe me made me realize I was wrong..."

"My father didn't forgive me for what I said, even after my mother explicitly told him to. He still couldn't accept that Materall was trying to establish an empire, dismissing it as ludicrous."

"Later that same day, I took them to the place where Materall and I practiced our magic—on a hilltop near the bay of Erkar. When we arrived, there was a large crowd gathered. I had misunderstood what Materall and Tannis had been discussing. I thought they hadn't yet gathered followers, but in reality, the deed had already been done. That place... that's where it happened. That's when my family fractured."

"Materall's followers consisted of humans and a tribe of Arkarnian outcasts known as the Valthurg. Tannis, you see, was from Astursis. His father, Vesta, had been a well-respected soldier who died in a disastrous war—one that had only happened because the King of Astursis abandoned his people to die. The humans Materall recruited were Astursians—renegades who wanted vengeance. He promised them that he would help them settle their scores, and in return, they gave him their loyalty and the keys to their kingdoms."

"My father was so blind that, instead of acting rationally, he approached Materall on his podium and demanded that he tell everyone to return to their homes and stop the 'nonsense.' He was blinded by love, thinking that Materall still respected his authority as a father..."

"That's when my mother and I realized Materall's soul was truly lost..."

Avery paused, climbing over a large boulder. Alan felt sympathy for him as he relived these painful memories. Once Alan joined him on the other side of the rock, he almost told Avery to take a longer break, but Avery continued.

"Materall gloated, saying it wasn't worth killing my father personally. With that, he had Tannis stab him in the back before he could do anything. Tannis left him just enough life to process the betrayal. I remember how my father looked at me and my mother one last time. It's a strange thing, but sometimes, I think back to that moment... bittersweetly, because I believe that might have been the only time I saw my father look at me with love."

Alan's heart sank as he realized the tragedy of Avery's past. "Avery... I... holy crap, I'm so sorry you lost your father like that..."

Avery patted Alan's shoulder. "Thank you, Alan... But what happened next? Did Materall attack you and your mother?"

Avery shook his head. "No... He knew that while he had focused on dark magic, I had excelled in other areas of magic. And with our mother now aware of his evil, she wouldn't be so easily dispatched as our father had been. He knew that if he attacked, we'd destroy him in anger over what he did to my father, but he also knew that if we destroyed him, his followers would overwhelm and kill us. I wanted to attack, but my mother took me by the arm and told me it wasn't over. We had to choose our battles carefully. We wanted to take my father's body, but Materall wouldn't let us..."

"Why wouldn't he let you take the body?"

"He needed it for an ancient forbidden ritual called the Tish. The Tish allows someone to access a person's memories through their blood. It's a perversion of nature—experiencing memories that aren't your own, to gain wisdom and knowledge from them. The process is incredibly risky, as it can cause the blood vessels in the brain to spontaneously burst."

Alan stopped, his eyes wide. "Did the Shadow-Lord do that to you?"

Avery shook his head. "No. He wouldn't be that careless. He knew he could torture the information out of me instead."

"So, Materall used the Tish to learn your father's magic skills?"

Avery nodded. "Yes, he did. He was one of the few to survive using the Tish."

"So, what happened next?"

"Materall attacked Astursis, turning the people against one another. He killed the King of Astursis and secretly journeyed to the Grotto of Life—he learned of its location from my father's memories. It was a place guarded by the Mystic Masters, known only to those deemed most trustworthy. My mother and I had no idea where he was. We were helping Astursis fight back against the rebels. But soon, we learned that the civil war in Astursis was a diversion—a way for Materall to distract us. It was during this time that my grandmother was killed by the Valthurg. That pushed my mother into a blind rage, and she hunted down and killed every last one of them. Her violent course of action only deepened the war between Astursis and Arkarnia."

"I parted ways with my mother. I felt she was jeopardizing our mission. Soon after, I received a message from Materall, telling me the location of the Grotto of Life. I went there and found the bodies of the dead wizards... Materall had killed them all to secure the Orbs of Livimor and Morimor, twin Arkarnian sorcerers from thousands of years ago."

Alan interrupted, "Wait, before you continue, I need to know—what are the Orbs?"

"The Orbs were created by Livimor and Morimor to focus their powers. They were the twin Emperors of the Ancient Arkarnian Empire, which they founded. At their peak, they controlled most of Whenua, except for Atilgoth, which belonged to a now-extinct species. They discovered that with the Orbs, they could create portal arches, first using them to shorten travel across their empire. Eventually, they realized they could use the Orbs to travel to other worlds. They spread their empire across many worlds, but when people began rebelling, they panicked. In desperation, Livimor reached out to isolated human civilizations on Earth, convincing them to join his empire. But once they arrived, the twins sealed the portals, leaving Earth isolated and untouched by the Arkarnian Empire. Livimor eventually betrayed his brother, joining the rebellion and helping to overthrow Morimor."

"After centuries of war, the Arkarnian Empire collapsed. Livimor and Morimor killed each other, trapping their souls within the Orbs. The Mystic Masters took the Orbs and created the Grotto of Life, guarding them so no one could ever wield the power of the twin emperors again. Livimor's body was taken to a remote location, buried in the Polar Regions, while Morimor's tomb is known to the Valthurg, though I don't know its exact location."

Alan nodded, processing the information. "So, Materall wanted to use the Orbs to conquer Whenua?"

Avery slowly nodded. "Yes, but he also wanted to open a portal to another world. He believed that by connecting Whenua to a more advanced world, he could create prosperity and unity. He led me to a cave where an ancient archway lay. He convinced me to help him open a portal... and we ended up on Earth, in Red Pine Forest, circa 1979. There, we met a confused young woman named Marion."

Alan smiled but then asked, confused, "So, your wife wasn't even born in your world? But I thought only people born in Whenua could use the portal?" "

Avery sighed. "Correct. She was from Earth, As for the portal that was something Materall did when he tried to trap me on Earth... and I would have been trapped, if not for Marion's bravery. She was terrified, but she helped me when Materall blasted me in the back with dark magic and stole the Orb of Livimor. I was too injured to move, so I asked Marion to help me into the cave, which she did. Materall was too slow with the spell he cast to seal all portals, thinking it would stop anyone from entering Whenua. But, after he fled, I realized the spell had the opposite effect."

"With a heavy heart, I had to tell Marion she was trapped in another world. She couldn't go back. I expected her to be devastated, but instead, she took it surprisingly well. She was confused, yes, but she accepted it."

"She explained to me that she'd been an orphan recently kicked out of foster care due to her age. She was homeless, with no money, just a worn-out tent. So, in a way, her situation hadn't changed much—except now she didn't have a tent. But I was offering to help her, and that meant something to her."

"It wasn't until after I brought Marion back to my family's home and spoke to my mother about what Materall had done that I realized I needed her help in the quest to stop him. We left for Arkarnia, following the faint trail Materall had left. Knowing we were pursuing him made him move faster, and he was less careful about covering his tracks. We followed him to an ancient necropolis beneath Arkarnia's capital, a fountainhead of magic and natural energies. That's where he intended to empower himself. We caught up to him there, fought through his loyal followers, and faced him at the center of the necropolis."

"The battle was painful for my mother and me. We couldn't stop Materall from using the Orbs to corrupt the natural energies of Arkarnia. The once-pure land was transformed by dark magic. The Arkarnian people fled and launched a desperate invasion of Astursis. The atrocities committed by Arkarnia led to its collapse, breaking into two factions: the Dinalo and the Rau-Trava. Those who stood by their actions in the war formed the Dinalo, while those who felt nothing but sorrow and repentance formed the Rau-Trava. The Dinalo traveled west from the land claimed by the Rau-Trava, establishing New Arkarnia, a territory granted by Wethen, who held the right to take resources from them at will."

"It took everything we had to defeat Materall in the end. As the necropolis collapsed around us, destroying the Valthurg and many of Materall's followers, my mother wrested control of one of the Orbs from Materall. She opened a portal just as the ceiling caved in. The three of us broke away from the fighting to escape, emerging at the very place where Materall had killed our father. My brother believed that because my mother had used the Orb, she would be tempted to join him, so he let his guard down. He tried to convince her to kill me and join him. But instead, without hesitation, she used the Orb to mortally wound him. She took both Orbs and vowed to return them to their shrines, where she believed no one would find them. She confided in me that she would enchant them so only my cousin, Alan Elwyn II, or his descendants, could ever use them and break the enchantment. She believed no one would suspect him, since he had chosen a life outside of magic. And so, she left me to deal with my errant brother."

"He was arrogant even in defeat. He believed he would survive because I would save him. But he was wrong. I knew he was dying from his injuries, so I waited. I watched as he realized no one was coming to help him. He tried to crawl away, and almost reached the exit of the hilltop ruins before he finally stopped moving. I buried him in an unmarked grave, in a place we used to play, so that none of his followers would find it."

"So, after all that history, you now understand why the Shadow-Lord needs you and/or Abigail."

Alan shook his head. It was a lot to process, especially with everything else he had learned.

"So... Shadow-Lord really was telling the truth? We are related?"

Avery nodded. "Yes. The Shadow-Lord is my great-nephew and your fourth cousin. His real name is Marik. I didn't know Materall had a son until Marik revealed himself to me. By that time, he had already decided to finish what his grandfather started—to find the Orbs and bend the world to his will."

"Two years after Materall's death, I was appointed to the Council of Elders and inherited my father's position in Wethen. And as you can probably guess, the group that tried to kidnap you and Abigail were Materall's former followers."

Alan considered asking Avery more about Mei and Tadashi's parents, but he decided it wasn't relevant to their current situation.

They walked in silence for several minutes. Avery wanted to give Alan a chance to absorb everything, and Alan wanted Avery to rest. Avery was exhausted in both body and mind. "I think we should stop for a few minutes so you can catch your breath."

Avery smiled. "Your concern is noted, but I'll be fine. Even though I may look old and weak, my magical abilities help regenerate my body. I should be good to go in about an hour. You do realize I'm only fifty-nine?"

Alan panicked for a moment. "I wasn't trying to say you look old! Honest!"

Avery chuckled. "Calm down, Alan. I was just teasing you. I know you didn't mean it, but if you had, you wouldn't be wrong. My hair is greyer than stone, and I've had a rough life. My appearance reflects that. So, yes, I look old, and mentally, I feel old at times. But physically, I like to think I'm still quite spry."

As they continued walking, Alan couldn't shake something Shadow-Lord had said. "So, about my grandfather... about Shadow-Lord needing me or my sister—one of us having magical abilities, but not both? How would we even know if we had this ability? Would we already have noticed? Would we know how to use it?"

Avery paused, then responded after a moment of thought.

"Everyone on Whenua is born with magic inside them. But not everyone can harness it. First, you have to decide if this is a path you want to take. Then, you'll need to be trained by someone adept in magic. Once we find the others and are safe, I can tell you more. If, after that, you want to see if you have the ability, I'd be happy to test you."

Alan accepted this and returned his focus to the task at hand: finding Abigail and the others.

The forest had grown thick with tall trees and undergrowth. Alan hadn't seen this part of the forest since he had fallen into the shaft and traveled underground. It reminded him of the Pine Tree Forest back home. There were no signs of the destruction they had seen days earlier. He stopped Avery to ask about it, and Avery replied, "We're still in the Northern Forest. When you arrived, you traveled from the south. We're almost at the secret entrance. Look through that patch of trees, and you'll see the fortress—Darkspire—in the distance."

Avery walked over to a sewer grate and started dragging it off. Alan began to realize what they were about to do. "Uh, if we're about to do what I think we're doing, I'd rather take my chances going through the front door."

Avery laughed. Then he walked over to a bush and pulled off several branches. "Here. Rub the leaves under your nose and keep the branch inside your shirt. It's mint, and it will help you endure the smells we're about to face. Once we're inside, we'll need to find alternative clothing."

Alan groaned, realizing this would be the worst part of this whole nightmare, but he did as instructed. When he dropped into the sewer, a loud splash echoed. "Aw, crap!"

"Quite literally," Avery laughed as he dropped down beside Alan.

Alan was relieved the waste was only a few inches deep and didn't have to be waded through.

Avery led the way through the sewer. "We should be coming to a three-way fork soon. If my memory serves me right, we need to take a right. About halfway down that channel, we'll need to find a ladder hanging down from one of the outlets."

Alan wondered how Avery knew his way around the castle's sewer but decided to let it go.

When they turned right, the sewer walls grew taller. Alan wondered if the channels ever filled up completely.

"There," Avery said, pointing to an iron ladder hanging about four feet from above.

"We might be tall guys, Avery, but there's no way I can reach that."

Avery extended his arm and, using magic, lifted Alan to the ladder. Then, he used the same magic to lift himself up.

Once they ascended the ladder, they found themselves in a room where clear blue water flowed into several pipes. Alan figured they were in a treatment room of some sort, and he was just relieved to be out of the waste.

"On the other side of those tanks, there will be a set of steps leading up to the dungeons," Avery said. "We'll check to see if Shadow-Lord has any prisoners. If so, they might be of use to us."

The dungeons were empty, and most of the cells didn't even have iron doors anymore. "Looks like Shadow-Lord never used this area. He must have only housed prisoners where he kept me," Avery muttered. "Let's check out the main floor, but we need to be quiet from here on out."

Alan followed Avery slowly up the stone steps. When they reached the wooden door, Avery cracked it open and peeked around. Satisfied that the coast was clear, he motioned for Alan to follow.

The first room they came upon was the dining hall. Avery peered inside. "Empty," he whispered.

This was how they proceeded—clearing each room, one by one, until the first floor was done. "I guess we head up next. You should lead now, Alan, since you know where you left the others."

Alan led them to the back staircase, remembering it was the closest to the room Shadow-Lord had given them. But as they moved, the silence began to disturb him. A feeling of dread crept in—he feared they were too late.

When Alan opened the bedroom chamber, he let out a sigh of defeat. "I was worried about this. They must have already left for the polar regions. This place has been abandoned."

Avery could hear the sadness in Alan's voice. "It'll be okay. We'll just have to catch up to them."

They made their way back down to the main hall and exited the castle. Avery wanted to take a quick look around outside to make sure no Morgs were waiting for them.

As they stepped outside, Alan initially missed two people standing in the courtyard. He ran toward the west, hoping to check for any hidden threats.

Avery smiled when he saw the two strangers. They ran over and embraced him. Just as Alan was about to yell out to Avery that the area was clear, he realized they weren't alone. He quickly ran over to see who they were.

"Who are you two?" Alan asked cautiously.

Elis smiled. "Don't worry, we're friends of Avery. I'm Elis, and this is Cinder."

Alan glanced at Avery, who nodded with a smile. "Elis is the Crown Prince of Wethan, and Cinder is a magically adept student of mine."

Avery's smile faded. "Wait... why are you two here? And where are your guards, Elis?"

Elis laughed nervously, scratching the back of his head. "Well, uh... that's a long story. But first, who's this guy?"

Chapter Sixteen

Elis and Cinder's Quest

The Market District of Overgate was bustling with activity as people went about their daily lives. The terracotta roof tiles of the buildings glowed a bright orange under the sun, contrasting sharply with the gray stone walls.

Prince Elis Belmont sat on a bench, watching the crowd bustle around him, seemingly carefree. At least, that's how it appeared at first glance. But as Elis observed more closely, he saw the weariness in their eyes—the struggle to make ends meet. Overgate's economy relied on trade with Kardica, but with horses requisitioned by the military, there were few left to pull wagons. As a result, crops and goods that once moved by land now had to be transported by boat, something that was no longer possible due to the Rau-Travan blockade. This blockade had severed trade routes between Kardica and Overgate, adding fuel to the growing conflict, turning what had been a cold war into a real threat of all-out war.

Seeing the hardship faced by the common folk troubled Elis, especially when he had ideas on how to ease their suffering. But despite being the son of the King of Wethen, his title as Prince granted him little real power within the kingdom. Yes, he could issue commands to civilians and guards, but he had no authority to make meaningful changes to improve the people's lives. His opinions carried little weight.

The King believed Elis too young and inexperienced to make decisions that affected the masses. However, this reality gave Elis the freedom to engage with the commoners in ways his father could not. He held gatherings where castle servants would bring food to share with the less fortunate, giving him a chance to speak with the people and hear their hopes and fears for the kingdom—things his father remained ignorant of. In time, Elis began to believe he could be a leader who could truly help his people, if only the kingdom remained intact long enough for his father to abdicate.

But today, as he watched the people, it wasn't their struggles that troubled him. For once, his mind was occupied with the rumors circulating among the castle's servants. The threat of the Shadow-Lord in the West was becoming undeniable. Rural villages were being targeted—crops burned, homes ransacked, and anyone unable to hide slaughtered. While it was the Rau-Travans carrying out the attacks, many in his father's council believed the Shadow-Lord had provided them with weapons.

Elis's hopes of stopping the Shadow-Lord and the Arkarnian faction from destroying Wethen were slipping away, especially after the capture of Avery Ambrose, his father's court wizard, a month ago.

To his horror, when Elis had approached his father about rescuing Avery, the King had explained that there was nothing they could do. Every available soldier was already fighting the Arkarnian faction led by Korvas. They simply didn't have the manpower to spare. It was bad enough that the scout who had delivered news of Avery's capture had succumbed to the Morgs' wounds.

As the Prince of Wethen, Elis felt it was his duty to protect his future subjects. Even if it wasn't his duty, he would still do everything he could to help those in need.

Currently, Avery Ambrose needed help. But Elis's desire to rescue him wasn't only because of his importance to the Royal Court; it was the deep friendship between the two that made the situation urgent in Elis's mind. The young prince found himself torn, arguing internally about what to do.

"If I do nothing, I'm not worthy of the title I bear... but if I leave Overgate... if I leave and they need me here..."

"No. I can't dwell on the what-ifs."

"They haven't needed me before. I doubt they will now."

"This is how I help my people. I do what I must, regardless of what my father says. I will search for Avery, and I won't return until I've freed him and brought him back to safety."

As Elis turned to leave the Market District, a familiar presence approached from behind. He turned, irritation creeping into his voice, "Cinder, I don't have any money for you to steal today."

The girl chuckled as she deftly lifted his coin purse from his pocket. "We both know that's not true."

Elis grabbed her arm, his tone serious. "I need my money, Cinder. Today isn't like most days. I'm going on a rescue mission."

Cinder stopped, staring at him for a moment before bursting into laughter. "Oh, that's a good one! I thought you were serious for a second! You—on a rescue mission! You crack me up!"

Elis didn't smile. "I'm not joking. No one's sending help to look for Avery. He's been gone too long. The reports of him being captured are true—he would have finished his investigation in the East by now. Since my father can't spare anyone, I'm going to find him myself."

Cinder handed him back the coin purse. "Alright, I'm in. You'll need my help. I can practice some of the magic Avery taught me when he was last here. There's not much room to practice in the city—it's too crowded. If I accidentally knocked someone over, they'd probably call the guards on me."

Elis took the pouch, knowing Cinder cared deeply for Avery. To her, both Avery and Elis were the closest thing to family. Cinder had grown up in Undergate, the crime-ridden undercity beneath Overgate, suspended above a deep, seemingly bottomless chasm. The only light she had known as a child was from lanterns and candles.

When Cinder was fifteen, Avery had caught her escaping Undergate into Overgate. It was then that he discovered her abilities. Since then, she had lived in Overgate as Avery's apprentice, protected and free from the dangers of Undergate.

"Avery is probably being held at Darkspire. We'll take a boat out to the bay and travel up the river to the Shadowed Lands. From there, we'll make our way to his fortress."

Cinder raised an eyebrow. "Do you have supplies for the journey? It'll take us several days just to sail up the river. Not to mention how long we'll have to walk once we get there."

Elis smiled. "That's what some of these coins are for. I was planning on hitting the market once I packed my things. Since you're coming along, I guess I'll need to grab some more coins."

Cinder nodded. "I'll head back to Avery's to get my things. Meet you in the market when I'm done."

They stocked up on dried meat and bread, then set out for the shipyards. Cinder was quiet during most of the walk. Elis knew she was worried about Avery, and he didn't blame her. If even half the stories about the Shadow-Lord were true, they had much to fear for him.

"How reliable do you think the reports are? Do you think Avery's still alive?" Cinder asked.

Elis didn't answer immediately, taking his time to gather his thoughts. "I think the reports are true. I believe he's been captured alive. The Shadow-Lord needs something from him—Avery knows too much. But how long he'll stay alive, I don't know."

They remained silent until they reached Erkan Bay. As they approached the pier, Cinder grabbed Elis's arm and pulled him back. "Stay low. We don't want to be seen. I didn't think there'd be this much activity here. I wonder what they're doing."

Cinder studied the men nearby. "Those guys have tattoos from one of the Under-gate gangs. They're probably picking up supplies—or should I say, stealing supplies. It's best not to mess with them. We'll wait until they leave. On the far side of the dock, Alban keeps several flatboats. We'll take the one farthest from shore. It'll probably go unnoticed until morning. We don't need anyone coming after us."

Elis shook his head. "Explain to me again why I can't just rent a boat? Why are we stealing one?"

Cinder gave him a serious look. "Okay, first off, gossip in this city spreads like fire in a dry forest. If someone sees you renting a boat, the rumors will fly. Now, I doubt they'd think you're going on a rescue mission, but your parents would definitely be displeased to hear you ditched your guards to take an unsanctioned boat ride in the bay—especially since the safety of these waters has been compromised by Arkarnians. Secondly, you're the Prince of Wethen. You can seize property whenever you feel like it, so stop being a wuss. It's better to get a head start so your parents don't have a chance to send people after you. It'll be easier to ask for forgiveness later, and besides, if we find Avery and bring him back, there won't be any consequences."

Cinder and Elis stayed hidden until dusk. By then, the area had cleared out, and Elis noticed how Cinder had subtly started taking control of the mission. He didn't mind—he trusted her experience and training far more than his own. She'd been like an older sister to him over the years, keeping him out of trouble when his guards were incapable of doing so. That's why he complied when she said, "Come on, Elis. Let's get moving. We need to make up for the time we lost."

Luckily, the fishing skiff they'd commandeered was a newer, faster design.

Elis and Cinder rowed together for a while, then alternated as the night wore on. By morning, they'd traveled more than sixty miles east and were approaching the outskirts of New Arkarnian Territory.

Elis, who had just woken up and noticed their progress, said, "We need to stay alert from here on out. We can't get too close to shore. If there are any Arkarnians nearby, they'll attack."

After a few more miles of paddling, Elis asked, "Hey, Cinder, have you learned any magic from Avery that can help us move a bit quicker?"

Cinder, who had been stuffing her mouth with dried pork, replied with her mouth full, "I can give it a whirl."

Elis raised an eyebrow. "Really?"

Cinder scoffed. "Hey, all I had to eat this morning was a stale slice of bread from Homer…"

She moved to the back of the skiff. "Alright, here goes nothing. I'm nowhere near as powerful or focused as Avery, but I can use an air spell to help push the boat along. I should've thought of this earlier, but Avery's always telling me not to use my magic when he's not around. I don't usually rely on it."

At first, Elis didn't notice any difference in their movement, but soon he could see that they were speeding up. "If Avery were here, I bet he'd give you one of those high-fives of his."

Cinder smiled nostalgically, reflecting on how far she had come since meeting Avery. "I have to admit, it makes me happy to think about how much control I've gained over my abilities thanks to him."

Elis scanned the southern shoreline, and after a few minutes, said, "I think you've doubled our speed. Based on the map, we should reach the first bend in the winding strait by midday and the tip of Southern New Arkarnia by dusk."

Cinder glanced at the map. "As long as everything goes smoothly, we should reach the shore by midnight."

They paddled in silence for a while. Just as they were about to suggest stopping for lunch, they spotted a group of six Morgs clearing a grove of trees along the southern shore.

"Try not to draw attention to us," Elis murmured. "We should be out of their sight in a few minutes. Do you think the stories about them are true?"

Cinder shrugged. "I'm not sure. Remember the run-in Avery and I had? One of the Morgs was actually friendly to me—guess he realized we weren't a threat. They're not very bright, but they'll do what their master tells them."

They paddled silently as they maneuvered around the winding channel. Suddenly, Elis broke the silence with an exclamation, "Aw, shit!"

Cinder turned to look at him, and he elaborated. "My parents... when they realize I'm missing and send scouts after me, I wasn't thinking about how this will detract from their efforts in the war. I should've been smarter..."

Cinder kept her eyes on the water as she steered, switching paddles. "Hey, you're plenty smart, Elis. You're just overthinking things. You go off a lot without saying anything, so there's a good chance they'll think this is just another one of those cases. Besides, considering they didn't send anyone for Avery, I doubt they'd risk sending anyone else into the Dark Lord's territory... even for their only son and heir."

Elis didn't reply. He still felt guilty. What if something went wrong and he never made it back? Yes, they aggravated him, but he still loved them. He began to wonder what would happen to Wethen if they were left without an heir.

As dusk approached, the river opened into a larger area. They would be on land within six hours.

When they reached the shore, they tied the boat to a large tree. "According to the map," Elis said, "it'll take us at least eight hours on foot to reach the castle. If we're lucky, we might find some horses along the way. But we need to stop for the night. We both need rest before we tackle the rest of the journey. We'll leave at first light."

The next morning, they woke early and ate breakfast. As they did, Cinder looked around at the landscape, clearly stunned by the contrast between Wethen and this place. She had heard stories of the destruction Shadow-Lord was causing, but seeing it firsthand was something else.

"Why is he doing this?" Cinder asked, her voice filled with disbelief. "Why destroy something so beautiful?"

Elis shrugged. "I don't know. No one does. It's all rumors and speculation. Like I said earlier, the laws between Kardica and Wethen prevent sending an army after him without proof..."

"And like I meant to say earlier, that's total bullshit—"

Elis silenced her by placing a hand over her mouth and pulling her behind a large rock. "Hush, I hear something!" he whispered urgently.

He removed his hand from her mouth just as she jabbed him in the ribs. She hissed in frustration. "Don't ever do that again!"

They watched in stunned silence as a dark-scaled creature with glowing red eyes hovered in the air before them.

It was the Mist—a legendary being from recent tales. Elis had dismissed it as a myth until he overheard his father discussing the real threat of Shadow-Lord.

The Mist hovered, its glowing red eyes piercing the darkness. A voice emerged from it, whispering, "Elwyn... Foster..." before vanishing into the water.

Cinder looked at Elis, stunned. "Isn't Elwyn the name of your godfather?"

Elis paced back and forth, troubled by the encounter. Finally, he stopped, shaking his head. "It's his surname... but I don't know who Foster is. Why would this thing be saying his name?"

Cinder shrugged. "I don't have an answer for that, but we need to move. Out of curiosity, don't you think it's strange that we haven't run into any Arkarnians yet?"

Elis closed his eyes, trying to shake off the unease. "Not really. I heard a group of them was moving toward the Northwestern shore of New Arkarnia. My father's working to build an army to protect Wethen's shores, and he's even reached out to Kardica for help."

Cinder quickened her pace. "Let's just hope our luck holds out."

About an hour later, they came upon a rocky area descending into a valley. This time, it was Cinder who grabbed Elis and pulled him out of sight.

"Good news and bad news," she whispered. "The good news is, we found two horses. The bad news is, those Arkarnians aren't about to give them up."

Ahead of them, two Arkarnians sat on a fallen log near a campfire that had yet to be lit, with their horses tethered to a dead tree.

As they got closer, Cinder and Elis could hear the Arkarnians speaking. Surprisingly, they weren't using their native language, allowing Cinder and Elis to understand them.

"Can you believe the nerve of Korvas? Leaving us out here high and dry just because we're hungry?" one Arkarnian said, his voice full of frustration.

The other Arkarnian shrugged and replied gruffly, "Do you realize how much of an honor it is to be nominated by your village to be trained by Korvas himself as an elite scout of New Arkarnia? You spoke out of turn. Besides, he didn't abandon both of us—only you. Now, I must prove my loyalty to the Rau-Trava... Forgive me, old friend..."

With that, the Arkarnian stood up and shoved the smaller Arkarnian to the ground, drawing a blade from his hip.

"W-Wait! Xevarus! We've known each other for years!" the smaller Arkarnian pleaded.

His cries were ignored as Xevarus raised the blade and brought it down on his companion's neck. Cinder and Elis winced as the headless body twitched, falling lifeless to the ground.

Xevarus grabbed supplies from the dead Arkarnian's horse, then moved toward his own steed.

Elis knew they needed both horses, so he quickly stepped out of hiding and called out to Xevarus, "Hello there!"

Xevarus spun around, confused. Before he could say anything, Cinder unleashed a gust of wind, sending him crashing into the rock wall behind him with a loud scream. Xevarus fell unconscious.

The two mounted the horses, and once they were far enough from the campsite, Elis called to Cinder, "If we ride as fast as we can, we should reach Darkspire in just over an hour. We can slow down every so often to give the horses a break."

As they rode, the conversation was light, mostly filled with comments about the landscape, but Elis couldn't shake his concerns. He kept wondering what would happen if he didn't make it back. Eventually, Cinder lost interest in his mumblings, focusing instead on riding her horse at a strong pace. She was eager to reach their destination. Elis noticed she wasn't paying attention to him anymore, so he fell silent and rode ahead. What started as a conversation became a quiet game of racing—each of them speeding ahead, only to fall back as the other surged forward. The horses seemed to enjoy it too.

By the time they reached the outskirts of Darkspire, Elis dismounted and said, "Let's scout things out first. We need to be careful here. We'll leave the horses tied up and keep our movements quiet."

As they drew closer, they saw that the gates were wide open, and the place was eerily silent. When they crossed the bridge to the fortress, it was the same—no one in sight. Cinder clenched her fists. "I don't think anyone is here. This place looks and sounds abandoned."

Elis, who had been thinking the same thing, nodded. "We still need to check inside, but I've got a gut feeling you're right. It's as if this place was abandoned... Wait, what's that?"

Cinder, distracted at first by kicking a bucket, muttered, "Avery isn't even here." Then she too became aware of voices nearby.

They stopped and listened. "Abigail!? Mei!? Tadashi!?" The voice was young—someone close to their age.

Elis ran toward the source of the yelling, his heart racing. He saw a boy around his age and an old man with long grey hair and a beard.

Elis turned to Cinder, excitement lighting up his face. "Could that be Avery?"

Cinder beamed. "Yeah, but who's the kid?"

They both ran forward and embraced Avery, relief flooding them as they reunited.

Chapter Seventeen

The Reunion

Avery led them back into the castle and into the great hall. "Let's sit here, and I'll explain who Alan is."

Once Avery finished, Cinder and Elis exchanged glances, then looked at Alan. Cinder scoffed, "I... Avery, I don't understand. Why didn't we know about this? Didn't you trust us? I can understand why it wasn't important for me to know—I'm your apprentice—but what about Elis? If Alan is the son of Elis's godparents, doesn't that make Alan and his sister a part of Elis's family? I understand wanting to keep the connection between worlds a secret, but why—"

Alan, eager to move on and find his sister and friends, interrupted. "Sorry to cut you off, but while I understand this is a lot to take in—trust me, it's more for me than anyone else—I wasn't born on this world. But we need to focus on what matters. Avery and I are in a rush to find my sister and my friends. Elis, can you explain why you're here so we can get going? We have to stop Shadow-Lord."

Cinder narrowed her eyes at Alan. She couldn't tell if he interrupted her out of rudeness or simply because he was impatient to move forward, but either way, his tone annoyed her. She decided she would hold onto her irritation until he gave her a reason to think of him as anything other than a mean-spirited ignoramus.

Avery placed a hand on Alan's shoulder. "Calm down, Alan. I promise you, we will find them. But the more information we have, the better our chances of success. We can't rush this. Now, what did you come all this way for?"

Avery gestured to Elis to continue. "A scout came back on his deathbed. He believed you'd been captured. My father didn't send men to search for you, mainly due to uncertainty about whether you were truly taken and the ongoing border conflicts with the Rau-Trava. Our forces are stretched thin. I waited a month to see if you'd return, but when nothing happened, I felt it was my duty to go after you. Cinder volunteered to come with me, and here we are, two and a half days later."

Avery stroked his beard, a knowing look on his face. "Let me guess... your parents have absolutely no idea where you are?"

Elis rubbed the back of his head, embarrassed. "Well... not exactly. They have no idea, but Cinder and I just wanted to find you. It's not like I have any pressing responsibilities that required me to stay at the castle."

Avery rolled his eyes, smiling and shaking his head. "Well... we needed to make a detour to Overgate on our way to the Polar Region anyway. I must speak with your parents, but more importantly, Alan needs to talk to his father—and his mother, if she even knows they're missing."

Elis stood up and told Cinder to fetch their horses, but Avery stopped her. "No, let them rest. We'll check the stables first to see if Shadow-Lord has left any horses behind. I'm sure the ones you rode in on are exhausted."

When they reached the stable, they were in luck—five horses. "We'll take all of them. Load up our packs on one, then mount up. Let's ride."

Chapter Eighteen

Gift's From Shadow

Later that morning, when the kids awoke, they could hear a voice speaking in a low tone. At first, it didn't sound like Marik at all, but as Mei strained to listen, she realized it was Shadow-Lord. She wasn't sure if his quiet tone was meant to avoid waking them or if he was trying to hide what he was saying.

Abigail glanced at her friend, who was eavesdropping, and shook her head. "Come on, let's just go out there. I need to see if he found Alan."

Mei pulled back the flap of the tent and saw Shadow-Lord suddenly turn toward them, as if he'd been surprised by their arrival. Quickly, he shifted from frustrated to a calm composure. "Ah... Good morning. Did you sleep well?"

Abigail scoffed. "Did we sleep well? How about you explain where Alan is? I thought you were going after him."

Instead of answering Abigail, Marik turned to Gorb and Glum. "Take down the tents and pack everything up, except for the food you prepared. Then, let the horses loose."

Abigail didn't like being ignored, so she called out, "I asked you a question! At least have the decency to answer me! WHERE! IS! ALAN?!"

Marik remained calm, unaffected by her outburst. "I thought we could sit and enjoy a meal together while I explain the events of last evening. As you can obviously see, Alan is not here. I was unable to catch up to him. It was as if he simply disappeared. Once I knew the Mist was no longer an issue, I reversed course and came here. Now, sit and eat. We need to leave as soon as possible."

Tadashi didn't need to be told twice. He grabbed some food and sat down. Abigail hesitated but followed. Mei, however, was still uncertain. "So you abandoned him? You left Alan in this unknown world to fend for himself... what kind of person does that?"

Abigail glanced back at Marik, wondering if he would respond. She felt a pang of guilt for not being the one to challenge him—Alan was her brother. Why, then, was her gut telling her to trust Shadow-Lord?

Marik shook his head. "I did everything I could to try and locate him. Take a good look at me—I fought that monster so it wouldn't come after you, nor could it continue to pursue Alan. By the time I defeated it, Alan was long gone. But know this, he's heading in the direction of civilization."

Mei studied Shadow-Lord. His chestplate had scorch marks, his cloak was torn, and as he walked away, she noticed a limp. Now, she felt guilty for questioning him. She walked over, grabbed some food, and joined him, sitting beside Tadashi and Abigail. "I'm sorry for being so direct with you. I'm just worried about Alan. Why did that thing want to attack us?"

Marik waved off her apology. "No need to apologize. I understand this whole experience has been stressful for you all. That Mist creature is an agent of Avery. It's probably pursuing Alan to bring him to his master... which, from what I understand, is Alan's wish... though a foolish one. I only hope that if Alan does find Avery, he'll come to his senses and trust your decision to stay with me." He coughed dryly, likely lying about his injury being minor.

Abigail extended her hand toward Marik, concerned that he was more injured than he let on. He nodded. "I'm fine. It looks worse than it is... and Alan will be okay. I believe he'll reach the Kingdom of Wethan, where they'll take care of him." He took a labored breath.

Abigail reached out again. "Why don't you use one of the healing potions? You're obviously more injured than you're letting on..."

Marik smiled faintly. "No, I won't waste a potion on myself. The safety of you and your friends is my top priority. Besides, I've been hurt worse than this before." He paused for a moment, then said, "Before we go, I have some items I'd like to give you all. Tadashi, please drag that black bag over to me."

Tadashi paused and looked around. "Wait a minute, we're back in a forest again? How did that happen?"

Marik rolled his eyes, shaking his head. "Evidently, you rode into it. Maybe you were asleep on your horse. Now give me the bag. Alright, everyone! Gather around!"

Abigail, Mei, Tadashi, and the Morgs crowded around Shadow-Lord, but when he noticed the Morgs had joined, he sighed heavily.

"I didn't mean the two of you..."

Gorb called to Glum, "He no give us gifts no more…"

Glum responded, "You not nice, you no specify…"

After the Morgs cleared away, Shadow-Lord reached into the bag.

"For Abigail…" He pulled out a short sword with a foot-long blade and carefully held it out to her, rummaging around for a sheath and belt.

Abigail took the items from Marik, adjusting to their weight. She was familiar with weapons, but short swords weren't her weapon of choice in her HEMA classes.

Marik reached into the bag again. "For Tadashi, I present to you this bow and quiver." The bow was perfectly sized for him, and the quiver was packed with arrows. "And if an attacker gets too close, you can use this dagger, which can be worn on your waist."

Shadow-Lord reached into the bag one last time. "For you, Mei…"

The others watched as he pulled out her weapon. Mei took it in her hands, only to look disappointed. It was a solid, pale-wood club with blades along the side, resembling the snout of a certain aquatic animal from Earth. "Wait, wait, wait… those two get weapons they've trained with before, but I get a sawshark's snout? Don't you have a sword or something in there?"

Shadow-Lord chuckled, clearly amused, though unsure of what a sawshark was. "Yes, I do, but it's not exactly easy to handle…"

He then pulled out a longsword—crafted from a very dark metal, unlike anything Mei had ever seen. The blade's ricasso flared, with serrated hook-like edges along much of its length, leading to a razor-sharp point. The hilt and the blade's surfaces were engraved with disturbing designs, like skulls and an alphabet that seemed unnatural. Mei realized this was Marik's sword.

Mei laughed nervously, intimidated by the sword's dark design. "Yeah… no, you can keep that one. I'll stick with the sawshark rostrum…"

Marik chuckled. "What you're holding is a Rau-Travan weapon. They use it to—"

Tadashi interrupted. "It looks like a weapon used by Ancient Mesoamerican cultures, like the Aztecs. They used it to knock people unconscious for sacrifices. I even read that some were sharp enough to decapitate."

Marik stared blankly at Tadashi. "Well, it serves a similar purpose. The Rau-Travan arkarnians use it to keep their cattle in line and for war. As for the name, you may want to use the proper term: bok-raht."

Mei's expression soured. "They beat their cows?"

Shadow-Lord shook his head. "I don't mean cows. The Rau-Travan arkarnians herd a different kind of livestock. Their 'cattle' are lerps they've domesticated… and humans they kidnap from villages."

Mei's face went pale, and she felt sick. "I know they were talking about eating people from what Alan said, but I didn't imagine it was that horrible…"

She looked back at the weapon in her hands. "Are you sure I can't have something that isn't used for something so… vile?"

Marik gave her a half-smile. "This weapon is brand new, never used. It's only vile if you choose to use it that way. Remember, Mei, a weapon isn't inherently evil. It's the wielder who decides its purpose."

Tadashi glanced at Marik's sword. "What about your sword? It looks pretty evil to me."

Marik clicked his tongue. "If you couldn't tell from my armor and helmet, I enjoy a more… edgy aesthetic. I know it doesn't help my 'good guy' image, but I simply can't resist. A nice outfit can make a person feel powerful in its own way. A little vain, I know, but you'll understand soon enough."

Gorb walked over at that moment, waiting until Marik finished talking. "Bring gear now?"

Marik nodded. "Yes, you can bring the items over." He turned back to the kids. "Gorb and Glum will be handing out armor. I know you're familiar with it, so please put it on without delay."

Glum first handed Mei and Tadashi Gambesons to put on, while Gorb helped Abigail with hers. Then came the next layer of armor.

Tadashi watched as Glum handed his sister a long leather-looking dress. "I don't want to wear a dress!"

Mei shook her head. "It's not a dress. It's a Brigandine. You wear it over the Gambeson for extra protection and warmth." She paused, then turned to Marik. "Are we near the Polar Regions? If not, we'll die from heat exhaustion in this armor."

Shadow-Lord, who hadn't been paying attention to Glum and Gorb, shook his head. "You're right, Mei. You shouldn't be wearing the Gambesons right now. We're still days away from the Polar Regions. Put on the Brigandines instead. Gorb, go get their bracers and bicep protectors."

Once everyone was dressed, Shadow-Lord stood and placed his helmet back on. "Now, we should leave at once. We're already behind. I'll do my best to protect you all, as will the Morgs, but I feel better knowing you're armed."

About half an hour into their walk, Tadashi began to complain. "This armor's heavy, and it keeps hitting the back of my calves. There's no way I'm going to survive this."

Marik took a deep breath under his helmet. He had to remind himself that these kids needed to stay alive, but Tadashi was really testing his patience. "Everyone stop. Tadashi, get over here."

Marik removed his helmet to inspect how Tadashi was wearing his armor, then glanced at Mei and Abigail. "My apologies, Abigail. You weren't supposed to get the shorter Brigandine. Would you please switch with Tadashi?"

With that, Marik put his helmet back on and continued walking.

As Tadashi and Abigail swapped their armor, Tadashi quietly muttered, "I don't think that guy likes me. The look he gave me was pure evil."

Abigail shook her head. "I think you're imagining things. But you might want to hold off on any more complaints or pestering questions for at least the next hundred miles."

Mei giggled. "I don't think that's possible."

Tadashi glared at his sister. "Fine, but I'm telling Sobo you made me wear a dress when we get home."

Mei exchanged a knowing glance with Abigail. They liked hearing Tadashi's optimism, but neither was sure if they would ever make it back home, not with how tough the journey had already been.

Mei glanced ahead and saw that Marik was now at least two hundred feet away from them. "Come on, guys, we better get moving, or else he'll start hating on all of us."

As they walked, they began to talk about the scenery.

"This place is really nice," Abigail said. "I mean, compared to where we've been so far in this world, this is the closest to normal we've seen—other than the Grotto."

Mei agreed. "Yep, had we been brought directly here, we might have never believed we weren't on Earth."

Mei turned to her brother. "What do you think, Tadashi?"

Tadashi glared again. "Oh, me? You want me to talk? Aren't you afraid I might complain or ask annoying questions?"

Mei rolled her eyes, and Abigail laughed. "Quit being a drama queen in that dress, and just tell us what you think."

Abigail laughed even harder, while Mei dodged a punch from her brother. "Sorry, just teasing. Trying to keep this situation light."

Tadashi quickly began to laugh. "Okay, you got me. That was funny. I do appreciate your effort to make things feel normal, but I think we all know we're far from normal. I know the chances of us returning home are slim, but I've gotta believe it's possible. Even if this area looks nice, it's not home. Earth is. I don't know if I'll ever feel at home here. And don't forget, this 'nice' area is where those lizard men come from. Who knows what the area we were born in is like?"

Abigail sighed. "Well, that was a short time keeping things light. I guess we all have the same things on our minds. This whole thing has been crazy, and all I want is to find Alan, maybe my dad. As for going home, it doesn't seem possible, so we'd better get used to that idea. If by some miracle we do get back to Earth, I'll be writing one hell of a book."

Mei laughed. "Book? I'm going to write a screenplay. I wonder who would play my part?"

Tadashi joined in the banter. They could worry about their troubles later.

***

After walking for four hours straight, Marik realized the kids were lagging further behind than usual. He called out to Glum and Gorb to stop, signaling for a short break.

Tadashi was the first to notice. "Hey, look! I think we're getting a rest break."

When they reached Marik, he gave them all a stern look. "You may rest for a short while. Glum and Gorb have food and water for you. But I expect you to stay alert from now on. No more casual strolling. I know we haven't encountered any opposition so far, but from here on, we need to be on guard. The rest of our journey is filled with perils."

Tadashi bit into a loaf of bread and mumbled, "Is it... lizardmen?"

Mei smacked her brother. "Who taught you manners? Don't talk with your mouth full." Then, turning to Marik, she said, "I believe my brother is trying to ask if we will be encountering the Lizardmen soon."

Marik, still wearing his helmet, rolled his eyes and ignored Tadashi. He focused instead on Mei and Abigail. "I'll remind you, the Lizardmen are called arkarnians. As for whether we'll encounter them, yes, they do reside in this area and beyond. What I didn't tell you earlier is that there are many factions of arkarnians. Some are more unpleasant than others. In these parts, most belong to the Rau Trava, who I've mentioned before. They are at war with Wethan and parts of Kardica. We won't encounter them until we get closer to the Wethan border, where most of them are fighting along the front lines. Once we reach the Polar Regions, we'll likely run into the Valthurg, who are far worse than the Rau Trava, but you needn't worry about that right now."

Abigail raised an eyebrow. "So are those all the factions, or are there others? Are any arkarnians actually good?"

Marik thought for a moment before replying, "Yes, there are others. The Boh-Rahl is a smaller faction living in the north of both Wethan and New Arkarnia. They don't fight the war. They're disorganized, small tribes constantly at odds with each other and those who threaten their way of life. They're generally suspicious of humans and raid any who get too close. As for peaceful arkarnians... There's the Dinalo. They were given land by King Alfonse of Wethan, but in reality, they're fenced in and oppressed by Wethan. Your mother was once the ambassador between Wethan and the Dinalo and also the advisor for Arkarnian matters. When she left this world to raise you and your brother, tensions between Wethan and the Dinalo worsened. They saw her sudden disappearance as a sign of hostility from Alfonse. I attempted to reach out to them for safe passage, but they're distrustful of humans. It's truly depressing. But once Avery's influence over Wethan is gone, I believe things will improve. Who knows? Maybe your disappearance will push her to return to this world and see the ruin she's caused. Then, she might knock some sense into your father."

Shadow-Lord raised his hand to stop any more questions. "Finish eating. We'll leave in ten minutes." He then turned to Tadashi. "Just so you know, we won't be stopping again until dusk. That's when you'll eat and sleep."

Marik walked over to Gorb and Glum, removed his helmet, and grabbed some food. Tadashi quickly snatched some more bread and fruit before stuffing his face. As he did, he noticed Mei and Abigail staring at him.

"What?" he mumbled, still chewing. "I don't know if I can go ten hours without food. This is barbaric."

Abigail didn't let Mei respond. "You know what, Tadashi? I know this is inconvenient, but stop and think. This isn't a luxury vacation. We're trying to save a world. A little sacrifice on our part is nothing compared to the destruction these people are facing."

Tadashi looked at the food in his hands, feeling guilty. "When you put it like that, I guess I can stop being so difficult. Maybe Marik will start to like me then."

They were ready and waiting for Marik before he even called out to them, which made him smile to himself. He knew they couldn't go ten hours without stopping, but he wanted to control when they did.

Gorb and Glum had just finished cleaning up and were standing by their boss's side. "What do we do now?"

Marik called out to Mei and Tadashi. "I want you both to start getting used to your weapons. Gorb and Glum will take the lead. If we encounter anyone or anything, they'll spot it first. Stay a little behind so you don't accidentally injure them while practicing your slashing and shooting on the forest growth. As for Abigail and me, we'll take up the rear so we don't encroach upon you."

Abigail was about to ask why she was being singled out by Marik, but he either intentionally or unintentionally answered her unspoken question. "I'll be teaching you about magic, and we'll find out once and for all if you're adept. Let's get moving."

Chapter Nineteen

Magic Awakening

Marik made sure to keep a considerable distance between himself and the others, not only to ensure that their conversation wouldn't be overheard but also out of caution. Teaching someone to draw on magic for the first time was dangerous, and he didn't want anyone getting hurt.

Abigail watched her friends practicing with their weapons, striking at vines, limbs, and even tree trunks. She stood by, patiently awaiting Marik to begin her lessons—lessons she wasn't exactly eager to start. Truth be told, she wasn't sure she wanted to learn magic at all. In fact, she feared it.

When Marik spoke, Abigail, who had been lost in thought, jumped. "So, Abigail... I'm sorry to startle you. Are you alright?"

Abigail let out a nervous laugh. "Yes, I guess I'm just a little apprehensive."

Marik removed his helmet for a moment and met her eyes. "I promise there's nothing to be nervous about. We'll start with some questions. From your honest answers, I'll be able to tell if you have the potential to tap into your innate magic."

"So, these abilities come from my father's side, right?" Abigail asked.

Marik shrugged, thinking carefully before responding. It took him a moment to find the right words.

"In simple terms, yes... but it's more complicated than that. Everyone born on Whenua has a connection to the natural world. The widely accepted story about magic originates from the arkarnians' beliefs. According to their religion, magical abilities come from Ora, the Spirit of Life, and the Four Pillars. These Four Pillars represent the magical elements, though the interpretations vary depending on which faction the arkarnians belong to. But that's not important right now. The key difference is that some believe anyone open to magic can learn it, while others, like myself, know that there's more to it than that."

He paused for a moment before continuing. "It's not just about being open to learning magic—you must also have a natural predisposition. That's where blood-lines come into play. I could be wrong, but I see the pattern in my family tree. And since you're part of my family, I believe you or Alan might possess that same ability. Does that make sense?"

Abigail mulled over his words. "I guess it sort of makes sense. But since you keep bringing up our family connection, I have to ask—how old are you? When you wear that helmet and speak, you sound like you could be hundreds of years old, but when I see your face, you look like you're not much older than me."

Marik laughed. "I'm 18, but I feel much older than that. I've had to grow up fast, especially after my father died when I was 13."

Abigail placed a hand on his shoulder. "I'm so sorry to hear that. I can't imagine losing a parent so young."

"Don't pity me," Marik replied. "Losing him forced me to mature quickly, and it set me on the right path. That's why I need your help."

Abigail felt a newfound sense of determination. "Then let's see if I can use magic."

Marik replaced his helmet and smiled to himself. This was going better than he had anticipated.

Further ahead, Mei and Tadashi were having fun. They'd turned their practice session into a game. Mei would point out a tree limb, and if Tadashi could hit it dead center, she would use her bok-raht to bring the limb down so he could recover his arrow. But if he missed, he had to climb the tree to retrieve it. So far, that had only happened once.

Wanting a break from swinging her weapon above her head, Mei decided to change things up. "Hey, Tadashi! Do you see that white tree trunk about a hundred feet away?"

"Yeah... what about it?"

Mei grinned. "I bet you can't hit it dead center, ten feet up from the ground."

Tadashi stopped and assessed the distance. Confident in his skill, he said, "I bet I can. But if I do, what do you have to do? There's no tree limb in sight."

Mei hesitated. Tadashi's confidence was overwhelming. "Uh, I guess I'll have to take the tree down."

Tadashi laughed. "Yeah, right. We don't have all day."

He aimed and released the arrow, and both of them watched as it soared through the air. There was a loud crack when it hit its mark.

"YES!" Tadashi shouted as they hurried to the tree.

Mei was kicking herself for making the challenge, but she knew it was now her job to fell the tree. The bok-raht had already chopped through a four-inch limb with one strike, so Mei figured a tree trunk about a foot in diameter would only take a few swings.

Tadashi stepped back, unsure of what would happen when Mei took her first swing.

"Here goes nothing," Mei said, stepping into position. She swung with all her might.

At first, there was a loud crack, and Mei felt confident. "I think I did it—wait, uh, this isn't good. Tadashi, come here... the bok-raht is stuck halfway in the tree, and I can't pull it out."

Tadashi glanced behind him, looking for Marik. Gorb and Glum were already several hundred feet ahead, but he was surprised to see Marik and Abigail almost catching up.

"Uh, Mei, don't look now, but Marik's just a few feet away, and he's waving his arms."

Marik removed his helmet and handed it to Abigail. "Evidently, they can't hear me. Those fools! STEP AWAY FROM THE TREE!" he yelled one more time.

Mei and Tadashi quickly ran to meet Marik and Abigail. Before Mei could explain, Marik muttered, "I said it could chop down branches and vines, not trees. You need that weapon to be sharp and ready for combat."

Mei just stood there, staring. Marik continued muttering as he tried to free her weapon. "I would've expected this from your brother, not you."

Abigail placed a hand on Mei's shoulder. "It's okay. You didn't know. It's not like he actually trained you."

Marik overheard this and knew that he was partly at fault. Just then, there was a loud snap, and Tadashi tried hard not to laugh. It seemed almost too unbelievable.

Before anyone could comment, Marik yelled, "Everyone, stand still! The tree's going down!"

As the tree toppled, crashing into other trees, Tadashi couldn't help but laugh. "Guess it was made to chop down trees after all."

Marik swung around, unable to be mad this time. "Your sister got lucky, that's all."

He turned to Mei. "You and Tadashi need to pick up the pace and catch up with Gorb and Glum. You can tell them you need a new weapon. I should have let you choose something you'd be more comfortable with, not what I thought you should use."

While Marik and Abigail waited for Mei and Tadashi to catch up, Marik held out his hand with a small rock. "I want you to concentrate on this rock and tell me if you can feel the energy within it."

Abigail shrugged. "That's just a rock, not a battery."

Marik fought the urge to snap at her but remained patient. "I can't teach you if you don't open your mind. Clear your thoughts and see if you can sense something from it. Close your eyes and concentrate. Take the rock from me."

Abigail picked up the rock and held it in her hand. At first, it felt smooth and cold, but as she held it, warmth radiated from it.

"I... I feel something," she said. "It's warm... I've never felt a rock do this before."

"That's because your senses have been dulled from being away from Whenua," Marik explained. "With time, you'll reconnect to this world, and your senses will become sharper. Now, I want you to throw it as far as you can with your eyes closed. Pay attention to it, and only it. Let the other sounds fade into the background."

Abigail paused for a moment, then gripped the rock tightly. She brought her arm back and threw it with as much force as she could muster, listening as it flew through the air. She focused on its trajectory and knew the exact moment it began to descend and hit the forest floor.

Marik watched as Abigail smiled. "Now, open your eyes and find your rock."

Abigail's voice shook with excitement. "I think I can..."

She walked ahead, replaying the sounds she had heard as she threw the rock. She looked at a branch she sensed had moved when the rock passed by. Then, she saw the exact spot where it had hit a tree limb. "It's right over here!"

Marik caught up to her, and she handed him the rock. He examined it. "Yes, this is the rock I gave you."

Abigail beamed. "How are you so sure it's the one I threw and not just another random one?"

Marik pointed to another rock nearby. "Pick that one up and compare it to the one you have."

Abigail did as he said and examined the second rock. "The one I threw is so smooth compared to this one."

"That's because I brought that rock with me," Marik explained. "It's from the moat at my castle. The smoothness comes from the years it spent being eroded in the water. Now, take this rock, hold it in your palm, and try to feel the connection again. But this time, I want you to lift it with your thoughts and the energy around you."

Abigail lifted the rock within her palm. "No, I didn't say to lift your palm," Marik corrected. "I said to lift the rock."

Abigail stared at the rock, unsure of how to proceed. Marik, growing impatient, took the rock from her hand. "Here, let me show you."

He raised the rock effortlessly off of his gauntlet—first a few inches, then higher, until it hovered well above their heads. He then gently lowered it back into his hand.

"Now," he continued, "I want you to let go of all your negative thoughts. You need to believe in yourself—that's the key. Accept that you have great ability. Let yourself connect fully to the world around you. Feel the air as it enters your lungs, hear the rustling of branches in the soft wind, listen to the silky rippling of water in the nearby creek... Feel at one with the elements, and they will bend to your will."

Abigail took the rock again, closed her eyes, and took a few calming breaths. As she concentrated on the weight of the rock, it slowly seemed to fade from her perception. Opening her eyes, she gasped in amazement, "Oh wow, I did it! This is incredible... What else can I do?"

Marik smiled behind his helmet. "That's for us to discover. There are four main elements in magic: Fire, Wind, Water, and Earth. So far, we've discovered your connection to Earth. Not everyone feels an attachment to all the elements. This may be the only one you're bonded with. But being skilled with Earth isn't just about lifting and finding rocks. Once we know which elements you're connected to, we'll begin your training. Next, we'll try Wind, then Fire, and once we find a larger body of water than the nearby stream, we'll explore that element too."

As Abigail listened, she continued to lift the rock in her palm. After a few moments, she began to feel nauseous and dizzy. "I need to sit down for a minute," she said, her voice weak. "I'm not feeling well."

Marik removed his helmet and sat down beside her. "I should've warned you. Using magic, especially for the first time, can make you feel unwell. It has to do with the give-and-take of manipulating energy. The symptoms should subside soon, and there are herbs that can help alleviate the effects. We'll find some as we travel. When you feel better, we'll catch up with the others. I think we all could use a break. Won't Tadashi be surprised?"

Abigail laughed. "Yes, I think he will be. Does this feeling get easier over time?"

Marik stood and offered his hand to Abigail. "Yes and no. It depends on how much you use at once."

***

It took Mei and Tadashi some time to catch up with Gorb and Glum, but once they did, it took even longer to convince them to stop so Mei could choose another weapon.

"Gorb, I promise you the Boss isn't going to be mad. My weapon got stuck in a tree, and it broke when he tried to retrieve it. He said I could choose a new one."

Gorb grunted. "Gorb not want trouble. Boss not nice when we not listen."

Tadashi sighed and rubbed his temples. "Trust me, I don't want him mad at us either. Just believe us, that's what he said."

It took Mei longer than expected to choose, considering the only options were another bok-raht or a pair of daggers she found. "What do you think, Tadashi? The daggers can be worn on my waist, but the bok-raht is heavy to carry."

Tadashi shrugged. "Go with what feels comfortable. You've used daggers before in our HEMA competitions. If they don't work out, you can always ask Marik for the bok-raht again."

Mei stared at him. "If they don't work, I'll be dead. You know, on second thought, he did say I could choose... So... I choose both."

Tadashi squinted into the distance. "Uh, I think we should get moving. Marik and Abigail are almost here, and I don't think Shadow-Lord will be happy if he sees we're lagging behind."

Gorb and Glum turned to see Marik waving his arm. They decided to wait for him.

Marik approached, still holding his helmet. "I've decided we should take a short break. You may eat." He then looked at Mei. "I see you've made an interesting choice. I'm glad you didn't give up on the bok-raht. I believe it will save your life one day."

After Abigail got some food from Glum, she sat down with her friends, away from Marik. Mei turned to her. "Do you think what he said about your mother is true? That she was a diplomat?"

Tadashi cut in before Abigail could respond. "Actually, he said she was an ambassador, not just a diplomat. While an ambassador is a diplomat, they're usually the highest-ranking one. So, calling her just a diplomat doesn't do her justice, if what Marik said is true."

Abigail smiled, and Mei rolled her eyes. Finally, Abigail responded. "I believe him. My gut tells me I can trust him. He's been really patient with me. If he was the bad guy, I feel like he'd be more pushy, trying to get me to learn darker things. Anyway, what made you choose the bok-raht again?"

Mei paused and thought for a moment. "I don't know. I guess I figured he had two of them for a reason. They're heavy, but I was getting used to the weight before I broke the first one. I thought it must be useful, or else he wouldn't have offered it. As for the daggers, they make me feel more secure, just in case the bok-raht fails. But enough about me—how did your magic training go?"

"It's slow going," Abigail admitted, "but so far, I've discovered I'm connected to the element of Earth. I did get a bit sick from trying it, which is why we're taking this break. Marik said the side effects will lessen over time, and there are herbs to help with them. I just hope I can learn this magic quickly enough to be of use."

Mei was about to lecture Abigail about not pushing herself too hard, but Marik approached before she could speak. "Okay, rest break is over. Let's get moving. Mei, no more hitting trees. Just get used to the weight of your bok-raht. I suggest you swing it as if there's an invisible enemy. Tadashi, I want you to run short sprints ahead of us. Gradually increase the distance, but don't get out of sight. We still don't know what we might encounter, and don't overexert yourself."

Tadashi hesitated, but couldn't help asking, "Just out of curiosity, why am I running sprints?"

Marik, less annoyed now, replied, "Because you need to build endurance, especially with all that gear on."

Tadashi stifled a groan. Though the thought of overexerting himself was unpleasant, he knew Marik was right. It was time to do his part without complaint.

Marik turned to Abigail once Tadashi had started running. "Okay, Abigail, I'd like you to just enjoy the journey for the next hour. But as you do, pay attention to the air. Feel how it moves, how it feels, and where it goes. After an hour, let me know if you can sense a connection with it."

He called Gorb and Glum over. "Now, let's set off. I'll take up the rear with the Morgs. Tadashi, don't get too far ahead. I need to be able to see you all in case anything happens."

CHAPTER TWENTY

Return to Wethen

The trip back to Wethen was mostly uneventful, unless you consider Alan's inner turmoil worth noting. He didn't openly discuss his struggle between wanting to save his sister and friends or confront his father about his true identity, but his irritability and bad attitude toward the others created tension within the group. By the time they reached the castle's outer wall, Cinder was about ready to strangle him.

"That kid is insufferable, selfish, whiny—" Cinder's tirade was interrupted when Elis grabbed her arm, preventing her from acting on her frustration. "You can't hit Alan. Instead, you need to look at things from his perspective. How would you feel if you found out that the past sixteen years of your life had been a lie? Isn't it bad enough that he and the others were transported from a completely different world? You've heard him grumble and complain about everything they've been through, right? I think he deserves some sympathy. If what Avery says is true and he's our world's best hope, we need to be there to help him, even if he is insufferable, selfish, and whiny."

Elis's remark brought a reluctant smile to Cinder's face. "Fine, but I don't have to like him."

As Alan gazed out from the side of the boat, he was struck by the sight of Wethan. It was nothing like anything he had seen since entering this world—it felt almost like he had traveled to Europe. The castle loomed above them on a rocky, mountainous landscape. The waterway they navigated was bordered by tall evergreens, but as they neared the port, the trees began to thin, revealing a small fleet of tall ships.

Alan's gaze drifted higher up the mountain to a part of the castle that jutted out of the side. "What's that, Avery? How would someone even get to that part of the castle? It's like they tried to build it inside the mountain."

"That's Undergate," Avery replied. "It's a prison city where criminals are housed for life. We also keep Arkarnian Prisoners of War there. You see that building? That's where the Warden of Undergate resides. There's only one way in and out, and it's heavily fortified. No prisoner has ever escaped."

Cinder coughed loudly off to the side, and Avery quickly added, "I may have misspoken—one person did escape, but they shouldn't have been housed there in the first place, so that incident was excused."

Elis steered the boat toward a shore just east of the main dock. "Elis, why aren't we getting any closer?" Avery asked.

Elis half-laughed. "I might not have permission to take this boat, and I'd rather speak with my father before I have to explain myself."

Avery shook his head as they disembarked and made their way down the docks toward the marketplace. Alan was reminded of a large flea market, though it was early enough that the stalls were still closed. Once they exited the market, Alan noticed a stone staircase leading up toward several inclined walkways that ascended the mountain.

It took them at least half an hour to reach the gatehouse. As they got closer, the sound of shouting filled the air. "Where the hell have you been, Prince Elis? The King is furious!"

"I—" Elis didn't have a chance to respond before the guards saw Avery and quickly allowed everyone to pass.

Once through the gate, they walked across a long bridge over a dry moat to a large stone building. "This is the armory and where the castle soldiers stay."

Alan took in the sight of the many weapons lining the walls as they made their way into a large courtyard filled with fountains and stone benches. In the center stood a man in royal garb with his arms crossed. It had to be the King. Elis slowly walked over to him with his head down.

"I should be mad at you," the King began, "but I see you brought Avery back. For that, I'm very proud of you."

Elis shook his head. "I didn't save him from imprisonment. That honor belongs to Alan Elwyn—he's Uncle James' son."

Alfonse nodded in understanding and called out to Avery, "I'm so glad to see you're safe."

Avery motioned for Alan to step forward. "Alan, I'd like you to meet King Alfonse Belmont, leader of Wethen. He's a very close friend of your father and your godfather, just as your father is Elis's godfather."

Alan extended his hand toward the King, surprised by Avery's words. The King waved it away and pulled Alan into an embrace. "Come here, lad. You're family, and I've waited far too long to see you again."

Elis watched the scene, trying to decide if he should feel jealous. Cinder, looking irritated by the King's gesture, nudged him in the ribs.

Noticing the group's appearance, King Alfonse called out, "You all must be starving after such a long journey. Elis, take Alan up to your room so he can bathe, give him some of your clothes, and make sure he's fed. Avery and I have much to discuss, and we'll meet with the rest of you later. Cinder, go with Lucinda—she'll show you to a guest room."

As the King and Avery turned to leave, Alan called out, "When can I see my father?"

"I've sent word of your arrival," the King replied. "Both of your parents are in negotiations with the Governor of Undergate. Once that meeting is finished, they'll come to see you. Be patient." He smiled, then walked off, leaving Alan to call after him, "My mother is here too?"

Alan took in his surroundings as they entered Elis's quarters. The space was warm and inviting, a stark contrast to the cold, sparse room at Darkspire.

The bath was luxurious. Instead of a fiberglass tub like the one back home, there was a small marble pool set into the floor. The water was surprisingly warm and soothing on his sore muscles. He could've stayed in the bath much longer, but was interrupted.

"Did you drown in there?" Elis's voice came from the door. "If you don't mind, I'd like to wash up."

Alan quickly apologized and, feeling out of place with Elis and Cinder—who, though his age, had lived very different lives than him—longed to be with his sister, Mei, and Tadashi again.

They later met Cinder in the dining hall. The room buzzed with activity, a sharp contrast to Darkspire, where Morgs were always lurking. Here, instead, they were greeted by a heavyset woman who led them to a lavish table filled with meats, cheeses, fruit, and bread.

Alan, timid at first, selected a small amount of food, but after seeing Cinder pile her plate with meat, he followed suit and stuffed himself. The meal passed in comfortable silence, and once they were finished, Elis led them to the King's library where they would meet with the others.

An attendant waited with a message. "Prince Belmont, your father wishes to inform you and your friends that he will join you shortly. Until then, please make yourselves comfortable."

Elis and Cinder sat on a leather couch, while Alan chose a high-backed leather chair for himself. He was about to close his eyes and rest when Cinder decided to play twenty questions.

"So, Alan Foster Elwyn," she began with a smirk, "I'm assuming you're a lowly commoner where you come from since you weren't introduced with a title. Is that right?"

Alan studied her for a moment, trying to gauge whether her tough attitude toward him stemmed from jealousy or resentment. He sensed she was close to Avery and might think he was encroaching on their relationship, but she had no idea how close he and the others had become. He decided to play along with the questions, as long as they didn't become argumentative. After all, he hadn't chosen this fate—it had been thrust upon him.

"First of all, don't call me Alan Foster Elwyn again," he said firmly. "That's too close to how Shadow-Lord refers to me, and it's unnecessary. Just Alan is fine. As for your question, where I was raised, we don't live under kings and queens. At least not in my country. I grew up in a democracy, not a monarchy. We don't live in castles, and those that do have been abandoned for hundreds of years—though some still stand. As for being a 'lowly commoner,' in my world, I guess I'd be considered middle class."

Cinder rolled her eyes. "So, in other words, you have no clue about war or what it means to fight for your world."

Alan took a deep breath, refusing to let her bait him. "I know all about war. I may not live on the front lines, but I don't live under a rock either. My world has many ongoing wars. Eventually, war affects everyone, whether they're a soldier or not. You can sit there and judge me, but you don't know me. Just like I wouldn't think to sit here and judge you. Since setting foot in the Forgotten Lands, I've fought like hell to survive. All I've ever wanted is to go home. If that means fighting for the world I was born in, then that's what I'll do. You may see me as an outsider, but apparently, you both know my father. So, if you respect him, I'd appreciate it if you gave me the benefit of the doubt."

Elis clapped his hands. "Well said, Alan. I have to say, my first impressions of you are making me like you. I can see us working well together."

Cinder huffed. "Whatever. Just stay out of my way, and we'll get along fine."

***

Madeline and James finished their meeting with the Governor of Undergate as quickly as possible, then walked across the hall to the King's office.

Avery stood to greet them. Madeline called out, "Avery, it's good to see you! But have you found the kids?"

Avery walked over and gave her a big hug. "Your son is here, safe in the castle. As for Abigail and the others, we need to go get them. I'll tell you more—let's take a seat."

Alfonse cleared his throat. "Avery, can you give us a quick update on the Arkarnia situation?"

Avery nodded and began, "As you know, I was on my way to the continent of Arkarnia to investigate rumors James heard regarding activity in the seemingly abandoned region. Obviously, I never made it to Old Arkarnia. I was intercepted by my nephew, Marik Ambrose, who I've learned is the true face behind the mask of the Shadow-Lord. He ambushed me when I tried to bypass New Arkarnia via the Shadow Lands. I have no doubt now that the strange happenings in Arkarnia were a ruse to lure me into a position where Marik could subdue me..."

He paused, then continued, "This brings us to our current situation. We must go to the Polar Regions—it's of the utmost importance. Time is of the essence, so whatever decisions need to be made, they must happen immediately." Avery turned toward James and Madeline. "Abigail, Mei, and Tadashi's lives are at stake. They're with Shadow-Lord."

Madeline gasped, and James looked to the King for support.

Alfonse saw the despair in his friend's face. "Okay, let's cut this short. I won't press you for more details. You know I trust you. But I'm sure James and Madeline will want more information and a chance to see their son, hear from him what's transpired."

James and Madeline waited patiently for the King and Queen to leave. Once they were out the door, James asked, "How much danger are they in? And why take them to the Polar Regions? How is it that Alan is here with you, but Abigail is not?"

Avery smiled. "You should be proud of all the kids, but especially Alan. I owe him my life. As for their purpose, according to Alan, Marik is trying to obtain the Orb of Morimor. It's as I feared when I first learned of my nephew's existence from his grandmother—he wants to fulfill Materall's plans. So, I don't think he'll bring harm to them, at least not until he obtains the Orb. The urgency is no less, though. So, come see your son. Then we must be off."

Madeline looked to James. He nodded, and she spoke, "Then I'll be off with you as well. I owe it to both Alan and Abigail to be by their side. I know they'll have lots of questions, and as you said, time is of the essence. That means we won't be able to explain everything right now. So, let's go see him."

As Avery entered the King's Library, Alan came running past him and embraced his mom. "It's so good to see you, Mom." When he let go, he added, almost as an afterthought, "Hey Dad, it's good to see you too."

James didn't take offense, of course. He understood the kids were closer to their mom—she had always been there for them. But he hoped to change that in the future. "I'm sorry you found out this way," James said. "We wanted to tell you and Abigail once you both finished high school. Since you and Abigail both have an interest in writing as a career, we figured it was something you could use to make a living in Whenua."

Alan chuckled. "Gee, what would you have done if one of us had been interested in computer science?"

James nodded, smiling. "Well, that was always a possibility we took into consideration. That's why it would've been presented as a choice—to continue life as it was on Earth or to start a life here."

Alan looked at them both, seeing the relief in their expressions. He realized they had expected him to be more confrontational. "Honestly... Mom's book prepared me, in part, for this. And if I'm being truthful, there were signs. I'm not sure about Abigail, but I never quite felt like I fit in back home. Not that I felt out of place among other kids—it's more that I never could get the hang of certain aspects of life where I thought home was. I get carsick easily, but riding horses and wagons doesn't bother me. This world... this city... it's breathtaking. I'd love nothing more than to call it home, like you and Mom, and to get to know the family I have here. But before any of that can happen, we need to save this world and find Abigail, Mei, and Tadashi."

Avery clapped his hands together. "All right then, let's get moving. All the supplies we may need are being readied. Shadow-Lord already has at least a two-day head start, but I think he'll have to travel behind the front lines along Albastru Bay.

The terrain will be slow going, so if we travel through the Arkarnian Reservation, we should make up much time."

Madeline, who had been the lead negotiator in allowing the Arkarnians to establish a village in North Wethen, spoke up. "They won't allow us to cross through their reservation so easily. We'll need to offer them something in return. I have an idea of what they'll accept, but it'll cause a small delay."

Avery scratched his head, considering this. "What offering are you thinking of?"

Madeline explained, "About a month ago, the son of Chief Pyramus got into an altercation with one of our soldiers over crops that had been growing on the reservation. Things escalated, and a fight broke out. The son was arrested and thrown into Undergate. If we free him and return him to his father, I'm sure they'll allow us safe passage."

Cinder interrupted, "So, a guy is arrested for standing up for what's rightfully his? Why would the King allow him to be imprisoned? I would think the soldier should have been punished instead. This just goes to show how unfair our laws are—innocent people are imprisoned for life in Undergate. It shouldn't be like that."

Madeline replied, "Alfonse didn't allow his imprisonment lightly. He tried using as many loopholes as possible."

She paused, then continued, "You see, while the treaty was written and agreed upon by both sides, there were some sections of it written by a now-disgraced associate of mine, Odereus Bilgeflow. He added paragraphs written in enchanted ink that wouldn't appear until hours after the treaty's ratification. While Chief Pyramus knew of this after we informed him, it was agreed that the deceit of Bilgeflow needed to be kept a secret to preserve peace. It was a miracle we managed to convince so many of Wethan's political leaders to agree to give them land. Undoing it and attempting to redo it would be impossible. Many humans still disagree with the creation of the Dinalo Reservation. One of Bilgeflow's paragraphs specifically states that if an Arkarnian uses force against a human—no matter if it's self-defense—they will be imprisoned."

Avery broke in. "When someone is imprisoned at Undergate, they become the responsibility of the Warden. Asking Alfonse for a pardon won't work because the King has no power over Undergate. The laws were written this way to prevent favoritism. I don't think we can risk it. We'll need to come up with a different plan."

Cinder, still visibly upset, asked, "Then how were you and the King able to keep me from going back?"

This statement piqued Alan's interest. He realized that Cinder was the one Avery had spoken of—the only person who had ever escaped Undergate.

Avery hesitated. "While you're indeed free... there's a slight possibility that the way your freedom was granted... wasn't entirely legal." Everyone froze, surprised by Avery's admission that he might have broken the law.

Feeling their eyes on him, Avery nervously chuckled. "Well, I may or may not have threatened the Warden... with a bit of a fib. You see, most people don't know how the Order of the Mystic Masters works. Some even think wizards have more influence than the actual King or Queen, which isn't true."

He continued, "I told the Warden that the bloodline of anyone who denies a Mystic Master from obtaining an apprentice would be cursed for ten thousand years. After he signed your release papers, he slipped, fell down the stairs, onto a servant's cart, and was propelled through a window, into a pigsty. Needless to say, I'm not very popular with the Warden. He thinks I cursed him out of spite. Not my fault he's a clutz."

Cinder blinked, "Huh... well... uh... we need to get moving. I'm pretty sure I can get us in and out of Undergate undetected. As for how we get the Arkarnian out, well, that I don't know."

Avery and the others took a moment to think it over, and finally, Alan spoke up. "Hey, Avery, do you know of any magic that could help with this? The way you controlled the wind on our way here was impressive."

Avery tugged at the end of his beard, a habit he often resorted to when deep in thought. "No, magic doesn't work that way. I can explain it later. For now, we're still left with the question of how to get the prisoner out."

Elis smiled. "I think I have a plan, but the timing could be tricky. I know where we could find another Arkarnian. If we can abduct one, we could swap them out, and I doubt the guards would notice."

Avery raised a hand, signaling caution. "That could be an option, but where are these Arkarnian's located? We don't have time to travel all the way back to the Shadowlands."

Elis shook his head. "No need to go that far. A small group has been spotted taking a defensive position on those unclaimed islands in Erkar Bay. They're about forty miles from the Wethan Docks."

Avery nodded thoughtfully. "That's a start. But how do you plan on subduing an Arkarnian without them fighting back or alerting the others? And how do you intend to reach the island undetected?"

Elis smiled again. "I didn't think that far ahead, but I'm sure if we travel at night, we can get ashore without being seen. As for getting to one without alerting the others... I'm not sure yet. I like to keep my options open, see how things unfold."

Madeline shook her head. "That may have worked for you in the past, and it could work again, but this mission is far too important to go in without a plan. I understand things may need to change along the way, but we need an overall strategy first."

Cinder scoffed. "We returned with Avery, didn't we? We had no plan then. I think you should trust us now."

Alan, feeling the need to defend his mother, spoke up. "May I remind you that you didn't find or rescue Avery? If you hadn't traveled that far, we would still be in Wethan. I understand that plans need to be adjusted, but having a clear idea of what we're doing is better than going in blind."

Cinder laughed, clearly irritated. "Who said you were going on this mission? Elis and I can handle it. This is our home. Just because you traveled hundreds of miles doesn't mean you're qualified to do anything."

Avery's temper flared. "Enough! Cinder, you've never crossed the Shadowlands. You've never faced the Shadow-Lord or the Mist. You have no idea what Alan and the others went through and survived."

Cinder, realizing she'd overstepped, regretted her words. She needed to salvage her standing with Avery, who looked disappointed in her. "You're right, Avery. I didn't think it through. Alan, I'm sorry for what I said. We need to stick together, and I guess we should have a plan in place."

Avery sighed, turning to Madeline. "Madeline, I'd like you to travel ahead and begin negotiations with the Chief. That will save us time once we get there. If he agrees with our terms, you'll need to arrange for supplies and a guide."

Madeline nodded. "I'll leave immediately." She turned to Alan. "I know we still have a lot to talk about, but we can do that once you all complete your part. Meet us at the reservation. Good luck." She gave him a quick hug before walking away.

Avery turned to the remaining group. "Cinder, what's your plan for getting into Undergate? How will we find the prisoner?"

"The sewer system is the easiest way in," Cinder explained. "From there, it's just a matter of navigating the tunnels. The Arkarnian prisoners are housed on the lowest level, away from the Wethan prisoners. Not many guards go down there. Usually, there's only one on duty to bring food, which he slides under the door."

Avery raised an eyebrow. "What makes you think the passages are still open after all this time since you escaped?"

Cinder hesitated. "Well, I may have gone back into Undergate over the years to sneak in goods for some of the prisoners."

Avery shook his head with a knowing smile. "That's a discussion for another time. For now, it works to our advantage."

Clearing his throat, Avery continued, "Alright, we've got part of the plan figured out. Now we need to decide how we'll get the replacement prisoner. Any thoughts on how to keep him pacified?"

Alan asked, "I guess magic isn't an option, since you didn't mention it. Are there any plants here that have sedative properties?"

Elis answered this one, trying to keep Cinder from getting too irritated. "Yes, we have several herbs used by our healers. When my brother was killed in battle, they gave my mother a mixture to calm her down. Maybe if we increase the dosage, it would knock the Arkarnian out. For my mother, it made her drowsy, and eventually, she fell asleep."

Avery smiled. "That's a perfect idea. I know which healer we'll approach. In fact, she may have something even stronger to help us. Alan, you can come with me to see her. Elis, Cinder, we'll meet you east of the docks. You can scout the area across from the islands until we arrive."

Alan reached into his backpack and pulled out a set of binoculars. "Here, Elis. I know I'm not supposed to introduce items from my world, but these binoculars are pretty powerful. They let you see long distances up close. Maybe you could use them just this once, and then we can get rid of them."

Avery nodded at Elis, signaling his approval. Alan showed Elis how to use the binoculars before handing them over. "Thanks. These are really cool. We have spyglasses, but these are amazing."

Avery smiled, relieved that at least Alan and Elis were getting along. He hoped Cinder would come around eventually. "Alright, we'll meet in about an hour. Do your best to stay out of sight. No need for anyone to figure out what we're up to."

Chapter Twenty-One

The Gnoglins

Tadashi was getting used to running in the armor; it was starting to feel like a second skin. As he sprinted forward, he'd cover about twenty feet before dropping to one knee to grab an arrow and shoot at a tree nearby. Then he'd spring back into a run, retrieve the arrow, and continue. He thought to himself, I hope Marik is paying attention to me. He'll be impressed with how my skills have developed.

Just as he had that thought, he glanced back to see where the others were, only to realize they were nowhere in sight. In that moment of distraction, he lost his footing, tumbled over a branch, and landed on the forest floor.

"Aw man, that hurt," Tadashi muttered aloud. As he began to sit up, he was shocked to find he wasn't alone. He slowly turned his head, trying to assess his surroundings. He was about to ask who they were, but the creatures surrounding him didn't give him a chance. They quickly encircled him, brandishing tiny spears.

Tadashi raised his hands slowly in surrender. "Hey, look, I'm no threat. I'm just a guy out for a stroll." He then poked one of the spears with a finger and winced when it drew blood. "Ouch, that hurt."

The creatures snickered but stopped as soon as one of their own approached. "Who do we have here? Why are you trespassing in our village? Are you a spy? And why do you wear such strange clothes?"

Tadashi was in shock. He wondered if he'd hit his head when he fell, because what he was seeing was almost too unbelievable, even for this place.

As he continued staring, the leader of the group prodded him with the other end of his spear. "I thought most hoomans spoke our language. Let me try speaking the language of the lizards..."

Tadashi slowly responded, "I... uh... I'm not an Arkarnian. I'm a human, not a hooman. I'm not a spy. My friends and I are traveling to the Polar Regions... trying to save the world. I wear this for protection. I'm sorry for entering your village—I didn't know it was here. The forest path just brought me in this direction."

The creature called over the others to huddle. While they discussed, Tadashi remained seated, trying to figure out what they were. One thing was certain: they were very short. The leader was at eye level with him while he sat. They reminded him of garden gnomes, but the one in his backyard wasn't furry or had clawed hands. Their ears were elf-like, and the whites of their eyes were enormous—almost the size of baseballs. Their fur blended well into the forest, various shades of green, with lime-colored beards of varying lengths. If they weren't pointing sharp spears at him, he might have thought them cute and cuddly. He could almost picture Mei picking one up and hugging it when she caught up.

The leader turned away from the discussion and approached Tadashi once more. "What do you call yourself? I'm Jord, Chief of this village. And if you're wondering, we're Gnoglins—protectors of the forest."

Tadashi nodded slowly. "My name is Tadashi... and I mean no harm to your forest."

Jord shook his head. "You injure our trees with your weapon. That does not make me happy."

Tadashi stammered, "I meant no harm to the trees. I was just practicing for when we have to battle. It's not like I chopped one down."

Jord held up his hand, silencing the other Gnoglins who began protesting. "Trees are living creatures, just as you and I are. I'll forgive your unfortunate mistake, but you must promise to never inflict pain on them again."

Tadashi sighed in relief. He just hoped Mei didn't show up swinging her weapon. "I promise I'll stop shooting arrows in the forest."

Jord nodded, accepting his promise as the others grumbled, knowing they must obey their Chief. "Now, that brings me to my request. We need help, and since you say you're on a journey to save the world, I'd like for you to start by saving our race."

Tadashi would have agreed immediately, but he knew it wasn't his decision to make. "Just like you're the Chief of your village, there's a man named Marik who's in charge of our journey. He'll be the one to answer your request. If it were up to me, I'd help right away, but you'll have to wait for them to catch up. I'd guess they'll arrive any minute."

Jord silenced his people again. "How many of you are there?"

"Just six of us—my sister Mei, our friend Abigail, the leader Marik, and his two Morgs, Gorb and Glum."

At the mention of the Morgs, the villagers became very vocal, and their worry was clear. Tadashi did his best to calm their fears. "Look, I take it you know what Morgs are, but I promise you, they're friendly. At least, they've been to me. The one you might want to worry about is Marik—he can get a little cranky."

Before Jord could respond, another Gnoglin came running from the forest, shouting, "Others are approaching! We must defend ourselves!"

Jord raised his arm to calm the villagers. "Do they look like this one?"

For the first time, the Gnoglin noticed Tadashi sitting on the ground. "Some do. Others are Morgs and a scary creature wearing a helmet. They all appear to be armed. You must hurry—they'll be here in a few minutes."

Jord turned to Tadashi, giving orders to his villagers. "Spread out, be ready to attack, but don't move unless I say so. We'll give these strangers a chance, just like we did with this one. Remember, they could be the answer to all our problems."

Tadashi called out, "Wait, why don't you let me talk to them first? I can explain what's going on so they don't feel threatened."

Jord thought for a moment. "Very well, but you'll need to remove your armor and leave your weapon behind. That way, I'll be sure you won't double-cross me."

Tadashi quickly removed his armor and handed his bow and quiver to the leader. He then ran off, calling back, "I promise we mean no harm, as long as no harm comes to us. Please, keep your villagers from attacking."

The Gnoglin had been right about how fast the others were approaching. It didn't take long for Tadashi to reach them, but before he could give his warning, Marik yelled, "What have you done with your armor? Where's your weapon?"

Tadashi, tired of being yelled at, stood his ground. "Stop and listen for once! There's a village ahead, home to a race called the Gnoglins. They're armed and ready to protect themselves, but I assured them we mean no harm. All we want is to pass through. They have a request for us—they need our help. It's best if you speak with Jord, the Chief. Oh, and one more thing: you should remove your helmet. They're a skittish group. Mei, you should probably store your weapon in Gorb's satchel."

Marik walked alongside Tadashi toward the village. "So, what happened to your stuff?"

"I negotiated with the leader to give you all a heads-up before they could attack. That way, you'd have a chance to defend yourselves."

Before Marik could respond, he stopped and began laughing. Not just a chuckle, but a full-hearted laugh. "These puny creatures are what you feared could attack us!? Ha! Ha! Ha!"

Mei, on the other hand, had a different reaction, just as Tadashi had imagined. "OH MY GOD, you guys are so adorable!" She dropped to her knees to greet one of the Gnoglins. But as she did, he jabbed her with his spear. "HEY! That could've hurt! I just wanted to be friendly and say hi!"

Abigail, trying not to laugh, glanced at the others. Though she thought the creatures were cute too, she held back, noting how serious they looked with their spears.

Jord stepped forward and addressed Marik. "We may be small in stature, but we're a fierce warrior tribe when we need to be. This forest is our home, and we will do whatever it takes to protect it."

Marik found it hard to take the short leader seriously, so he knelt on one knee to meet Jord at eye level. "So, if you're so fierce, why is it you need our help?"

Jord called out to his villagers, "I need time to speak with our new friends. Go back to your duties, and I'll call on you again if needed." He then turned to Marik and the others. "In case Tadashi hasn't told you, my name is Jord. Please, take a seat on those tree stumps, and we can begin our discussion."

Marik glanced at the tree stumps arranged in a circle. "Gorb, Glum—go rest by the tree line for now. You're not needed just yet."

Mei sat down and called out, "By the way, I'm Mei, Tadashi's sister, and this is Abigail, our friend."

Jord nodded, then, once everyone was seated, he spoke. "Before I ask for your help, can you tell me more about how you intend to save Whenua and what the Polar Regions have to do with it?"

Marik turned and glared at Tadashi before replying. "The details aren't important. We're trying to stop a bad man from destroying all the beauty of this world. If we fail, even this forest will be gone. Now, what is it that you need? Time is something we're running out of."

Jord smiled and scratched his claws together. "I can help make up for the time I've cost you, but only if you help us stop the Myklins. Otherwise, you may end up lost in this forest forever."

Marik shook his head. "Are you trying to threaten us into helping? We've made it this far without anyone's help. What makes you think we aren't capable of finding our way through your forest?"

Jord laughed and kicked his legs out. "What you've traveled through is nothing compared to the forest ahead. Without a guide, you could end up going in circles for days, or worse, into the boglands. Many of my people, as well as Myklins, have perished there."

Marik didn't want to waste more time. It would be easier to help and move on. "So where are these Myklins, and why are they targeting you?"

"You won't have to search for them—they'll come to us later today," Jord said. "A particularly aggressive group attacks every ten days, and today is the tenth. They kidnap our people for forced labor, and when they're no longer useful, they kill them. The Myklins eat their meat and skin their bodies to make armor."

Marik needed more information. He'd never encountered a Myklin but had heard of them. While he thought they mostly kept to themselves, he knew they could be ruthless. "How many of them invade your village? What weapons do they use? And how long has this been happening?"

"It started a few months ago. Each attack costs us an average of five villagers. There are ten Myklins, armed with clubs, and they stand as tall as you. That makes them difficult to fight, but not impossible. I'm just tired of losing my people."

Marik glanced at the others before coming up with a plan. "We can help, but first, I want to know how you can help us save time."

Jord studied the group, then met Marik's gaze. "We navigate this forest through a network of secret tunnels. I can get you past the swamp and save you a full day's journey."

Marik considered it. If it saved them that much time, it might be worth helping the Gnoglins. "Are there many arkarnians near these tunnels? They're Lizardmen, if you're not familiar with the term."

Jord twirled his mustache. "I've never been there myself, but I have a scout who has. It's important for our security to keep track of all the forest's entrances and exits. As for the arkarnians, we've heard of them. Before we spoke with Tadashi, we called them Lizardmen, as they hardly resemble the divine protectors of nature they were once known to be in the chronicles. Yes, they've been spotted in that area."

Marik nodded, impressed by the Gnoglins' ability to remain hidden. He hadn't known about them until now, and their knowledge of the ancient arkarnians' peaceful role as stewards of nature surprised him. The secret existence of the Gnoglins made him wonder what else he didn't know.

Jord excused himself to inform his people of Marik's decision, leaving Marik to speak with Mei, Abigail, and Tadashi.

Abigail didn't wait for Marik and spoke first. "This is perfect! We can all practice fighting, and I can work on my earth magic..."

Marik stood and raised his hand. "NO! You never go into battle thinking it will be easy. War is serious. I've never faced a Myklin, but I've heard the stories. From what the Morgs have told me, they are merciless..."

Tadashi interrupted. "Then why don't you have Gorb and Glum come over and fill us in?"

Marik couldn't be annoyed this time—Tadashi had made a good suggestion, even though he'd planned to do that himself. "Good thinking." He called out, "Gorb, Glum, come over here!"

Gorb smacked Glum on the arm—Glum had taken Marik's advice to rest a bit too far and had fallen asleep. "Why you wake me?"

"Boss wants us. No make him wait."

Gorb and Glum bounded over. "Yes, Boss," they said in unison.

"Have either of you encountered the Myklins in your travels?"

Gorb spoke for them both. "Yes, Boss. But that was before you came to live with us at Darkspire."

Glum added, "Yeah, when we take you in and feed you."

Marik gave them a stern look. "I remember it differently. You were in need of someone to show you the way, and I kindly obliged."

Glum nodded. "Okay, Boss, what you say."

Marik rolled his eyes. "So, Gorb, tell us about your encounter."

Gorb grinned. "Oh, it wasn't just one encounter. We had many. They try to capture Morgs, but they're unsuccessful. We pound them into dirt."

Marik had heard differently and wondered if Gorb was exaggerating. "Are you sure the fight was easy? I've heard Myklins can be a bit of a challenge."

Glum punched Gorb in the arm, and Gorb punched him back. Glum shoved him and said, "You tell or I will."

Mei, Abigail, and Tadashi struggled to hold back laughs at the antics between the Morgs. Marik, however, was losing his patience. Glum sensed it and spoke quickly. "Fine, we didn't pound them into dirt. Those Myklins are savage. You show them you can beat them, then they leave you alone."

Marik saw this as an advantage. "Then we'll make sure they see you two first. With the rest of us and the villagers, we should be able to stop this."

Jord returned with a group of male villagers. "I've sent the women, children, and a few of our men into the tunnels to hide."

Marik nodded. "Good. Do you have some scouts who can tell us which direction they're coming from and when?"

Jord smiled. "We always have scouts on duty. That's how we were prepared for your arrival."

Marik glanced at Tadashi, thinking he might need to ask him about what had happened when he first entered the Gnoglin village.

CHAPTER TWENTY-TWO

The Plan

Avery and Alan walked through the City of Wethan. As they moved, Avery explained who they were about to see. "We have several healers here in and around Wethan, and many more who travel to the front lines to tend to injured soldiers. The woman we're visiting was our only healer for a long time until she trained others. She learned from her mother, who, in turn, learned from her own mother. So, in other words, this healing knowledge has been passed down through generations."

Alan asked, "Why do you think she'll help us without alerting anyone to what we're doing?"

Avery smiled. "Because she's Mei and Tadashi's mother."

Alan stopped. "So that's what you meant by them having commitments to Wethan?"

Avery nodded. "Exactly. Their mother, Nori, is one of the finest healers in the entire kingdom. Their father, Hiroto, isn't a healer, but his role is just as vital. Nori and Hiroto must be worried about their children. The King was supposed to send word to them, but I think your visit will do more to ease their concerns."

Alan began walking again, his mind heavy. "I don't know how much hope I can offer, though. After all, I'm the one who left them with that monster."

Avery shook his head. "Don't be so hard on yourself. You can give them encouragement about how well Mei and Tadashi have handled everything. I'll reassure them that Shadow-Lord needs them and will protect them, at least until he gets the orbs. That should suffice."

Alan nodded, then Avery asked, "By the way, I think it would be easier if we just called Shadow-Lord by his given name, Marik. You haven't called him that yet."

Alan shrugged. "In my mind, he has no name. He's the one who started all this. I never knew him as Marik—he's just Shadow-Lord... and besides, he claims to hate the name."

Avery thought for a moment. "I understand. But underneath the mask and all his lies, he's still Marik Ambrose. And I believe we may have a chance to save him."

Alan was shocked. "You're serious? You think you can change him?"

Avery understood Alan's skepticism. "If you knew the whole story of Marik's upbringing—how there were things beyond his control—you might see things differently. I have to try. And if I'm wrong, then we'll destroy him."

Avery stopped just outside a door. Alan looked at him, still uncertain but willing to keep an open mind. "Alright, let's go give some parents hope."

As soon as Avery stepped inside, Nori Mikan approached him and wrapped him in a tight hug. "I was so happy to hear you're safe! Do you have any recent news about my children?"

Once Nori stepped back from the hug, she noticed Alan standing nearby. Without waiting for Avery to reply, she asked, "Are you Alan?"

Alan stepped forward slowly, still weighed down by guilt. "Yes, I am. I'm so sorry..."

Nori didn't let him finish. She pulled him into another tight hug. "I've heard so many wonderful things about you from my mother. My husband and I are so grateful for the friendship you've shared with our daughter and son."

Alan smiled when she released him. "Abigail and I are the lucky ones. Mei and Tadashi mean a lot to us. You'd be proud of how well they've handled themselves through all the challenges we've faced since arriving here. Unfortunately, they still believe you're dead, but when they learn you and Hiroto are alive, they'll be overjoyed."

Nori's expression darkened. "I hope you're right. Hiroto is currently on the front lines of the war. He's a general in the King's army. The King did send word to him, so he knows about their situation."

Avery interrupted. "We're here to ask for your help, but what we're asking must remain secret from the King. Is that something you're willing to be involved in?"

Nori didn't hesitate. "If this involves getting Mei and Tadashi home safely, then yes, I'll help with whatever you need."

Avery smiled. "That's exactly what I hoped to hear. Let's get down to business."

Avery explained their mission, and Nori listened thoughtfully before responding. "I have several things that will help. It will take me a few minutes to gather what you need, but it should work. Your journey is dangerous, so I'll also give you some herbs to aid in healing if necessary. I wish I could do more, but I promise to keep all of this to myself. I won't even tell Hiroto."

Avery thanked her. He and Alan were about to sit down and wait when Nori asked, "Alan, would you like to learn how I process the herbs? It could come in handy on your journey."

Alan glanced at Avery, who nodded. "Sounds good to me."

Nori pulled a large basket from a high shelf. "This herb is called Anglonium. See how the flowers are a pale purple? That's when it should be picked and dried. If you ever find it with deep purple flowers, don't touch it. It will burn your skin. I use it in small amounts as a painkiller, and it can also reduce stress. In larger quantities, it's used as a sedative during surgeries. Too much, though, and it can be fatal."

Alan looked concerned. "How do we determine the correct dosage?"

Nori placed some of the Anglonium into a mortar and began grinding it with a pestle. "Arkarnians are mostly built the same, so for someone of his size, you should use enough powder to coat the palm of your hand."

Alan scratched his head. "How are we going to get him to ingest this?"

Nori smiled. "I'm sure Avery has some ideas. But the way I administer it is through food or drink. Luckily, Anglonium is tasteless, so it won't be detected."

She filled a small pouch with the ground Anglonium. "This pouch contains enough to sedate him. Once he consumes it, it will take a few minutes to take effect, and then he'll be out for at least two hours."

Nori tied a third string around a second pouch. "This one contains more, in case you need it later. Don't confuse the two."

She pulled out another herb. "This is Yuchimiln. It's found all throughout Wethan. I'll give you a small piece to keep with you to help identify it. I won't make a powder for you, but I'll show you how to use it. Take the yellow flowers and grind them in the palm of your hand, like this."

Alan followed her instructions. Nori grabbed a small amount of dirt from a pot. "Once it's ground, add a little dirt and mix it. Then, add water to make a paste. This will heal any wound, so make sure you have enough to cover it. You can also use this herb in other healing potions, but Avery will have to teach you that, if the need arises."

Alan nodded. "Thank you. I hope we never have to use any of this."

Nori smiled and hugged him again. "When you find my children, please tell them that their Oya and Chichi love them very much and are so sorry for leaving them. But it was the only option we had."

Alan looked at Nori. "I'll tell them, but can you explain why you and Hiroto didn't do what my parents did? I'm sure they'll wonder as well."

Nori sighed deeply. "It was a difficult decision. Ultimately, it came down to a choice between myself and my Oya. Hiroto, their father, had to stay as a military general. My mother, an even better healer than I am, could have fled with me, but I couldn't risk her life by running away. That's why we decided that she should go, and I would stay."

Alan nodded thoughtfully and gave her another hug. "They'll understand. Before I go, can I ask you something about what Shadow-Lord told us?" Nori nodded, and Alan continued, "He claimed that Avery was responsible for the deaths of you and Hiroto, and in the same breath, he said you were friends with his father, Viktor Ambrose. Is that true?"

Nori shook her head in disbelief. "Oh, no. The only Ambroses Hiroto and I ever knew were Avery and his late wife. What he's saying about my children... it worries me."

Alan and Nori re-entered the room where Avery was waiting. "Thank you, Nori, for everything. I promise we'll return Mei and Tadashi to you, but it may take some time."

Nori smiled softly. "You've given me hope. That's something I've been missing for far too long. Now, go on. I'll see you again."

Alan and Avery made their way back through the streets of Wethan. "So, Avery," Alan asked, "now that we have what we need, how are we going to use it?"

Avery smiled. "Everyone needs to eat and drink at some point. We just have to wait for the right opportunity."

Later, Avery and Alan found Elis and Cinder behind a tree along the shore. Avery called out, "So, what have you two observed while we were gone?"

Cinder motioned for Elis to speak. "First off, these binoculars are amazing. We need to get our craftsman to make some of these."

Avery shook his head. "Get on with the report, Elis."

"Sorry. At first, we didn't notice anything. But just a few minutes ago, we saw three arkarnians walking along the eastern side of the island. They were gathering wood near the shore, then headed inland. We didn't see any boats, so if we head to the north shore, we should be fine."

Avery took a moment to consider. "Let me have a look through those binoculars... Yes, these are very useful. We've got some time before sunset. The next step is to get a few more things we need. Elis and Alan, up the road to the west, you'll find an old boathouse. Bring back two canoes, while Cinder and I find a cart to haul the Arkarnian."

Before long, they were all together again. "Good work," Avery said. "We'll hide the cart with these branches. The docks have cleared for the day, and the guard is eating dinner, so now's our chance."

Alan and Avery took one canoe, and Elis and Cinder took the other. Avery and Cinder used their magic to manipulate the wind, making their canoes move quickly across the water. Before they knew it, they reached Erkar Island.

Alan and Elis moved the canoes farther onto the beach. "No talking unless I say otherwise," Alan whispered. "If you see something, use a hand signal."

The group moved quietly across the beach and into the tropical vegetation. Avery led, using his magic to part the plants as they walked. After about ten minutes, the smell of smoke filled the air—Alan knew they were getting close.

Another ten minutes passed, and they began to hear voices.

"I don't understand why Korvas keeps changing his mind," one voice grumbled. "First, he sends fifty of us to attack the Port of Wethan, then pulls us back and leaves just the three of us to watch. What's the point?"

"I agree, Zalvic. I just want to kill something. It's been days since I last ate a human, and I'm tired of eating these stinky fish. We need a 'tree dangler,' at least they've got more meat."

Alan, Elis, and Cinder recognized the third Arkarnian voice—Xevarus.

"Both of you remind me of a friend," Xevarus said, his tone serious. "He complained constantly about his belly and questioned Korvas's orders. Do you know what happened to him a few days ago?"

Zalvic lowered her head. "Did Korvas kill him?"

"No," Xevarus replied, his voice sad. "Korvas gave me an order—to prove my loyalty. I followed it. I cut my friend's head off and dedicated the kill to Korvas. Watch yourselves, or one day, someone you know might have to do the same to you."

The group ducked behind a large bush, observing the three arkarnians sitting around a campfire, roasting fish and drinking. Avery noticed a large keg nearby and suspected it contained Kynoka, the fermented drink the arkarnians were known to enjoy. It gave him an idea, but first, he kept listening.

"Okay, okay, we get it, Xevarus," Zalvic said. "But Korvas isn't here. What do you say we leave this place together, and be done with him?"

Xevarus looked at Zalvic and Mydauk. "You have no idea what happens to deserters. I'll stay. I'll turn a blind eye to your desertion and report to Korvas that there was an ambush and you two didn't survive. But you better get moving. With how erratic Korvas has been lately, there's no telling when he might show up."

With that, Mydauk and Zalvic left.

Avery waited a few moments and then used his magic to project his voice from a distance. "Rarrha... rarrha... rarrha..."

Xevarus immediately tensed. "Well, since no one's around, I guess I can grab myself a tree dangler."

Once Xevarus left, Alan whispered to the others, "That's the guy we encountered when we saw Korvas for the first time."

Cinder nodded. "Elis and I witnessed him kill his friend."

Avery ignored their exchange. "We need to move quickly. Alan, give me the pouch with the Anglonium. I'm going to put it in his Kynoka. It should work faster since it's mixed with fermented drink."

Soon, Xevarus returned, looking in a foul mood. "Damned tree dangler. Guess these fish will have to do." He sat down, devoured the fish, and washed it down with Kynoka. After finishing, he refilled his cup from the keg and chugged it down. Elis smiled—this was going to be easy.

As soon as Xevarus started to wobble, Avery and the others emerged from hiding. They wrestled him to the ground, bound his hands behind his back, and gagged him.

Elis and Alan grabbed his legs, while Cinder and Avery each took an arm, leaving Avery's hands free to part the vegetation again.

By the time they reached the canoes, Xevarus was unconscious.

At the shore of Wethan, they unloaded him from the canoe and placed him in the cart. Cinder covered him with blankets.

"The next part is up to Cinder and me," Avery said. "As for you two, travel west of the city to the rural farms. Here's some gold—buy us horses and wait for us at the old fishing hut. We'll be quick."

Elis turned to Cinder. "I know you'll be with Avery, but please be safe."

Cinder rolled her eyes. "You're the one who needs to be safe. You're with him."

Avery cut in before Alan could respond. "Enough, Cinder. Let's go."

Chapter Twenty-Three

Undergate

As Avery and Cinder walked toward Undergate, Avery decided it was time to address the subject of Alan. "Cinder... it doesn't take a wizard to see you're upset by Alan's presence here. If you want to talk about it, I'm always here for you."

Cinder sighed in exasperation. "I don't know... Maybe it's the way he spoke to me when we first met. He was in a crappy mood, and I get why—I do. He's just trying to find his sister. If I had a sibling, I'd probably be the angriest person alive if something happened to them. But deep down, it's not just the way he spoke..."

She paused, debating whether to share her feelings, but decided to open up. "Listen... don't think poorly of me, but I guess I'm jealous of him. At least, I think that's what it is. A part of me always thought I was the only one who could call you family—besides Elis and his folks. But now it feels like there are so many others who could say the same thing. What I mean is... I thought I was special."

Avery smiled inwardly, understanding her feelings. He knew he'd become a father figure to Cinder after all she'd endured growing up, and he was one of the few adults she trusted. He understood the hurt of thinking you're not as important as someone else, having experienced that himself with his father. "You are special, Cinder. Not just because you're my student. I don't prefer one of you over the other. Listen closely—I'm proud that you trust me. The relationship I have with you is like the one I have with Alan, but I'm not a father figure to him the way I am to you. He has someone else to fill that role. You don't need to feel threatened."

Avery continued, sensing it was important to address one of Cinder's concerns. "As for your doubts about Alan's importance, he's just one piece of the puzzle. So are Elis, Abigail, Mei, Tadashi, and you. No one person can save the world. I believe that the fate of our world rests in the hands of people like you and Elis, who love this world too much to let it fall without a fight. I only hope the others will come to care enough to stay and see this struggle through once the Orb of Morimor is retrieved."

Cinder was quiet for a long time after Avery spoke. It wasn't until they reached the secret entrance to Undergate that she finally said, "Thank you, Avery. I get it now. Where we both fit in. And when you put it that way... it makes me realize I should cut Alan some slack. Of course, I'm not going to go easy on him—we won't be pals overnight—but I won't be purposely mean anymore."

Avery smiled. "I'm glad to hear that, Cinder. I think, in time, you'll come to see Alan's unique personality. I believe you two will become good friends... maybe even something more."

Cinder froze, her head jerking toward Avery. "What was that last part?"

Avery smirked playfully. "What? Me? I didn't say anything beyond the fact that I think you two will become good friends."

Cinder rolled her eyes and shook her head. "Yeah, right... But, you know... even if that happened, it'll be a while. I'm not in a hurry for any lovey-dovey stuff. Though, I'll admit... he's somewhat easy on the eyes—" She froze immediately, muttering dreamily, "You... didn't hear that, right?"

Avery's voice came from behind the cart. "Oh, I'm sorry, Cinder. I didn't hear anything. I'm just busy trying to lift this rather heavy fellow all by myself."

Cinder took the hint and went over to help Avery lift Xevarus out of the cart. Once they set him on the ground, Avery turned to her. "From here on out, we'll use air magic to lift him."

Cinder blinked. "Wait... Why didn't we use air magic to get him out of the cart in the first place? Did you only think of that after we struggled to lift him?"

Avery paused, looking slightly embarrassed. "You know... I think I might have heard that last thing you said. Something about someone being a sight for sore eyes..."

Cinder stopped teasing Avery and used her magic to levitate the unconscious Arkarnian's body. As they both used their abilities, they floated him between them and entered through the sewer exit. This particular sewer had long been abandoned due to years of waste flowing over the mountains and falling hundreds of feet into what was once a beautiful valley—now an uninhabitable wasteland.

As they moved through the dark tunnel, Avery spoke to Cinder. "I'll float the Arkarnian on my own from here. You should practice producing flame from your palm. It'll help light the way. Just remember, concentration is key to keeping it burning."

Cinder took a deep breath and tried, first summoning a small flicker that quickly died. On her second attempt, a larger flame appeared, and she felt a surge of pride. "How far must we travel before we reach the cells?"

The flame flickered out again as Cinder worked to reignite it. "Sorry about losing concentration. We're about fifteen minutes away."

Avery smiled. "No need to apologize. You reacted quickly and corrected it. It will take time and practice. Let's keep moving."

A few feet before reaching the exit to the prison section, Cinder extinguished the flame and whispered, "We're here."

Avery set Xevarus down. "Now we need to locate the Chief's son. Any ideas?"

Cinder thought for a moment. "The way the cells are designed, we can see into the wire mesh windows, but the prisoners can't see out. We'll have to go cell by cell and call out his name."

Avery nodded. "Alright, but I want you to stay with Xevarus while I search for the correct cell."

Avery's first attempt at asking for Silvyn's whereabouts only resulted in grunts from behind the door. Moving on, he tried another cell, and this time, a voice responded. "Why do you want that traitor? Is it time for him to die?"

Avery kept moving, and halfway down the corridor, he found who he was looking for. "What do you want with me?" Silvyn asked.

Avery didn't want the other prisoners to overhear, so he used magic to unlock the cell door. Unlike the door he had been kept behind, these weren't imbued with dark magic.

Once unlocked, Avery conjured enough light to reveal himself.

Silvyn took a step back, wary. "Who are you?"

Avery whispered, "I'm the man who's going to return you to your people. All will be explained once we're out of earshot of the other prisoners."

Silvyn hesitated, still unsure. "But the guards... when they find me missing, they'll send word. The warden will come after my family."

Avery smiled reassuringly. "Don't worry. We have someone who will take your place here. When the guards find the prisoner in the cell, they'll think he's been found and arrested."

Silvyn nodded. "Alright, wait here. I'll return with the prisoner, then we can leave."

Avery quickly returned with Cinder and Xevarus. Once they set him on the floor of the cell, Avery locked the door, and the three of them fled into the sewer.

Once outside, Avery introduced himself to Silvyn. "I'm Avery Ambrose, Wethan's Court Wizard, and this is my protégé, Cinder. We need you to climb into this cart so we can safely move you through the city. We'll meet up with two others who will have our transportation back to your reservation. We need to move quickly."

Silvyn eyed them cautiously but climbed into the cart.

***

Elis and Alan were waiting at the fishing hut with the horses, just as planned, when Avery and Cinder arrived, pulling the cart. "Did you get him?" Elis called out.

At the sound of the question, Silvyn leaped out of the cart, immediately taking a defensive stance.

Avery held out his hands in a gesture of peace. "We don't intend any harm. This is Elis and Alan. Alan is the son of Madeline Elwyn. I believe you're familiar with her name—she's done much negotiating with your father and even came to your defense when you were arrested. Madeline is currently en route to your father, Pyramus. We seek your help in traveling to the Polar Regions, and we broke you out as a gesture of goodwill. Please relax. You are safe."

Silvyn looked from one person to the next, his stance softening. "You say you need my help, but will I be imprisoned again once you've gotten what you want?"

Avery smiled. "No, but you'll need to avoid contact with Wethan soldiers from here on out. If you're caught again... Let's just say it would be bad for all of us. What we're doing is illegal, but we're desperate for help."

Silvyn nodded in understanding. "Then I shall do my best to assist you. I will ensure my father complies with your request."

Cinder's impatience was evident. "I hate to break up this chit-chat, but we need to get moving before the soldiers start their patrols."

Avery reached into the cart. "Here, Silvyn. Put on this hooded robe. It will help disguise you as we make our way to the Dinalo Reservation. We'll ride through the farmland and stay west of the city."

Soon, all five of them were mounted on their horses, heading northwest.

***

Madeline had not set foot on or seen the Dinalo Reservation since she was pregnant with Alan and Abigail. As she approached the gate, one of the Arkarnian guards recognized her, his eyes widening in shock. She turned to the younger guard and said, "Go tell Chief Pyramus that Madeline is here. Go at once!"

It didn't take long for the young guard to return, and with him was Chief Pyramus, his face breaking into a shocked smile as he saw Madeline.

"I—I can hardly believe it. Madeline Elwyn... alive, a little older, but alive. It's as if nothing has changed..."

Pyramus's smile slowly faded. "What happened to you, Madeline? We needed you. Do you realize that, in your absence, King Belmont has made things more difficult for us?"

Madeline bowed her head in silence for a moment. "I'm sorry, but when my children were born, the King felt it was in their best interest for me to stay at the castle, rather than risk my life traveling as his consultant. I wanted to inform you personally, but Alfonse wouldn't allow it. To be honest, he felt my friendship with you was a conflict of interest."

Pyramus considered her words before asking, "If our relationship was a conflict of interest, why has he chosen to send you to see me now? What could he possibly want?"

Madeline smiled. "He hasn't sent me. I've come of my own accord. I need your help, and I promise I can offer you something you won't be able to refuse."

Pyramus extended his hand toward Madeline. "I'm intrigued by what you're offering. Let's talk somewhere else."

With that, Chief Pyramus led Madeline through the large village. She looked around, noting how much had changed in the sixteen years since she had last been here.

"Where is Rissa? And young Melmar? She'd be what, twenty now?" Madeline asked.

Pyramus's expression hardened. "Yes... Melmar would be twenty... if she were still with us. Five years after you left, we were attacked by an enemy faction—not the Rau-Trava or Boh-Rahl—who they were isn't important. What matters is that they... they killed Rissa and Melmar, along with many others..."

Madeline paused and hugged her old friend. "I'm so sorry. I... I can't even imagine what that feels like."

Pyramus briefly returned the hug before stepping back and continuing to lead her toward the village center.

"It was my fault," he said, his voice heavy. "I became desperate to escape King Belmont's oppression. I invited the faction here, thinking they might make us appear stronger, so he'd take our pleas seriously. But these other Arkarnian factions... they had no interest in helping."

Madeline's heart sank. She wondered if her departure had contributed to Pyramus's desperate actions, but she quickly pushed the thought aside. It was clear that Pyramus didn't blame her. If he had, he wouldn't have allowed her in.

They finally reached the village center, where Pyramus's hut stood. They entered through a tarp covering the doorway and sat on the floor around Pyramus's firepit.

Madeline began, "Avery and I need your help. A dark force seeks the sacred Orbs of the Twin Emperors. He is on his way to the Polar Regions to obtain Morimor's."

Pyramus nodded slowly. "Yes... I recall rumors of a rogue wizard who took the sacred Orbs of Livimor and Morimor from the Grotto of Life, where the Mystic Masters had safeguarded them for eons. He used them to attack a great center of magical power in Ancient Arkarnia, and those Orbs brought about the destruction of the Kingdom of the Rau-Trava. After the rogue wizard's demise, the Orbs were returned to the tombs of their creators. We know of the Shrine of Morimor. Our scouts have seen it, but I've forbidden them from entering. I wouldn't risk unleashing any untold terror..."

Madeline nodded as she listened, then explained further.

"The rogue wizard was Avery's brother, Materall. He's the one responsible for the war that led the Dinalo to break away from the Rau-Trava. His ultimate goal was to use the Orbs to conquer all of Whenua and create a new world order. Morgana Ambrose killed Materall, took the Orbs back to their sacred shrines, and told Avery that she'd place a powerful enchantment on the Orb of Morimor. The enchantment would only allow magically adept descendants of my husband's father to release it from its resting place. This secret remained until Avery realized that the Disciples of Materall somehow learned of it. That's when I had to send my children into hiding. The location of the Orb of Livimor is lost to history, but there's a chance the Orb of Morimor can locate its other half."

Pyramus's eyes widened with horror as the realization hit him. "They've taken your children. That's why you've come out of hiding."

Madeline nodded. "Yes. My daughter and two of her friends have been taken by the Shadow-Lord, who dwells in the Shadow-Lands of Astursis. He's Materall's grandson, trained by the Disciples of Materall. He's bringing my daughter to the Polar Regions. Avery, my son Alan, Prince Elis, his friend Cinder, and I are on a quest to rescue them. The Shadow-Lord has a head start, but he'll travel through New Arkarnia, which should slow him down. What I need from you is safe passage through the reservation and, possibly, through the Polar Regions."

Pyramus stared at Madeline, thinking over the request. "I want to help you, Madeline. But helping Avery Ambrose and the son of King Belmont is another matter entirely. They took my son from me, Madeline. They locked him up and threw away the key... just to humiliate an already broken old man."

Madeline paused before replying, "About that... the others I mentioned are working toward breaking Silvyn out of Undergate. We help get your son back, and you help me get my daughter back."

Pyramus looked shocked. "Are you going behind Belmont's back to do this?"

Madeline smiled. "We both know that when your child is in danger, sometimes doing what's considered illegal and breaking trust is necessary. The King is unaware of what we've done. I honestly don't know how he'd react if he found out, and quite frankly, I don't care."

Pyramus sighed. "If you and the others succeed in bringing my son back, then yes, I'll help you. But won't the King send an army here once they realize what's happened?"

Madeline's smile grew wider. "If all goes according to plan, no one will ever be the wiser. Arkarnian prisoners in Undergate have no contact with anyone. They're in solitary confinement, which is why breakouts have never happened. Once they're locked up, they never leave their cells. We've replaced your son with a member of the Rau-Trava. Don't worry, Avery's plans seldom fail."

Pyramus closed his eyes for a moment, his breaths shaky. When they reopened, Madeline saw something missing before: hope. Hope she had given back to him. Finally, he said, "We'll be ready when they arrive. Until then, let's plan your journey."

CHAPTER TWENTY-FOUR

The Dinalo

The journey to the Dinalo Reservation proved to be easier than they had anticipated. The farms were quiet, with very few farmers working their fields. Avery surmised that it had something to do with King Belmont putting his citizens on high alert for a possible attack by the Rau-Trava Tribe.

As they rode, Alan noticed many of the animals his mother had written about in her book. First, he spotted arkhogs—pink-scaled, lizard-like mammals resembling pigs. Then there were blovi, creatures like cows but larger, with bison-like faces and near-furless bodies.

As they continued onward, Alan and Elis talked. Elis shared stories about how Alan's parents had impacted his life. "Sometimes, when my parents were busy, your mom would help me with my studies," he said. "I like to think that's why I didn't end up copying my father's views. Both my mom and yours encouraged me to find my own path. That's why I'll always strive to become the king I choose to be, not the one my father wants me to be."

Alan nodded. His mother had always made it a point not to decide things for him or Abigail, always encouraging them to choose what was right for them. But a thought crossed his mind. Had this created conflict between his mother and King Belmont? He asked, "And your mom and mine didn't get into trouble for undermining what your father wanted?"

Elis chuckled. "My dad knows better than to butt heads with either of them. He knows he'd be chewed up and spit out. But that doesn't mean he's not bothered by the fact that he couldn't influence me to think all his choices as king were the right ones."

Elis paused, realizing he might give Alan the wrong impression. "My father is complicated. He's not a bad man. He's just not always right, and I wish he'd admit when he makes mistakes instead of just rolling with them."

Alan nodded again. "One day, I think your father will realize you'll be a great king."

Elis smiled. "Thanks, Alan. I'm glad we met. Hopefully, when this is all over, you'll get to know my parents like I've known yours. My dad's a mostly wholesome guy when he isn't busy."

The more Alan learned about Elis, the more he liked him. He felt they would have a lasting friendship, which made him wonder how their fathers had met. Had they, too, once gone on a quest like the one he and Elis were on now?

Further ahead of Alan and Elis, Avery and Silvyn were also talking, but their discussion focused on the dangers awaiting them in the Polar Regions.

"Silvyn, I've only heard stories of the Polar Regions, but they're old tales," Avery said. "The problem with legends is that they're often watered down or changed with each retelling. Can you give me an idea of what we'll actually face once we get there?"

Silvyn nodded. "I haven't been there personally, but Baldric, a trusted voice within our tribe and a friend of my father, has told me of his many experiences over the years. It will be tough. It's very cold, but with proper clothing, we should be able to travel during the day. However, I wouldn't recommend traveling at night. I've heard the temperature drops dangerously low."

Avery raised an eyebrow. "We?"

Silvyn nodded again. "Yes, we. You've risked your reputation to help me, and while I know you needed me as a bargaining chip, I feel honor-bound to see this through."

"Back to the Polar Regions," Silvyn continued. "The terrain is mostly flat, save for rocky outcrops scattered across the tundra. As we approach a frozen lake, the land rises. The shrine is said to lie at the center of the lake, but we'll need to find a way to cross it without falling in. Baldric never attempted to cross it. When my father learned that the Shrine of Morimor was likely in the Polar Regions, he forbade any Dinalo Arkarnian from entering it. Their reasons for staying away are irrelevant to us, though. Still, we're getting ahead of ourselves. Surviving the journey is no small task. If it were easy, many others would have tried."

Avery wasn't concerned about the cold. "The cold doesn't matter. We have warm clothing, and I can use magic to keep us from freezing. I agree, we'll rest at night."

Silvyn sighed. "When I consider our chances, it's not just the cold that worries me. I thought you'd have heard of the Valthurg..."

Avery scoffed. "I've not only heard of the Valthurg—I've seen their brutality firsthand. They met their end at the hands of my mother. Morgana wiped them out years ago. What's that got to do with anything?"

Silvyn's expression grew serious. "While it's true the Valthurg were decimated after their alliance with a dark wizard, they were never fully gone. They fled from Astursis back to the Polar Regions, where they once fought amongst themselves due to lack of strong leadership. But in recent years, they've united. Under what banner and for what purpose, we don't know. There are fears they're preparing for expansion. If you think the Rau-Trava are bad, you've seen nothing. The Valthurg are the most brutal beings I've ever encountered. A decade ago, when I was only six, my tribe's compound was attacked by them. My mother and sister were killed. My father and I are lucky to be alive, and that's thanks to Baldric."

Avery fell silent. Worry crossed his face. How was he going to keep everyone alive against the Valthurg? The Valthurg weren't like the other Arkarnians he knew. The Dinalo had empathy and kindness. Even the Rau-Trava cared for their own unless one dishonored Korvas. But the Valthurg were cold, bloodthirsty, and hateful—even toward their fellow Arkarnians. All of it because of the ancient tragedy surrounding their founder, Morimor.

Silvyn could tell Avery was disturbed by what he had just shared. "I know our odds of survival have gone down, but I do believe we can succeed. I promise I'll fight to the death to get you to your destination. We just need to be very careful. As long as we're smart, we might be able to avoid running into them. Do the others have any fighting skills? If not, it might be wise to leave them with my father."

Avery shook his head. "No, that's not an option. It's imperative they come on this journey. Elis and Cinder have faced many Rau-Trava in the past and both have come out victorious. As for Alan, he's skilled. I'm told he's been training in the art of longswords since he was thirteen. He also survived traveling through the Shadow-Lands without any weapons, avoiding conflict and coming out unharmed. While he's never faced an Arkarnian before, I believe his past, coupled with some additional training from you, Elis, and Cinder, will better prepare him. It will also give everyone insights into what to expect."

Silvyn wondered why it was so important for the others to come along, but it wasn't his decision. He figured there was more to the quest than he knew, though he didn't concern himself with it. At the moment, he had his own worries. His father would not be happy with his decision to join this journey, and Silvyn knew he'd have to argue his case. There was also more to the story of his mother and sister's deaths at the hands of the Valthurg, but Silvyn didn't want to divulge a secret to Avery that wasn't his to reveal. Years ago, Pyramus had mistakenly trusted the Valthurg, hoping to come to an agreement that would free the Dinalo from Wethen's subjugation.

But instead, the Valthurg slaughtered many Dinalo, and Pyramus had abandoned all hope of freeing his people.

They rode in silence for much of the way, both deep in thought. So when Elis suddenly yelled, "Looks like we're here!" both Silvyn and Avery were surprised.

Silvyn removed his cloak. "This is the main gate on the south side. The village center is just past the gate, and it's a short walk to where my father resides."

The guards at the gate were surprised, but happy to see Silvyn. "It's good to see you. Your father has eagerly awaited your arrival."

Avery dismounted and walked over to Elis, Cinder, and Alan, who were ensuring their horses drank from the trough before entering the reservation.

"Alan, your father told me you took HEMA classes, specifically in longsword fighting. How well would you say you can fight?"

Cinder raised an eyebrow. "What's a HEMA class? Even if it's combat training, it sounds goofy."

Alan sighed and addressed Cinder. "It stands for Historical European Martial Arts. 'European' refers to a culture and ethnicity from Earth. I'm guessing it's one of the human groups brought here since a lot of the armor, weapons, and architecture I've seen combine Eastern European, Eastern Asian, and Middle Eastern influences."

Cinder chuckled. "That's a lot of Easts. Anyway, what's an ethnicity?"

Alan was puzzled by her question. "Well, it's like... how you can trace where someone's bloodline originated by their skin pigment and other traits?"

Cinder shrugged. "Skin pigment?"

Alan scratched his head. "Well, never mind. That's not really important if it's not a thing here."

Avery nodded. "No, racial labeling is a concept that humanity's enslavement by the Ancient Arkarnians erased for the humans of Whenua. Earth is unnecessarily complicated and divided in that regard. Arkarnians come in different shapes and scale colors, but they don't have names for those differences. They're all Arkarnians, and the only thing that separates them is the same thing that separates the people of Whenua: the banner they're under."

Elis raised an eyebrow. "Wait, wait, wait... You mean people on Earth have different names for humans with different skin tones? As if they were different species?"

Alan nodded. "Unfortunately, yeah, that sums it up. Mei and Tadashi got picked on by nasty kids at school... speaking of them, that reminds me. I should get back on topic and answer Avery's question. Yes, Abigail, Mei, Tadashi, and I were all involved in many HEMA competitions. I started when I was thirteen. To put it simply, I think most of us were adequately trained—Abigail, Mei, and I had three years of classes, while Tadashi only had one. The thing is, we never used it in a real life-or-death situation. It always felt like a real fight, but I never really thought I was in any genuine danger. So, I can't say for certain how good I am in an actual fight."

Cinder held back a scoff and asked, "So, you grew up learning all of this and never used it once?"

Alan nodded. "Yeah. The reason for that is, on Earth, people don't usually have to fight for their lives. And when fights do happen, swords aren't used for war anymore. Usually, it's ranged weapons—things that spit metal at high velocities, like a bat out of hell."

Avery cut in. "Okay, that answers my question. I'd like you to train with Elis and Cinder on the way to the Polar Regions. Maybe you'll even teach them something. Now, let's get back on our horses and follow Silvyn to the village center. The sooner we rendezvous with Madeline, the sooner we can officially get started on this journey."

Cinder muttered under her breath, "I highly doubt he'll teach me anything I didn't already know."

***

Madeline and Pyramus were reviewing the final details of the plan they had spent the past few hours developing.

"So, it's agreed then?" Pyramus said. "Sobek will lead your group to the Mortass River. There, you'll board a flatboat operated by several skilled navigators. Sobek will ensure your safety with them, as they're not very accustomed to humans. Once you reach Kurlo Pass, you'll disembark and head to Grimsby. From there, you'll need to round up a few of the wild Durbos to ride the rest of the way. Don't worry, they're very tame and don't mind humans."

Madeline still had doubts about the river route's safety. "Are you sure it's safer to travel upstream rather than through the forest? The river's many obstacles seem extremely dangerous, and the Arkarnians operating the boat don't exactly align with your non-combative beliefs."

Pyramus placed a hand on Madeline's shoulder. "I understand your misgivings, but I assure you, traveling by land would be ill-advised. No matter how skilled your party is in battle, there are too many different factions of Arkarnians, not to mention the many dangerous creatures roaming the land. Yes, traveling by river will also be dangerous, but at least you'll know upfront what those dangers are, and where they are located along the river. As for the navigators, as long as Sobek speaks with them and offers them a tribute, you won't need to worry about them—they will honor their agreement."

Madeline smiled up at Pyramus, but before she could express her trust in his judgment, the Chief turned toward a familiar voice. "Father, I've returned."

Pyramus stepped forward and pulled his son into a tight embrace. "It's so good to have you back home."

Looking to the others, Pyramus continued, "Thank you for returning Silvyn to me. As you may have overheard, I've agreed to assist in your journey to the Polar Regions. Madeline has the details, and I've offered to send Sobek, one of our clan, to be your guide."

Silvyn interrupted, "Sobek? He's never once left the Reservation. Baldric would be a far superior guide, especially since he's already been to the Polar Regions."

Pyramus sighed. "My son, that's not for you to decide. I have faith in Sobek; he's skilled. Besides, Baldric is older than I am. Asking him to join this venture would be inappropriate."

Silvyn shook his head. "I've already sworn to help Avery Ambrose and the others. They risked their reputations, maybe even their freedom, to rescue me. If you send Sobek with them, so be it. But I'll lead them instead. At least I've memorized all of Baldric's stories of the Polar Regions."

Pyramus closed his eyes, bowing his head for a few moments. When he looked up, his eyes were filled with deep sadness. "I just got you back... Please, I beg you to reconsider. The only reason your imprisonment was bearable was knowing you were at least alive. I can't bear to lose you as I lost your mother and sister."

Silvyn placed a hand on his father's shoulder. "I do not plan on dying. This is something I must do. I'm sorry, but my decision is final."

Pyramus nodded slowly, accepting his son's choice. He turned to Avery and the others. "I don't like the idea of my son taking this journey, but he's correct that he knows the Polar Regions better than Sobek. However, Sobek will still accompany you. He can learn much from the experience. Madeline, I will leave you to discuss the plan with the others."

After greeting Alan and the others, Madeline began explaining the route they had agreed upon. "We'll leave here early tomorrow morning on foot. It will take us two days to reach the Mortaas River. This area is a safe zone, allowing us time to train and plan our defense. Once we reach the river, we'll board a flatboat with our supplies. The boat will be navigated by a group of Arkarnians who don't align themselves with the Dinalo. However, Pyramus has guaranteed that they won't attack us as long as we're with Silvyn and Sobek."

Silvyn nodded in agreement.

Madeline continued, "Once on the river, which flows north to the Acheron Sea, we'll face several obstacles. And before you ask, no, traveling by land is not an option—it would be even deadlier."

Avery looked from Madeline to Silvyn. "Please explain these obstacles so everyone can hear."

Silvyn motioned for everyone to take a seat. "While I haven't crossed into the Polar Regions, I have traveled up this river to Grimsby. The journey north has several challenges, but I'm confident we'll make it through. That being said, I believe the area has been cursed by very dark magic."

Avery raised his eyebrows but said nothing, waiting for Silvyn to continue.

"As we travel up the river, there are areas where it narrows, here and here." Silvyn pointed to the map they were using. "When the river narrows, the jungle-like vines growing along the banks come alive."

Avery interrupted. "What do you mean by 'come alive'? Are we talking about nature playing tricks on the eyes, or something else?"

Silvyn cut him off. "When I say 'alive,' I don't mean optical illusions. I mean truly alive. I've seen many warriors disappear into the jungle as the vines cling to their arms and legs. It takes brute force and a lot of luck to break free. That's another reason why traveling up the river is safer than on foot. We just need to take defensive positions on either side of the boat as we make our way through that area."

Avery didn't ask any more questions. He knew all too well the dangers of dark magic. They would need to be prepared.

Silvyn continued, pointing at the map again. "Once the river widens, we'll be clear of immediate danger, but that's when we'll encounter a different kind of threat.

Scattered throughout this area are Arkarnian tribes that follow a more aggressive warrior culture called the Boh-Rahl. They aren't unlike the Rau-Trava, but they don't share the same beliefs in Korvas's teachings. They're less militant and content with their territories, but they distrust outsiders—especially humans. They believe us weak, and anyone they catch crossing their land becomes a target. Unless, of course, the travelers can prove themselves strong warriors. In that case, they'll break off their attack and let you pass."

Silvyn paused and glanced around at the others before continuing. "The danger comes from the archers. They nest high in the trees and can shoot arrows from far distances, pinning anyone who crosses into their territory while the raiders board the boat, kill the crew, and steal the cargo. The boat has a wooden canopy, but we must remain vigilant, or we risk being shot while we defend ourselves. If luck is on our side, they'll be far in the forest and we'll travel undetected."

Silvyn gave the group a moment to process the information. He didn't see fear on their faces but rather determination. He nodded and pointed to a fork in the river. "This is where we need to ensure we turn northeast, or we'll end up in the rapids leading to the Acheron Sea. Once we hit those rapids, there's no turning back, and we'll be stuck in the ocean with nothing but a flatboat. Trust me, the creatures we'd face in the ocean are far worse than anything on the river route."

Avery raised an eyebrow. "Is it more dark magic?"

Silvyn shook his head. "No, it's worse. There are giant crab-like creatures in that area. They prey on anything that moves on the water or near the shoreline where they spawn."

Alan spoke up for the first time. "So when you say giant crab, do you mean about this big?" He spread his arms about three feet apart.

Silvyn shook his head. "Not unless you're talking about a baby. The adults, when they expand their legs, can reach eight feet."

Avery took a moment to consider. "Is there any other option? Could we go ashore sooner and continue on foot?"

Silvyn was firm. "No, it's still safer on the water. These navigators have made many successful runs through this area. It's all about timing, or so they say."

Avery paused, then asked, "Is that everything? Are there any other dangers?"

Silvyn thought for a moment before sharing one last piece of information. "This entire river is known as Death's Door. You'll hear voices coming from nowhere, the voices of dead Arkanians who once lived in the area. If you look closely in the water, you might even see their bones."

Alan looked at his mother, concern on his face. He was a teenager, old enough to protect her, and he'd meant it. "I've got your back, Mom. Don't worry."

Madeline smiled at him. "And I've got yours." She knew the time would come when she'd need to explain more about who she was—and who Alan was—but for now, it could wait. "If that's everything, I think it's best to take a break. We still have things to prepare before we leave tomorrow."

Avery nodded. "Yes, most importantly, we should eat, then the three of you need to practice your swordsmanship. Once we're on the water, there won't be much time to train."

Silvyn led the group to a tent his father had set up for their visitors. Inside were several cots and a table laden with assorted meats, fruits, and bread. Beside the table stood a keg filled with water. In the corner, a curtain hung. "Behind that curtain, you'll find a bathing tub. Just light the wood with flint; it heats quickly. It might be a while before you get another chance to bathe, so take advantage while you can."

As the group ate, Alan asked Avery, "Do you have a plan for dealing with the obstacles along the river?"

Avery nodded. "Yes, I've been thinking about it. As you know, I have magical abilities, and some of those will help. But I won't be able to do it alone." He turned to his protégé. "Cinder, I know we haven't spent as much time as I would've liked honing your skills with fire, but if you follow my lead, I think you'll catch on quickly. We'll need your help with the vines. As for you two," he glanced at Alan and Elis, "you need to be ready to attack any vines Cinder and I can't handle."

Cinder smiled, proud to be playing a major role in the defense, but also curious about Avery's other plans. "What about the giant crabs?"

Avery shrugged. "I'm tempted to think magic alone will help with everything, but remember, the vines are enchanted with dark magic. And while Silvyn says the crabs aren't evil, I have a feeling he might be wrong. Dark magic is difficult to defend against, so we'll have our hands full. With that said, you'll be able to draw from both fire and wind to help. I can use all the elements, but it's going to take a lot of fighting skills from all of us to survive."

They ate in silence, each person deep in thought. When the meal ended, Alan, Elis, and Cinder grabbed their swords and headed outside to begin practicing. They were surprised to find Silvyn and Sobek waiting for them. "We thought it would be best if you sparred with someone of the same physical stature, as that's who you'll be up against."

Elis considered this. "That sounds reasonable, but if Alan here lacks experience, I think I should train him."

Silvyn and Sobek exchanged glances. "Why don't we just see how you all do? Who wants to go first?"

Cinder stepped forward. "I'm sure Alan will need the most help. I'll go first, followed by Elis, and then you can spar with this novice."

Silvyn wasn't pleased with Cinder's assumption of superiority and decided to teach her a lesson. The team needed to trust one another and work together. "All right, but first, put down your sword. We'll begin with hand-to-hand combat."

Cinder was taken aback but complied. "All right, big guy, show me what you've got."

Silvyn studied her stance carefully. As she began to move, he paid attention to how she shifted her body and limbs, knowing he could predict her attack. Cinder, too, observed, waiting for the right moment to strike.

She stepped forward with her right foot, drawing back her right arm. Just before delivering the blow, she turned her body slightly to the left, planning to follow with a cross-kick to Silvyn's left knee. Confident, she thought she could knock him down.

But as soon as she moved, Silvyn anticipated her strike. With a quick elbow block using his left arm and a right-arm follow-through across her chest, he had her pinned to the ground in seconds. He pulled her back up to her feet.

Cinder dusted herself off, but instead of taunting her, Elis and Alan said nothing. Silvyn spoke, "I can tell that had you succeeded in hitting me, the force behind your punches would have been enough to knock me down. However, you need to be able to change tactics quickly if your opponent outsmarts you."

Cinder's ego was bruised, but knowing the others weren't judging her helped her refocus. She resumed her stance, but Silvyn stopped her. "You'll get your chance to practice again soon. I'd like to see how the others do first. Then Sobek and I will demonstrate the fighting techniques we may encounter from different factions. Each one fights differently, and it's important you all study this."

Cinder sat down as Elis stood up, taking his place across from Silvyn. He'd been watching closely, knowing Silvyn would likely anticipate Cinder's moves. Elis knew this would be more of a challenge now that Silvyn had an idea of what to expect, so he planned to switch things up—fighting more like the Rau-Trava.

Elis kept circling his opponent, changing direction every so often, to the point that Silvyn was growing tired of the dance. As Elis prepared to shift directions again, Silvyn charged forward, grabbed Elis around the waist, and flipped him over his right shoulder, pinning him to the ground.

Cinder let out a small laugh, not mocking Elis, but simply enjoying the moment. "Glad it wasn't just me who got humbled. Come on, Alan, it's your turn to eat some dirt."

Alan didn't take offense. For the first time, he felt he was on the same level as the others, but he also knew he was still unskilled in hand-to-hand combat.

Silvyn watched Alan closely, trying to predict his movements, as he had done with the others. But there was something different about him, something that Silvyn couldn't quite place.

Alan waited, quickly planning his attack and committing to it. He took several quick steps forward, closing the distance between himself and Silvyn. This forced Silvyn into a defensive stance. Silvyn struck out with his left arm, aiming for Alan's jaw, but Alan was quicker. The two exchanged a flurry of counterblows, each one more rapid than the last. Silvyn was impressed by Alan's skill, but that momentary distraction allowed Alan to thrust his knee into Silvyn's chest. Stumbling back, Silvyn quickly reached for his club, but Alan was ready. As Silvyn swung, Alan grabbed the club with both hands, threw it aside, and flipped Silvyn onto his back.

Alan took a deep breath, still processing what had just happened. He had always trained with a sword, never in hand-to-hand combat. A tinge of fear crept into his mind, but he pushed it aside and helped Silvyn to his feet.

Silvyn locked eyes with Alan. "You have much skill, which impresses me. But what impresses me most is that you're not arrogant about it."

Alan nodded, careful not to reveal how surprised he was by his own success. "Well, when I learned sword fighting, I was taught that fighting is about discipline. It's not about winning or losing, but about being true to yourself and those around you."

Cinder and Elis listened to Alan's words, and they hit home. Maybe they had been trying too hard to show off. It was time to learn how to fight together.

Silvyn and Sobek spent the next hour discussing the different fighting styles of the various Arkarnian tribes. While the styles were similar, each had its own nuances—especially the Valthurg. Their actions wouldn't be easily predicted.

Once the sparring was over, Silvyn and Sobek bumped their foreheads together, an act Alan assumed was akin to a handshake. Silvyn then whispered something to Sobek, who hurried into a nearby tent.

"Okay," Silvyn said, turning back to the group. "I want you all to get some more sparring practice in. Elis, you'll spar with Sobek when he returns. Cinder, I'd like you to spar with me." He glanced toward the tent, noting Sobek's return—but he wasn't alone. A tall, muscular Arkarnian walked over to the group.

Silvyn nodded at Alan. "Alan, this is Baldric, my uncle. I'd like you to spar with him. He's survived many encounters with the Valthurg and is one of our most skilled warriors."

Baldric glared at Silvyn. "Don't get any ideas, Silvyn. I'm too old to go looking for a fight. But I will do my best to keep this lot from getting themselves killed. Have you told them about the trials they'll face before reaching the Polar Regions?"

Silvyn nodded. "Yes, but feel free to offer any insight. You've traveled Mortaas more times than I have."

Alan followed Baldric to their sparring spot. As he was about to ask if they'd be using weapons, Baldric suddenly spun around and aimed a punch at Alan's chest. Alan quickly raised his left arm, deflecting the blow. Baldric smiled. "Very good. I just wanted to see if you could react quickly to a surprise attack. From here on out, never let your guard down—that's what will keep you alive."

Alan nodded. "Other than the archers, what types of weapons do the Arkarnians use?"

Baldric shrugged. "It depends on the faction. As you said, the Boh-Rahl use bows and arrows. The raiders in their group carry a variety of close-combat weapons—hand axes, daggers, and homemade wooden shivs. Their style is a rapid flurry of stabs and jabs. But I've fought the worst faction of them all—the Valthurg. They're brutal. Their strength alone is enough to frighten you. I once witnessed a man have his skull crushed between the hands of a Valthurg. Close combat with them is not advisable, which is why swordsmanship becomes crucial. They don't use quality swords like the ones you'll carry—they use bone swords. And trust me, the name says it all—they're made from the bones of their dead."

Alan thought this over. "So, we just need to be quick on our feet and ready for anything. You may be able to predict their moves, but knowing what they're thinking is not an option."

Baldric nodded. "Exactly. Now, let's stop guessing and just practice."

After about an hour of sparring with Baldric, Silvyn called everyone over. "Alright, I have to say Cinder here has improved greatly since her first match with me—she gave me a run for my money. Sobek is equally impressed with Elis. So, we'll switch things up after a short break. Alan, I'll spar with you. Cinder, you'll spar with Sobek. Elis, you'll spar with Baldric."

Once the next sparring session ended, Alan, Cinder, and Elis were exhausted. Silvyn, unaffected by the physical strain, decided to call an end to the training. "You three did well today. There will be food waiting for you in your tent once you've bathed. Eat, relax, and get some sleep. We leave at first light."

Chapter Twenty-Five

The Myklins

Waiting was the hardest part for Mei, Tadashi, and Abigail. In the past week, when they had encountered obstacles, they were able to make quick decisions and move forward. But since joining Marik, everything had changed. It was no longer about group decisions; what Marik said was law.

Abigail glanced over her shoulder to check if Marik was nearby before voicing her frustrations to the others. "I don't understand why Marik won't let us scout with the Gnoglins. It would've been good practice—something that could really benefit us in the coming days. Instead, all we can do is sit here and wait. The longer we wait, the longer it'll take to find Alan."

Mei looked over both her shoulders before responding, "I agree. If we each went with a Gnoglin Scout, we could stop them before they even reached the village."

Tadashi, without bothering to check, spoke up. "Yeah, this waiting game is exhausting."

Mei and Abigail exchanged a glance of mild concern. "Marik is right behind me, isn't he?" Tadashi's question was answered when a hand slapped him on the back of the head.

"OUCH! Really?" Tadashi yelped.

Marik, now wearing his helmet, glared through the small slits. "You should be mentally planning different attack strategies. That's what a smart warrior does. This village may not be ours, but it's what we know, and that's why we stay here. It'll give us the advantage. If we head out in all directions, we lose the element of surprise."

Before Marik could continue, a Gnoglin Scout came running from the north side of the forest. "They're very close. I can see about twenty of them—armed with swords and clubs. Some are wearing armor, others are not. We Gnoglins can target their legs, though. They're not armored there."

Marik had to calm the villagers down—they were getting too excited, and he couldn't afford to lose the element of surprise. He ordered Gorb and Glum to position themselves on either side of the village, just within the treeline. Marik then gave Tadashi a boost into one of the taller trees. Tadashi would sit on a wide limb and begin shooting once Marik gave the signal. The Gnoglins would spread out—some hiding behind trees, others behind rocks. Mei and Abigail were also in trees, but not as high as Tadashi. They would jump down to fight when Marik called for them. As for Marik, he stood in the village center with the Chief, preparing to give the Myklins one chance to leave peacefully. If they refused, they would be killed.

Just as Marik was about to tell the Chief that he would handle the negotiations and that the Chief should stay out of his way, another Gnoglin came running from the west. "About fifteen Myklins are armed and headed this way. They're not far behind!"

Before Marik could alter his strategy to try and sway the Myklins from attacking the Gnoglins, all hell broke loose. The Myklins charged into the village, intent on maiming and kidnapping the villagers.

Marik bellowed, "Mei, Abigail, drop down and fight! Tadashi, aim for their necks and shoulders. If any of them grab a Gnoglin and run, hit their legs!" Drawing his sword, he ordered the Chief to get out of the way as he rushed to fight the nearest Myklin.

Tadashi noticed a Myklin heading north with a Gnoglin under each arm. "This should be easy," he thought. He aimed his arrow in a downward trajectory, just a foot in front of the Myklin, and released the bowstring. He watched as the arrow made contact, embedding into the Myklin's calf. The creature staggered, dropping one of the Gnoglins. However, Tadashi's confidence quickly faded. The Myklin's grip on the other Gnoglin didn't falter. Instead, the Myklin reached down, broke off the arrow shaft, and kept running. Ignoring the Gnoglin who had escaped, the Myklin continued his retreat, the freed Gnoglin raising his arms and letting out a high-pitched scream as he returned to the village.

Tadashi quickly climbed down the tree and took off in pursuit on foot. He wasn't about to let the Gnoglins be kidnapped.

***

Mei didn't drop down the moment Marik ordered them to. Instead, she waited for a Myklin to move directly below her. She planned to land on top of him, using her body weight to knock him unconscious. However, just as she formed her plan, the Myklin spotted her in the tree and had one of his own.

Mei was taken completely by surprise. As she made her jump, the Myklin moved quickly forward, and she realized too late that she wouldn't land on top of him. She tucked her head under her left arm and performed a somersault, rolling onto her shoulder and propelling herself into a standing position as she hit the ground.

Before she could fully recover, the Myklin was upon her, swinging his club. Mei took a blow to her chest, knocking her off balance for a moment. She recovered quickly, reaching for her Bok-Raht, and swung haphazardly at the Myklin. In the heat of the moment, fear clouded her mind, and in her fight for survival, she forgot much of what she had learned. Her attacks were sloppy, lacking the discipline she had spent years honing back home.

The Myklin noticed her unpredictable technique and realized she was panicking. He pushed forward, forcing her into a defensive stance, not giving her an inch to strike back. He studied her movements, looking for an opening to deliver the final blow.

Mei wasn't sure how much longer she could keep deflecting his attacks. In a last-ditch effort, she quickly raised the Bok-Raht above her head and used her remaining strength to bring it down at the Myklin. He hadn't anticipated this, and she made contact with his face, the blades streaking across his cheek and opening a deep gash.

The Myklin grimaced, pressing one hand to his wound, but he retaliated with the other, striking Mei's left side. Mei stumbled backward, hitting her head on a small, moss-covered log, and everything went black.

The Myklin looked down at her unconscious form and chuckled. "Such smooth skin… I'll use your hide to make myself a canteen…"

He pulled out a dagger and approached, but before he could make a move, a sharp crack of a branch behind him froze him in place. Before he could turn around, a hand clamped over his mouth, and an arm wrapped around his neck. He tried to scream, but the man behind him was too fast. With a sudden jerk, the Myklin's neck snapped, and the body collapsed to the ground next to Mei.

The man knelt beside her, quickly pulling a flask from his satchel. He poured a red liquid into her mouth, helping her swallow it. The potion was simple but effective. If any more time had passed since her fall, it would not have worked. The potion was a healing elixir, designed to undo internal bleeding and reverse possible brain damage if used in the early stages of head trauma.

The man stood up and scanned the area, ensuring no one had seen him. He had taken a risk intervening to help Mei, but allowing her to die would have defeated his purpose in following Marik and the others he had manipulated into joining his quest. Satisfied that his presence remained concealed and that no more Myklins were near, he retreated into the treeline. For the past few days, he had followed and watched... and he would continue to do so.

***

Abigail wasn't faring any better than Mei or Tadashi. She had started off holding her own against the Myklin raiders, but as the battle wore on, fatigue began to set in. Her arms grew heavier with each swing, and the exhaustion was starting to take its toll.

She dodged an incoming strike and swung her blade over her head, bringing it down on her attacker's weapon, forcing him to drop it. Seizing the opportunity, she surged forward and tackled the Myklin into a nearby creekbed, knocking him unconscious. As Abigail rose, she climbed out of the stream, leaning on a tree. Her sides burned from exertion, and her breathing was ragged. She had hoped to earn herself a moment to recover, but as she relaxed, another Myklin appeared from behind a shrub, snarling at her, ready for more.

Abigail stepped forward, ducking just in time as the enemy swung his blade sideways. Her reaction was sluggish, and she felt the jagged metal pass just above her scalp, severing several strands of her brown hair. If she hadn't been having a bad hair day already, she certainly was now.

Quickly, she thrust her sword forward, aiming for the Myklin's chest. To her surprise—and eventual horror—she hit her mark. Thick, warm purple blood spurted onto her hands and clothes as her weapon pierced the Myklin's skin and several vital organs, driving through his entire torso and out the back.

Throughout the fight, Abigail had taken care to subdue her opponents, avoiding taking their lives. It had made her feel better, knowing she had kept her hands clean despite the chaos around her. But now, instead of feeling victorious, she felt sick. The Myklin dropped his blade, writhing on the ground as he struggled to breathe. Blood poured from his mouth, and within moments, he collapsed, his body convulsing as more blood spilled out.

The fight felt like it dragged on for hours to Abigail, though it was only a few seconds. The Myklin's body went still, leaving her staring wide-eyed in horror as she realized she had just taken a life.

Meanwhile, Tadashi had just returned to the village after rescuing the remaining Gnoglin. The adrenaline from his leg wound had subsided, making it easier to take down the Myklin. As he drew closer to the village center, he immediately saw that Abigail was in trouble. She was facing several Myklins, her back turned as they raised their swords over her.

Tadashi quickly notched and released several arrows at two of the Myklins, forcing them to recoil. The arrows weren't fatal, but they bought enough time for Marik to close the distance and swing his sword, bisecting the two raiders in one swift strike.

Just then, five more Myklins came charging in, furious at the loss of their comrades.

"Tadashi! Keep them off me while I talk to Abigail!" Marik shouted.

Tadashi nodded, firing more arrows at the advancing raiders. But soon, he was forced to draw his dagger as the Myklins surrounded him. Despite this, he kept his eyes on Marik and Abigail, hoping to help when needed. Fortunately, Gorb and Glum arrived to assist him, easing the pressure.

Marik placed a hand on Abigail's shoulder. "Abigail, snap out of it! Yes, you took a life, but do you think he would have hesitated to take yours? What you did was self-defense."

Abigail closed her eyes, her voice trembling. "I... I know... I just... I didn't expect it to be so warm... all the blood... and the sounds it made..."

Marik turned her away from the body of the Myklin and forced her to look into his eyes. "Abigail, this won't be the last time you'll have to take a life. Just remember, you're defending your life and the lives of those you love."

Abigail nodded faintly, and just then, Marik whirled around, throwing his arm back to backhand a Myklin across the face.

"Dammit, Tadashi! I said keep them off us!" he barked.

Tadashi looked at Marik and muttered something, but the noise of the battle drowned him out. For Tadashi's sake, it was probably a good thing Marik didn't hear him.

The fighting could have continued, but Gorb had taken a Myklin into a chokehold, ready to snap his neck, when a loud voice rang out, "STOP! EVERYONE STOP! WE WILL RETREAT!" The voice grew calmer as the Myklin continued, "We will leave, but only if you put down my only surviving son."

Marik nodded to Gorb, signaling him to let go but to keep a hand on the Myklin. He then approached the Myklin leader, slowly and deliberately. "I am Marik, I speak for the Gnoglins. Now, tell me, you disgusting creature, who are you?"

"My name is Krognol, and that is my son Krika," the Myklin replied, gesturing to another Myklin lying on the ground. "The one over there was my youngest, Kirik..."

Marik didn't offer any condolences. "What kind of fool brings both his sons on a raid like this? His blood is on your hands, Krognol. These people are innocent—they pose no threat to your existence. If it were up to me, I'd end your son's life just so you could feel some semblance of the pain you've inflicted on the Gnoglins..."

Krika whimpered, pleading with his father, but Krognol held up his hand, "It'll be alright, Krika, steel yourself... As for you, Marik, I will not tolerate your judgment. You have no right—"

Marik cut him off. "So be it. Gorb, kill Krika."

Krognol's eyes widened. "WAIT! STOP! I'm open to negotiation! Don't kill my son, I beg you!"

Marik's face remained cold. "How many Gnoglins begged you to let them go home?"

Krognol remained silent, and Marik scoffed. "You want to negotiate, fine. You and I will. Jord, come here. I think you should be part of this."

As Jord approached, Krognol raised his hand. "No, I will negotiate only with you. You say you speak for them, so go ahead and speak."

Marik's lips curled into a bitter laugh, but he considered Krognol's demand. A plan formed in his mind, and he realized the Myklins could still be useful to him. "You assume my mercy has no bounds, but I have little against hurting filth like you. Fine, you and I will negotiate. First, you'll send all of your warriors, living and dead, back to where you came from. Your son stays in Gorb's hands until we reach a compromise. And if you insult the Gnoglins again, I'll have Gorb rip your son's out."

Krognol nodded reluctantly. "I agree, as long as the Gnoglins disperse."

Marik turned to Jord and the others. "Jord, have your villagers return to their homes and tend to the wounded. Abigail, Tadashi, go find Mei. I'll meet you by Jord's house once I'm done here."

Abigail and Tadashi realized they hadn't seen Mei for some time. They exchanged a look and sprinted off in search of her.

Tadashi called to Abigail as they ran toward the spot where the fight had started. "Where did you last see her?"

Abigail replied, "To be honest, once I jumped into the fight, I didn't see either you or her."

Tadashi's stomach tightened with worry. "Alright, you stay on that side, and I'll cover this side. Just shout if you see anything."

Abigail found the tree she had been in earlier and walked over to where she had last seen Mei. The ground was littered with leaves, and a trail of purple blood marked the spot where a Myklin had fallen. Abigail's heart sank—she hoped Mei hadn't gone through what she had when killing that Myklin. It was harder now that she knew he had a name.

Before she could fall further into her thoughts, she heard Tadashi yell, "I found her, she's over here!"

Abigail ran toward his voice and found Tadashi helping Mei into a sitting position, leaning her against a tree. A dead Myklin lay next to her.

Mei was rubbing the back of her head, smacking her lips at the strange medicinal taste in her mouth.

Abigail and Tadashi sat on either side of her. Tadashi asked, "Are you okay? What happened?"

Mei chuckled softly, but the movement made her head and body ache. "Let's just say the plan I had didn't go quite as expected. The big guy sensed it coming, and I think I held my own for a few minutes, but honestly, I need more combat training if we're going to keep fighting..."

Tadashi shrugged. "Hey, you did good. You killed the guy, didn't you?"

Mei looked to her right and saw the Myklin she had fought lying dead, his head twisted backward.

"What? I didn't kill him. When I fell and hit my head, he was still alive... Besides, how could I break someone's neck like that? I couldn't even if I tried."

The three of them glanced around, and Abigail spoke first, "Maybe Marik saved you?"

Mei shook her head. "No, he'd have lectured me by now about my clumsiness. Besides, didn't you two have to look for me? If Marik knew where I was, he wouldn't have left me here. Let's not mention this to him. Whoever it was, maybe it's the person Alan thought was following us at the beginning."

Abigail's face clouded with concern. "What if it was Avery...?"

Tadashi chuckled. "What? You think an old wizard just walked up behind this bat-looking guy and broke his neck like some kind of assassin?"

Abigail rolled her eyes. "You might have a point about the wizard part, but Avery's not that old. He's probably only in his fifties. Alright, we can keep this from Marik for now, if that's what you want."

Mei nodded. "It is. Thank you, Abigail. So, tell me, what happened? Did we win?"

Abigail hesitated. "I'm not sure if we can call it a win yet, but the fighting seems to have stopped for today. Marik's negotiating with a Myklin named Krognol."

Abigail's words took a more somber tone. "I killed Krognol's youngest son, Kirik. You should be happy you got knocked out—killing someone is not a feeling I would wish on anyone."

Mei could tell Abigail was wrapped up in guilt. "Yeah, it sounds like I missed a lot. But I'm just happy I woke up and found I wasn't dead."

Mei turned to her brother. "Did you have to kill someone too, Tadashi?"

Tadashi squirmed slightly. "No, but not for lack of trying. The arrows just aren't sharp enough. They did some damage, but I didn't take any lives." He then turned to Abigail. "I can't imagine what you're feeling, but just remember, those guys wouldn't have thought twice about killing you."

Abigail felt the weight of her guilt lift just a little. In the past hour, she had started coming to terms with what had happened. She had to agree with both Tadashi and Marik. "Yeah, you're right about that. Marik said something along those lines too. But just remember, if either of you ever kills someone in battle, I'm here to talk about it."

Just then, Marik approached, and Tadashi noticed first. "You negotiated that quickly? Are they going to stop terrorizing the Gnoglins?"

Marik raised his hand, calling out. "Jord, please come out and speak with me."

Jord emerged from his house, blowing into a horn to signal the other villagers.

Once everyone had gathered, Marik spoke. "You no longer need to worry about the Myklins. As for those of your people still alive and enslaved by them, they'll be returned to you by tomorrow."

The villagers cheered, but Jord remained skeptical. "How did you accomplish such a thing?"

Marik smirked under his helmet. "Oh, don't worry about the details. Just know that they'll be leaving this forest for good, moving on to find a new home. And Krognol won't break his agreement with me."

Jord still seemed unsure, but he decided to give Marik the benefit of the doubt. "I thank you, and my people thank you. Tonight, you will rest and enjoy a feast that we will prepare for you. At first light, Nòr will escort you through the tunnels. I wish you well on your journey."

That night, they ate and enjoyed music performed by the villagers, then drifted to sleep under the stars, their minds at ease for the first time in a long while.

CHAPTER TWENTY-SIX

Journey to Mortaas Begins

The morning after training with the Dinalo, Alan awoke in a cold sweat. His dream had been strange—he had found himself staring up at a void, but within it, he could feel something staring back at him. Initially, Alan thought it was Shadow-Lord and called out to him, but the presence watching him did not reply. As he sat up, he wondered if it had just been a typical dream.

Glancing around the tent he shared with Avery and his mother, he noticed they were nowhere to be seen. Quickly, he put on his shoes and shirt before stepping outside to find them.

The sun was just beginning to rise, casting a beautiful orange hue across the sky. In the distance, he spotted his mother sitting with Avery and started walking toward them.

Avery, sensing someone approaching, turned to Madeline. "We will have to continue this conversation another time."

Madeline looked up and saw her son coming toward them. "Good morning, Alan. Did you sleep well?"

Alan could tell he had interrupted a private conversation. He wondered what it was about—perhaps it concerned him—but he knew better than to ask. If it were important, they would tell him. He already had enough on his mind.

"Good morning, Mom. Avery. Yes, I slept well. Had a weird dream, but nothing like the ones Shadow-Lord used to plague me with. Honestly, it was the best sleep I've had in a week. I think everything finally caught up to me. I know you wanted to talk last night, Mom—sorry I dozed off."

Avery nodded knowingly. A long-overdue conversation needed to take place between mother and son, but just then, he noticed others beginning to exit their tents. "How about we go eat a big breakfast? Pyramus has prepared an enormous meal as a send-off. His people are loading the wagon with our supplies and the weapons we'll use as payment for transport along the river."

Madeline saw in her son's eyes that he wanted to talk. Standing, she gave him a proper good-morning hug and kiss, then held his face in her hands. "I promise, we'll make time to talk. We have at least two days of quiet before things become... hectic."

Alan laughed. "Yeah, Mom, I think 'hectic' is putting it mildly."

They walked arm in arm toward the wooden building where a feast awaited. A long table had been set with enough chairs for everyone. As they entered, they greeted the others and took their seats.

Once everyone was seated, Pyramus remained standing and spoke. "I wish you all good fortune on your journey. Your success is our success. The fate of this world rests in your hands. After much internal struggle, I now see the importance of the Dinalo people standing with you and offering aid where we can. I am proud to have my son leading you on this perilous task, and I know Sobek will also be of great help. From this day forward, I extend an offer of brotherhood between the Dinalo people and those of Wethan. We share one common goal: the survival of this world."

Just then, Baldric entered the room. "Excuse my interruption, Chief, but I also wish to offer my skills. I could not live with myself if I stood by and did nothing to ensure the success of their mission."

Silvyn stood and approached his uncle, bowing his head slightly as he touched foreheads with him. He spoke the phrase, "Mak te Wairusa ori Koek e tiakis." Sobek followed suit, repeating the words.

Alan watched the display, finding it both touching and informative. The Arkarnians of the Dinalo tribe were deeply respectful toward one another. Since meeting Silvyn and observing the Dinalo, he had noticed a stark contrast between them and the Rau-Trava. Korvas was worshipped fanatically by his people, and any disrespect toward him was met with punishment. The Dinalo, however, revered their chief while treating him as an equal. In return, he treated them the same—everyone had a role, and everyone was valued.

Alan decided he wanted to develop that same kind of mutual respect with Cinder. Until now, they had been too competitive, too judgmental of each other. It would be difficult to sway Cinder, but he was willing to try.

Pyramus waited for the men to sit back down before addressing Baldric. "We have endured much together, brother. Your presence and guidance will be missed, but I will honor your request. May Ora guide you." He then touched foreheads with

Baldric and repeated the same phrase as before. Alan made a mental note to ask Sobek about its meaning later.

Everyone ate in silence, focusing on their meal. When Avery finished eating, he spoke. "We will travel on foot for two days until we reach the river. Our supplies will be transported by wagon, and we'll take turns driving. Along the way, we will train—swords, knives, sticks, and hand-to-hand combat. Now that Baldric is joining us, it will allow for a better training practice

Avery continued, "Silvyn, I think you and Alan will work well together. Elis, I want you to partner with Baldric, which leaves Cinder and Sobek. I will also need to work with Cinder on her magic, so during those times, Madeline, you can get some refresher training with Sobek." At that, Avery winked at Madeline. Alan didn't miss the gesture.

"Now, if everyone is finished, grab your packs and meet by the wagon. It's time to leave."

***

Madeline held the reins of the two horses pulling the wagon as they left the camp. "I'm glad Avery allowed us to ride in the wagon first. He knows how important it is for you and me to talk. I'm sure you still have plenty of questions, even though Avery mentioned he filled you in on a few things. He also said that Marik has given you many half-truths—if not outright lies—so I want to clear the air and ensure you fully understand everything."

Now that Alan was finally alone with his mother, he struggled to figure out where to start. "I don't know where to begin. I mean, I know we sort of talked about this earlier, but... I realized something. You raised us differently from our friends, made sure we never became too dependent on modern conveniences. I get it now—it was all to prepare us for the choice. That's why we started learning self-defense at such a young age, why we walked to stores more than we drove, and why hiking and climbing were part of our family outings. That's why you wrote The Book of Whenua. I'm grateful for how you raised us. That said, I do have questions."

Madeline smiled. Alan had always been a good kid—responsible, understand-ing—but self-confidence had never been his strong suit. He excelled at everything he tried, yet never saw it in himself. But now, something had changed. The trials of the past few days had made him more sure of himself.

"Ask away," she said warmly. "But know that I am, and always have been, so very proud of you."

Alan looped his arm through his mother's as she held the reins, resting his head on her shoulder. "Thanks, Mom... About the whole thing with either Abigail or me—maybe even both of us—having magical abilities because of Great-Grandpa Elwyn... Do you have any idea which one of us it is?"

Alan lifted his head, listening as Madeline answered.

"No, I don't know which of you might be able to connect with the elements. That's something only another magically adept person can help determine. Avery wanted to get my permission before working with you. Once someone is identified as having the ability, their life can change in many ways. Not everyone who has the potential chooses to develop it."

Alan nodded. "So, magic is a give-and-take kind of thing, like in your book? That must be why someone wouldn't want to use it."

Madeline hesitated before replying. "Exactly. Magic can take a toll on your body if you overextend yourself. And beyond that, it's a lifelong commitment. Once you learn to draw from it, it becomes your responsibility to pass that knowledge on—to one day train others. And with that comes a heavy burden: the knowledge that you could be teaching someone who may use their magic for evil. I told Avery I would let you decide if you want to know for sure. And if you do, it will be your choice whether to pursue it."

Alan nodded again. "I understand. And I promise to think this through before making any decisions... something I don't think Abigail will get the chance to do."

Madeline's smile faded. "You and Abigail are both too strong-willed to be pressured into making choices. But I do fear that she could be tricked into choosing a path she would normally know is wrong. Listen to me, Alan. There are worse things hiding in the shadows than those like Shadow-Lord. These creatures... well, I never wrote about them. They aren't commonly mentioned or seen. Most people in Whenua assume they're just Arkarnian ghost stories..."

Alan's expression grew serious. "What could be worse than Shadow-Lord, Mom? The Mist? Is that what you're talking about?"

She shook her head. "No, Alan... not the Mist. Not exactly, anyway. I can't confirm or deny the nature of that beast."

Madeline paused before continuing. "Arkarnians call them Ak'spir. They are insectoid creatures from another world. From time to time, they manage to contact people and manipulate them into granting them form. Once that happens, they wreak havoc—until someone puts a stop to it. However, some forms of dark magic allow people to summon and even command them.

"The Ak'spir can range in size from that of a two-story building to that of a common insect. One of the smallest species is known as a Ctotles—capable of entering a person's body and influencing their intuition and instincts. Earlier, when your father wasn't around, I spoke to Avery about the possibility that Abigail may have been under the sway of such a creature. Avery said that Shadow-Lord isn't strong enough to summon, let alone control, an Ak'spir. I want to believe he's right... but he's been wrong before."

Alan patted his mother's shoulder. The revelation that such creatures existed was chilling, but he wasn't about to let it ruin their mood.

"Don't worry," he reassured her. "Mei and Tadashi are with her. They wouldn't let Shadow-Lord put some devil-bug in Abigail's head. Everything will be okay, Mom."

Madeline's smile returned as she steered the conversation back to the choice Alan would one day have to make. "If you ever need a sounding board, you know where I am. But might I suggest talking to Cinder? She can probably give you more insight into what it truly means to learn magic than I can."

Alan scoffed. "I don't know about that. She doesn't seem to like me..."

His expression softened as he admitted, "Though that might be my own fault."

Madeline nodded. "It will take time, but I'm sure she'll come around. Cinder has had a difficult life, and trust isn't something she gives easily."

Alan nodded again. "I have another question—something Avery told me. He said that on the day Abigail and I were born, the Disciples of Materall tried to kidnap us."

Madeline took a deep breath and exhaled slowly. "Yes... but there's more to the story than what Avery told you. It started toward the end of my pregnancy. Avery came to your father and me with a warning—the Disciples of Materall had learned what his mother had done to prevent the Orb of Livimor from falling into the wrong hands. The Disciples had made it their mission to hunt us down, to take you and Abigail, raise you under their influence, and indoctrinate you. If neither of you had the gift, they would have simply waited for you to grow up, have families of your own, and tried again with your children."

She paused for a moment before continuing, "After you and Abigail were born, the castle was attacked by two different groups—the Disciples of Materall, as Avery mentioned, and a faction of Mystic Masters who had gone rogue. They feared another evil like Materall rising again and sought to end our bloodline entirely.

Many soldiers and guards of Wethen lost their lives protecting our family... It was then that Avery convinced us to flee to Earth."

Alan processed her words in silence before asking, "What about the rest of our family? Is Grandpa Alan Elwyn II still alive? Was I named after him? And what about your side of the family—are they still living?"

Madeline sighed. She hated the web of deception she had spun around her children for so many years. Even though it had been done to protect them, the guilt still weighed heavily on her. "I'm sorry, Alan. I know this must be difficult—to hear about more lies we told. Yes, you're named after your grandfather, as well as your great-grandfather. Both Alan Elwyn I and II are still alive. They live in the Elwyn family manor in the Highlands of Yure'tein, which is in Kalnia on the Eastern Continent.

"As for my side of the family... I never knew my biological parents, but that's okay because my adoptive parents were amazing. I'm proud to be their daughter. They're Arkarnian—part of the Kalko Tribe. They live on the southwestern shore of Kardica with the rest of our tribe. It's safe there, and they live a simple life."

Alan's eyes widened in surprise. "So that's why Pyramus trusts you so much—you're a member of an Arkarnian tribe. No wonder you wrote in such detail about the Arkarnian people over the other kingdoms. You wanted me to understand them because... I'm one of them, aren't I?"

Madeline smiled. "Indeed. You are a member of the Kalko. Your Ramri—your grandmother—and Ranri—your grandfather—inducted you and Abigail into the tribe when you were born, before we were forced to leave."

Alan scratched his head. "I don't remember much of what you wrote about them, other than the fact that they're peaceful. My knowledge is mostly limited to that... and what Shadow-Lord said about their role in humanity's escape from the Ancient Arkarnian's rule. Can you tell me more about them?"

Madeline nodded. "Of course. The Kalko are a peace-loving society who live off the land and sea. Since the fall of the Arkarnian Empire, they have never once been involved in a war. Because of this, the Kalko have always been regarded warmly by Kardica, and many Eastern nations accept Kardicans as official citizens. That's not the case for all Arkarnian tribes—the Dinalo, for example, have been struggling to earn the same respect."

She sighed. "Kardica and the Kalko have never fully accepted the Dinalo because of their history. You see, the Dinalo originally belonged to the Rau-Trava, until they broke away during the Arkarnian Civil War. Because of this, the Dinalo were never allowed to leave the reservation and join the Kalko."

Alan felt a mix of emotions—happiness at knowing he had more family, but also emptiness at the years lost. "I always wondered what it would have been like to have grandparents. I mean... Avery feels like a grandfather to me, but he wasn't there for so many years, so I still missed out on that in a way."

Madeline placed a comforting hand on his. "When this is all over, I promise we'll travel to Kardica so you can meet your grandparents. And one day, we'll go to Kalnia so all three Alan Elwyns can meet. By the way, you share their middle name—Alban." She smiled. "Now... do you have any other questions for me?"

Alan hesitated. He knew he had to address the obvious. With a deep breath, he ripped off the bandage. "I... want to apologize for leaving Abigail in the hands of the Shadow-Lord. At the time, I felt I needed to find Avery. The others weren't convinced that he was trustworthy. They didn't know who to believe and wanted to give Marik the benefit of the doubt... but I couldn't accept that."

Madeline had been waiting for him to bring this up, and she was glad he finally had. "Let's get one thing straight—I do not hold you responsible for what happened. Sorting out who to trust after everything you had been taught must have been incredibly difficult. I'm just glad you're here with me now. And together, we will find Abigail, Mei, and Tadashi."

Alan shook his head. "But they're in danger because of me..."

Madeline turned to face him. "No, Alan. I don't believe they're in any danger. Marik will make sure nothing happens to them—he needs them. He'll say and do things to convince them he's on their side. And when we find them... they may still not believe you."

She saw that Alan was still unconvinced, so she decided to share more. "Did you know that Avery thinks he can bring Marik back? That he can convince him to return to being his nephew—that Shadow-Lord will cease to exist?" She shook her head. "Marik started life just as you did, but his father pushed him down this path. This is all he knows. Avery believes he can reach him, but... I don't. Not after what he's been through."

Alan glanced toward Elis, who was walking with the Arkarnian group. Life had changed so much in the past week. A part of him wished this were all just a dream, but another part—one he couldn't explain—was glad it wasn't. It felt... right, even if he was still facing the unknown.

"I met Mei's mother the other day," he said after a moment. "I understand why she stayed behind, but it won't be easy for Mei and Tadashi when they find out their parents weren't actually killed. They'll be confused, but also excited. She asked me to tell them when I find them... but I don't think it's my place to rip off that bandage, especially when we'll already be facing Marik."

Madeline nodded. "As a mother, I understand her desire for her children to know she and their father are alive. But in the end, you and Abigail know Mei and Tadashi better than anyone else—except perhaps their Sobo. So, I trust your judgment."

She pulled back on the reins, slowing the horses. "We need to let them rest. Our ride is over for now."

Alan stepped off the wagon and held out a hand to help his mother down. "I have one last question... If we can't save this world... what then?"

Madeline shook her head. "I don't believe it will come to that. Not while so many of us are willing to fight for it."

At that moment, Avery approached. "Alan, why don't you feed the horses and grab a snack? The others need to rest for a few minutes... as do I."

Alan knew he was being dismissed, but that was fine. He felt better after talking with his mother. There were still things he wanted to ask, but none were urgent. He looked forward to walking and training.

Once Alan was out of earshot, Avery turned to Madeline. "I overheard Alan asking if everyone on Whenua knew about Earth. I think you handled it well for now, but one day, I'd like to explain to him why Earth and Whenua are connected."

***

As Madeline began to pull away with the wagon, Avery gathered everyone together.

"Cinder, I think it would be best to work on some magical training. Elis, you can use this time to spar with Silvyn, Sobek, and Baldric. As for you, Alan, I want you to practice rolling out of the way of imaginary incoming attacks. Sometimes, you'll face weapons and strikes that can't be blocked by your blade. Alternate between running and rolling for the next half hour. Then, you'll be ready to spar with Silvyn—who will be a tad bit stronger than any opponent you've faced before. Now, go ahead and begin. And remember, one must always be prepared for the unexpected."

Cinder walked over to Avery, knowing she would need his guidance for the journey ahead.

"What should I focus on first?" she asked. "Fire magic? Wind magic? Or, since the vines we'll be facing were given life by dark magic, do you want to discuss ways I can try to break the enchantment?"

Avery smiled—Cinder had already guessed most of what he was going to say.

"Indeed. We need to discuss how to handle the vines. You've never encountered dark magic before, and removing a curse created by it is no easy task."

Cinder frowned. "So how are we supposed to break the spell?"

Avery shook his head. "We're not going to try. Instead, we're going to manipulate the enchanted vines."

Cinder's brow furrowed. "How is that different?"

"Well," Avery explained, "it's possible to manipulate cursed or enchanted things without breaking the spell binding them. Think back to my lessons on using the energy within yourself to connect with the energy in fire and wind. That connection will allow you to resist the energy within the vines. You won't be able to destroy the curse that animates them, but you will be able to stop them from harming us."

Cinder nodded slowly as she processed his words. "So, if a vine comes down to grab one of us, I could use wind magic to push it away—or fire magic to burn it."

"Exactly," Avery said with a smile. "And if you master this within the next two days, you may even learn to use both elements at the same time."

Cinder's eyes widened. "At the same time?"

"Yes. Imagine several vines attacking in unison. If you generate both energies at once, you could create a swirling blaze of fire using your wind magic."

Cinder had never considered that possibility before, and the thought of it filled her with excitement.

"Now," Avery continued, "let's start with wind. I think it's time Alan got a firsthand demonstration of what it's like to encounter magical elements."

A mischievous grin spread across Cinder's face as she realized where Avery was going with this training. Deep down, she had a feeling she was going to enjoy it.

Meanwhile, Alan was completely unaware of their conversation. He continued practicing his rolls, dodging imaginary attacks, but after several consecutive tumbles, his head started pounding. Suddenly, a powerful gust of wind surged from behind, catching him off guard. Instinctively, he turned to see where it had come from—but that was a mistake.

The combined force of his turn and the gale caused his momentum to spiral out of control. Before he knew it, he was lifted off his feet, spinning through the air with a startled yelp. The wind carried him a few feet before setting him gently back down. Dazed, he looked around to find Cinder grinning and Avery stifling a laugh.

Avery called out, "I just wanted you to get a small taste of what to expect when facing Marik's abilities. Of course, he won't be nearly as kind—he won't set you down so gently. But don't worry, there will be no more sudden surprises. I'll warn you before any future magic defense training sessions."

***

Elis walked between Silvyn and Baldric, with Sobek on the other side of Baldric. The wagon was at least thirty feet ahead, far enough that their conversation wouldn't be overheard.

"If my father's seer had ever told me that one day I would be taking a friendly walk with several Arkarnians, I wouldn't have believed it," Elis remarked.

Baldric let out a hearty laugh. "I imagine Ora is having a good laugh as well. Though we generally don't quarrel with humans, the Dinalo came into being because we opposed Korvas's desire to subjugate them. Ironically, despite abandoning him, our past as former Rau-Travans has made us targets for the people of Wethen—those who have lost loved ones to the border raids and skirmishes instigated by Korvas and his followers. I fear the ill will toward our people will linger, even if Korvas and his forces are driven back into obscurity."

Silvyn cut in, "Even if all of Wethen refused to forgive us, I would still be wrongfully imprisoned. While it's true that many citizens refuse to accept us—especially since King Belmont won't consider granting the Dinalo official citizenship—I believe Prince Elis sees us differently. Am I wrong, Elis?"

Elis listened carefully. While he often disagreed with his father's choices, he also knew he had to ensure his father wasn't blamed for something beyond his control.

"I'm sorry you were imprisoned and treated the way you were, but it wasn't my father who sentenced you, despite what Pyramus believes. The King of Wethen doesn't hold the power to decide judgment in criminal cases."

Silvyn frowned. "Why? If he's King, how is that possible?"

Elis sighed. "Because toward the end of my grandfather's reign, he became corrupt, and the people of Wethen lost faith in the crown. So, when my father took the throne, he wanted to prove he wouldn't abuse his power. He established a system where twelve citizens vote on the guilt or innocence of an accused person."

He continued, "But even with this system, I believe it's flawed. If those twelve citizens are prejudiced against Arkarnians or Dwargs, then the accused stand little chance of a fair trial, and the cycle of corruption continues. As for the Dinalo gaining citizenship, I do agree that you deserve the opportunity—but it must be done with care. Your history as a peaceful people is still relatively recent."

Silvyn considered his words and nodded. "I see your point—humans need time to trust us. But how can we prove ourselves if we're forbidden from interacting with the citizens of Wethen, except when they're harassing us?"

Elis thought for a moment. "I think you've already taken the first step by helping us on this quest. If we succeed, I'll make sure word spreads across Wethen about how the Dinalo Arkarnians stood against the Shadow-Lord. As Prince of Wethen, I'll do more to make your voices heard."

Silvyn gave Elis a rare smile. "Thank you. I truly hope you can convince the people of Wethen—and that one day, we'll be able to live freely among them."

***

Avery watched as Cinder worked to combine both wind and fire. For the past hour, she had been focusing on generating energy within each element, and Avery was impressed by the skill she had achieved.

Suddenly, a small ball of fire shot backward, striking the edge of Avery's robe. He quickly brushed it off, but Cinder's face turned red with embarrassment.

"I'm so sorry, Avery! Are you alright?" she asked anxiously.

Avery waved it off. "I'm fine, but I think it's time for a rest and—"

Before he could finish, Cinder cut him off, worried she had done something wrong. "No, I'm fine! Let's keep going."

Avery chuckled. "Relax, Cinder. Look—Madeline has stopped. The horses need a break. Go sit down; I want to speak with her."

***

Alan finished feeding the horses before heading over to join Elis and the arkarnians. He decided to save his conversation with Cinder for later—once he had built up the courage. As he approached, he overheard Baldric speaking.

"This bovine leg is delicious, but not quite as good as a freshly roasted lerp cooked over an open fire."

Sobek noticed Alan's expression and burst into laughter. "Baldric, I don't think Alan agrees with your choice of meat."

Alan sat down and raised an eyebrow. "So, you eat lerps? When we find the girls, I wouldn't let them hear that—especially if you eat the young ones. They got kind of attached to one."

The three arkarnians laughed heartily. Once they settled, Sobek grinned. "No, we don't eat the young ones. We like them big and meaty. Maybe one day I'll cook one for you."

Alan shrugged. "If you ever do, just don't tell me what it is until after I've tried it. I think that'll help me stomach it better."

He grabbed a bovine leg from the fire. It was a bit gamier than beef but still quite tasty.

Madeline, overhearing the conversation, worried that Alan's surprise might make the arkarnians suspicious. Casually strolling by, she added, "Yeah, good luck getting this one to try anything different. Back home, his diet was mostly fish, and I never acquired a taste for lerp, so he never had the chance to try it."

Silvyn nodded in understanding. "Ah, that makes sense."

Just then, Avery called out from the wagon. "I want everyone in full gear. You need to practice moving with the extra weight."

Elis and Cinder retrieved their own armor, while Alan turned as his mother handed him his.

"This is a little different from what you're used to," Madeline said, passing him a long-sleeved chainmail shirt. "But it should feel similar to when you competed."

Alan pulled the chainmail over his head, the hem falling five inches past his waist. His mother then handed him a breastplate and backplate made of leather. As he slipped them on, she moved behind him.

"Here, let me secure the buckles," she said. "They need to be tight."

Alan took a moment to adjust to the pressure against his ribs. The leather armor felt different from the polycarbon plastic he was accustomed to, but he knew this would offer better protection for the challenges ahead.

Next, Madeline helped him secure the greaves over his shins and knees, then the spaulders over his shoulders, and finally the vambraces, which covered his hands and forearms. The vambraces fit snugly like gloves, fastened just below the elbows with three buckles.

Flexing his arms, Alan nodded in approval. "This feels good. But where do I put my scabbard?"

Madeline walked to the wagon and returned with a scabbard holding a longsword, along with two leather belts.

"This scabbard is designed to be worn on your back," she explained. "It has a special side opening on the right, so you can unsheathe and sheathe your sword with ease. The blade itself is made of Gavrite, a composite of iron and gothite ore—gothite being native to Atilgoth. Your great-grandfather forged this sword. He wasn't sure if he'd ever get the chance to meet you, so he left it with your father and me in Overgate. The pommel is engraved with the Elwyn family crest. I'd tell you what it means, but... well, your father and I might have slightly forgotten. You'll have to ask your great-grandfather when you meet him."

Alan took the sword and examined the scabbard. He had always been taught to wear a sword at the hip. One of his instructors had even scoffed at the idea of back-drawing, calling it a fictional concept.

"I'm guessing this is common here?" he asked.

Madeline nodded. "Yes. The art of back-drawing was taught to humans by the Kalko when they were still warriors, many centuries ago. While not every human kingdom adopted it, it's quite common in the east—where the Elwyn family originates. The Kalko haven't been warriors for a long time, so no one will find it suspicious if you struggle with it at first."

Alan examined the scabbard more closely. "Ah, the opening is on the right because I'm left-handed. You kept Great-Grandpa up to date on us."

He wondered whether left-handedness was more or less common in Whenua. If most swordsmen here were right-handed, he might have an advantage.

Swinging the scabbard over his back, Alan adjusted the straps across his chest. Then he looked at the two leather belts in his mother's hands.

"What are these for?"

"The longer one goes around your waist—it'll hold a knife on your left side. The smaller one attaches to your right thigh and will hold another knife. We want all of you to be well-armed in case anything happens."

Alan nodded and carefully drew the sword.

He rested the flat of the blade on one hand while supporting the pommel with the other. The craftsmanship was remarkable. The handle was wrapped in burgundy leather, reinforced with black rings. The black pommel was circular, engraved with the Elwyn family crest—a cat standing atop a crescent moon. The sword's guard was subtly angled and black, contrasting against the silvery sheen of the thin, elegant blade. Alan assumed the gothite in the alloy was responsible for its distinct coloration.

Sliding the sword back into its scabbard, he turned to his mother with one final question. "With all this armor, how are we supposed to stay warm in the Polar Regions?"

Madeline pushed aside the emotions of seeing her son fully armored. She needed to stay focused—just as Avery had advised.

"The warmer clothes you'll wear under the armor should be enough," she reassured him. "Leather retains heat well. We should all be fine."

Alan watched as the open farmlands they had just traveled through abruptly came to an end. The next leg of their journey led them into a dense forest, but at least there was a dirt road to guide them.

Alan walked alongside Silvyn as the others kept pace with their training partners. Though they were separated, they remained within speaking distance—only Sobek and Cinder, who were driving the wagon, were out of earshot.

Avery called out, "We're about to enter the forest. It's a good time to practice using your swords to chop at the vegetation. Swing high and low, alternating movements. You'll need to be ready for anything."

Alan drew his sword from its scabbard and gazed at it. The blade, crafted for him by a great-grandfather he'd never met, filled him with a sense of pride. It was a reminder of the unconditional love and support within his family. Were it not for the lives of his sister and friends hanging in the balance, Alan might have been tempted to cast aside all the responsibility placed on him and visit his family. But at that moment, his greatest desire was to bring his sister and friends back.

Alan had chosen the longsword for its versatility. It was short enough to wield one-handed for quick slashes while leaving the other hand free—useful for sword and shield combat. However, it was also long enough to be wielded two-handed, allowing for more powerful strikes. Both techniques had their strengths and weaknesses, but the longsword was a well-rounded, all-purpose weapon.

What Alan wasn't used to was wearing the scabbard on his back and drawing the sword from it. It was something he needed to practice. He began drawing and returning the sword repeatedly. The first few times, he accidentally hit himself in the head with the guard, a mistake that caught his mother's attention—especially given the string of colorful expletives escaping his mouth, some of which surprised even her.

Madeline smiled, trying to remain serious as she called out, "Watch your language, Alan."

Alan turned to look at her, catching the smile on her face and knowing she wasn't too upset. "Yes, Mother." That's when he noticed she was holding a dagger in each hand. "Why those, instead of a normal sword?"

Madeline's smile widened. "These aren't the only weapons I'm carrying. I also have an arming sword. The daggers are for close-quarters combat. Just as you have two knives and a longsword, I prefer these daggers."

Alan nodded, still puzzled by his mother's skills with weapons. "Hey, Mom, if the Kalko are pacifists, who trained you to use those?"

Madeline gave Alan a half-smile, knowing this day would come but hoping for a more relaxed moment to share her past. With the danger they faced, she knew she could only give him a brief overview. "My background is a complex story. One day, I'll tell you everything. For now, I'll give you an abridged version."

Alan nodded in understanding, and Madeline continued, "When I was sixteen, I underwent a Kalko rite of passage called the Akoreila."

"As I traveled beyond my village, I encountered a mercenary group that offered to take me in and train me. I had run low on provisions, so I accepted. It meant a warm bed and food, and that's where I met Eshe Wicket—Elis's mother."

"The mercenaries were called the Senten'ari Keepers. It was an all-female warrior group, named after the goddess of Skatchator, where they originally served as royal guards. They were the protectors of Skatchator's queens, until assassins broke the line of succession. We trained in hand-to-hand combat and a variety of weapons, proving ourselves in countless jobs. We had a lot of fun back then, traveling from the West to the East. I even spent a week in the Sands of S'Yhor."

"A few years later, when Eshe and I were eighteen, we were hired to protect the Queen of Wethan as she traveled to Kardica. The Queen was Alfonse's mother."

"On the fifth night, our group was attacked by Rau-Travans. They were swift and efficient in assassinating the Queen. I had been asleep when it happened, but their assault didn't end with her death. They didn't want witnesses. You see, the Rau-Travans had diplomatic ties with Wethan, so they planned to leave evidence that would pin the assassination on Kardica, hoping to bring two of their enemies against each other."

"There was little we could do but survive. Fighting back wasn't an option. Of the Queen's detail, only Eshe and I managed to escape and return to Wethan. We took a huge risk to bring her body back, and though we both felt guilty, honoring her in that way eased some of it."

"The King was deeply grateful, so much so that, driven by rage and sorrow, he entrusted Eshe and me to lead a group of mercenaries after the men who killed his wife. He even offered a hefty reward if we brought back the head of the one who ordered the attack. We took the job and promised we wouldn't return until the task was complete."

"It took months for Eshe and me to replace the fallen members of our team. Even though we made decisions together, Eshe asked me to lead the new group. I was hesitant, but I did it out of respect for her."

"Once our plan was set, we headed east toward New Arkarnia. Early in our travels, we met two men—one of whom we soon recognized as Prince Alfonse. He was traveling with his best friend, a knight in the King's army. They'd defied the King's orders to seek revenge, despite his warning to avoid risky missions. Alfonse couldn't live with himself if he didn't try to avenge his mother. The knight, on the other hand, seemed unimpressed with us 'money-grubbing mercs,' as he called us."

Alan smiled, suspecting who the soldier was. "Let me guess, that's how you met Dad."

Madeline smiled as well. "Yes, though we didn't get off on the best foot. It didn't take long for him to see that we were skilled and determined. The Queen's assassination changed everything for Eshe and me. It became less about making money and more about helping others and seeking justice."

Avery's voice called out again. "Let's get to practicing. We can save the rest of the story for our breaks."

Madeline nodded at Avery's request and turned back to Alan. "I'll finish this story another time. Go train with Silvyn."

Alan and Silvyn picked up their pace, moving ahead of the others. Alan watched Silvyn draw his weapon—an impressive machete-like sword, similar to a dao. Alan had a feeling he recognized it from his mother's book. "That's an interesting weapon. Is it a zizha?"

Silvyn held it up. "Yes. I've trained with these for years—well, except when I was imprisoned. Zizha are incredibly useful. A strong enough wielder can chop down a tree, split an animal in half, or behead an enemy in a single swing. They're useful both as weapons and tools."

Alan's eyes widened. "Wow. I think I'll stand at least four feet away from you."

Silvyn laughed. "Don't worry. I'm very skilled with it. I'll be careful."

Silvyn swung at a hanging vine, then Alan tried to chop through one nearby. "Success!" he called out.

Silvyn lowered Alan's excitement a bit. "Yes, you got one vine. Now try a few more and see how your arm feels after several."

As Alan continued chopping, Silvyn observed him carefully. "Is your arm sore?"

Alan didn't want to seem weak after just one task, so he answered with a strained voice. "Nope, I'm fine."

Silvyn saw through Alan's pride but said nothing. Instead, he suggested, "For the next group of vines, alternate between one-handed and two-handed swings. Don't reach up and down; instead, chop at a slight angle, alternating left and right."

Alan followed Silvyn's advice, then commented, "This method takes less energy. Using two hands on the backstroke lets me apply more force, and chopping at angles keeps my shoulders from overexerting."

Silvyn was pleased with Alan's openness to learning. He had feared Alan might be too set in his ways. They were going to make a great team. "Keep going like that for the next five trees, but this time, stick to the right side. I'll take the left. This will help you get used to someone fighting in close proximity."

***

The training Baldric was doing with Elis was different. Instead of focusing solely on chopping down vines—something Elis was already comfortable with—Baldric aimed to test how well Elis could handle two tasks at once. Elis wielded a short sword, his eyes fixed on a vine. Out of the corner of his vision, he noticed Baldric coming toward him, the sight of the three-foot-long machete making his heart race. Elis quickly followed through with his stroke against the vine, spun around, and blocked Baldric's incoming weapon.

"What the hell? Are you trying to kill me?" Elis exclaimed, heart pounding.

Baldric sheathed his weapon and looked at him seriously. "You need to focus more, Elis. This isn't the time to drop your guard. You never know when an enemy will strike."

Elis scoffed, speaking through gritted teeth, offended by Baldric's words. "You don't think I'm focused? How so? I still have my head, and I blocked your attack."

Baldric huffed. "Incorrect. I simply stopped my swing. If I'd wanted to, I would've followed through—fast and forcefully. You'd have lost your head. If a Rau-Travan or Boh-Rahl were fighting you, this wouldn't have ended with a block. And if it had been a Valthurg, that block would have done nothing to defend you—you would have been cut down."

Baldric's tone remained stern. "You might be attacked from multiple sides, and you need to be prepared for that. Even after you blocked me, you should have closed the distance and gone for a closer contact position. Now, get back to chopping the vines, but stay alert. I promise you, I'll attack again when you least expect it."

Frustrated, Elis wasn't angry with Baldric—he was angry at himself. Though he knew they were in a safe area, he should've treated the training as if his life depended on it, because in less than forty-eight hours, that's exactly what they would face. He smiled and nodded at Baldric, patting him on the shoulder to show he understood.

"Okay... yeah, you're right. I should've been more focused. Sorry I raised my voice."

Baldric shook his head. "You don't have to apologize. I understand this isn't what you're used to, and it's not your fault. I'm being hard on you because I want you to survive."

***

Avery and Madeline were walking several hundred feet back from Elis and Baldric, who were walking about the same distance away from Alan and Silvyn. In the beginning, Madeline tried to watch her son and Silvyn while they were training, but after about ten minutes she gave up especially

after Avery spoke, "You need to trust him, Madeline, he doesn't need you as his mother right now, he needs all of us to be focused at the task at hand. He is more than just your son right now, he is part of the solution. You will need to treat him and the rest of us as equals, do you understand that?"

Madeline scowled at Avery, feeling a pane of irritation, "You mean like how your mother treated you as an equal? Just because that worked for you, does not mean it will work for Alan..."

Avery sighed, "I apologize if I've overstepped myself, but deep down, you know I am right..."

Madeline looked ahead blankly for a moment, "Fine, I'll do as you ask... only for as long as I deem it appropriate, just don't get into the habit of telling me how to act towards my children, how would you like it if I lectured you about how you act towards your daughter?"

Avery felt like he had been punched in the gut, but he realized how cold he must have come off when he had told Madeline to not treat Alan as her son, so he felt that her harsh words were deserved, "I am sorry Madeline, I did not mean to sound so terribly aloof in my request, of course I am not trying to tell you how to parent Alan, I simply mean to warn you against making him feel too comfortable on this journey, now let's put this behind us and get some practice in, I will move the vines, and you can get used to having those daggers in your hands once again."

Madeline gave Avery a half smile, she felt silly for becoming so aggressive, but, she would not apologize for what she said, "Yes, let's put this behind us."

***

Cinder kept trying to close her eyes to rest while Sobek drove the wagon, but he seemed oblivious to her desire to sleep. Instead, he kept asking her questions she wasn't comfortable answering. It wasn't that she was uneasy with lying, but in the past, her lies had always been well thought out and planned, making them convincing. The backstory Avery had given Cinder and Elis about Alan and the others was a quick explanation with few details, leaving Cinder uncertain about how credible she could sound.

"Where did Alan grow up?" Sobek asked. "He seems very familiar with the types of weapons Arkarnian's use, but only in name."

Cinder coughed, clicking her tongue against the roof of her mouth before replying, "I don't know Alan that well. I only met him a few days ago, but he's a good friend of Avery's, and you know his mom—her parents are Arkarnian from the Kalko tribe. From what I've gathered, he was raised by them. Alan probably heard the terms for Arkarnian weapons without seeing them firsthand, since, I mean, the Kalko are pacifists. The few who actually believe in self-defense weapons prefer to use human weapons. Beyond that, I don't know much about him. I find him a bit of a weirdo, so I try to avoid him. Not because he looks strange, I just don't like him."

Sobek chuckled. "I see. Well, regardless of how he looks, I find it strange that I haven't seen him pray to Ora. Being Arkarnian by birth, I would've thought he would have been raised to believe in Ora."

Cinder looked up at the sky, took a deep breath, and tried not to sound annoyed. "Firstly, I never said I didn't like how he looked. Secondly, who says he doesn't believe in Ora? Some people are just more private about their beliefs. Besides, with how they've integrated into Kardican society, they likely let their members worship whatever they want. Alan might believe in a different religion—after all, his father would've been raised on Wethan's faith. Beyond that, I can't help you. I'm not the person you should be asking these questions. I've had very little interaction with Alan, and the times we did talk only led to arguments. If you're that interested in him, why not ask someone who knows him? It's not like I watch his every move. Try asking Avery, his mother, or I don't know, maybe Alan himself. I don't mean to be rude, but I'm exhausted. Doing magic drains both my brain and my body. So, if it's okay with you, I'd like to close my eyes for a while."

Sobek wasn't offended at all. He now understood how tired she was. "It's I who should apologize. I didn't realize you needed rest."

With that, Cinder closed her eyes and let herself drift off to sleep.

***

By the time they were ready to stop for the evening, Avery and Madeline had taken over driving the wagon. During their hour together, Avery gave Madeline an update on everyone's progress with their training.

"You should be proud of your son," Avery said. "Silvyn is very impressed with his skills. He seems to have a natural ability to pick up the techniques Silvyn is teaching him. Elis is doing well too, but we can't forget he's the heir to the throne. We need to take extra care to ensure his protection. As for Cinder, after a slow start, her ability to use both fire and wind together is now fluid. I'm confident she'll be able to handle herself. The more she uses her magic, the stronger she'll get. At this point, I think she's ready for more advanced training, though that may have to wait until after this journey."

They continued riding for another twenty minutes before Avery pointed to the left. "Look, there's an open area that could make a good campsite. We should stop here and call it a day."

Madeline turned the horse's reins, leading them off the main road and further into the forest. "Sounds good to me. I think everyone's ready for a rest."

Baldric and Elis worked together to prepare the evening's meal, which consisted of smoked Blovi, dry bread, and a salad made from various greens and berries.

Once Sobek had plated up some food, he made his way toward Alan. "Do you mind if I join you, Alan? I'd like to hear about your life in Kardica."

At that moment, Avery approached. "Sorry to interrupt, but I was hoping you could join Madeline and me so we can discuss what needs to be done tomorrow. Silvyn and Baldric will also be joining us."

Sobek couldn't shake the feeling that Avery had purposely interfered with his desire to ask Alan about his past. But he began to question whether it was just his paranoia, the innate distrust of humans that fueled his suspicions. Nonetheless, he stood and followed Avery, knowing he could speak with Alan later.

Elis and Cinder, noticing that the arkarnians, Avery, and Madeline were eating together, walked over to join Alan. Cinder hesitated for a moment before speaking. "Just a heads-up, Sobek has taken a real interest in where you're from. I'm not sure if he believes you were raised in Kardica."

Alan had been worried about this since Avery mentioned they needed to be careful about what they said. He knew he'd slipped up a few times, asking questions someone from Whenua should already know the answer to.

"Did you tell him anything? Did you stick with the story?" Alan asked, a note of concern in his voice.

Cinder rolled her eyes, a bit offended by the question but replied, "What do you take me for, Alan? Don't worry, I mostly stuck to Avery's story. But like I told Sobek, I don't know you, so I can't speak about you. Unfortunately, he started asking why you seem unfamiliar with arkarnian terms since you grew up with the Kalko in Kardica..."

Elis narrowed his eyes at Cinder. "What? Why did you say you don't know him? I thought we agreed that you and I would vouch for Alan, say that we knew him because of his father..."

Cinder sighed. "Listen, I can't just say I know someone when I don't. Lying is not my strong suit. Sobek would have seen right through me. In the end, I told him to ask Avery, his mother, or just ask Alan himself if he was so curious."

Elis shook his head disapprovingly. "You could have tried."

Alan shrugged. "It's not that big of a deal. The only part that matters is that she stuck with the bit about me being raised by my grandparents in Kardica."

Cinder was surprised by Alan's defense of her, especially regarding something that could come back to bite him later.

Elis then turned to Alan. "Did your mother ever tell you anything about Kardica?"

Alan nodded. "Yes, I know a bit from what my mom has told me, and from what she wrote about in the book. I would've grown up in a simple life, probably in a fishing village. So, I guess I spent a lot of time fishing, boating... and swimming?"

Cinder couldn't help but smile at how Alan stalled as he worked through his backstory. There was something innocent about it. She quickly hid her smile and asked, "Alright, how about your religion? Sobek was really focused on the fact that he hasn't seen you pray to Ora. So, tell us, where you grew up, did you practice any religion?"

Alan thought for a moment. "Well, we weren't raised with an organized religion or any named god. However, my mom, along with Mei and Tadashi's grandma, instilled in us a belief in respecting nature and the idea that there is a higher power of some form. But there was never really any name for our beliefs, and no one we specifically prayed to."

Elis nodded in understanding. "I think she was probably teaching you the faith she was raised with by the Kalko. I don't know much about the arkarnian faith specifically, but all I know is that it involves someone named Ora. I couldn't tell you what their god is called unless maybe the Kalko don't have a name for their god, or maybe Whenua is their god. You should ask your mom before Sobek has a chance to talk to you."

Cinder joked sarcastically, "Or you could lie and tell Sobek you're a godless heathen who was still accepted by the Kalko."

Alan laughed heartily at Cinder's words, which took her by surprise. The fact that she had made him laugh gave her a warm sense of accomplishment. Alan then looked between Cinder and Elis. "Well, what religion do the people of Wethen follow? Maybe I could just say I follow that one."

Elis replied, "Wethan follows a religion called Tolism. We have two gods—Ignetolis and Apoktolis. Ignetolis is the god of balance, truth, hope, good, and life."

Cinder added, "And Apoktolis is the god of chaos, secrets, despair, evil, and death."

Alan rubbed his chin. "I might just go with that if I can't talk to my mom before Sobek comes to talk to me. If he's that set on asking me questions, I mean."

Elis looked over his shoulder to make sure they were still alone. "So, can you tell us what living on Earth is like?"

Cinder rolled her eyes but stayed put, clearly curious about Alan's life.

Alan wasn't sure how much he should share. He didn't know if there was some unwritten rule he was violating, but he needed to offer an olive branch, at least toward Cinder. So, he replied, "Well, you already know I didn't grow up in a castle. We live in houses. I don't live in a big city, nor do I live in a rural area. It's sort of in between. I go to school five days a week and have only two more years until I finish and move on to college, which is a more advanced school. Then again, I don't know if I'll ever go back. When I'm not in school, I hang out with my sister and friends. We enjoy hiking, martial arts, reading books for fun, playing games, and just talking. There are other conveniences that we enjoy, but the technology would be too hard to explain, not to mention, I don't think I should be telling you about it."

Cinder, curious as ever, asked politely for once, "What does your world look like?"

Unbeknownst to the teens, Silvyn had been nearby, listening to everything they said.

Alan smiled. "Earth is made up of seven continents and five oceans. It has one moon and one sun. Life is very different on each continent—the weather, the people, the languages. Some places have lots of snow, others have deserts, jungles, big cities, rural areas with farming, and just so many different cultures. I see a lot of similarities to this world, but also many differences. I don't really know how to describe it other than that."

Elis nodded. "Yeah, I get it. You really need to experience something firsthand to understand it."

Silvyn slowly and carefully stepped away from where he had been standing. This new information was something he needed to think about. It confused him, but it also stirred up old stories he'd heard growing up—stories passed down by his ancestors for centuries.

Once dinner was cleaned up, everyone spread out to find a comfortable spot to rest for the night. Tomorrow they would continue on their journey.

Chapter Twenty-Seven

The Dark Depths

The next morning felt like it came too soon for Mei, especially since Abigail kept waking her up every few hours to ensure she was okay and didn't have a concussion. Yes, Mei had a pounding headache, but she wasn't nauseous or dizzy. However, when you're tired and someone keeps waking you to ask who you are and where you are, it gets irritating. Naturally, Abigail diagnosed her with a mild concussion due to the headache and irritability.

"For the last time, I'm fine," Mei pleaded with Abigail. "I don't think I have a concussion."

Abigail pressed on, "I'm just worried about you. You're showing several signs that indicate a mild concussion."

Mei was too tired to argue but added, "Yes, I have a headache, but I'm not sick to my stomach. Yes, I'm tired because you kept waking me. I'm irritable because my sleep was broken into short segments from your constant questions, but if taking it easy will stop you from worrying, I'll do it. It's really because I'm too exhausted to fight with you."

Just then, Tadashi woke up and stretched. "Morning! You guys look awful—didn't you get any sleep?"

Mei gave him a look and walked away. Tadashi glanced at Abigail, "What did I say?"

Abigail sighed, "I stayed up and checked on your sister, only resting my eyes for short moments. Neither of us really slept. Now, get your stuff together. We're having breakfast, and then we're moving on."

Tadashi felt guilty for having had such a restful sleep while Mei and Abigail hadn't. He knew he didn't need to feel bad, but he wanted to make it up to both of them.

Tadashi had to wait until after breakfast to check on his sister, as Jord and Marik were introducing them to the Gnoglin who would lead them on the next leg of their journey.

Jord gestured toward a Gnoglin standing beside Marik. "This is Nòr. He used to be a miner in the tunnels you're about to enter. This part of the mine has been abandoned for a while, but we still use it to travel. There are some resources we like to gather. I know you need to be on your way, so I want to thank you again for your help and wish you well on your journey. If you're ever in this area again, you'll always be welcome. I now leave you in Nòr's hands."

Nòr bowed to his chief and then turned to the group. "I don't want you all thinking the tunnels are safe just because they're abandoned. They're far from safe. I'll do my best to guide you through, but you need to heed my warnings: watch your footing and stay on the path. Any questions?"

Mei looked around at the others to see if anyone would ask Nòr anything. When no one spoke up, she asked, "Since it's an abandoned mine, are there still mine carts we could ride to the exit?"

Marik, not wearing his helmet, stared at Mei and shook his head. Nòr answered, "The carts were all destroyed, but the rails remain. Unfortunately, we can't use them. Also, we won't be following the tracks the whole way—doing that would lead to almost certain death."

Gorb, who had grown close to Tadashi, punched him on the arm and asked, "Tracks no good. How are we gonna see?"

Marik didn't immediately reply. He was looking back into the treeline, sensing something—or someone—was watching them. He'd had the feeling of unseen eyes on him for the past few days, but as his mind swirled with possibilities, he wasn't sure if it was something to be worried about. He snapped back to attention when he realized Gorb had spoken again. "Sorry, can you say that again? I was distracted by my thoughts..."

Gorb repeated his question, and Marik shook his head. "I believe Jord mentioned there are lanterns in the tunnel. Now, we need to leave. You'll see for yourself what it looks like soon enough. Just stay close and don't touch anything."

Nòr led them to a hatch on the ground. Marik reached over the short Gnoglin and pulled the handle up. "Jord told me there's a ladder that extends down into the mine. It's about twenty feet to solid ground. From there, we'll be walking down a steep incline. The tunnels and mine system are about a thousand feet underground. Just take your time on the ladder, and make sure to hold on with both hands."

Abigail raised an eyebrow. "If we're going that deep, is there going to be enough fresh air? Mines aren't exactly known for their good airflow."

Nòr nodded. "The mine is part of a natural cave system, so yes, there's plenty of fresh air. There are also natural streams with clean water down there."

Marik motioned for Nòr to go first. Once Nòr had descended five rungs, he signaled for Tadashi to follow. Next was Mei, then Abigail, and finally Marik, who closed the hatch above him before descending.

Once they were all standing together at the bottom, Mei noticed the bright glow coming from a lantern on the wall. "Wow, that's a bright light. What is it?"

Nòr gestured for the group to follow him as he answered, "Those are light stones. They're one of the resources harvested here. They not only provide light, but they can also generate heat. The more stones you have, the larger the area of heat. While embedded in the earth, they retain both heat and light. But once removed from the rock in the mineshaft, they gradually lose their energy. When a light stone dies, all you need to do is take it to the surface, and the sun's energy will replenish it."

"Watch your step as you walk," Nòr continued. "The ground is steep and uneven. This tunnel is also very narrow, so stay in a straight line. Marik, bring up the rear."

Mei kept apologizing to Tadashi every time she accidentally stepped on the back of his shoe. Tadashi, however, didn't seem upset. The true culprit was Nòr's short stride, which caused the group to walk much slower than they were accustomed to. By the time they reached the lowest part of the mine, even Abigail felt frustrated with the slow pace. Her gut told her they needed to move faster.

As they continued deeper into the mine, Mei marveled at the vast open chamber. The walls glowed with numerous light stones, filling the area with a brilliant light. "Why did they abandon this mine? It still has so many stones left in the walls. Do the different colors mean anything?"

Nòr replied, "When we mine them, we have to leave a large amount behind. The light stones regenerate over time as long as they're left in their natural habitat. I believe there will be enough to harvest again in about twenty years, at which point this mine will be more active. Until then, we only mine small quantities of other materials. As for the colors, no, they don't have any specific meaning, except that they emit different temperatures and colors of light."

Marik asked the obvious question, "What kind of monsters live in these mines? Is that the reason Jord said this path could be dangerous?"

Nòr stopped and turned to face the group. He twisted the end of his beard in his hand, making it curl like a corkscrew before he spoke. "Yes, but also no. We rarely have issues with the monsters in this area, but occasionally, they can become a problem. When that happens, we miners usually hide, because some of them are much larger than us, or they come in large numbers."

He paused, then continued, "Most of the danger Jord mentioned was due to the terrain and the layout of the tunnels. However, it's important to note that we are definitely not alone down here. First, there are venomous insects called Xel'lum that make their nests in the rock of the walls, ceilings, and floors. Their aggressive burrowing can trigger rock slides and cave-ins if the area becomes unstable. Further down, there's a predatory fish species that lives in an underground river. We'll need to cross it before reaching the exit. These creatures aren't friendly, so we'll need to be quick when we cross. Gnoglins usually travel alone, so we're fast enough to avoid them, but with all of us, I don't know if we'll be that lucky."

Tadashi muttered under his breath to Mei, "He thinks he's quick? I'd hate to see what he considers slow..."

Marik, trying to process their risks, spoke up. "Abigail, I want you to take up the rear for now. I need to talk to Nòr about these dangers as we walk."

Tadashi moved to walk behind Marik, eager to hear every detail of what they might encounter.

As Nòr continued leading them through the narrow path, he answered Marik's questions while deftly maneuvering around rocks jutting out from the ground. For someone roughly two feet tall, these rocks must have seemed like boulders, but for the others, all taller than five feet, it wasn't a problem.

"We won't reach the river until tomorrow morning. You'll have time to plan for the Kae'Kulie then, and we can discuss them over dinner. Right now, we need to focus on the Xel'lum. You must know that if we disturb a hive, we need to run fast—their stings are very painful and difficult to remove."

"Is there one area where they're more prevalent, or can they show up anywhere?" Marik asked.

Nòr chuckled. "Since the mine is mostly rock, they can show up anywhere."

Marik opened his mouth to ask another question, but Nòr kept talking. "And before you ask, yes, there are more creatures down here, but most prefer the deeper, abandoned parts of the tunnels, where it's darker."

When Nòr fell silent, Marik asked, "How often have you come across the Xel'lum or the Kae'Kulie during your travels?"

Nòr let out a soft laugh. "Almost every time I've traveled through here. But I'm quick on my feet, so the Kae'Kulie can't catch me. As for the Xel'lum, after the first time I got stung, I started wearing leather armor. It's not foolproof, but it helps. Your armor should protect you too, but don't think that makes you invulnerable. Those pests are persistent. I've been stung at least twenty times, but luckily, I'm not allergic—unlike my brother Zòr. We found him three days later, still unconscious."

Tadashi, who had overheard everything, couldn't keep quiet anymore. "Unconscious for three days? I'm allergic to every bug bite under the sun! They say I have sweet blood, which makes me a target. And I don't have any bug spray!"

Marik spun around to face Tadashi, who immediately realized his mistake. "What? Bug spray is what I call the potion you make. You don't happen to have any, do you?"

Marik shook his head. "No, I don't have any bug potions. Now quit eavesdropping. I'll tell you and the others what you need to know later."

Mei smacked Tadashi's arm after Marik turned back around. When he glanced at her, she was simply shaking her head.

***

Nòr stopped once they reached level ground. "This is where the tunnel begins. We'll go left and follow the tracks from here. As you can see, the tunnels are much wider than the path we just came down. It's safe to walk together now, but make sure you're watching your step. I'll do my best to warn you of any dangers. Also, as you can tell, it's much cooler down here than up above, but with what you're wearing, you should be fine."

"So, how long will it take to reach the exit?" Mei asked as she began walking between the iron rails.

"We'll reach the exit in about two and a half days. Tonight, we'll stop to eat and sleep just before we reach the river. That's when I'll discuss what we'll face—something you'll need to be rested and alert for. It's also the hardest part of the journey. Now, let's get moving and pick up the pace. We've got a lot of ground to cover," Nòr replied.

After an hour of walking with little progress, Marik called out for Nòr to stop. "We appreciate you guiding us through this mine so we can make up for the time we lost helping your village. But at the rate we're going, it's going to take us much longer to reach our destination. In the past hour, we've probably only covered about a mile, if that."

Nòr stood silent for a moment, stroking his beard as he thought it over. Then, as if struck by an idea, he nodded. "I see how my shorter legs are slowing us down. I think I have a solution." He turned to Marik and added, "You'll carry me on your back. I probably don't weigh as much as the backpacks the morgs carry."

"I agree that's the best option we have," Marik said, bending down to let Nòr climb onto his back.

Once Nòr had settled with his legs around Marik's neck, he grumbled in pain. "Your helmet's going to be a problem. Can you please take it off?"

Already frustrated by the lack of progress, Marik took a deep breath and removed his helmet. "Gorb, can you carry this for me?" he asked.

"Sure, Boss. Is it okay if I wear it? It would be easier," Gorb offered.

"No. Just carry it. Now, everyone, let's get moving and finally make some progress. No more unnecessary rest breaks from here on out."

***

After pushing forward as quickly as they could through the tunnel, Nòr realized that they weren't going to take as long as he had originally thought. His focus, however, was on how close they were to the river, which distracted him from noticing the hive hanging down from above until it was too late.

"LOOK OUT!" Nòr shouted. "I've disturbed a hive! Prepare to defend yourselves!"

The group drew their weapons as an onslaught of Xel'lum erupted from the hive. Marik, however, couldn't draw his sword fast enough with Nòr still on his back. By the time he managed to reach around, grab Nòr by the neck, and set him down, it was too late. One of the Xel'lum had already flown down onto Marik's neck and back. As he tried to swat it away, the insect, which was the size of his hand, injected its stinger into the muscle between Marik's neck and shoulder.

Marik fell to his knees with the creature still attached. Reaching around with his right arm, he used his remaining strength to snap off the bottom half of the Xel'lum.

Abigail saw Marik collapse from the corner of her eye, but she couldn't help him at that moment. She and the others were busy fighting off the insects. Nòr noticed that the group was making quick work of the hive, so he rushed to Marik's side.

Marik groaned quietly. "I can hardly feel my muscles. It's like I'm paralyzed from that sting."

Nòr looked at the stinger still embedded in Marik. "We need to get this out—it's spreading poison throughout your body."

Marik barely managed a whisper. "Gorb..."

Nòr shouted, "Gorb! I need your help! Now!"

Gorb bounded over, leaving the others to finish off the last Xel'lum.

"I'm here, boss. What you need?" Gorb asked.

Nòr pointed to the stinger. "You need to pull this out as quickly as possible."

Once the stinger was removed, Nòr rubbed an orange paste into the open wound. "This will help your body feel more normal, but it will take time before you fully regain your strength."

The others approached, watching as Nòr tended to Marik.

Reaching into his waist pack, Nòr pulled out green herbs and a brown root. "Gorb, give him some water. Marik, sit up and chew these leaves, then wash them down with the water. After that, chew on this root—it'll help you feel better."

Mei looked at Nòr and asked, "What are these things you're giving him?"

"The orange paste is a mixture of water, yuchimiln flowers, and dirt. It's a healing agent," Nòr explained. "The leaves are from the menta and okalip plants. They'll help ease the pain. The root is koh. If you chew on it slowly, it'll relieve nausea."

Mei watched as color returned to Marik's face. "I'd love to learn more about healing plants. How did you learn about them?"

Nòr smiled. "A very kind woman visited our village years ago. She spent a few days teaching us about the properties of the plants around us. We're very grateful to her. Since then, we've saved many lives. Actually, you remind me of her—she had beautiful black hair, just like you. Maybe you'll be lucky enough to meet her as you travel. If you do, tell Nori that Nòr says hello and thank you."

Tadashi, always the comedian, laughed and said, "Nòr, Nori... that's kinda funny. If you get into herbal remedies, Mei, you might need to change your name. How about we drop another letter and just call you 'No'?"

Mei turned and smacked her brother on the arm. "Very funny."

Marik found the strength to stand. Once on his feet, he said, "Nòr, I want to thank you for your help. I owe you a debt of gratitude." He then turned to address the others. "Abigail, Tadashi, and Mei, you'll take the lead, but be careful not to disturb any more hives. Stay alert. Glum will stay close behind you in case you need help. I'll do my best to keep up, but until I regain my strength, I'll be moving slowly. Gorb and Nòr will stay with me."

Nòr shook his head. "It would be wiser to stay together. They don't know the way. Up ahead, there will be a fork, but I'll need to see the landmarks there to know which path we should take."

Marik waved him off. "They'll be fine. I don't want them slowing down for me. They need to maintain a fast pace so their bodies get used to it. Once we leave these tunnels, they'll have a long distance to cover. Think of this as part of their training."

Nòr finally agreed, watching as the group moved forward.

A few hours later, Tadashi, Mei, and Abigail reached the fork Nòr had mentioned. Just as Mei was about to ask which path they should take, Tadashi took off running down the right tunnel, shouting, "I can hear running water! It must be this way!"

Abigail tried to get him to stop. "Tadashi, slow down! Wait for us!" But his mind was made up, and there was no stopping him. So, Abigail, Mei, and Glum sprinted to catch up.

***

An hour after the kids had left them, Marik's condition took a turn for the worse. Gorb quickly scooped Nòr off the ground and swung him onto his back. Then, without hesitation, he picked up Marik and carried him in his arms, running as fast as he could to catch up with the others.

***

The tunnel Tadashi chose turned out to be a dead end. "From now on, Tadashi, we make decisions as a group. No more running off. Who knows what you could have encountered?" Abigail lectured.

Mei swatted her brother's arm as she added, "Yeah, don't race off anymore, but I have to admit, this place is pretty. Who would've thought we'd find a small waterfall and pond? The water is so blue, yet you can't see through it. It's amazing, but we don't have time for this. We need to head back and make sure we mark the right path for the others."

Tadashi shrugged. "I guess it was kind of stupid of me, but can we at least walk back? I think I pulled something in my calf from running the whole way down the tunnel."

Glum, who usually just waited for direction, spoke up, "We hurry, Boss be mad if he find out mistake made."

Mei looked up at Glum. "Sorry, Glum, we don't want Marik mad. And if he does find out, we'll make sure he knows it was Tadashi's mistake."

"Hey!" Tadashi yelled as the others left him standing there. They may not have run back, but they were definitely moving quickly.

Once they returned to the fork, they could hear bounding footfalls fast approaching. Tadashi saw Gorb and yelled out, "Don't go that way, it dead-ends into a pool of water!"

But Gorb didn't slow down. Instead, he ran even faster toward the spot Tadashi had described.

The others ran after him but couldn't keep up. When they finally reached the pool with the waterfall, they all yelled out in unison, "NO!" as Gorb dropped Marik into the water.

Gorb then set Nòr on the ground. He and the others stared at the water, waiting for Marik to surface. Gorb and Glum exchanged confused glances, not understanding why the others were upset.

After about ten minutes, Marik finally emerged from the water, completely healed. "Thank you, Gorb. You saved my life."

Abigail just stared at Marik and the water. "But how?" she asked.

Marik smiled. "Water has healing properties when combined with magic. This seems like a good spot to take a break. Gorb, Glum, get everyone something to eat and drink while I spend some time with Abigail."

Mei, Tadashi, and Nòr walked a few feet away from the pool and sat down, leaving Marik and Abigail alone.

Marik smiled at Abigail. "This would be the perfect opportunity to see if you're skilled in water magic. Reach out and try to connect with its life force."

Marik watched as Abigail closed her eyes and extended her hand toward the water. At first, nothing happened, but after a few minutes, Abigail pulled up a sphere of water. Marik told her to open her eyes. She smiled when she saw what she had done.

Tadashi, being as nosy as ever, interrupted her thoughts. "Hey, if you want to try healing someone, how about getting rid of the pain in my calf?"

Abigail smiled to herself, then tossed the sphere of water directly at Tadashi's face.

Mei and the others burst into laughter as Tadashi yelled out, "Very funny! But that is so cool that you can do that."

Marik was impressed by what Abigail had accomplished on her first try. He was convinced she would be a powerful wizard one day, but he kept that thought to himself.

***

Now that the group was back on the right path, Nòr, who was once again sitting on Marik's shoulders, said, "We're about four hours away from the river, where the Kae'Kulie spawn. It would be best if we stop for the night just before we get there. We'll want to be well-rested in case we have to face them."

***

After walking for a little over three hours, Nòr called out, "Stop. This is where we'll spend the night."

Tadashi noticed a carved image on the tunnel wall and asked, "Who drew this? Is this the creature you were talking about?"

As Nòr confirmed that the image indeed depicted the Kae'Kulie, Mei commented on what they saw. "It looks like it has a mole's face, but also a bit like an oarfish. Those usually stay close to the bottom of the water. Are those arms? Why does a fish have arms? Is the size shown here an actual representation?"

Nòr, now standing on his own again, waved everyone over. "Sit, sit... I'll tell you all about them."

Marik, who had already asked Gorb and Glum to distribute food for their dinner, motioned for them to hurry up and join the group. They would need to listen to Nòr as well.

Once everyone had settled, Nòr began. "The Kae'Kulie are an aquatic species that live in the deep rivers of this cave. From what we've learned, they're blind, like all cavefish. They navigate by sensing movement and currents in the water. The image you see on the wall isn't an accurate representation of an adult, but of a baby fish. An adult's length is roughly the height of two Gnoglins. For the most part, the Kae'Kulie aren't predators, but when they're spawning, they become very protective of their eggs. They spawn twice a year, and where we're crossing is one of their spawning grounds. If we're lucky, we'll have missed it, but if not, we'll need to stay vigilant."

Marik asked, "What kind of behavior have you seen from the Kae'Kulie if they feel their young are threatened?"

Nòr shivered. "They're terrifying. Their mouth is like a large suction, clamping onto the threat with immense force. Then, they use the claws at the end of their arms to wrap around the victim, pulling them deep into the river. I've seen it happen myself. I lost a brother and several friends to the deep abyss."

Abigail asked, "Will we get any kind of forewarning, or will they just attack?"

Nòr thought for a moment. "The air... yes, the air. If it smells very fishy, that's how we'll know they're spawning."

Marik called out, "That seems pretty straightforward. We'll all need to stay alert tomorrow—armed and ready. Finish your dinner and get some sleep. Whoever wakes up first needs to wake the rest of us."

***

As Abigail lay sleeping, her thoughts drifted to her brother, Alan. Soon, she found herself back with him. They were sitting outside a tent around a campfire. She faced a river, marveling at how beautiful the trees and sky were, illuminated by the bright full moons of the night. Alan was talking with the others, but she had trouble seeing their faces. She realized she was dreaming, but wasn't ready to wake from it. So, she calmed her mind and allowed herself to fall deeper into the vision.

When she looked again, she saw several arkarnians, and Alan was smiling, even laughing with them. Abigail tried to stand, wanting to grab Alan and run, but she was frozen in place—helpless, speechless, like an outsider intruding on someone else's thoughts. Before she lost sight of Alan, she saw a woman walk over and sit beside him, rubbing her hand on his back. Abigail quickly awoke, calling out, "Mom!"

Luckily, no one else was awake. She hadn't disturbed anyone. The dream—or vision—left her unable to return to a deep sleep, so she lay there with her eyes closed, just resting, as her mind tried to make sense of what she had just experienced.

Meanwhile, Mei was also dreaming, but she was alone. She was lost in the tunnels of the cave. Gone were the bright stones that lined the walls, and now the only light came from the torch she held in her hand. Its flickering flame was dying. Mei knew she was losing oxygen, the walls pressing in on her. She needed to find a way back to the surface or risk suffocating. Her heart beat wildly in her chest, the panic threatening to drive her mad. She wondered if she was buried alive, destined to die here, never to see her loved ones again.

Her thoughts were interrupted by a strange sucking sound, like someone drinking through a straw. She turned and screamed as she saw a Kae'kulie sucking on her back. Mei woke abruptly, just like Abigail, and thankfully, she hadn't disturbed anyone. After taking a few calming breaths, she closed her eyes and drifted back to sleep.

Tadashi, on the other hand, had been having several different dreams—ones he would probably forget upon waking. Most had been pleasant, some bizarre, but right now, he was dreaming that he was asleep. As he slept, he felt a heavy weight pressing down on his chest. With every inhale, it became harder and harder for his chest to expand, and when he exhaled, it felt as though his body was being pushed further into the ground. This continued until Tadashi could barely take a breath.

Suddenly, he woke up, gasping for air. Instead of screaming, he lay very still, staring directly into the eyes of a hairy beast. The creature was sitting on top of him, watching him as he struggled to breathe. Tadashi slowly turned his head to the left, looking for help. Standing by his side was Nòr, smiling.

"It seems Troll has taken a liking to you," Nòr said. "He's a cave cat. Not that he lives down here, no. He usually hangs around the woods of our village. I guess you could say he's a friend. He comes and goes as he pleases."

When Tadashi didn't respond, Nòr added, "Well, don't just lie there. Everyone else is awake. It's time to get moving."

Troll glanced at Nòr, then back at Tadashi. He quickly licked Tadashi's face before jumping off his chest. Tadashi coughed and gasped as he took in deep breaths, filling his lungs once again.

Abigail, still disturbed by her dream, didn't pay attention to Tadashi's encounter, but Gorb reached out and helped him up. "That creature means no harm. He's friendly."

Tadashi nodded. "Where did he run off to?"

Nòr replied, "Troll doesn't stay long. He's very independent. We gave him some bread, and now he's off doing whatever it is that they do."

Marik cut in, "You better eat something. We're leaving."

Mei handed him some bread and his water bag. Tadashi took up the rear with Gorb and Glum. Nòr was back on Marik's shoulders, leaving Mei and Abigail in the middle.

Marik looked at the river and then at the rock path across to the other side.

"... I don't like this. Are you sure there's no other path?"

Nòr stroked Marik's ear. "Yes, this is the only way to get to the other side of the cave in a timely manner. The only route that avoids the river is miles out of our way, and extremely dangerous."

Marik sighed, then swatted at Nòr. "Stop that!"

Nòr giggled. "Sorry, but your smooth-skinned ear fascinates me. We Gnoglins, as you can see, have very hairy ears."

Marik just shook his head. Then he noticed that his Morgs weren't following the plan, which made him even more irritated. "Damn... Gorb, go across first. Stop at the larger rock platform. Then Glum will go across to the other side. That way, there'll be a halfway point for Abigail, Mei, and Tadashi to steady themselves with your help, and then Glum will help them across. Do you think you can remember that?"

"Uh... are you sure, boss? Those rocks look slippery..."

Marik snapped at Gorb, suddenly poking him with each word. "If I didn't think you could do this... I... would... NOT... ASK IT OF YOU! Just do as you're told!"

Nòr's eyes bulged as he nearly fell off Marik's back, grabbing onto his hair to steady himself, as Gorb stepped back in surprise and fear. "I'm sorry, boss!"

Abigail put a hand on Marik's shoulder, shaking him out of his angered stupor. "Calm down! He just said the rocks looked slippery! That's all he said!"

Marik appeared to calm down, glancing around at everyone with a look of shame. He took his helmet back from Glum and put it on, apparently to hide his embarrassment.

"I... I'm sorry. I'm just... stressed about this whole thing... that's all."

Abigail smiled understandingly, and Gorb put an arm around Marik. "It's okay, boss. We're all stressed. Tired of the cave. We don't mean to say bad things. Like the other day, I told Glum he looked like our Mawmaw, but then I took it back later, because our Mawmaw's not ugly like him."

"Hey! You said I wasn't ugly like Mawmaw!"

"I told you what you wanted to hear! You know I never say anything bad about Mawmaw!"

Everyone laughed at Gorb and Glum's banter for a moment before refocusing on the task at hand.

Gorb walked carefully across the stones and stopped at the middle platform. Glum followed.

"So far, so good," Nòr muttered. "But I worry that your outburst, combined with our laughter, may attract the Kae'Kulie..."

Marik replied grimly, possibly still angry with himself. "As do I..."

Tadashi moved up to Marik's side. "Short people first! Come on, Nòr! I'll carry you across!"

Nòr chuckled and hopped onto Tadashi's shoulder.

Tadashi began to cross slowly. When he reached Gorb on the center platform, Nòr glanced over at the water and froze.

"Be still, Tadashi..." Nòr whispered.

A Kae'Kulie swam past the stones, part of its head above the water. Its blind eyes seemed to lock onto Tadashi's, making him shift uncomfortably.

Nòr quickly put a hand over Tadashi's mouth as his lips began to quiver. "Shhhh-hh..."

The Kae'Kulie slowly descended back into the water.

Nor removed his hand from Tadashi's face and whispered, "The danger has passed for now..."

But then, with a sudden yelp, Nòr was grabbed by a Kae'Kulie that leapt from the water, pulling him in. Tadashi was knocked off balance and fell toward the ground, but thankfully, Gorb caught him mid-fall and held on tight as a massive group of Kae'Kulie became visible in the water.

"Uh oh... no good..." Gorb whispered to Tadashi, encouraging him to keep moving. "Stay close..."

Behind them, Mei screamed, "No!!" as Nòr was dragged off Tadashi's back. Her outburst gave the other Kae'Kulie their location. Mei stopped, frozen, as a swarm of the monstrous fish came flying toward them. Abigail, quick on her feet, pulled Mei behind her, drawing her short sword to protect them. She began slicing and slashing at the creatures as they lunged at her. Mei shook off the shock and quickly began defending herself as well.

Marik, still at the river's shore, began shouting orders as he made his way to the large rock platform. "Settle yourselves and use your skills wisely! Do not panic! That will only bring harm to you and the others!"

Marik's commanding voice did its job, and soon some of the Kae'Kulie shifted their attention away from Abigail and Mei, redirecting it toward him.

With a fierce swing, Marik cleaved through four of the Kae'Kulie, dark red clouds swirling in the clear water as their bodies split in half. Their entrails spilled out, some floating to the surface, while the rest sank into the depths.

Shadow-Lord backed away from the water, watching the next wave of Kae'Kulie frenzy at the blood now floating on the surface. Marik wasn't sure whether they were unintentionally or intentionally feeding on the organs of their fallen brethren, but he didn't have time to dwell on that. His focus had to be on helping the others, who were struggling against the onslaught.

As Marik continued to slash and cut through the Kae'Kulie, he noticed Gorb doing his best to protect both Mei and Tadashi, who were struggling to hold their ground. Meanwhile, Glum had moved in to shield Abigail, who was attempting to use her newfound connection with water to push the monsters back.

Mei screamed in pain as one of the Kae'Kulie leapt at her, its sharp, finger-like appendages sinking into her arm, its teeth biting into her like a parasitic lamprey from Earth's oceans.

Tadashi turned at the sound of his sister's scream, stabbing the Kae'Kulie with his knife and forcing it to release her. The wounded creature fell back into the water, but another leapt at Tadashi, slashing at his chest with its claws, causing him to stumble. Gorb quickly reached out, catching Tadashi with one arm while using the other to bat away the Kae'Kulie that was about to latch onto Tadashi's neck. In the process, Gorb received a deep, painful bite. He howled in agony, then grabbed the monster by its skull, crushing it with one hand until it finally released its fangs from his arm, its blood pouring onto his hand.

The battle was far from over. Gorb threw the dead fish at another Kae'Kulie that was about to leap at Mei, sending it crashing back into the water. The pain in his arm was overwhelming, so he took a moment to assess his wound.

Mei, horrified by the sight, asked, "Are you alright?"

Gorb winced, grimacing as he replied, "Uh oh... hope no disease from it..."

"GORB!" Marik shouted, "Get them across! I'll handle the rest. Abigail! Tend to the wounded."

It didn't take long for Marik to finish off the remaining Kae'Kulie. Soon, he was joining Abigail in tending to the lacerations. "You've caught on quickly, Abigail. I had a feeling you'd be powerful with magic."

Abigail didn't smile or acknowledge Marik's praise. She was too focused on sealing the deep wound on Mei's arm, holding back the tears that threatened to surface as she worked on her dear friend, who had passed out from the pain and blood loss.

While Abigail used her magic to encase the wound in water, Marik finished healing both Gorb and Glum. He was about to tend to Tadashi's lacerations when he saw that Mei's wound was not closing properly.

"Abigail, I'll take care of Mei. You go help Tadashi. This wound is too severe to treat this way—I'll need to cauterize it."

Abigail slowly stepped back, watching as the Shadow-Lord snapped his fingers, summoning a fire that sparked in his palm like a lighter. Tadashi, covered in lacerations on his face, neck, and hand, made his way over, watching as Marik closed the wound on Mei's arm. He tried to speak to Abigail, who seemed frozen, mumbling over and over, "Please be okay, please be okay, please be okay..."

Tadashi touched her shoulder with his good hand, startling her. Abigail turned, and for the first time, she allowed the emotional wall she'd built around herself to fall. She pulled Tadashi into a hug, letting the tears she'd been holding back finally flow.

Marik stood up, calling out, "Mei will be fine. The wound is sealed, and once she wakes, she'll need food to regain her strength. Until then, Glum, I want you to carry her. We need to move away from this river. Losing Nòr has put us in a difficult position. We don't know where the exit is, but I'm hoping that by following the path he set us on, we'll find it. So keep your eyes open."

Abigail finally released Tadashi from her tight grip, and he let out a small whimper. "Do you think someone could tend to my wounds before we head out?"

Marik gave Abigail an exasperated look, then walked over to Tadashi and pulled him toward the edge of the riverbank. "Kneel down and put your wounded hand in the water," he ordered. Marik then shoved the back of Tadashi's head, submerging it in the river. After a few moments of Tadashi flailing his good hand in the air, Marik released him. "All better?" he asked.

Tadashi shook his head, "Yeah, all good."

Abigail smiled, feeling better knowing her friends were alright. But then, a dark thought crossed her mind. They'd survived this time... but what about next time?

***

About an hour after leaving the river behind, the group reached what seemed like a dead end. The tunnel they had been following opened into a large cavern, and on the far side, three more tunnels branched off, presenting them with a decision.

Marik glanced over at Glum as Mei began to stir for the first time. "We'll stop here for all of you to eat and rest. Gorb, Glum, and I will each venture down one of the tunnels for about ten minutes. When we return, we'll decide which of the three is our best option. For now, Abigail and Tadashi, you need to make sure Mei eats well."

As Marik and the Morgs left, Abigail and Tadashi took to mothering Mei, each trying to get her to eat what they handed her.

"Really? Can you guys give me a minute to breathe? I appreciate the concern, but I'm starving! So trust me, I'll eat. I suggest you worry about feeding yourselves or I'm going to eat your share too," Mei joked.

Abigail and Tadashi laughed, both chiming in at once, "Yep, she's back."

Meanwhile, on the other side of the cavern, Marik was giving Gorb and Glum instructions on what to look for as they scouted the tunnels. "We'll make our decision based on what we observe, so I need you both to pay attention to the details. Go about 1,000 steps, then report back here."

Less than half an hour later, Marik, Gorb, and Glum returned to the others. As they sat down, Abigail handed out food to the group. Marik, having already spoken with Gorb and Glum about their findings, addressed the group.

"It seems we're down to two options. Gorb reported that the tunnel he was in had little to no light, while the other two are well lit. So now, it's about the terrain to determine which way we go. I had hoped one of the tunnels would incline toward the surface, but from what we saw, none of them showed that feature. That leaves us with a toss-up, except for one thing. Glum mentioned seeing what looked like an arrow etched into the wall of his tunnel. Based on that, let's take a vote."

After everyone voiced their opinions, they gathered their belongings and crossed the cavern. Glum's tunnel had won the vote.

As the day wore on and they still hadn't found an incline, the others suggested turning around and trying a different tunnel. But Marik shook his head and called for everyone to stop and be silent.

"Listen... and smell the air. Do you sense that? We're approaching water. I hope we're not walking in circles. Nòr never mentioned more than one river down here."

No one voiced their concern, but the fear was evident on their faces—no one wanted to face the Kae'Kulie again.

A few minutes later, the tunnel opened into a vast cavern, and the water came into view. It wasn't a river, but a large lake stretching out before them.

"Thank God it isn't the river," Tadashi exclaimed.

Marik squinted, looking across the walkway. He couldn't believe his eyes. "Nòr... is that you?"

The group grew excited as they raced ahead, ignoring Marik's warning to be careful.

Sure enough, it was Nòr, sitting by a small fire, eating what appeared to be a roasted Kae'Kulie.

"Wow, I can't believe you're alive! Looks like you had the last word in that fight," Mei exclaimed.

Nòr smiled, but when Marik approached, he spoke. "Ah... your missteps have become my fortune. I never thought I'd see you all again."

Marik stared at the Gnoglin, his curiosity piqued. "First, how did you survive? And secondly, what do you mean by 'misstep'? Is this not the way out of here?"

Nòr grinned. "I outwitted the scaly beast, and as you can see, it's fed me well. Would you like some?"

Marik didn't question Nòr, though he had a hard time believing the little Gnoglin had bested the Kae'Kulie on his own. He briefly felt the same sensation he had before they entered—the feeling of being watched. He suspected that Nòr had been rescued by whoever was stalking them, but Marik wasn't sure if it was just the after-effects of dark magic. Years ago, his teachers had warned him that, if he wasn't careful, he might start experiencing hallucinations. So instead of voicing his suspicions, he simply replied, "No, thank you. But if you're done with your meal, we need to move on. My group has had enough of these caverns and wishes to see the sky once again. Do we need to go back the way we came? You still haven't answered about our misstep."

Nòr could tell the humans were shaken by their experience with the river monsters—it was written all over their faces. He worried his next words might trouble them further. "I'll lead you out of here, but you should know that you're farther from the exit than you were before. We won't reach the surface before nightfall, and that's the worst time to leave. The arkarnians are more active then. It would be wise to get back on the correct path and stop for the night. From the looks of it, everyone could use some rest."

Tadashi and Abigail groaned, but Mei replied firmly, "Fine, but let's move quickly. No wasting time."

Nòr climbed onto Marik's shoulders to avoid slowing them down. "Continue heading this way. We'll come to a fork soon—take the left path."

An hour later, Marik could tell the kids were slowing down, so he called for a rest. "We'll continue once everyone's had a good break."

The next morning, they were all rested and eager to leave the mine. They quickly ate and set off again. Nòr assured them the exit was only a few hours away.

"Here we are," Nòr said, pointing ahead. "Just climb these steps, and you'll be in a small cave. Walk through the hanging vines, and you'll see the sky once again. But be careful and make sure no patrols remain. It was an honor to meet you all, and thank you once again for helping with the Myklins. I wish you well on your journey."

Abigail knelt and hugged Nòr. "Thank you for your help. Where will you go from here? Are you heading home?"

"I must head north to a small village to collect supplies before I can return home, but I'll continue my journey underground—it's safer for me. If you're ever in the area again, please come to our village and say hello."

Once they exited the cave, they were relieved to find the area was free of arkarnians. Marik took in their surroundings. "We're not far from where I arranged to meet the other Morgs. Let's get moving—the sooner we get there, the sooner we can start riding horses again."

CHAPTER TWENTY-EIGHT

Journey to Mortaas Continues

The second day began just like the first: breakfast followed by a half-hour of walking before any rigorous training. It had been decided the night before that the focus would be on battle training, with even Cinder joining in.

The group was geared up as they had been the previous day. As they walked, Alan noticed the similarities and differences in the arkarnians' armor. Like theirs, it was made from leather, but they didn't wear chainmail or individual pieces of armor. Instead, they wore long leather jackets tightly secured around their torsos.

Alan, Cinder, and Elis sparred with their partners and with each other throughout the day, breaking only once for lunch. By the time they reached the Mortass River, the sun was just starting to set. Avery called out, "We'll set up camp over there. Eat something, relax for the night, and when you're ready, turn in. This may be the last solid night of sleep you'll get for a while." He turned to Silvyn, Sobek, Baldric, and Madeline. "Is this the right spot? I don't see any boats at the dock."

Silvyn looked at Sobek and Baldric, then turned to Madeline. "Who did my father send ahead to make the arrangements? I never thought to ask him."

Madeline appeared puzzled as she walked toward the dock. "Lesnik was supposed to meet us and introduce us to the navigators. Maybe he had to travel farther up the river to find them."

The Dinalo seemed calm, which was enough for Avery to say, "I'm sure there's no need to worry. We'll wait until midday tomorrow. If they haven't arrived by then, we'll head north up the river to meet them. For now, let's eat before the younger ones finish everything."

Alan grabbed some food. Since his mother had wandered off with Avery, he decided to go in search of Cinder. He felt it was time for that conversation.

He found her sitting alone on the riverbank, with Elis nowhere in sight. Alan approached cautiously. "Hey, mind if I join you? I was hoping you could help me with a few questions."

Cinder nodded, simply saying, "Sure."

Alan could feel something strange in the air between them. He didn't understand it at first and thought it was just the chill of dismay he assumed Cinder felt for him. "Alright, out with it already," he said.

Cinder raised an eyebrow. "Out with what? I thought you had questions for me."

Alan shook his head. "I'll get to those in a minute. But first, you need to explain why you've had such an attitude toward me. Every time I talk to you, it's like there's this icy barrier. Especially when I catch you staring at me sometimes."

Cinder blinked, surprised he had noticed her glances. She panicked inwardly, not wanting to cause any bad blood between them. She thought her earlier joke had made Alan aware she was letting her walls down, but now, she wasn't sure. She quickly shook her head, replying defensively, "Look, I don't know what you're talking about. I have better things to do than glare at you. I don't have a problem with you, at least not one big enough to dislike you. But if you keep accusing me of something I didn't do, we might just go back to square one."

Alan narrowed his eyes. "I'm not asking you to like me or be my friend. All I'm asking is that, for the sake of this quest, we agree to get along and work together. That means we need to trust each other and be civil. Do you think you can handle that? Because if not, I don't think we'll succeed in stopping Shadow-Lord."

Cinder listened carefully. She hadn't meant to make him feel this way. She regretted many of the snide comments she had made before. The friendship she had with Avery and Elis was different from the one she wanted with Alan. She had never met someone she could trust so quickly, and that scared her. There were things she hadn't shared with anyone, even Avery, but she felt like she could tell Alan. Still, she wasn't sure how to say that, especially with all the misunderstandings between them so far. She took a deep breath before replying slowly, "Listen... I know I come off as harsh or mean sometimes. I don't mean to act like I dislike you. It started when I got irritated by the way you talked to me when we first met. You know what they say about first impressions. But you're just passionate about protecting your friends and your sister... I'm sorry I held that against you and said all those stupid things. It was petty. So, let's just... forgive and forget, okay? I wouldn't mind counting you as one of the few friends I have."

Alan blinked a few times before nodding, surprised at how much Cinder's attitude had changed. Mentally, he kicked himself for not being calmer when they first met—it would have saved them a lot of trouble. "Yeah, that would be nice. I'm sorry for my role in this."

Cinder nodded. "And I'm sorry for mine. Now, on to your question."

Alan took a breath. "Avery mentioned I might have the potential to learn magic. First, I need to know if I'm capable. Then, if I am, I need to understand if it's worth it. Avery said not everyone with magic potential is obligated to learn it. For example, why did you choose to learn magic?"

Cinder thought for a moment before answering. She didn't want to go into too much detail, so she gathered her thoughts on how to explain her journey. "Alright... I'll give you a quick rundown. Back in Undergate, I developed a basic ability to manipulate fire. It was a tool I used to survive, and eventually, it helped me escape. At that point, it was more about using it to stay alive than about any real choice."

She continued, "After breaking out of prison, I ran into Avery, who was investigating the breakout. He let me explain my side, and that's when he realized I was adept. He offered me the chance to become his student and avoid living a life on the run."

Cinder paused, looking at Alan. When he didn't interrupt, she resumed. "Avery gave me something I hadn't had in a long time: hope for a better life. So I took a chance and accepted his offer. During my training, I realized I had the ability to make a difference. What was once a tool to protect myself could be used to protect others. To help people who suffer."

"So, the first question you need to ask yourself is this: Do you want to commit to a life of magic? You'll have a responsibility to devote yourself to this world and its people for the rest of your life. I suspect you'll need time to think about that. But if you want, I can help determine if you have the potential. Just take your time and do some soul-searching."

Alan stood, his plate of food in hand. "You're right. I have a lot of thinking to do. Thanks for your honesty. Have a good night. I'll talk to you tomorrow."

Before Alan could join his mother and Avery around the campfire, Cinder spoke up, "You know, you could stay and eat with me, if you want."

Alan smiled. "Yeah, sure." He sat down next to her by the riverbank. As they ate, their conversation drifted to small things—nocturnal birds, training tips, and advice on improving their skills.

Eventually, they said goodnight, and the nature of the air between them, which Alan had previously mistaken for chill, became more apparent as something else. Yet, the feelings were still a mystery to him. He thought about pondering it, but instead, he reflected on what Cinder had said about magic—that learning it would come with an obligation to Whenua and its people.

As he lay in his tent that night, Alan felt fear—not from leaving Earth, but from the realization that he was more scared of abandoning the home he had known than of leaving its comforts behind. Maybe it was because he had learned about the family he now had here—grandparents, godparents, cousins—a family he never had back home. In a world straight out of the stories that once brought him comfort.

***

The next morning, the boat still hadn't arrived, and plans were being made to head upriver. The concern was timing—if they didn't encounter the boat soon, there was no way they would reach the shrine before Shadow-Lord.

Since Alan wasn't involved in the decision-making, he stood on the dock with Elis and Cinder. Their task was to keep an eye out for the boat. As they stood there, Cinder turned to Alan with a comforting tone. "So, were you able to sleep last night? I know you're carrying a lot on your mind, and now you also need to decide what path you want to take with magic."

Alan wasn't sure if he wanted to have this conversation in front of Elis, but with the arkarnians nowhere in sight, he figured now was as good a time as any to answer her. "Yes, I slept okay—well, as okay as I've been. I've made my decision, and here it is: regardless of whether or not I'm adept, I will commit myself to Whenua. Not only is this my birthplace, but it's where my parents belong. My grandparents live here, and I have a family I never knew existed. I want to meet them, but more than that, I want to keep them safe. My decision is made easier by an ancient saying from Earth: 'Home is where the heart is.' My heart is with my family, so this world is my home. I will gladly sacrifice all the comforts and conveniences Earth offers, for them."

As Cinder listened to Alan's words, she felt a pang of admiration for him. His willingness to leave behind the life he knew for a world he owed nothing to only deepened her interest in him, leaving her wondering what was going on inside his head. But before she could say anything, Elis called out, "Look! I can see a boat headed this way!"

***

The Arkarnian captain and Lesnik stepped onto the dock, heading toward a group of arkarnians who were waiting. As the captain got closer, his expression darkened with rage. He turned to Lesnik and began shouting. "You want me to transport humans!? You didn't tell me about this!" Then he turned to the other arkarnians, spitting out, "You can keep your weapons. We don't do business with the likes of them!"

Silvyn spoke up, his tone calm but firm. "These are not just any humans. We're escorting Avery Ambrose, Elis Belmont, and Madeline Elwyn to the Polar Regions. Our journey is important—important enough that you should set aside your feelings about humans and focus on the bigger picture."

The captain's eyes widened. "Ambrose?! Belmont?! Are you kidding me?! That's even worse than if they were just random human peasants! And don't get me started on the Elwyn woman! Just because she was raised by those dimwitted pacifists in Kardica doesn't make this slick-skinned one of us!"

Alan glanced at his mother. Her eyes were narrowed, brows furrowed, and a sneer was starting to creep onto her face. He had only seen this expression once before—when she witnessed an older boy harassing him outside of school. Alan quickly reached out and rubbed her back. She looked at him, meeting his gaze, and he shook his head, silently urging her to calm down. After a moment, she relented and said nothing in reply to the captain's insult.

Elis, not willing to let the captain dismiss them without a fight, spoke up. He knew he had to say something, and he hoped the captain would hear the honesty in his words.

"Listen, sir, I know my father's treatment of arkarnians isn't fair. I like to think he's making the right choices for everyone, but the more I see, the more I realize he's only making the best choice for the people in Overgate. I think he's a good man at heart, but I don't always agree with him. One day, I will be king, but that won't be for a while. I promise I'll try to convince my father to do more for everyone in Wethen, to help the Dinalo and other non-threatening Arkarnian tribes thrive. But I can't do any of that if you don't take us to Kurlo Pass. If it's more weapons or money you want, I promise I'll get it for you, as long as we're successful in our quest."

Silvyn stepped forward, his voice steady. "I'm not sure if Lesnik told you, but it was these humans who helped me escape from Undergate. They knew my punishment was wrong, and they risked treason against the king to help me. I give you my word—they are sincere in their support of the Arkarnian people."

The captain studied the humans for a long moment. "Prince Belmont, I'll take heed to Silvyn's words. It was bold of you to go against your father. One day, when you rule, we may all be at peace. If this journey takes us in that direction, then I'll help you reach Kurlo Pass. Now, bring the weapons and follow me."

They walked over a thick wooden plank to board the watercraft. The boat creaked beneath them, and for a moment, it wobbled heavily, causing Alan to grasp Cinder's arm to steady himself.

Cinder helped Alan steady himself, then continued walking aboard with him. As soon as they reached the more stable deck, Alan released her arm.

"Sorry about that..." he said, feeling a bit embarrassed.

"Don't worry about it," Cinder replied. "You were just trying not to fall."

"Well, yeah, but I still feel like I should apologize for grabbing you. I doubt you would've wanted to fall in with me."

"Nah, I wouldn't have been mad about falling in," she said with a grin. "I just would've been disappointed that I didn't get to see you scream and fall in."

Cinder jabbed him lightly with her elbow, still grinning. "I kid you not, I once got hit by an angry ram in the bum, which caused me to roll down a hill and into a river while Avery was teaching me about patience. He picked the farm with the most belligerent sheep."

Alan chuckled. "That's a cute story. Maybe, once we settle in here and aren't dealing with vines and hostile arkarnians, we could exchange stories like that."

Cinder nodded. "Yeah, I'd like that. By the way... what you said about whether or not you have magic—I respect that you're committing yourself to..." She paused, choosing her words carefully so none of the arkarnians overheard, "...being the kind of person who helps others, even when it isn't your problem."

Alan smiled, unable to find a response that wouldn't betray his cover story.

Instead, he focused on the boat they were now standing aboard. It reminded him of a pontoon barge—no sail, no rudder, no wheel. It seemed that the boat was moved and directed by a set of three poles, one on either side of the ship, with tall and burly Arkarnian crewmen holding them, apparently waiting for the order to set off.

The captain noticed his men glaring at the humans and raised a hand. "Calm down, it's okay. These humans helped Silvyn escape from Undergate. They can be trusted, so we'll protect them on this journey."

He then turned his attention toward the newcomers. "Now, before we disembark, we should come to know your names."

At this, Avery stepped forward, taking charge. "I am Avery Ambrose. This is Elis Belmont and Madeline Elwyn. To my right is her son, Alan, and next to him is Cinder. I don't think our Dinalo friends need any introduction."

Once everyone was settled, Alan continued to observe the wooden barge. He had a sense of how the logs were held together, though it seemed the boat should have simply fallen apart and sunk to the bottom of the treacherous River Mortaas.

"Hey, Silvyn," Alan called, "when the Dinalo and Rau-Trava were one, didn't they invent a black adhesive paste that becomes nearly invisible after it hardens? I remember my grandma complaining about how they never taught the Kalko how to make it."

Silvyn responded, "Yes, Timir'ent is what it's called. It's quite strong and durable, but impossible to clean if you accidentally get it on your skin or clothes. I've met many craftsmen and builders who've been permanently disfigured trying to remove it. As for why the Kalko weren't taught to make it, well, I suppose my forebears didn't see a reason to share it with them. It only works for river water, and the Kalko mostly use the seas. Of course, it became a point of contention between our tribes in the past..."

Alan raised an eyebrow. "That sounds like a risky thing to use... I'm kind of glad it doesn't work with seawater and we didn't use it."

Silvyn smiled. "Without risk, there would be little reward—not necessarily in the results, but in the satisfaction that comes from the attempt."

Alan nodded, understanding what Silvyn meant. Much of what he had experienced and endured had given him a sense of accomplishment, especially when he found Avery on his own.

Standing on the boat, Alan gained a better perspective of the river's width. It was narrower than he had expected, so he asked Silvyn, "You said we'd run into the vines when the river narrows, but the river is at least 20 feet wide here, and this boat can't be more than 10 feet wide. How much narrower does it get?"

Silvyn smiled. "It narrows quite a bit more. Right now, neither of us could reach out and touch the vegetation along the bank, but in about eight or ten hours, we'll reach a point where the distance to the shoreline will be only about two feet on either side."

"Why the two-hour difference?"

"Traveling by flatboat depends on many factors—weight, number of paddlers, and the speed of the current. We're fortunate to be heading north with the flow. Paddling against it is difficult and requires very strong men."

Just then, Avery walked over to join them. "Baldric has made sure the crew knows they won't have to worry about protecting us, and that they won't be alone in protecting the boat from harm. On a more somber note, Baldric learned that the captain lost four crew members on his recent travels up and down this river. We must stay vigilant at all times on this tide."

Silvyn nodded, and Avery walked away to the opposite side of the boat to join Cinder. He grasped her shoulder and whispered something Alan couldn't hear. If he had to guess, it was likely a repeat of what Avery had just told them.

An eerie stillness hung in the air, and there was an uncomfortable silence among the crew. They all knew the journey ahead was treacherous, and many would enter the River Mortaas but never leave, claimed by the cursed and haunted waters beneath the boat that carried them upriver toward impending danger.

Soon, everyone gathered under the canopy to discuss their positions. Avery decided that since there were eight people in his party and eight crewmen—including the captain—it only made sense for his group to defend each crewman's post. The flatboat was maneuvered with three oarsmen on both the port and starboard sides, the seventh man at the aft controlling the rudder, and the captain at the fore, steering the wheel.

As Alan considered where he would like to be stationed, the captain called out, "Rist, it's time to cast off. Everyone else, get to your oars. As for our passengers, steady yourselves until we're on our way. The current can be rough, but once you get used to the movements, you should be able to walk around with ease."

Alan took a deep breath. This was it. There was no turning back now.

Chapter Twenty-Nine

Northbound

Abigail, Mei, and Tadashi felt lighter and happier for the first time since leaving Darkspire. Their contentment seemed to be having a positive effect on Marik as well—he had been humming a cheerful tune for the past few miles. Unfortunately, that came to an end when Tadashi asked, "Hey, Marik, what's that song? It sounds really beautiful."

Shadow-Lord stopped immediately. "I didn't realize I was doing that out loud. And while it is a beautiful song, as you call it, it is a personal melody that my mother used to hum to me when I was a boy."

Tadashi, without thinking, spoke again. "Yeah, I never thought about a scary guy like you having a mother, let alone being a boy."

Mei and Abigail were both shocked by Tadashi's comment and simultaneously slapped him on the back of his head.

Marik didn't react with anger. Instead, he said, "I too forget that I once had a somewhat normal life. Unfortunately, my happiness was taken from me, and I had to grow up much faster than you. Now, look ahead—Yerk is waiting for us at the top of the slope. You all can rest and eat while I get an update from him. The information he has will help me determine what obstacles we may encounter. Tadashi, when you're finished eating, please help Gorb and Glum place our supplies on one of the horses."

Without waiting for a response, Marik turned and moved on. Tadashi, wearing a huge smile, turned to the girls and said, "See? I'm starting to grow on him. He wasn't insulted by what I said, so you two shouldn't have head-slapped me."

Mei rolled her eyes as she watched Tadashi scarf down bread and berries. He was now in a hurry to attend to Marik's request. Mei was about to comment to Abigail but noticed her friend looking down. "Hey, what's wrong? Don't worry about hitting Tadashi. He was in the wrong."

Abigail shook her head. "No, it's not that. I know I shouldn't feel this way, but I really thought I was becoming Marik's right hand, that I was earning his trust and could help him. But ever since I couldn't heal you back at the river, he seems to have distanced himself from me. He was impressed with how quickly I grasped magic, but then I failed him. I screwed up in the fight with the Myklins by overthinking what it meant to kill someone, and I couldn't even save you. If it hadn't been for Marik, you'd be dead. You shouldn't even be talking to me right now."

"Cut it out, Abigail! I think Marik has a lot on his mind right now. I don't think he expects you to be an expert in magic, just like he doesn't expect Tadashi and me to be skilled warriors. What he expects is for each of us to do our best, to help him without complaint, and to learn from our mistakes. Why does it matter so much to you to be his right hand anyway? That's what bothers me a bit. I think we all have something to offer. We may not have magical abilities, but Tadashi and I have been right there with you through all of this."

Abigail felt even worse after hearing Mei's words. She was right. Wanting to be the one most needed by Marik wasn't important, but the feeling of being important was something she always craved. It came from the envy she had over Alan's relationship with their mother. She needed to apologize and explain herself. "I'm sorry, Mei. You're right. We're all in this together, and none of us should be favored over the other. It's just that back home, Mom always seeks out Alan to do things—she never asks me, only him. I love them both, but it hurts to think she trusts him more than me. They have this strange bond, and I feel left out most of the time. With Alan nowhere around, I thought this was my chance to shine. And once we see them again, I could be the hero. I know this is all wrong, but it's a feeling I've struggled with for years. I can't just snap my fingers and make it go away. Even in my dreams, Mom is by Alan's side, helping him fight. If Alan has magical abilities, I'm sure he'll be far more advanced than I..."

"Abigail, STOP! Get out of your head for a minute. None of this is going to help us save this world or return to our own. You and Alan may be twins, but you're each your own person. Yeah, you both have this weird twin connection, and yes, Alan is a momma's boy, but you know you and your mom have a bond too. She doesn't ask Alan to go shopping with her or decorate the house for the holidays—that's all you and her. I could say more, but I don't think I need to. What I want to know more about is this dream you had of Mom fighting by Alan's side. Was it on Earth or here?"

Abigail took a deep breath, feeling lighter. "Thanks for what you said. You're right—I do stay in my head too long and overthink things. As for the dream, it was really strange, and I was going to talk to you about it, but then the whole Kae'kulie mess happened, and the moment never felt right after that. Anyway, it felt more like a vision, as if I was on the outside looking at something happening somewhere else in this world. I know it took place here because, well, this place is unique. Alan was wearing armor, as was Mom. They were sitting together by a river, and the weirdest part was that they were with arkarnians."

"Oh my God, Abigail, are you saying you think they're prisoners? We should tell Marik right away."

Abigail glanced over her shoulder to ensure Marik wasn't paying attention to Mei's outburst. When she was sure he hadn't heard, she turned back to Mei. "No, I don't think they were prisoners. In fact, I think Alan was laughing and having a good time with them. It was very strange, and I don't think we should tell Marik—at least not now."

Mei scrunched up her nose, considering it. "I guess you're right. It could have just been a dream. You've never had visions of Alan before this, right? I mean, it's not a twin thing? So unless you have more of these dreams, it may just be a fluke."

Just then, Marik and Yerk walked over, calling out to Tadashi, Gorb, and Glum to join them.

Once everyone was seated and Marik introduced Yerk to the group, he spoke. "The journey north will be uneventful for the first three days. There are no arkarnians in sight until the fourth day, when we approach the front lines of the war. We'll ride hard during that time. During the first two days, as long as we're making good time, I'll allow a few longer breaks so you can continue practicing your fighting abilities and so Abigail can advance in her magic. Yerk will ride ahead with Gorb, and one of them will return each night to give us an update on their scouting, so we won't be taken by surprise. Any questions?"

Marik didn't wait to see if anyone had any questions. Instead, he stood and said, "Good. Saddle up. We leave in a few minutes."

***

Marik had been right—the first three days were uneventful, save for their training. During this time, Abigail's fears were further eased as Marik showed patience, teaching her new ways to use her magic.

Everything had gone according to plan. They had even managed to avoid any confrontation with the Rau-Travan arkarnians. Eventually, they passed through villages ravaged by conflict, abandoned by their inhabitants. The evidence of destruction and death still lingered, but not so viscerally that any bodies could be seen. Even Tadashi couldn't find a way to lighten the mood as they traveled through the gloomy, war-torn countryside. He did, however, make things worse by wondering aloud whether the lack of bodies was due to the arkarnians eating them, a remark that everyone chose to ignore.

Yerk and Gorb had just returned from their scouting. After speaking with Marik, he held up his hand, signaling for everyone to stop. He dismounted and walked over to them.

"It seems we're within half an hour of the frontline," Marik said. "You'll dismount now, and I'll go over the plan."

"First of all, we won't be making this journey during daylight. We'll set out after dusk. Crossing when we can be seen is no problem for me, but you haven't faced an arkarnian in battle before. They make Myklins look like small rodents. Look at this map—we're here. After we cross the area where the war is being waged, from here to here, we won't be truly safe again until we reach this path. It will take us to a mountain where a subterranean passage cuts through. It was abandoned for good reason, and there may be untold horrors within, but it will still be safer than taking the other paths, which are riddled with sentient vines—another group of arkarnians who are even more indiscriminate with whom they kill than the Rau-Travans—and giant crabs. But make no mistake, whatever lies inside the passage we take could be far worse than even I fear."

Mei raised her hand. "What about the horses? Won't they make a NEEEIGGGGHHH sound?"

Marik stared at her for a few moments. Abigail could've sworn she heard him giggle quietly under his helmet, though it was hard to hear over Tadashi's hysterical laughter. Once Tadashi quieted down, Marik replied.

"They're trained to remain as calm and quiet as possible. I'm not sure if you've noticed, but the horses have been fairly silent ever since we've had them. They're also highly intelligent. Horses can react to the demeanor of their rider, even just by looking at facial expressions or the touch of a hand."

Tadashi, still giggling, added, "I wonder if Mei's horse is offended by her impression!"

Marik shook his head, his words laced with a mix of frustration and amusement. "Enough, Tadashi. We're lucky your laughter hasn't made our presence known to every arkarnian in a fifty-mile radius. Come on, we have some time before dusk, so we might as well make ourselves comfortable for the next few hours before we begin our arduous journey."

Tadashi nodded and slowly brought his laughter to a halt, grateful that Marik hadn't yelled, instead maintaining some semblance of calm that made him feel like the progress they'd made hadn't been squandered in that moment.

They set up camp soon after, sitting in a circle. Tadashi looked to Marik and asked, "Can we make a fire for some heat?"

Marik shook his head. "No. We're far too close to the frontlines. We don't need anyone to see the smoke and think we're enemy scouts. However, why don't you take out one of the light crystals you swiped from the caves? Those provide some heat without giving off any smoke."

Tadashi scratched the back of his neck nervously. "Wha—? I don't know what you're talking about! I certainly didn't take any of those light stone thingies!"

Marik tilted his head, clearly unimpressed.

"Okay, okay! I grabbed a couple of them! But I took them to give to my Sobo! So it isn't stealing!"

Marik rolled his eyes. "It's not even stealing by your strange reasoning. Those mines arguably belong to no one. It's not like the Gnoglins carry tiny little pickaxes and chip away at stone. I mean, not anymore, at least. Come to think of it, if they had a mining operation, they'd be less likely to cause cave-ins... They're small enough to gain access to ore with more precision and— Just take out the largest light crystal you have already!"

Tadashi gave a slight smile as he took out a light crystal and placed it in the center of their circle.

After a short while of sitting quietly, Mei broke the silence. "Can you believe that just a few days ago my biggest worry was my grades?"

Tadashi snickered and replied, "I thought your biggest worry was whether someone else would ask Alan to the dance."

Mei narrowed her eyes and jabbed Tadashi in the arm. "Ouch!"

Abigail chuckled before speaking.

"The bright side of all this for me is, I don't have to help the junior high teachers anymore. I just want to reiterate how much I hate the fact that we have one composite school for all primary education instead of multiple different schools... Ever since I filled in for Mrs. Eggbert when she had hip replacement surgery, the junior high teachers have been trying to get me to substitute for their classes whenever they want time off. Those classrooms are always full of rowdy sixth graders, with zits all over their faces..."

Tadashi cringed. "Ew... you know, I don't think that'll happen to me."

Mei and Abigail laughed. "Give it time, Tadashi. You'll get at least one pimple one day. You're just a late bloomer."

Tadashi shook his head. "No way! I watch my diet and keep my face clean—well, I *was* before we came here... when we could bathe regularly..."

Mei shrugged. "You know, with all the stuff we've been through, I would've thought we'd smell horrible by now without a bath."

Marik cracked a smile. "You three are just used to the stench, but trust me, you're all incredibly... for lack of a better word, *ripe*..."

Everyone, including Marik, chuckled quietly. As the laughter faded, Tadashi spoke again.

"One thing's for sure—I do *not* miss Algebra tests. I'd rather fight Myklins than take one of those again."

The mention of fighting Myklins made Abigail uncomfortable, and the memory of when she killed Kirik replayed in her mind. She stared off into the distance, past Marik and the horses, her eyes focusing on the horizon.

Mei glanced over at Abigail, noticing her distant gaze. Reaching out, she touched Abigail with her right arm and swatted Tadashi with her left.

"Oh my God, Abigail, Tadashi speaks without thinking sometimes. I know what you had to face was awful, and I really hope I can make it through this without having to experience what you went through."

Abigail turned to Mei, noticing Tadashi rubbing his arm. She smiled as she said, "That's not it, really. Yes, the mention of Myklins stirred up some emotions from when I killed Kirik, but I know it had to be done. Before this is over, I'll probably have to kill more than just him. At least with the Myklins, I won't have to know their names, which makes it a little easier, I think. What's really bothering me is... I'm wondering if Alan has had to go through this—the anguish of taking someone's life in order to survive. He once got all choked up just from hitting a bird during driver's ed... Can you imagine how he'll be if he kills something that walks and talks like a human?"

Marik cut in. "I know emotions can mess with your mind, but you all need to clear your heads. You need to be ready for anything. If you're going to think about something, think about how to plan your defense. But before that, let me give you a piece of advice: those you may have to kill won't hesitate to kill you."

He paused before continuing. "Now, here's a more detailed plan for crossing the frontlines."

"We'll split up. Abigail will cross first with Glum, then Mei and Gorb, and finally, Tadashi and Yerk. I'll follow from behind to ensure I can help anyone who gets caught by unforeseen events. Any questions?"

Tadashi raised his hand. "Why can't we all go at once?"

"Good question. If too many of us cluster together, we'll be spotted. Smaller groups, however, may go unnoticed."

"Always keep one hand on your weapon, the other on the reins..."

Tadashi raised his hand again. "Shouldn't I have both hands on my weapon? It's not like I can pull and shoot with just one."

Marik sighed. "Use your knife if necessary. That's what Yerk is there for."

Now Abigail raised her hand. "When will we be safe again?"

"The majority of the war is to the south. Once we cross, it should only take about half an hour to get to safety, as long as the arkarnians haven't left a few men behind to cover their flank. If there's nothing else, get ready to leave at the first sign of darkness."

***

Tadashi gave a thumbs-up to Abigail as she and Glum prepared to make their crossing, silently praying in his head that she would be safe. After a few minutes, it was Mei's turn to saddle up and head out with Gorb. But before she had a chance to put her foot into the stirrup, Tadashi bolted over and gave her the tightest hug he'd ever given her in his life.

"Be safe, sis. I might not say it much, but I love you!"

Mei hugged him back and patted him on the head. "Don't worry, I'll be fine. Just like I know you'll be fine. Besides, we've got Marik watching our backs if anything happens. And I love you too."

Yerk picked Tadashi up and placed him on his horse. "We go in few minutes."

"Okay, okay, but I can get on the horse by myself. I'm not that much shorter than Mei!"

A few minutes passed, and it was finally Tadashi and Yerk's turn. Tadashi gave one last look at Marik and called out, "Hey Marik, if you get into any trouble, just yell. I've got your back too."

Marik smiled to himself. It seemed he had won Tadashi over, so he replied, "I appreciate that, Tadashi. You've come a long way since we left the castle, and that makes me proud."

Tadashi smiled, then he and Yerk rode off, leaving camp behind.

The horses were quiet, just as Marik had promised. They slowed as they entered the encampment, carefully watching their steps to avoid alerting any half-awake arkarnians.

Tadashi glanced around and took in the sight: the arkarnians had made their camp in a series of old stone ruins. What he saw next nearly made him gag. A tanning rack with what could only be human skin, with buckets of raw meat tucked beneath it. But as he looked closer, his stomach dropped. He saw skulls resting in front of the buckets—this was definitely human.

Tadashi's mind raced back to his earlier theory about the humans in the village they passed through. He whispered to himself, "I rarely hate being right... but in this case, I do."

Yerk glanced at the eerie sight and whispered to Tadashi, "You no think that's Mei and Abigail, do you?"

Tadashi's heart raced. "What?! No!"

The horses stopped walking, and both Tadashi and Yerk went dead silent. Their eyes widened as they froze. The silence was soon shattered by the shrill screech of an arkarnian who had woken up and spotted them.

The arkarnian shouted in a language unfamiliar to Tadashi, but if he had to guess, it sounded like "Intruders!"

"Run for it, Yerk!" Tadashi yelled. Yerk immediately dismounted and began running.

"No, not literally, Yerk! With the horse! Wait! Come back!"

Yerk darted down some stone steps as Tadashi dismounted, his heart racing as he tried to catch up.

Tadashi rounded a corner, calling out for Yerk while drawing his bow and nocking an arrow. "Yerk! Come back! We need to get back to the horses before—WAAH!"

Out of nowhere, an arkarnian appeared in front of him, swinging an axe down at him. Tadashi backpedaled and quickly pulled back on the drawstring, releasing the arrow. It struck the arkarnian in the head above the eye. The lizard warrior swung horizontally at Tadashi, but he ducked, pulling out his knife. He plunged it into the arkarnian's thigh, causing the creature to stumble. Tadashi yanked the knife out and stabbed the arkarnian in the stomach, twisting the blade and pushing his attacker to the ground. He repeatedly stabbed the arkarnian in the stomach and chest until the creature's limbs fell limp.

Breathing heavily, Tadashi tried to process what had just happened. He felt the stone wall next to him for support as he stood up. He reached down, trying to remove the arrow from the now-dead arkarnian. After a few tugs, he finally freed it from the corpse. He stared at the dead body, then looked at the green blood covering his hands and knife. He closed his eyes, taking a deep breath to calm himself. "It's just like Marik said. He was the evil idiot. He tried to kill me. I did what I had to do, just like Abigail did..."

Tadashi refocused on the task at hand, trying to find Yerk. So far, he'd been lucky—no other arkarnians had followed him, and the one he had just killed had been alone.

He moved cautiously through the ruins, keeping quiet to avoid drawing attention. As he turned a corner, he almost bumped into Marik, who was holding the reins to both his and Yerk's horses.

Marik looked behind Tadashi, then at the dead arkarnian. He glanced at Tadashi's blood-covered hands and said, "Impressive."

Tadashi nodded, feeling a small sense of pride. It felt good to hear that from Marik instead of disappointment. "I'm just glad the moons are bright tonight, or I would never have been able to see what I was doing. Anyway, we need to find Yerk. I told him to run for it... and he took it literally. He got off his horse and headed through the ruins over there."

Marik handed the reins to Tadashi. "Go catch up with the others and tell Gorb to stop once he reaches the fortress. Once I find Yerk, I'll meet you there. But take it slow. I won't have your back this time—unless, of course, I find him quickly."

Tadashi nodded without comment. He didn't want to bring attention to the fact that Marik hadn't had his back during the fight with the arkarnian.

Marik rode his horse slowly over the rocky ground, with Yerk's horse following close behind. The ruins still had partial walls, providing plenty of places for an enemy to hide. But Marik couldn't afford to waste time—he needed to find Yerk as quickly as possible. This delay could prove fatal to the others.

As Marik reached the end of the ruins, he spotted Yerk standing over four dead arkarnians. Yerk hadn't noticed him yet. He turned quickly, sword in one hand and a dead arkarnian's war hammer in the other, ready to strike down the next enemy. But when Yerk saw Marik, he froze. Marik waved his arms and shouted for him to calm down.

"Sorry, Boss... I'm real stressed out by these no-good lizards."

Marik lowered his arms and patted Yerk on the shoulder. "Don't worry about it... we all get that adrenaline rush in situations like this. Life or death makes us act crazy sometimes. Now we need to hurry and get back to the others. They may be in danger—"

Marik stopped midsentence, his attention caught by the sound of a war horn—one he knew all too well.

"Uh oh, Boss... bad things happen when I hear that noise..." Yerk muttered.

"We need to find them now!" Marik yelled.

The armor-clad soldiers of Wethen stormed into the camp, swinging their weapons across the bodies of arkarnians, their battle cries echoing as they quickly advanced. Marik and Yerk turned to head back toward the area where Marik had last seen Tadashi. As they moved, they heard a human soldier shout to the others.

"The Shadow! He is here! Retreat!"

"Captain, we do not retreat! Everyone advance on the Shadow-Lord! Forget taking down this camp! He takes priority!"

Yerk ran ahead of Marik, who slowed as a small group of Wethen soldiers cut him off from the morg.

Tadashi peered through the crack in the stone wall he was hiding behind, straining to focus on the leader of the human soldiers. The man who had yelled for them to find Marik looked almost like an older, more rugged version of Tadashi's father—the only image he had of him, a photo his sobo kept of both his father and mother.

Suddenly, Tadashi heard loud footsteps approaching from behind. He turned to see Yerk standing over him, looking down with a childlike innocence.

Tadashi pressed a hand to his chest, silently recovering from the proverbial heart attack Yerk had just given him.

After a few deep breaths—like he had seen Alan do when he was stressed—he calmed himself and refocused on the task at hand.

"Yerk, I'm glad to see you... I know where we need to go to catch up with Mei and Abigail... but... there's a group of arkarnians in the way."

He pointed past the stone road they were on to what might have once been a city center. Now, it was lined with wooden defensive barriers, and arkarnians stood guard, alert.

"This is all just conjecture, but I think Mei and Abigail made it through before the arkarnians were fully awake and guarding those barriers. Otherwise, we'd have probably found them fighting—or seen some dead arkarnians."

Yerk looked at the arkarnian bastion, then held his sword out to Tadashi.

"I don't know what 'extra pollution' mean, but you take... I got dis." He raised the large war hammer he'd taken from the arkarnians.

Tadashi nodded and took the sword, which was heavier than expected for the young boy to hold. But he knew it would deal more damage than his knife and save his arrows for when they were truly needed.

South of their position, Marik was surrounded by at least ten soldiers. They held their swords at the ready but did not approach him.

Marik scanned the area past the soldiers, closing his eyes as he tried to feel the earth beneath him, determining how far away Yerk and Tadashi were. Once he was sure they were far enough that they wouldn't witness anything, he reached up and grasped the hilt of his sword with one hand, using his other to steady the sheath. Slowly, he drew the sleek, jagged-edged blade. The soldiers held their ground, but Marik could see the fear in their eyes—the sweat dripping down their brows to their chins. The open-faced helmets betrayed their effort to appear confident in the presence of a man infamous for his cruelty.

The Shadow-Lord held his sword at his side with one hand and began to move his fingers with the other. Several soldiers shifted their focus to his free hand, panic flooding their minds as they assumed he was preparing some sort of evil spell to curse them.

But it was a ploy. As soon as one soldier took a step back in his panic, Marik struck. He swung his sword in both hands, ducking under the spear tip of one of the panicked soldiers. With a swift slash, the jagged edge of his blade tore through armor, crimson blood spraying onto another soldier. She backed away in terror, unable to comprehend how quickly Marik had dispatched her comrade. Marik seized the spear from the first soldier's dead hands, turning quickly to slam it into the skull of a soldier approaching him with a greatsword. The man's helmet flew off as the spear pierced his skull. Marik swung his sword in defense against the female soldier, who had been frozen by fear, and released the spear, letting the dead soldier slump over.

The other soldiers had regained their composure and began to close in on Marik to help the woman. But Marik was faster, and he easily outmaneuvered their attacks. In a swift move, he grabbed the woman from behind, locking his arm around her neck and holding her as a human shield.

The soldiers paused, unwilling to risk any more of their comrades' lives.

"Let her go!" one of them shouted.

Marik stabbed his sword into the ground and pointed his free hand at them, still holding the woman in a chokehold.

"We won't fall for that one again!" the soldier yelled.

Marik smiled beneath his helmet, forming a fist with his hand. He held it over the ground, and as he released his grip, the dirt under one soldier's feet liquefied, causing him to sink. When the soldier's head was fully submerged, Marik clenched his fist again, causing the earth to solidify and bury the man alive.

The remaining soldiers gave up on trying to protect the woman and rushed at him. Marik threw her aside, grabbed his sword, and plunged it into the chest of the first soldier to reach him. He then used magic to unleash a burst of flame from his palm, hitting the next soldier.

The woman lay on the ground, still alive, though blood dripped from a head wound she had sustained when Marik had forced her down.

Marik turned his attention to the remaining four soldiers. They exchanged looks, then turned and fled.

Marik looked down at the wounded woman, turned her over, and pulled some water from a nearby puddle to heal her head wound.

"Get moving... and remember that on this day, you were given mercy that your comrades did not receive. But don't feel guilty... It was mere luck that you survived. If anyone should feel guilty, it's the four gutless worms who abandoned you to save their own miserable lives. Now, go tell General Mikan... that if he sends anyone after me... I cannot guarantee the safety of Mei and Tadashi. Do you understand? Repeat it to me, so I know you understand."

She stuttered for a moment but then spoke as calmly as she could, "Tell General Mikan... not to send anyone after you... because you can't guarantee the safety of Mei and..." She hesitated. "Tadashi."

Marik nodded, standing and pulling her to her feet. "Good... now go."

She started walking back but turned to glance at Shadow-Lord. By the time she looked back, he was gone. General Mikan and a group of soldiers ran up to her.

"Are you alright, Lieutenant?" he asked.

"I—I don't know, sir... he... wanted me to tell you something..."

The general grasped her shoulders. "Go ahead... You're safe now. Just tell me what he said, and I'll have these men escort you back to base."

"He said, if you send anyone after him, he can't guarantee that Mei and Tadashi will be safe..."

Mikan's eyes widened. His arms dropped from her shoulders, and he looked behind her, taking a deep breath before speaking.

"Escort the lieutenant back to basecamp... and make sure everyone knows not to engage the Shadow-Lord or pursue him... We're falling back."

One of the soldiers turned to the general, confused. "But sir! What about the arkarnians?!"

"I said we're falling back. I won't say it again."

***

Tadashi peeked over a pile of rubble at the arkarnians' makeshift barrier. So far, the Rau-Trauva hadn't noticed him and Yerk.

As Tadashi tried to come up with a plan to sneak past the bastion, Yerk poked his back, catching his attention.

"Sometimes it's better to go back before moving forward."

Tadashi thought it over for a moment and realized it made more sense to try and find a way around than to risk another confrontation with the arkarnians.

"Alright, Yerk. Let's go."

From that point on, Yerk led the way as they climbed over pillars covered in vines and thick vegetation. The sounds of fighting had faded as they moved deeper into the ruins.

"I hope Marik is alright... I haven't seen him since he went off to look for you," Tadashi muttered.

Yerk whispered back, "He find me earlier. Last I see, he get chased by hooman soldiers."

Tadashi glanced back, scanning the path they'd come from, but saw no sign of Marik.

"I'm sure he'll be fine. Let's keep moving, Yerk."

A little later, Tadashi spotted a crumbled section of a large, decrepit stone wall ahead. It had collapsed to a low enough height that he and Yerk could climb over it, hopefully leading them out of the ruins.

As they neared the wall, Yerk grabbed Tadashi and pulled him down behind a large stone block, causing Tadashi to momentarily release the reins before quickly grabbing them again and pulling the horses behind their cover.

"I hear lizardmen... over by the wall," Yerk whispered.

Tadashi strained to listen. He could faintly hear voices, though he didn't understand their language.

"Yerk," he whispered, "Do you understand what they're saying?"

Yerk paused and listened intently. "First one say... 'I swear I saw two humans and two of those green guys from down south. They came through here on horses. One of them reached out and made the wall come crashing down. Can't you smell the lingering scent of horses?' Other one say... 'There are wild horses that come by here on their way to a nearby creek. As for any humans, I wouldn't worry about them. We've got them on the run back to their nearby city. Come on, let's go back to the camp commander and see what he wants us to do.' Now they walking away."

Tadashi looked at Yerk in surprise. "You just spoke like a human? I didn't know you could do that."

Yerk grinned. "We Morgs choose to speak like this. It makes us unique. If I repeat what the lizardmen say in the Morg way, you wouldn't understand it as well as you can when I say it like this. But I don't like the lizardmen. They call me 'green.'"

"Would it be better if I spoke the Morg way when talking to you guys?" Tadashi asked.

"I can teach you if you want, but it doesn't matter to us how any human or lizardperson speaks," Yerk replied.

The two of them emerged from their hiding place and approached the fallen section of the wall.

"Wow... Hard to believe Abigail did that," Tadashi remarked.

Yerk shrugged. "That's how Boss made Darkspire. He took apart the old damaged castle we Morgs call home and made a new one for us all. He was scary when I first saw him, but he became kind to us."

Yerk gave Tadashi a boost, helping him climb up the rubble. Then, Yerk climbed up after him. From the top, they saw that beyond the wall was indeed the way out of the ruins. The horses, with their strong legs and agility, climbed up on their own, not needing Yerk's help.

After climbing down the other side, they remounted and rode off toward the mountain in the distance that Marik had mentioned.

A few minutes later, they slowed as they saw the others resting under a large, umbrella-shaped tree.

"Mei!" Tadashi called out.

"Tadashi!" Mei's voice rang out in response.

Tadashi dismounted and ran over to his sister, who nearly tackled him in a tight hug. "I was so worried about you when all that fighting started behind us!"

"We're okay, but we lost sight of Marik... Hey, what happened to Abigail?" He pointed at Abigail, who was sleeping against the tree.

"She used her earth magic to make a wall fall for us to escape... It took a lot out of her. So Gorb and Glum said to rest here and wait for you two and Marik."

"Guess what! I fought an Arkarnian! And won!" Tadashi grinned proudly.

Mei's eyes nearly bulged out as she looked at the dried green blood splattered on his hands. "What? How? Are you alright?"

"Don't worry! Your warrior brother's got nerves of steel. You should see the other guy!" Tadashi said with a grin.

Mei hesitated for a moment, unsure whether to be concerned or relieved that her brother had fought and killed an Arkarnian so well. But since he still seemed to be his normal self, she decided to be relieved—for now. In the back of her mind, however, she made a note to watch him more carefully. She didn't want this journey to change him, as she had seen it nearly change Abigail earlier.

They all sat down, and Tadashi and Yerk began recounting their adventure in detail.

Chapter Thirty

River Escapades

As they made their way up the river, Avery and Silvyn devised a plan for how the group should position themselves on the boat. Now, it was time to share their strategy with everyone.

Alan, Elis, and Cinder had been conversing openly with Sobek, Baldric, and Madeline when Avery cleared his throat to grab their attention.

"All right, according to Captain Yarba, we should be nearing the Lair of the Vines in no more than ten hours, and no less than eight. That gives us about two hours to practice our game plan. Silvyn and I have already decided on our defensive positions. Cinder, you'll stand at the port bow."

Cinder interrupted, "And where would that be exactly? I don't think many of us know boat terms."

Avery cleared his throat, looking a little sheepish. "Ah, right. Sorry about that. Cinder, you'll be in the northwest corner of the boat, just in front of Javik. I'll be a few feet to the right of you, alongside the captain. Baldric, you'll take the northeast corner, a few feet in front of Poglu."

Avery turned to Elis and Sobek. "Elis, you'll be on the east side, just in front of Raphas. Sobek, you'll be on the opposite side, a few feet in front of Rist."

Alan, who had been anxiously awaiting his position, finally heard his name. "Alan, you'll stand in the southwest corner, just below Truvik. Madeline, you'll be in the back center, just behind Kreka, who will control the rudder. And finally, Silvyn, you'll be in the southeast corner."

Avery glanced around at them all. "I know you all know how to fight, but since you'll be close to others, I want you to practice your swings in the next two hours, making sure you don't hit the oarsmen. They'll be armed too, but their main job is to move us upriver as fast as possible. Now, get to your posts and begin."

Cinder swung her rapier over Javik's shoulder, testing how close she could get with the thin blade without injuring him.

The arkarnian, nervously rowing, spoke up. "You're proficient with that blade, right?"

"Relax," Cinder said, swinging the rapier again. "I've only accidentally injured a sparring partner twice. Just stay still and calm, and I'm sure I won't hit you."

Javik raised his eyebrows—more like spiked ridges along the tops of his eyes—his concern evident. Noticing this, Cinder added, "Don't worry, I've got your back."

Avery walked over and asked, "Ready to practice using your magic?"

Cinder swung her rapier again, this time from another angle, swooping around Javik's back. "Yeah, I'm ready."

Avery moved to the edge of the boat, farther down from Javik, and motioned for Cinder to join him. "I want to teach you the technique I used to get us back to Wethen. Instead of using it to move a boat, you'll use it in combat. In other words, I'm going to show you how to manipulate water using your air magic."

At the other end of the boat, Alan and Silvyn had been conversing as they practiced swinging around their assigned oarsmen, who, much like Javik, seemed just as uncomfortable with the situation.

"Have you ever been to the Shadow Lands, Silvyn?" Alan asked.

Silvyn swung around Droga's nose. "No, I haven't. The closest I've been is when I was on a boat in Erkar Bay."

Alan swung by Truvik's leg, stopping near his back. "There are pools of a red acid-like substance, and everything is gray and black—devoid of life. Well, except for Lerps. My friend Mei picked up a baby one because it was so cute. It just started yelling 'LERP! LERP! LERP! LEEERP!' as it wiggled its way out of her arms. The next thing we knew, the mother came charging at us! We jumped into the bushes and got the heck out of there!"

Silvyn let out a hearty laugh at Alan's tale. Cinder's concentration broke as Alan's outburst of 'LERP!' rang through the air.

Silvyn replied, "Oh my, Lerps. As I said before, there are so many ways to cook them. My personal favorite is to bread and season a slice of Lerp, then smother it with sauce and cheese, nestling the lovely meal between two slices of arkarnian bread..."

Alan sighed. "Silvyn, you're going to make me hungry over here. I take it you enjoy cooking?"

Silvyn nodded enthusiastically. "Oh, no, Alan. I don't just like cooking, I love it! I'd love to open an eatery someday where everyone can enjoy it. I mean, if one of those Dwargs can open a place in Overgate, I don't see why I couldn't in a town or city that's more accepting of arkarnians—maybe Kalnia or Opral."

Meanwhile, Captain Yarba waved Elis over, his eyes trained through a spyglass. As captain, it was his responsibility to scan the horizon for danger.

Elis walked over. "Yes, Captain?"

"I wanted to let you know that I trust what you said before," Yarba began. "You seem quite different from your father, at least from what I've heard about him."

"Thank you, Captain. I honestly wish that weren't true, though. I don't want to strive to be someone my father isn't. He can't seem to see things the way I—and so many others—do. I've tried talking to him, sharing my views and what I see as the future of Wethen, but he seems to think I'm not old enough to understand how things 'need to be.'"

Yarba gave a thoughtful nod. "Well, we have time. Why don't you share with me what your vision for the future is?"

Just then, a splash of water hit both Elis and Yarba. They turned to see Cinder, who called out, "Sorry!"

Elis smiled and then turned back to Yarba. "A total, lasting peace across all of Whenua isn't realistic, as sad as it is to admit. There will always be conflict over something. But I believe what's possible is unity between arkarnians and humans. When I'm King, I'll be in a position to slowly but surely integrate the Dinalo into Wethen's society and culture."

Yarba nodded in agreement. "There will be those who oppose you. The worst of your opponents won't likely be humans, but rather the Korvas and the Rau-Trava. They believe that peaceful coexistence would be a slow death for their way of life. They think there's nothing to gain from being allies with humanity—not since your grandmother's assassination and the counter-assassination of Korvas's father. Their ignorance and unwillingness to make peace with the past, along with the fact that the Dinalo were once part of the Rau-Trava, will make it difficult. They won't allow the Dinalo to join with humans easily. They will resist."

Elis looked down, his mind weighing the captain's words.

"I can't speak for the other arkarnian tribes, nor for my own people. Even though my small tribe leans toward the beliefs of the Dinalo, we don't align ourselves with any tribe. Many call us the Trovec, but we never gave ourselves a name. Our lives revolve around trade. We supply both sides of the war efforts, as well as everyday villagers. We may not like most humans, but that doesn't mean we think your race should be wiped out, as Korvas preached to his followers."

Elis looked down again, contemplating the weight of the captain's words. "Sure seems like trying to sway the Rau-Trava is a lost cause, from what you say..."

The captain took a moment to look through his spyglass before replying.

"They're not beyond swaying. In any conflict that drags on for as long as this one has, soldiers eventually begin to question what they're fighting for and may lose sight of what they once thought important. On both sides of this struggle, many have lost their brothers in arms—and their families. While humans don't exactly eat dead arkarnians, they are certainly guilty of their share of attacks on Rau-Travan villages, just as the Rau-Trava have attacked innocent towns in Wethen. It's been a long and painful road. Korvas won't live forever, and I doubt he'll remain unchallenged should enough Rau-Travans question his brutal commandments. That's why you do have a chance at changing their views."

"Do all Rau-Travans eat humans?" Elis asked.

The captain chuckled. "Well... not exactly. But the practice of eating humans goes back to the legends of the Ancient Arkarnian Empire and the belief that humanity is inferior. You see, there are stories, told through pictures etched across ancient, forgotten structures, that explain how humanity came to exist."

The captain continued, "In New Arkarnia, there are five mystics who claim to be as old as the ancient empire. They are called the Prophets of Haarkyne. The Prophets say the stone carvings tell history and claim that humans were brought to Whenua through a series of ancient portals. When these humans arrived, they were enslaved, forced to serve as soldiers against those who resisted the will of the ancients. Eventually, humanity revolted against their overlords. They were given asylum by arkarnians who were ancestors to the present-day Kalko, the now-extinct Atilgothins, and the other species they had once been forced to fight. Livimor and Morimor, the twin immortal emperors of the ancient empire, were divided. Livimor's beloved, stricken with grief over how non-arkarnians were treated, ended her life. Her death led Livimor to aid all non-arkarnians in the war, and with his help, the empire fell.

My ancestors were not innocent in the history of Whenua. Humanity repeats the same mistakes we made. Nothing has improved. The suffering continues, and the only real change the world has seen is a role reversal. Those who were conquerors are now the conquered, and vice versa."

"Well, you've certainly given me much to think about... thank you for the conversation," Elis said, before turning to join the others, who were resting under the canopy.

***

The trip down the river had been quiet for many hours as Avery and his group rested, but that silence was soon shattered when Poglu exclaimed, "We've just passed Krimshaw's Rest! We're less than an hour from the Lair of the Vines!"

Yarba shouted at the top of his lungs as he moved to the bow. "EVERYONE, TO YOUR POSITIONS!"

Alan, who had nodded off, jerked awake at the sound of Yarba's yell. He hit his head on a hanging fish trap and cursed as he rubbed the sore spot. He saw everyone scrambling to their positions and quickly, remembering their situation, walked over to grab Silvyn by the arm, holding him back as the others moved.

"Silvyn, I need your help to make sure my mom is safe throughout all of this," Alan said. "I know we have to protect our assigned oarsmen too, but I can't lose her. Can I count on you?"

Silvyn nodded, gripping Alan's shoulder and pressing his forehead against his. "Don't worry, Alan. I swear I'll keep your mother safe. After all, what are friends for?"

Alan smiled. "Thank you, Silvyn. Good luck."

"To you as well, Alan," Silvyn replied, and the two moved to their positions.

Captain Yarba climbed up onto the canopy, making sure he was visible and audible to everyone on the barge.

"Once we enter these waters, we'll have little to no respite between the dangers we'll face. They'll come in quick succession as we make our way up the river," Yarba announced. "Yes, there will be some brief downtimes, but they won't be long enough to fully restore our energy—not until we reach the safety of Kurlo Pass. After we clear the Lair of the Vines, we'll have a rest period before we enter Boh-Rahl territory. If we continue at this pace, we'll encounter them under the cover of night, which might help us avoid conflict—if we stay quiet and mask our scents. Their archers have poor eyesight in the dark, but we arkarnians have a strong sense of smell. They'll likely follow us along both sides of the river, but it all depends on where their scouts are patrolling."

Yarba climbed down from the canopy and returned to his position at the front of the boat with Avery.

Alan, now regretting that he hadn't been assigned to the front, thought that would've given him an advantage in spotting danger ahead. Instead, he kept yelling to Elis and Cinder every few minutes, "SEE ANYTHING YET?" To which they took turns replying.

As the river narrowed to the point where any of them could leap off the boat onto the bank, all hell broke loose. The first vine made its presence known, slapping its wet, green tendrils onto the side of the deck near Alan. He yelped and swung his sword down, cutting the tendrils off as the rest recoiled into the water. Alan heard others shouting as similar incidents unfolded across the vessel.

Avery used his staff to channel a combination of fire and earth magic, pulling sand up from the riverbed and using it with flames to entrap the vines in glassy ropes, bundling the tendrils so Yarba could smash them with his sword.

Cinder, focusing on the lessons Avery had taught her, used air magic to encase the incoming tendrils in water like a force field. After holding them back, she used her fire to turn the water into scalding steam, burning the vines' skin and exposing their vascular stems. The tendrils became brittle and crumbled into the water, still partially aflame.

Elis, who had no magic, simply swung his sword and slashed at the vines, sometimes stomping on them and cutting them down, being careful not to damage the boat or himself.

Meanwhile, Silvyn was moving back and forth between his oarsman and Madeline's position, just as Alan was, trying to maintain his composure as the surreality of their situation weighed on him.

In the midst of all this, Cinder, focused on her magic, didn't notice when a vine grabbed hold of Javik's oar and began coiling up toward him.

Sobek, spotting the danger, quickly leapt over and cut the tendril off the oar. However, he miscalculated the force needed, and the oar snapped in half.

Javik fell to the ground, and Sobek helped him up.

"There's another oar under the canopy!" Javik said, shaking his head in frustration. "I'll go get it!"

"No time," Sobek replied. "Unsheathe your sword and go help Alan. It looks like he's being overwhelmed back there!"

Javik looked over and saw Alan struggling to fend off several tendrils while trying to protect Truvik.

Alan, drenched in sweat, swung his sword repeatedly, cutting into the tendrils. He glanced at his mother and Silvyn for a split second, but that moment was enough for a vine to slap him across the face, knocking him to the ground and loosening his grip on his sword. It flew across the deck, landing out of reach as tendrils wrapped around his legs and began dragging him toward the edge of the boat.

Madeline screamed, "COVER ME, SILVYN!"

Madeline jumped over the vines pulling her son, sliding across the deck. She drew one of her daggers and severed the tendrils before using it to change her direction, sliding around Alan. She reached out, grabbed his sword, and held it out to him—all in a matter of seconds.

Alan took his sword and stared at her. "That was awesome! I wish I'd known about your fighting skills years ago. You could've helped me prepare for my tournaments."

Madeline smiled, relieved that her son was safe for now, and replied as she moved back to her position at the rudder.

"I'm sure I can still give you some pointers along the way if you want. But I must say, I've been impressed and proud of how well you've adapted to new fighting styles. It doesn't stop me from worrying, but it does give me some room to breathe."

Javik ran over and joined Alan, cutting down a tendril that had shot up from the water toward Truvik.

"Sobek said to help you!"

Alan nodded in appreciation, though inside, he didn't feel as confident as he appeared.

He had asked Silvyn to help protect his mother, but now it seemed like he was the one who needed saving.

This realization, combined with Sobek sending Javik to help, made Alan feel like everyone saw him as a lesser fighter.

Was it just him, or were Cinder and Elis struggling too?

As Alan fought back the incoming vines, self-doubt began to overtake him. He feared that if anything happened to Abigail, Mei, or Tadashi, it would be his fault—that he was too weak, and would fail everyone, including Avery.

But then, as a vine slapped Alan across the face, he turned and, in slow motion, saw Cinder struggling against the tendrils. Her position faltered as they pushed back against her magic. Seeing her struggle gave Alan the strength to silence his inner voice of self-loathing. Seeing someone his age fighting just as hard reminded him that it was okay to struggle.

Alan turned back to the vine that had struck him, waiting to see how it would move next. He watched it coil like a snake, assessing its options. These were not just ordinary vines—they were displaying intelligence, choosing where and how to strike. He now realized that the simple term "Living Vines" meant they were sentient.

Instead of attacking them like he would any normal vegetation, Alan shifted his mindset—he needed to treat them as opponents, as he did during HEMA matches.

Now, Alan was in his element. Confidence returned, and he and Javik excelled in fighting back the vines in their corner of the boat.

Using not just one, but two separate magics at once for nearly an hour had started to take its toll on Cinder. As she finished burning another couple of vines, she yelled out to Yarba, her voice strained, "How long until we're away from these psychotic vines?"

Yarba briefly took his eyes off the fight, relying on his reflexes as he surveyed their surroundings. "We still have about an hour at the rate we're moving until the river widens enough for us to be safe."

Cinder groaned, and Avery noticed. He could tell she was mentally exhausted. She had performed more magic in the past hour than she usually would in a week. Avery glanced back at Alan. He seemed to be handling himself better, but Cinder needed help. He called out, "Javik! Come up here and help Cinder! Cinder, stop using magic and switch to your sword! The strain will cost more than it's worth if you keep going like this!"

Elis, still focused on defending himself and Raphas, had momentarily zoned out. That split second proved to be a mistake when a vine wrapped itself around Raphas' waist, attempting to pull him overboard. Elis quickly moved to hit the vine, but another tendril shot up, taking the brunt of his attack, seemingly protecting the vine grabbing Raphas.

Yarba noticed the situation and glanced at Avery, who immediately understood what Yarba was asking. "Go," Avery ordered. "I'll be fine. We cannot afford to lose anyone."

The captain quickly ran over to Elis and cut through two vines that had wrapped around Elis's arms, holding him back from helping Raphas. Once the tendrils withered from being severed, Elis was able to cut through the vine pulling on Raphas' midsection. Raphas, who had been pushing back against the deck to resist the vine's pull, collapsed onto his back, but his oar remained in his hand.

Yarba and Elis helped Raphas to his feet, and he quickly returned to his oar. Elis patted Yarba's shoulder with thanks.

"I don't know what I would've done if you hadn't been so quick to react. Thank you—you saved my life."

Yarba shrugged. "Ah, well, I don't doubt you would've figured something out. The wizard keeps killing all the vines near us before I get a chance to slash them. I just didn't want you to have all the fun."

Raphas, from behind them, interrupted. "Captain! I really think you two can talk later! When we aren't being attacked—AH!" Raphas shrieked as a vine swiped at him, missing by inches.

"Well," Yarba said, "we better stop talking before Raphas ends up in the same position he was in before."

Elis nodded and swiftly returned to his duty, slashing his blade at a tendril as it swung toward Raphas. The vine fell, dying, and Elis quickly regained his deep, trance-like concentration.

Captain Yarba nodded, watching Elis' skillful swordplay, content that the young prince would be fine for the moment. He returned to Avery's side.

Avery, having overheard Yarba's remark, smirked. "You know, if I'm killing too many of these violent plants for you to keep up, I could always take a break and let you have all the fun."

Yarba chuckled. "No, no, I'm quite content with the current state of things, Mr. Ambrose. If we keep this up, I'm optimistic about our chances of reaching the Boh-Rahl without any losses."

Avery didn't reply, but the atmosphere had lightened. After the first few hours, the vines had become predictable, and thus posed less of a danger. Once Alan had changed his mindset, Cinder relied less on her magic, and Elis fell deep into his focus, the rest of the Lair of the Vines had become more of an annoyance than a serious threat.

A little further up the river, they began to notice that fewer and fewer vines were sprouting from the water. Soon, they had gone a full ten minutes without a single sighting. Satisfied with this, Yarba climbed onto the canopy to address everyone.

"Alright, great work, everyone. We've passed the Lair of the Vines and earned ourselves a few hours of rest. Take it easy, because these hours will fly by. Soon enough, we'll be tested again when we enter the Boh-Rahl's territory..." Yarba said before climbing down.

Alan walked over to his mother. "Hey, Mom, I'm going to lie down for a bit... try to catch some shut-eye."

"Okay, Alan, but... I want you to know... I'm so proud of you. You did really well today."

"Thanks, Mom. But you were the one who did the cool, badass moves and saved me."

Madeline chuckled and lightly pinched his ear. "Language, honey."

Alan laughed to himself as he went under the canopy to lie down on one of the cots. Sleep found him instantly.

Chapter Thirty-One

Visions

Leaning against the tree trunk, Abigail stirred, her sleeping mind consumed with disturbing visions.

She found herself standing in the middle of a desolate, ice-covered lake, a blizzard raging around her. Despite the snow howling fiercely in her face, Abigail could sense she wasn't alone. An unsettling presence hovered nearby, carrying with it a great, terrible hunger—an emptiness that felt familiar. It was a loneliness she knew all too well, mixed with the desire to be important.

Abigail scanned her surroundings, unable to pinpoint the source of the feeling.

"No... I don't want this... I don't want this feeling... go away... just go away!"

She screamed and turned, feeling the entity closing in. But just before the shadowy mass reached her, the ice beneath her cracked, and she fell into an abyss of nothingness.

Abigail fought to swim back to the surface, but with every attempt to rise, she sank deeper. Soon, her lungs burned for air, and as water filled her chest, she began to lose consciousness.

Abruptly, Abigail stirred and opened her eyes, dripping wet. She found herself on a boat, floating down a river of thick, bubbling blood. Lizardmen screamed in agony, their writhing forms occasionally rising to the surface. The sky above was a fiery red-orange, and the dark blob that had been stalking her on the ice lake floated ominously in the sky.

On the deck of the boat, Abigail saw her mother, lying on the ground, screaming as a giant crab approached her. Abigail wanted to shout out to her, but she froze when she saw the next horrifying sight.

Alan was there, his limbs ensnared by black, brambly vines that tugged at him as he screamed. The dark shape of emptiness descended from the sky, enveloping Alan's body before passing through him, leaving nothing but tattered, burnt clothing and a charred skeleton.

At that moment, Abigail awoke with a scream, but she still wasn't fully awake. Instead, she was pulled into another vision—one where the dark presence was gone.

Abigail wasn't sure if the earlier vision was a glimpse of her future, but she doubted it. Instead, she felt that it was her inner self trying to send a message—telling her to stop letting jealousy of her brother control her. If she allowed herself to be ruled by negative emotions, she'd destroy her relationship with Alan and everyone else, ultimately finding herself alone, just as she had been on the ice lake.

She paused her self-reflection as the current vision took her full attention. In this one, Abigail saw Alan on a boat again. However, there was no river of blood. The arkarnians were rowing the boat instead of writhing in the water, screaming in agony, as in her first vision. Her mother and brother appeared to be safe, but they weren't the only ones Abigail noticed. Avery was there too, and his presence made her seethe with anger.

Abigail walked over to where Avery was speaking with one of the arkarnians. She couldn't understand what they were saying, but she was certain he was poisoning the lizardman's mind with lies, just as he had done to her parents and brother.

"I know you can't hear me... but you... you will pay for everything you've done," she thought bitterly.

"For being responsible for Mei and Tadashi losing their parents... for manipulating my family... all because of your selfishness..."

"Marik, me, and my friends, we'll stop you... and I'll save my family from you."

"You'll be sorry after we're through with you."

Abigail turned away from Avery and scanned the ship.

Two other humans stood on the boat, besides her mother, brother, and Avery. A girl and a boy, both clad in armor. The boy wielded a weapon, but the girl appeared to be using air magic to manipulate water. Abigail recalled what Marik had said about abilities—that those who are magically adept are typically strong in a few elements, but not all of them. She smirked, finding it amusing that the girl had to use air to manipulate water while she herself was fortunate enough to command water.

The girl looked frustrated before turning away from the edge of the boat. She glanced past Abigail and seemed to smile slightly at something. Abigail's eye twitched when she realized the girl was smiling at Alan, who was speaking with their mother.

Before Abigail could voice her disgust, she felt herself being pulled out of the vision, waking from the trance.

***

As Abigail opened her eyes, she glanced around. It was daytime now, and Mei and Tadashi were sitting nearby, eating breakfast.

"Mei... I had another one of those 'dreams.' I'm convinced it was a vision. It felt so surreal. My mom was there, Alan was there, so was Avery, and... a strange girl was ogling Alan, too."

Mei narrowed her eyes. "What do you mean, 'ogling' Alan?"

Abigail sighed. "Really? That's what you're focusing on? Not the whole 'I had another vision' thing?"

"So... other than the girl, what else happened in the vision?"

"They seemed to be sailing on a river through a forested area. Some arkarnians were rowing the boat, so I guess they must've been heading upstream rather than downstream. That girl... she seemed to be practicing magic. Avery was talking to one of the arkarnians, but I couldn't hear any words—only the sounds of the water and trees. It must be because I'm adept in those areas of magic."

Mei frowned. "On the plus side, if these visions are accurate, Alan and your mom are okay. But on the downside, it means they're still with Avery. That either means they haven't realized Avery isn't who they think he is... or it means we've been deceived."

Abigail huffed. "Mei, Marik has nearly died for us how many times already? Of course, they haven't realized what Avery really is. But we'll save them from his deception."

Mei didn't argue, though she couldn't help but feel uncertain. She knew neither Alan nor his mother was that gullible. She thought back to when they all agreed to remain neutral, not choosing sides between Marik and Avery until they had all the facts. But, as of that moment, Mei felt like she was the only one still holding out hope that Alan's departure wasn't a reckless decision.

Nearby, Marik was cleaning his sword in a creek. He smiled, seeing that Abigail had become the polar opposite of her brother, but frowned as he noticed Mei seemed to be playing devil's advocate. He pushed his concerns about Mei's commitment to the mission to the back of his mind and focused on Abigail's visions, wondering if they could help slow Avery's progress.

After finishing the cleaning of his blade, Marik walked over to them.

"Now that Abigail is awake, we can proceed. Mei, why don't you take the lead with Gorb? Tadashi and Yerk will follow you. When you see Glum, you'll know when to stop. As for you, Abigail, I want you to ride with me. There are some things we need to discuss."

Mei reluctantly nodded and walked over to her horse. She wasn't sure if splitting up and leaving Marik alone with Abigail was a good idea, but she knew not to make an issue of it. She'd just have to do her best to keep an eye on her friend.

***

Marik rode closely beside Abigail for a few minutes before breaking the silence. "Forgive me for intruding, but I couldn't help overhearing your conversation with Mei regarding your... visions."

"I think, if you feel comfortable talking it out with me, I might be able to offer some insight into what you're experiencing. Of course, you don't have to tell me anything if you don't want to... I wouldn't want you to feel as though I'm manipulating you."

Abigail sighed. "Don't listen to Mei. She trusts you, I'm sure. She just likes to stay neutral because of Alan. I don't think she wants to consider herself on a different side than him. As for my visions... I don't think it would hurt to discuss them."

"A couple of days ago, I had a surreal dream. Alan was sitting with our mother in front of a campfire with some arkarnians. They looked like they were laughing and having a good time... It felt like I was watching them in real life. Then, last night, I had two visions. The first one was... abstract, to say the least. It's not even worth discussing, to be totally honest..."

Marik shook his head. "When it comes to visions, there are rarely pointless dreams. If you're not comfortable discussing this 'abstract' vision, that's fine, but don't discount it as meaningless."

Abigail paused. "I was alone in the middle of a frozen lake. Snow was blowing all around me, and I could barely hear myself think. But I could feel something... something stalking me. It looked like the creature that attacked your castle, but... it was different. It ran toward me, but just before it could get me, the ice beneath me gave out, and I sank into freezing water."

Marik put his hand to his chin as he pondered. "Continue."

"I then found myself emerging from the water, on the deck of a boat. The sky was this horrible red-orange color, and the water surrounding the boat wasn't water at all... it was blood. Arkarnians were floating in it, screaming in pain. I saw my mother being attacked by a giant crab, and Alan was held down by vines. The shadow that was chasing me passed through him, and he was just... a burnt corpse. Then I woke up and had the second vision—the one that made sense."

Marik lowered his hand. "I think the vision you just described is a warning of what could happen if we fail. If Whenua is destroyed, as Avery unknowingly plans, the arkarnians will suffer. The shadow stalking you could represent your self-doubt or the concerning trust Alan has placed in Avery—or perhaps even Avery himself. Either way, we must be cautious when we reach the polar regions. For Alan's sake, two of those possibilities suggest he could be harmed—or worse—by Avery's hand. Sorry... go on, explain your other vision to me."

"I was on the same boat as before, but the water was normal this time. I saw Alan with my mother, safe. There was also this... girl practicing magic. She was... well, looking at Alan with googly eyes when he wasn't paying attention."

Marik spoke without turning his head. "Did this girl have auburn hair? Green eyes? About your height?"

Abigail nodded, then realized Marik wasn't looking at her. "Yes. Do you know who she is?"

"In a manner of speaking, I've seen her from a distance, but I've never spoken with her. Her name is Cinder—a play on her skill with fire magic and a shortening of her birth name, Cynthiana."

"She's a very dangerous individual. Recruited as a student of the magical arts straight out of prison by Avery."

Abigail's eyes widened. "She's a convict?"

"Oh, yes. As I said, a very dangerous one. She was arrested for burning down an orphanage with people inside. She's a pyromaniacal apprentice—perfect for Avery to exploit in his self-centered quest to save his wife."

"Anyway, continue. Tell me what else you saw."

Abigail continued. "I also saw Avery talking to an arkanian. In fact, arkarnians were rowing the boat. I couldn't hear anything they were saying... and honestly, that was it."

Marik nodded. "They're traveling up the River of Mortas... now I understand why you saw vines and a giant crab in your previous vision. Both are dangers travelers face along those cursed waters. We must move quickly if we're to reach the polar regions before them."

Marik then thought to himself, "At our next rest... I'll have to visit Alan. Avery's presence will make it difficult, but I think I can risk a confrontation to relay a message..."

He moved his horse closer to hers and patted her on the back. "It will be alright, Abigail. We just need to stay focused. Your brother is a smart person, just like you. And if you believe it's from your mother that you inherited that trait, then you won't need to worry about either of them."

"Remember, worry and self-doubt are your mind's enemy. They strike fear and paranoia into your heart. If you don't learn to control them, they'll dominate and control your life for as long as you let them. I know it can be hard and seem impossible, but these feelings can be controlled if you gather enough strength to push them back. That strength can be found by thinking of those you know you can always count on, like Mei and Tadashi. Trust that Alan will see reason and return to your side."

Abigail nodded. "Thank you, Marik. You know, after all this is over, you could be a therapist. You always know the right things to say to make a person feel good about themselves."

Marik smiled and chuckled to himself. "And that's why I'm so good at manipulation."

CHAPTER THIRTY-TWO

Under the Cover of Darkness

Alan looked around his room. His sleeping mind had created a place where he always felt safe, but something wasn't right. There was a feeling, a sense, that he was not alone.

He got out of bed and approached the door. As he opened it, he narrowed his eyes, determined not to be afraid this time. He finally understood what was happening.

Outside his room stood the forest he had first visited in his dreams—a forest that had eventually become reality and marked the beginning of his current adventure, ever since the day they crossed over from Earth.

"I know you're here. Where are you, Shadow-Lord?" he called out.

He heard his enemy's familiar voice in the distance. "Oh, Alan, I already told you, I despise that title… Feel free to call me Marik. It's what your sister and your friends call me. Or do their opinions mean nothing to you anymore now that you've got your mommy back? Or maybe you feel like you don't need anyone else now that you've got your new girlfriend, Cythiana? I wonder how poor Mei will feel about that."

Alan scoffed. "Oh, shut up. Like I care what you want to be called. As for my friends, their opinions will matter once they stop believing your lies. And… wait, I don't have a girlfriend. Who's Cythiana?"

He heard Marik chuckle. "Oh, she didn't tell you her actual name is Cynthiana? That would be Cinder's legal name. Perhaps the Undergate records are wrong, and I'm mistaken. I guess you'll just have to ask her sometime about it. I'm shocked that you deny she's important to you…"

Alan narrowed his eyes as he searched for Marik. "I deny that she's my girlfriend because she isn't. So if you think taunting me with the mere mention of someone I just met is going to intimidate me, you don't know me very well."

There was a pause before Marik replied. "Interesting… My intention was not to taunt or intimidate, but rather to manipulate. However, hearing you now, I realize you're either telling the truth or lying to yourself. After hearing your sister's description of the way Cinder looks at you, I thought she was something more. So if you fail to die before we meet again, I'll make sure she dies quickly and painlessly."

Alan turned a corner and found Marik alone, sitting on a chair in front of a stone table covered in overgrowth. There was an empty seat across from him.

"Please, sit down. I want to have a chat... I promise this won't end like the last two times we've spoken like this," Marik said.

Alan crossed his arms and scowled at the man he considered his mortal enemy. "You'll have to forgive me if I prefer to stand."

Marik tilted his head. "My, my. You've come a long way. You were so afraid last time I entered your dreams, but now... you're stronger. Being home has awakened something inside of you. That's good, Alan. It means if Abigail fails me, maybe I can count on you as a backup. But you see, I still hold all the cards. Even if you get the orb and manage to sway Mei and Tadashi back to your side, I will still have your sister."

"Abigail and I are much more similar than you think. We both had a father who neglected us, a mother who tried to love us but failed, and someone like a brother—literally, in her case—who stands in the way of our destinies. But I believe I have adequately... let's say, persuaded her to stay on this path."

Alan nodded slowly as he moved around the table behind Marik, speaking as he went. "Abigail is nothing like you. She has a heart and a soul, while you have neither. You're just a power-hungry bully pretending to be some dark lord. I can only pity those who can't see past that and actually fear you."

Marik chuckled, quickly stood, and grabbed Alan by the throat. "Do you pity Avery? He feared me. After months of berating him, cutting him, depriving him of food and water... I broke that old fool in ways my grandfather never could. So don't speak to me as if I am lesser than those who wore this mask before me. I've carefully planned this quest for Morimor's orb, and little has strayed from the path I carved. You may think you have an advantage, but you're traveling along one of the most dangerous rivers in Whenua, just as I predicted. I can assure you, even if by some manner of luck you and the others survive, many will still face their final moments at the Shrine. For some, it will be quick, but for you... I promise your fate will be crueler than death. Here's one idea I have swirling around in my head: maybe I'll force you to watch as your mother is ripped apart by the Valthurg. Or perhaps, I'll convince Abigail that your mother is a villain and make you watch her kill your beloved mommy. I won't let your life fade away until I can feel your throat in my hand and look into your eyes to see your fear."

As Marik moved to choke Alan and end their connection, Alan reached up and pressed his thumbs into Marik's eyes. As he did, Marik vanished from view, and the world around Alan turned white as he awoke.

***

As soon as Alan's eyes opened, he jolted upright on his cot, drenched in sweat. His head spun, lightheaded and dizzy from the sudden awakening.

"Argh!" He choked out a cry of frustration, pressing his hands to his throat, rubbing away the lingering pain.

His outcry was heard by Cinder and Madeline, who had been talking outside the canopy. Both rushed in with weapons drawn, Cinder clutching a ball of fire in her other hand.

"What happened!?" Madeline asked urgently, kneeling by her distressed son.

Alan didn't meet her gaze at first. He took a moment to gather his thoughts, to find the words to explain what had happened, before finally speaking.

"Shadow-Lord... he came to me. He knows we're on this river. He said he has control over Abigail..." Alan sighed, frustrated. "Not only that, but he claimed everything is going according to his plan. We're just doing what he expected. He said we've already lost... he threatened you, Mom. Said he'd convince Abigail that you're corrupted by Avery, that you're too far gone, and that she would need to kill you... He said he'd make me watch. When we meet him, I won't care what Avery says about there still being good in Shadow-Lord. I'm going to kill him."

Madeline wrapped her arms around Alan, hearing him speak of wanting to kill a man was foreign to her. But she couldn't judge him. After all, her life as a mercenary had involved a great deal of killing—though not all of those she killed had been as deserving of their fate as the dark lord's heir apparent. Cinder, too, didn't think less of Alan. She could only shudder at the thought of how horrid it must feel for him, to have someone maliciously invade his sleeping mind to torment him with threats to his loved ones.

Madeline pulled away and looked Alan in the eyes. "Listen to me, Alan. Marik is full of it. I don't believe for a second that he's predicted our every move. He cannot see everything. There's some other reason he knows where we are. It has to be. As for his threats—toward me, or his claim that Abigail is under his control—he's just trying to anger you, to unbalance you, so you'll lose focus and fail to reach the Polar Regions. Believe me, Alan, I'm just as angry as you right now, but we have to control that anger. If we don't, it will get us killed."

Alan nodded. "Okay... Are we almost to the Boh-Rahl territories?"

Cinder answered him. "Yeah, your mom and I were talking about whether to wake you up or wait to see if you'd do it on your own."

"Okay... I'll be out in a minute. I need to compose myself."

Madeline kissed Alan on the forehead before standing and leaving the canopy. Cinder lingered for a few moments longer, her gaze fixed on Alan. "Hey... we're going to get your sister back. I promise you can count on me to be there, with you and your mom."

Alan gave her a half smile. "Thanks. I appreciate that." With that, Cinder finally left him alone.

Alan took several deep breaths, standing up and strapping his sword and sheath to his back. He fastened his bracers, and when he felt ready, stepped out onto the deck. He saw Madeline and Cinder talking to Avery and Elis. He guessed they were informing them about the development—that the enemy somehow knew of their progress.

"This is most concerning..." Avery mused, stroking his beard. "The spell Marik performed to invade Alan's dreams should not allow him to see memories, or sense his location. That was part of the reason he kidnapped me. He needed me to tell him how to perform the spell, and then, when he realized that while he could find Alan in his dreams, he couldn't in reality, he tortured his location out of me... Unless this isn't that spell... but something more..."

Avery's eyes widened. "Of course! Abigail!"

Alan walked up to them. "What about her?"

"Abigail must have seen you. It's a rare ability, one my mother had. She could see my aunt—her twin sister—in the waking world, in her dreams, no matter how far apart they were. The connection only ended when my aunt passed away. When underdeveloped, it's like a one-sided mirror, with one twin looking in on the other. But when properly developed, it can work both ways, a means to communicate when far apart... It's a magical ability unique to those who shared a womb room, if you will."

Elis and Cinder both laughed quietly, holding back only because of their imminent approach to the Boh-Rahl. Cinder, still chuckling, said, "Womb room? What the heck is a womb room?"

Avery sighed, allowing himself a brief chuckle. "Forgive me, I've yet to eat, and for some reason, that's the first thing that came to mind to describe twins..."

Alan spoke up. "Do you think I could use this connection to spy on Shadow-Lord, the way he's using Abigail to spy on us?"

Avery shook his head. "No, not unless you've made a connection to at least one of the elements. That means Marik has indeed begun to train Abigail in the magical arts. For now, we must focus on the task at hand. We need to stay alert and keep our wits about us."

Just then, the captain and two crewmen approached, carrying five buckets. They walked past, taking them into the canopy, and shortly after, the arkarnians emerged. Yarba approached the humans and spoke.

"To mask your scents and cover your pores, you will each need to remove your armor and clothes to ensure your bodies are completely covered in mud. Then, quickly put your clothes and armor back on. Take turns, so each of you has privacy. Buckets of mud have been placed in the canopy for you."

"Well..." Avery started. "Who wants to go first?"
After about half an hour, everyone had finished. Alan struggled to resist scratching the areas of his body that itched from the mud.

"I suppose it could be worse," Madeline said. "It could have been mud with insects living inside it... At least the arkarnians were kind enough to make sure the mud they gave us was clean... or as clean as mud can be, anyway."

Yarba glanced from Madeline to Avery, his eyes wide. "Yes... clean..." He then whispered to Avery, "It was more luck that there weren't any bugs than anything else."

Everyone fell silent as they entered enemy territory. The stillness was so profound that all Alan could hear was the water lapping against the boat. The arkarnians had decided to let the river carry them forward, directing the boat only when necessary to avoid alerting the enemy.

Alan sat between his mother and Cinder, hoping there would be no fighting. The humans had all opted to remain together in the canopy, sitting in silence. The atmosphere remained tense for at least an hour.

He wanted to ask Cinder about the name Shadow-Lord had called her, but he knew this wasn't the time or place for such a discussion. Plus, he wasn't sure it would be appropriate to bring up something so personal.

Alan closed his eyes for a few minutes, figuring that no one would notice if he stole a bit of sleep, given how dark it was under the canopy.

***

As Cinder thumb-wrestled with herself to pass the time, she suddenly felt pressure on her shoulder. She slowly turned her head to see what it was and felt her chin brush against something.

She smiled as she realized Alan had fallen asleep and was unwittingly resting his head on her. A warm, fuzzy feeling washed over her knowing he was there, which made her wonder why this didn't feel weird. Alan was the first person in her life who hadn't felt like a sibling, a parental figure, a means to an end, an enemy, or a rival—at least not recently, for the latter.

Elis was like a brother, always looking out for her when Avery wasn't around. As for Avery, he was a mix of the father and grandfather she had once pretended were real, the ones who had been there for her when she fought back against the depression and loneliness that had gripped her in Undergate, when it had just been her and her mother, struggling to survive.

Her smile turned bittersweet, then faded into a frown as she thought about her poor, dead mother and the things she had gone through to keep her little girl safe, fed, and alive.

Cinder often battled intrusive voices that told her she wasn't good enough, that her mother had endured things no woman should, only to do so for nothing. But now, standing on a quest to save the world, she had the strength and determination to silence those thoughts. She knew, deep down, that her mother's sacrifices had given her opportunities she had never wasted, and that she had made something of herself.

She felt that her mother, even in death, was proud of her. Maybe it was because of her connection to magic that she could still feel her mother's love, reaching her from the world beyond life.

***

Elis sat with his hands behind his head, his legs stretched out in front of him. The urge to yawn was powerful, but he quickly suppressed it, reasoning that yawning might get them all killed.

He spent his time imagining what would happen when they made it back to Wethen and the conversation—more like the argument—that would follow with his father. He knew his mother would be just happy to see them all safe and sound, but his father was another story. He would yell at Elis for the example he was setting for the youth of Wethen, then angrily berate him and Avery for freeing a prisoner from Undergate. After that, he'd explain to Madeline how disappointed he was in her, pointing out how many laws and protocols she'd broken.

Elis then mused that Alan, who seemed just as protective of his mother as Elis was of his own, would likely forget that Alfonse was the King of an entire country. Alan would probably rip into him verbally, bringing up the terrible conditions the Dinalo were forced to live in, and the corruption of Undergate—saying everything Elis wished he could, but without dishonoring his father. Of course, his little prediction lacked the knowledge of how his father would react. Maybe Alan wouldn't say those things, or maybe he'd be wrong and his father wouldn't blow up. Perhaps he'd direct his anger at Elis instead of anyone else.

Elis considered that if they captured or killed Shadow-Lord, his father's reaction to their quest might change. But, he predicted, the enemy would slither his way out of danger when faced with defeat.

Before Elis's thoughts could go any further, he heard a sound he hoped he'd never hear: an Arkarnian trilling for help. The trill was animalistic, disoriented, and off in a way that made him realize a Boh-Rahl Arkarnian had likely been woken by the boat and was now alerting nearby forces.

Alan woke instantly as the loud shriek pierced the air, the canopy slightly illuminated by the moonlight. He realized he had been resting on someone's shoulder and lifted his head, expecting to see his mother in the pale light. His heart skipped a few beats when he saw Cinder instead. They stared at each other for a moment in silence, but the awkwardness faded when Alan briefly saw what might have been a smirk on Cinder's face.

Avery stood up and yelled, "Come on, we must take defensive positions!"

Everyone quickly rose and followed him out.

Alan stayed close to his mother until a bright, hot projectile flew between them, stabbing into the deck. He looked at it, eyes wide.

"TAKE COVER!" he yelled. "THEY'RE SHOOTING FLAMING ARROWS!"

Volleys of blazing projectiles whizzed past, striking the deck or the riverbanks, but luckily missing everyone for now.

The one good thing about flaming arrows at night, Alan noted, was that they were easier to see, making it easier to dodge them. Unfortunately, some of the arrows launched from farther away were extinguishing before they reached the boat. Rist shouted in pain as one of the arrows pierced his leg. He fell over as Alan, Elis, and Silvyn rushed to him.

Silvyn dragged the wounded man back to the canopy while Alan and Elis stayed behind, exchanging concerned looks as the arrows ceased flying.

Then, they heard Yarba yell, "They're going to board us now! Get ready for combat!"

The boat had become partially engulfed in flames, making it easier to see Boh-Rahl Arkarnians armed with makeshift swords and hatchets leaping from both sides of the river onto the ship.

Alan and Elis drew their weapons and engaged the nearest attackers. The adrenaline rush was different from the one they'd felt battling the vines—it was far more intense. But both of them steeled their minds, determined not to be driven by pure instinct like their attackers were.

Elis faced the nearest invader. He slashed at the woman's chest, but she raised her sword to meet his, baring her rows of sharp teeth as she roared in his face. The stench of her last meal made him wince, but he pushed against her, forcing her backward and off the boat. He looked down as she was grabbed by vines and dragged under the water, struggling. He felt a brief pang of sympathy but reminded himself it was her choice to attack them.

Meanwhile, Alan ducked as a Boh-Rahl wielding a hatchet swung at his neck. He gripped his sword with both hands and attempted to slash the lizardman's stomach, but his blade bounced back after cutting through only a thin layer of fabric. It had no effect on the armor underneath.

Alan rolled away as the Boh-Rahl swung again, performing an uppercut to the invader's left leg mid-roll. This time, his sword sank into the warrior's leg, likely stopping at the bone. However, with his sword stuck, Alan was now vulnerable. The Boh-Rahl moved to bash him in the skull with the hatchet, but Elis intervened just in time, slicing through the invader's weapon hand before it could strike.

Alan ripped his sword out of the Boh-Rahl's leg and plunged it into the warrior's chest, killing him. He looked down at the fallen body for a moment, feeling a brief sting of remorse, but quickly suppressed it. He wouldn't feel bad for someone who wouldn't have hesitated to kill him.

"Thanks, Elis!"

"You're welcome! No time to stand around! There's more of them!"

Elis and Alan turned to face four incoming warriors. "Stay closer to me this time, Alan. We have a better chance of overpowering them if we work together."

"Alright, I just hope everyone else is doing okay!" Alan replied.

Despite their best efforts in fighting off the invading Arkarnians and defending the remaining oarsmen, the boat slowed.

Madeline looked around amidst the chaos after stabbing a Boh-Rahl under his jaw and into his skull. Fear gripped her as she searched desperately for Alan. Overwhelmed by the sheer number of enemies boarding the ship, she finally breathed a sigh of relief when she saw Alan, unharmed and alongside Elis. However, her concern for her son distracted her from hearing Silvyn yelling her name in warning. A large Arkarnian swung a wooden club, striking her in the chest. If it hadn't been for her armor, she would have been dead. As it was, she lay on her back, wind knocked out of her, alive but in immediate danger.

Alan looked over when Silvyn shouted his mother's name. A boiling rage unlike anything he'd ever felt consumed him as he saw a brutish lizardman standing over her.

He sprinted across the deck, a deep cry of fury ripping from his throat. The Arkarnian turned away from Madeline, barely having time to react as Alan swung his sword. The momentum of his strike cleaved through the man's bone and well-developed muscles, stopping as it struck the side of his ribs. But Alan wasn't finished. He pulled his sword free and slashed back and forth across the beast, tearing through cloth, armor, scales, and muscle. He didn't stop until the Boh-Rahl had fallen to his knees. Then, with a powerful swing, Alan brought his sword down into the Arkarnian's skull, splitting it and ensuring the creature would never harm his mother again.

While the humans who witnessed Alan's brutal execution of the Boh-Rahl's chief wore expressions of shock and horror, many of the Arkarnians on both sides stopped fighting to watch in awe. The incredible violence did not deter their admiration, save for Silvyn, who, remembering the terrible night his family had been slaughtered, saw the same emotional defense mechanism in Alan's eyes. The violent acts that his father had committed to avenge his family's death had broken him for years, and Silvyn feared Alan might be heading down that same path.

Alan withdrew his sword from the warrior's head, dropped to his knees, and rested his forehead against the pommel, breathing heavily as his eyes closed in an attempt to comprehend what he had just done.

Suddenly, a deafening noise drowned out all other sounds. The Arkarnians still fighting stopped, just as their brethren had. Everyone turned to see who was blowing the war horn, and that's when Elis noticed a female Boh-Rahl walking toward them, her arm raised as though ordering them to stop. As the horn stopped, an eerie silence filled the air as the female warrior approached Alan. She reached out and helped him to his feet, supporting much of his weight.

"You... are a strong warrior," she said, her English not as fluent as the Dinalo's, but far better than Alan remembered the Morgs' language being.

"We will fight no longer... you have killed our greatest warrior, our chief. Now tell me, where do you travel?"

Avery approached cautiously. "We are heading to the Polar Regions... why do you ask?"

She looked at him, her gaze steady. "As the new chief, by order of our laws and customs, I will pledge myself and some of our strongest warriors to your cause. We will help you on your way."

She turned back to Alan. "What is your name? It is our tradition to remember this day and retell the tale in song, out of honor to you."

Alan could hardly speak. His mind was in two places at once—trying to understand what she had just said, and struggling to stop reliving the brutal killing of the Boh-Rahl chief.

The woman tilted her head, trying to understand why he remained silent.

Madeline, helped to her feet by Sobek, went to Alan's side and put her arm around him for support, allowing the Arkarnian to release him.

"His name is Alan, Alan Elwyn," Madeline said softly.

The Boh-Rahl warrior nodded, understanding the situation better. She raised her voice for all to hear. "Then let it be known that we will recount the tale of the warrior Alan Elwyn, who bravely and honorably slew our Chief, Akelneu, to protect his mother!"

Madeline helped Alan to the canopy, and Cinder and Elis both approached, wanting to console him, but Avery stopped them and entered first.

Alan gagged and grabbed a bucket, vomiting as the images of his actions flashed in his mind.

Madeline rubbed his back gently. "It's okay, honey. I understand. You just... lost control. I know you wouldn't have done it that way if you could have helped it."

Avery paced, his voice hard. "It's not okay."

Madeline shot him an angry glance. "Avery! He didn't mean to do it!"

Avery's expression softened with concern as he looked at her. "The fact that he didn't mean to be so violent is exactly why it's not okay. Alan, do you realize what you did?"

Alan's voice was ragged as he fought to hold back another wave of nausea. "I don't know... I was angry... scared... I didn't realize what happened until I was kneeling."

Avery sighed and kneeled next to him. "Alan, you used magic. The speed and strength behind those attacks were not natural. And no offense, but you don't have the physique needed to pull off a move like that... What worries me more is that the magic came from your anger, triggered by fear."

Alan looked up at Avery, his eyes filled with guilt. "I'm sorry... I didn't mean to..."

He broke down, sobbing uncontrollably. "What's wrong with me?"

Avery closed his eyes, realizing how harsh he had been. He reached out, grasping Alan's shoulders. "Alan... I'm so sorry. I'm just worried about you. I don't want you to get lost in the same darkness that took my brother... I've always had control over my emotions, so I can't even help you with that. I'm not mad at you... I'm mad at myself. If I ever seem harsh, it's only because I care deeply about you. My relationship with my daughter and grandchildren... it's strained, and I've accepted that. While I may never have a friendship with them, I will always consider you like a grandson. And I can understand if you hate me, or if you think you wouldn't be in this situation if it weren't for me..."

Alan threw his arms around Avery, holding him tightly.

"You always were the grandfather I never had growing up... Why do you think I had to leave Abigail and the others? They didn't understand that I thought of you that way. They didn't understand how important you are to me. Despite the pain I felt when you left, I'll always love you and think of you as one of the greatest people I've ever known—mistakes and all. I'll never hate you."

Madeline wiped her eyes as she watched them embrace.

Outside the canopy, Elis caught Cinder sniffling as they eavesdropped. "Are you... crying?" he asked her.

Cinder punched him in the arm, choking out, "Not one word."

After a while, Alan chuckled. "This is probably a bad time to mention it... but you've got some puke on your shoulder now. Sorry."

Avery laughed. "That's quite alright, Alan... quite alright."

Chapter Thirty-Three

Into the Abyss

After Abigail's visions of Alan, their journey had been relatively uneventful. Marik continued to lead them toward the mountain, and a thick fog had settled around them, making it difficult to see their surroundings.

Abigail moved up beside Marik. "So, Marik, I've been meaning to ask—where did Avery and your grandfather learn to use magic?"

Marik glanced at her before answering. "Primarily, they learned from their parents, Morgana and Aiden. But if there was anything they couldn't teach, they must have learned it from other wizards within the Order."

Abigail frowned, puzzled. "The Order?"

"The Order of the Mystic Masters," Marik explained. "They are the most well-known group of wizards in all of Whenua. They make and enforce laws regarding which magic is safe to use, and they also research new forms of magic and alchemy. For the most part, they're a fine group, with many noble members who are wise and well-versed in the ways of magic. Their goal is to help others and continue the pursuit of knowledge within reason. Most of the world's kingdoms have a member of the Mystic Master's Lesser Council as an advisor on all matters of magic. The Lesser Council serves as backup leadership in case anything were to happen to the Arcane Council, who handles the day-to-day operations of their fortress and country. I'll give you one chance to guess who represents the Lesser Council for the Kingdom of Wethen..."

Abigail scowled. "Avery."

Marik nodded. "Yes... Avery. He took the position from his father, Aiden, after he killed my grandfather. That was when he began consolidating his power, bribing officials, and paving his way toward his dark quest."

"Thank you for telling me this, Marik," Abigail said quietly.

"You need only ask," Marik replied. "I have researched much of this world in my efforts to undermine Avery's corruption."

As they continued their journey, the fog began to lift. Abigail could now make out the mountain, and ahead of them stood a massive stone archway. As they drew closer, the details of the large, impressive gateway became clearer. Symbols unlike any they had seen before in the Forgotten Lands were carved into the arch's border.

They had arrived at the mysterious mountain passage Marik had spoken of before their encounter with the Rau-Trava.

Marik suddenly stopped, raising his hand to signal them to halt and listen.

"This door leads down into a ruin far older than the mines the Gnoglin escorted us through," Marik said, his voice low. "It doesn't have a name—at least none spoken by the living. Most people I've spoken to refer to it as the Abyssal Cathedral. It was built long ago, probably by a group that worshipped the darkest forms of magic, judging by what explorers have claimed to have seen, heard, and found in the deep darkness of this forgotten chapel."

Tadashi laughed. "Hey, we're in the Forgotten Lands, so why not check out the Forgotten Church?"

Marik allowed a brief, audible chuckle to escape but quickly regained his composure. "This place is no laughing matter, my friend. Archaeologists, scholars, and explorers once came in scores to this place. They stopped coming because of the Rau-Trava's aggression. But even when they did visit, they rarely descended past the first three floors... and those who did... well, they joined whatever evil lurks in the unholy bowels of this cold, cavernous hell."

Mei chimed in. "No offense, Marik, but why are you so scared? I thought you used dark magic?"

Marik nodded. "It's true I've dabbled in dark magic, but I primarily use shadow magic. There's a difference between the two, though it's slight, narrow, and hard to explain. Shadow magic isn't considered illegal by the Order of the Mystic Masters. It's seen as a 'justifiable' form of dark magic because it's less potent, less raw, and far less torturous to the soul than true dark magic."

Abigail studied him with sympathy in her eyes. "You're speaking from experience, aren't you?"

Marik met her gaze. "Indeed. I've dabbled in dark magic in the past... but it feels like a lifetime ago."

He continued, his tone darkening. "I've heard the rumors from those who visited this place and returned. If the stories are true, a great many terrible things were done here... ritualistic suicides, humanoid sacrifices, and far worse. Things you'd sleep better never knowing."

Abigail stared at the gateway. "Why would people do such horrible things?"

Marik chuckled bitterly. "In this world, it's easy to feel suffocated and powerless under corrupt rulers. It's easy to walk paths best left untouched. They were drawn in by promises of power and forbidden knowledge—promises made by twisted entities called the Ak'spir. These people believed they could tap into the hellish planes of existence where the Ak'spir reside, and gain the power they desired. Instead, they allowed the Ak'spir to enter our world... and the surviving cultists all met grisly ends. I don't know if the stories are true, but there's a reason this place is abandoned. Why else would such a massive underground complex be left behind? This cathedral would make a lovely fortress for any would-be warlord. Hell, I would've taken refuge here if not for the stories."

"The Ak'spir—Strigua, as they're known in my homeland of Kalnia—generally can't manifest physically beyond their homeworlds without help. Their influence is usually limited to faint whispers and visions too horrifying for an unprepared mind to handle. But thanks to the Order of the Mystic Masters, such incidents have become rare. There was a disturbing case in my village where a man butchered his family. He claimed to be innocent, saying he remembered nothing after seeing a terrible vision. The Order sent representatives to investigate, and they determined his mind had been invaded by a parasitic species of the Ak'spir, called the Ctotles."

Abigail looked down, troubled. "That's horrible... were they able to save him from the creature?"

Marik nodded solemnly. "Yes, but he could never live with the knowledge of what he had done. It pains me to recall, but my friends and I were the ones who found his body... we were barely eight years old at the time. He was my mother's brother, my uncle. I lost many people that day—my aunt, my cousins..."

Abigail placed a hand on Marik's shoulder. "I'm sorry... Tell me about your friends."

Marik sighed. "It was a friendship not unlike the one you have with Mei, Tadashi, and your brother. There were three of us—Wulf, Luna, and myself. I... I do miss them sometimes. Our parting wasn't... ideal. They didn't agree with my decision to leave Meri'duus. Things were said that couldn't be unsaid, and the actions that were taken can never be undone..."

Tadashi walked up and gave Marik a hug. "Don't worry, you're one of us now, Marik. We'll stick with you through all of this."

For a moment, Marik felt a deep tug of guilt in his heart. For a few precious seconds, he felt a humanity in his soul that he had long ago decided was a distraction. But that humanity quickly faded, returning to what it had been for so long—a ruse, another deception in his long history of lies and manipulation. He knew that, by the end of this quest, they would eventually betray him just as Luna and Wulf had done so many winters ago in Meri'duus.

"Thank you, Tadashi. You're a good friend... all of you are," Marik said quietly. "The world would be better with more people like you. Alright, we need to get closer to the entryway. Once there, we'll need to turn the horses loose. Those caves won't be a place for our fair equine..."

Tadashi looked at Marik, surprised. "Wait a minute, you know Latin? I thought 'equine' was a Latin word for horse."

Marik chuckled. "I also know English, but you never exactly questioned that."

Marik paused for a moment before continuing.

"The last fifty-some generations of humans in the Forgotten Lands were born here. However, as Alan and I discussed, their ancestors were not. The two languages adopted by the slaves of Arkarnia—and later by the other species of Whenua—were primarily English and Latin. This was because the language of the Atilgothin people was most similar to both. Nowadays, English is the primary language of most species."

Marik stopped for a moment, ensuring they had heard him, then continued.

"The original people of Atilgoth weren't exactly human, but they were very similar. So much so that they've lost their identity as a separate species over the years. They've become rare due to how often they, for lack of a better term, mated with humans. It was because of the Atilgothins that humans here can potentially develop the ability to use magic."

Abigail's eyes widened. "You're saying that all humans born here—me, Alan, Mei, Tadashi—can trace our bloodlines back to these... Ardaldolphins?"

Marik sighed and corrected her. "Atilgothins, not... whatever it was you just said. But yes, you, Alan, myself, and all other magic-using humans can trace our lineage to the Atilgothin race."

Abigail nodded slowly. "That makes sense. But why didn't humans ever try to go back to Earth?"

"The knowledge of Earth is like a distant, fading memory. Few humans know of their homeworld, and many just assume humans are some evolved or devolved form of the Atilgothins. Besides... the humans of Earth tainted their world. Their reliance on nonrenewable technologies, and their lack of magical properties, will be their undoing. Those people have set themselves on a path toward the collapse of society and the decay of the natural world, all without dark magic. Mark my words—one day, they'll destroy themselves in seconds with the push of a shiny red button. What use is a world like that to humans who have it better? But, that's of no consequence. We're just about at the door now..."

Abigail, Mei, and Tadashi didn't quite know how to feel about what Marik had just told them. Marik's opinion of Earth was unsettling, but Abigail felt that, perhaps understandably, he could not find a place so different from his own home as beautiful or valuable. She also thought, maybe somewhat morbidly, that he was right—Earth's problems had been caused by humans. Whenua's problems, on the other hand, seemed to have stemmed from dark magic—something not man-made.

The three of them came to similar conclusions as they rode in silence, pushing thoughts of Earth from their minds. All save Abigail, who briefly wondered if Alan had been thinking of home, or if he had renounced Earth and come to accept Whenua as his true home. She felt conflicted. While she knew she had been born in Whenua, she had never connected to the story their mother had written for them as deeply as Alan had. But that wasn't her only issue—Abigail still had friends on Earth. It wasn't just Mei, Tadashi, and Alan who mattered to her; she had made many friendships over the years, and those people meant a lot to her too. But perhaps Whenua was where she belonged, despite all that.

As she continued to wrestle with her thoughts, she recalled an indescribable feeling that had always plagued her—a longing, a call to be part of something greater than herself. That feeling had faded when she first arrived in Whenua, but now, it was creeping back. She feared that if she accepted Whenua as her home, she would never return to Earth. But could she even bring herself to go back once the journey was over? Even if she wanted to?

This same fear plagued Mei, but Tadashi remained unaffected. His fear, however, was the opposite of theirs. Unbeknownst to him, it was the same fear that Alan had secretly carried with him along the Mortaas River. Alan and Tadashi feared that, when their journey was over, something would happen beyond their control that would force them to return to Earth.

Marik dismounted from his horse, and the others followed suit. Tadashi scratched his horse behind the ear and asked Marik mournfully, "Will they be able to survive out here?"

Marik walked over to Tadashi and placed a reassuring hand on his shoulder. "Worry not. My horse, Brarum, is no ordinary steed. He will guide them back to Darkmount with ease."

Marik paused, his gaze shifting to the distance. Once again, he felt the unmistakable sensation of being watched. He briefly wondered who, beyond Avery's many friends and allies, would risk their lives to follow him. The only certainty he had was that his source within the Order of the Mystic Masters had confirmed that no other wizard, aside from Avery, was present on the western continent. Kardica's mystic master was currently in Atilgoth for an important meeting regarding the ongoing Amphinarian War in the east.

As his thoughts deepened, Marik realized something more troubling than not knowing the stalker's motives: whoever this figure was, they were deliberately allowing Marik to catch glimpses of them, as if to taunt him. The figure was skilled in staying hidden—every time Marik tried to investigate, there was no trace of anyone following.

He began to wonder if he was simply becoming paranoid. Perhaps the knowledge that he was so close to achieving his goals was burdening him, subconsciously making him afraid of slipping up. But as soon as those thoughts took root, he rejected them. "I am the heir to Materall," he reminded himself. "I will not slip up, nor shall I fail. Whoever the fool is who follows us, it is inconsequential. They will not survive the horrors that lurk within the Abyssal Cathedral."

The massive entrance loomed before them. In stark contrast to the humid, stagnant air that had preceded it, a cold draft emanated from the darkness beyond, both refreshing and spine-chilling at the same time.

Tadashi pulled out a light-stone and stepped forward. Yerk followed closely behind to keep him safe, while Mei, Abigail, Marik, and the other morgs brought up the rear.

Mei glanced at the stone masonry along the walls. "This kind of reminds me of that diorama Alan made for his little medieval dolls."

Tadashi grunted. "They were figurines, Mei, not 'little medieval dolls.'"

Abigail chuckled. "In her defense, they were both tiny and medieval-themed..."

Tadashi muttered something under his breath and fell silent.

They continued down the dark, dusty hallways. The floors, made of solid stone blocks, had aged remarkably well compared to the state of Marik's fortress.

Many of the walls were covered in spider webs—both abandoned and occupied. Thankfully, the spiders were not excessively large and seemed mostly uninterested in the humans and morgs passing so close to their lairs. Mei kept shuddering and brushing herself off as she imagined invisible critters crawling on her due to the sheer number of spiders.

The light-stone grew brighter the further they ventured from the entrance, until the darkness outside of its glow was almost complete. Marik's only worry was that the dangers within the subterranean church would prove too much for the teens. It might have been safer to have taken the longer route, one that would have given Alan and Avery more time to prepare, but it was too late for second guesses. They had already entered this horrible, abysmal place, and now only time would tell who would leave with their life and who would succumb to the forgotten secrets waiting inside.

CHAPTER THIRTY-FOUR

Death's Door

Alan sat in front of the canopy entrance, watching as Avery and his mother spoke with the Boh-Rahl female, whose name they had learned was Ohk-Kwha-Mha. However, she insisted they simply call her Okama. She had picked up their language quickly—so fluently that one might think she had been raised speaking it. Alan had a feeling she had spent time among humans before.

When Okama learned of the Valthurg's presence in the Polar Regions, she selected fifteen warriors to accompany them. The fact that they had been unaware of the threat had surprised Baldric.

Elis waited patiently for Avery and Okama to finish their conversation about the remaining trials of the river. Now that they were no longer fighting, he was eager to speak with her—he wanted to learn more about the cultural differences between her people and the Dinalo from her perspective.

As Avery wrapped up his conversation, he glanced at Elis. "If you have a moment, Elis would like to speak with you about your people's culture—if that's alright with you. We have some time before we reach Death's Door..."

Okama nodded as Avery and Madeline walked away.

"What do you want to know?"

"I understand you follow a warrior way, like the Rau-Trava?"

Okama immediately shook her head, dismissing the comparison. "No! Never like them. They follow a different path than we do. We believe in Ora, the Spirit of Life, just as all Arkarnians do, but we sing songs to the four great spirits—the elemental spirits that make up Ora."

"First, there is the warrior, Fierdros—Lord of Flame. Then, there is the guide, Arn'ris—the Wind-Mother. Next is the builder, Rokdier, Master of Earth, who tends to the soil and nature. And finally, the singer, Osienna—bringer of life and Chieftain over the Sea."

Elis stroked his chin thoughtfully. "So the difference between you and the Dinalo is clear—they believe in Ora as one spirit. But how do your beliefs differ from the Rau-Trava?"

Okama nodded. "There was a time when all Arkarnians followed six great beings who made up Ora—each representing an element: fire, air, earth, water... and dark. The one who represented light has been forgotten, lost to time."

She lowered her voice slightly. "But we do remember the name of the pillar of shadow. He is the shunned one, a bringer of darkness and evil, a dweller of murky, long-forgotten depths. He is... G'thul, the Keeper of Forbidden Knowledge. It is said that G'thul became one of the Ak'spir—that his once squid-like humanoid form has twisted into that of an insect that walks upon two legs."

Her expression hardened. "We of the Boh-Rahl do not sing songs to G'thul. But the Rau-Trava treat all six as equals. And the Valthurg? They are truly unforgivable... They sing only to G'thul and forsake all other elemental pillars."

Elis tilted his head. "So you believe these spirits actively influence the world around us?"

Okama considered the question for a moment. "Whether the pillars exist as individual beings is up to personal belief. What we do know for certain is that Ora and the Four Pillars exist. Whether they are independent of each other or simply different aspects of the same source of magic, we do not know. But we do know there is a force of dark magic separate from Ora and the Four Pillars. Magic comes from somewhere, that much is clear. And throughout history, dark magic has shown a will of its own.

"As for the Order of the Mystic Masters, I do not know what they believe. Perhaps they understand more, given their long history of studying and using magic. But we will follow our traditions—singing songs to Ora and the Four Pillars—until we can sing no more, regardless of whether our faith is ever proven to be mere myth."

Ever since Okama had offered to help them, an idea had been forming in Elis's mind. He decided to ask, "Do you think your tribe would ever consider allying with the Dinalo? And, eventually, Wethen? Not in a way where you kneel to Wethen, but in a way where we help each other stand."

Okama thought carefully before answering. "The Boh-Rahl are different from the Dinalo and Rau-Trava in more ways than just religious and spiritual beliefs. We are divided, spread across different areas of this region. We respect each other, but our treatment of outsiders varies from group to group. My people are the most forgiving due to our sense of honor. But had you encountered the group to the east, they would not have stopped—even if you proved yourselves to be honorable warriors. I admit, my own people may not have stopped either, had I not ordered it."

She sighed. "Perhaps, with patience, effort, and a proper meeting between the leaders of each Boh-Rahl group, the Chief of the Dinalo, and the King of Wethen, an alliance could be reached. But I could just as easily see things going terribly wrong... Perhaps even sparking a war between the Boh-Rahl and everyone else at such a meeting."

Elis nodded, understanding the weight of what she was saying. "Yes... I can see that happening, too. And maybe... my father shouldn't be the one attending that meeting."

Okama's eyes widened as she suddenly put the pieces together. "You are the Prince of Wethen?"

Elis chuckled nervously. He was so used to people immediately recognizing him that he hadn't considered how isolated the Arkarnians were from the rest of the world. "Well... yeah. I guess I forgot to mention that."

She studied him for a moment, then smiled. "To hear a royal of Wethen speak of unity is... unexpected. I will not neglect to share your idea with the other Boh-Rahl groups. If they know the next generation of Wethen's leadership favors an alliance, they may be more willing to consider it. And if I vouch for you, they might actually take you seriously."

Elis was surprised at how much that meant to him. It made him feel like he wouldn't have to wait for his father to abdicate—or worse, pass away—to start making a difference.

"So... since you are now the chief of your group, does that mean... your father was the one who died?"

Okama's expression darkened. "...Yes, he was my father. But any tears for his death would be undeserved."

Elis's eyes widened. "I—I'm sorry. I had no idea he was that terrible when I asked."

"It is not your fault," she said simply. "You had no way of knowing unless you could see my thoughts."

She exhaled slowly. "There was a time when my father was an honorable man. But that changed when a human clad in black came to our village. He smelled wrong—not like any other human I have ever met. He offered my father a deal: if he would destroy any human who dared to cross this region, the man's strange, bumbling minions would bring us precious gems in return. Many of us opposed the deal—it was made without consulting the village. But the first, and only, one of us to openly defy him had his skull crushed."

She clenched her fists. "After that, no one dared to challenge him. In our tradition, if someone opposes the chief, they must fight him one-on-one. Even if there are several challengers, they must face him one at a time. No one believed they could defeat him alone."

Elis let that sink in, then asked, "If you only just became chief, how do you know your people will be willing to work with humans? I'm sure you're a skilled warrior, but some of the others are much larger than you. From what you said, they could have easily defeated you in a one-on-one challenge."

Okama chuckled. "So you think I couldn't defeat someone twice my size? I don't blame you. I didn't think Alan could defeat my father when I first saw him. And yet, here we are."

She smirked. "A larger opponent will only overwhelm you if you let them. Strength is important, but too much muscle can hinder your ability to react quickly. Not all warriors are clever, but if you use your mind, you can overcome any obstacle." She shrugged. "That only partly answers your question, though. My fellow warriors and I had already discussed overthrowing my father's rule—but many lacked the confidence to challenge him. We believed that, together, we could defeat him. But our customs did not allow it."

She then gestured toward the camp. "Would you like to meet the others?"

Elis nodded, and the two walked over to the group of Boh-Rahl warriors.

Meanwhile, Alan had retreated under the canopy. Though his conversation with Avery had helped, he was still grappling with the violence he had unleashed. The images remained fresh in his mind—every graphic detail of flesh severing from bone. He tried meditation, then distraction, imagining one of his favorite fictional characters wiping the floor with Shadow-Lord, but that only worked for a few minutes.

Leaning against the wooden wall, he closed his eyes and took deep breaths, determined to banish the trauma by focusing on the happiest, most wholesome moments of his past.

Cinder stood at the canopy's drape-like entrance, watching him. It felt a little creepy, but she reasoned that it was normal to stare at someone when you were worried about them and didn't want to disturb them.

She remembered her own first kill in Undergate. She couldn't recall her exact age—only that she'd been searching for food and had somehow wandered into Cannibal District. Cannibalism among humans was rare, so rare that any criminal convicted of it was sent to Undergate. That day, one of them had found her.

He was horrifying—nearly naked, his own body and face mutilated to the point of looking inhuman. She never learned his name, and she never gave him the chance to kill her. When he charged at her on all fours like a wild animal, she scrambled up a nearby lamppost, clutching the lantern that hung from it. When he tried to climb up after her, she knocked the lantern down. Oil spilled over him, and even at her young age, she knew what oil plus fire meant. With no other choice, she used her untrained magic to set him ablaze. If the fire hadn't killed him, the fall from the platform surely had.

But she knew that what Alan had done was different. He had gone beyond self-preservation—beyond protecting himself and his mother. Not that she blamed him. If she'd ever found the man who murdered her own mother, she wasn't sure she wouldn't have done the same... or worse.

Still, she understood how dangerous the thirst for revenge could be—how it could break someone's spirit.

Cinder sighed, shaking off the memory. Her feelings toward Alan had changed in ways she didn't quite understand. At first, she had found him annoying and out of his league in Whenua. But over time, she had seen that he was capable of being the person Avery believed in. And now... now, she felt something foreign—something she wasn't ready to name.

Maybe talking to him would help both of them.

She walked over and knelt across from him. "Hey... how are you doing?"

Alan opened his eyes and looked at her. He smiled, but Cinder could see the truth in his eyes—the haunted look of someone trapped in their own mind.

"I'm fine... how are you? You didn't get hurt during the fight, did you?"

Cinder shook her head. "Nope. Had a few close calls, but I'm good." She hesitated, then continued. "Listen... I may not know exactly how you feel, but I understand. And I don't think you should beat yourself up over it. You're not a bad person. I get wanting to protect your mother. I would've done the same thing in your shoes."

"Thanks..." Alan hesitated, then asked, "Hey, can I ask you something?"

Cinder's heart skipped a beat. Was he about to ask if she was single? "Uh—" she stammered. "S-sure."

"When Shadow-Lord visited me in my dreams... he said your full name was Cynthiana. Is that true? If you don't mind me asking, I just want to figure out how much of what he said was real."

Cinder exhaled, relieved. She wasn't ready to deal with that kind of conversation—not until she understood these strange feelings.

"...My full name is Cynthiana Král. My mother was the only one who called me Cynthia or Cynthiana. After she died... well, I wasn't comfortable going by either of those anymore. Everyone else just started calling me Cinder after I started burning anyone who tried to hurt me. And it stuck."

Alan looked down. "I don't think I ever told you—I'm sorry about what happened to your mom."

Cinder smiled and touched his shoulder. "I appreciate that. And... I don't mind talking about her. In case you're worried you brought up a touchy subject. You seem to overthink things a lot." She smirked slightly. "I just don't like talking about her with most people. But you're not most people. Besides, if I stopped talking about her altogether, it'd be like she never existed."

"She would've found the bright side of every trial this river has thrown at us so far," Cinder continued, her voice softer. "She was great at that—finding light in darkness. I remember telling her that once, and she said... I was her light. I thought it was silly at the time. But I get it now."

Alan smiled. "She sounds like she was a wonderful person."

"She was..." Cinder's expression darkened. "The day she died, I—I went through a flurry of thoughts. And... first, let me explain something about Undergate. The whole city is built over this massive chasm. If there's a bottom, no one's ever seen it. After she died... I went to the lowest point, where they were building a new area for prisoners. I've never told anyone this—not even Avery—but... I almost jumped."

Alan's breath caught, his eyes wide with emotion.

"I missed her so much," Cinder admitted. "And I was scared. But I couldn't do it. It was like... like there was an invisible hand holding me back. I like to think it was her. That her spirit is still somewhere near, watching over me, making sure I don't do anything stupid."

Alan sniffled and pulled her into a hug, understanding how much she must trust him to share something so personal.

Cinder hugged him back, still unsure of her feelings toward him, but grateful. She had always kept her past and emotions locked away, even from Elis. But now, for the first time, she had let someone in. And as she embraced Alan, she felt a weight lift from her soul. A pit that had long existed in her stomach was filled by the warmth spreading from her heart.

***

Madeline sat down with Avery at the rear of the boat, her thoughts dwelling on Alan and Abigail. Alan's anger had gotten the better of him, and her son was usually the last person in their household to become frustrated with a difficult situation. She worried how Abigail was handling her abilities, especially when Shadow-Lord would likely fan those particular flames.

She glanced over to Avery. "Do you—do you think that—" Madeline struggled to find the words, but Avery seemed to sense what question she was intent on asking.

"Do I think that Abigail can still be led away from the path Marik is trying to lead her down?"

Madeline nodded silently, and Avery answered her. "Between the twins, I have long since concluded that Abigail is more likely than Alan to first think things through with her heart and then with her head lastly. That said, I believe she has a very good heart, and that should keep her out of trouble long enough for her to think it through with her very intelligent mind, which I might add she inherited from you. I'm not telling you not to worry, but I am saying that you should do so to a lesser extent than you have been, if that is even possible for you as her mother. I will say this—you are what I wish my own mother had been. While you and Alan are closer than you and Abigail are, you still treasure them equally, and I know you'll do whatever it takes to protect and save them, and that you'll never give up on them."

Madeline sighed, thankful for Avery's kind words. "I wonder though... if it would have been better to have told them sooner. Abigail is so sensitive... she might perceive keeping everything from her as a slight against her personally—"

Avery raised his hand to stop her. "We cannot alter a choice once it's been made, Madeline. In the end, we only have three choices we can make when confronted with the guilt of the past: stand by our convictions, strive to correct them if we can, or instead allow the mistakes we made yesterday to inform our choices today, rather than tether our minds to memories that are warped by guilt as the finer details fade and change with time."

Madeline nodded, and they remained silent.

They had finally reached Death's Door. Spine-shivering chills ran through everyone—even the most muscular of the Arkarnian warriors aboard.

Alan looked down into the river. His left eye started twitching, and he reached up to place his finger on his upper cheek and pulled on it, finally ending the nerve-racking movement.

He felt better after his conversation with Cinder. The fact she trusted him enough to have told him something so private, despite his brutal action earlier, had eased his wandering mind greatly, and the intrusive thoughts had subsided ever since.

Suddenly Alan felt someone touch his shoulder lightly. He turned, expecting one of the Arkarnians, his mother, Cinder, Avery, or Elis—but instead, he saw nothing. He looked around, and his eyes started to bug out. Since his arrival in the Forgotten Lands, he had traveled landscapes that were dying due to a malignant force of magic, was attacked by sentient vines, fought reptilian humanoids, had been chased by an angry Momma Lerp, and stalked by a Mist Monster who, now that he thought about it, was likely still out there hunting him from a distance. Sure, he thought, why not add ghosts to the list.

As much as he had respected the word of their guides, he doubted the possibility of ghosts, and he was realizing in hindsight how his suspension of belief was raised by the presence of poltergeists, despite everything else he had seen.

He heard a whooshing noise behind him. As he turned and looked down over the side of the boat, there was a skull floating alongside the ship, presumably Arkarnian due to its shape and the remnants of blood and scaly skin still attached. A wispy black and red glow was swirling around it as its rotted eye sockets began to glow. The jaw began to move, and a deep voice started to vocalize.

The skull spoke in a guttural language, something that reminded Alan of the Arkarnians' language, but more archaic. He surmised that the skull itself was not ancient, so whatever force had brought it to life was perhaps a spirit of a bygone era. Alan turned to call out to Avery, but the world around him darkened as a blanket of shadow spread out across the boat, and the voice—and the sounds of the river and jungle—all fell silent.

"...Avery?... Mom?... Cinde—" He stopped as he heard the sound of heavy breathing. It was all around him. He felt a strange sensation, akin to when he was speaking to Shadow-Lord in his dreams, but he didn't feel the aura of dread that Marik seemed to exude in those visions. So if he was with him, he was trying to hide it.

"Who's there?"

The same voice that had spoken through the skull echoed around Alan once more, but this time, he understood it perfectly. The words reverberated off invisible walls, carrying a tone that was kind, gentle, and patient. If not for what it was saying, he might not have felt so uneasy.

"Thy acrimony is powerful... I wonder, now that thou hast tasted the darkness within, how will thee turn away? Don't deny it—deep down, thou felt joy when thou took that man's life. After all thee have endured, it felt good to unleash thy fury upon something... and what better excuse than doing so to save thine mother?"

Alan's fists clenched. He looked around, his voice sharp. "I'll be ready to let it loose again if you don't shut up."

The voice chuckled, unbothered.

"Very well. I do not seek to antagonize thee, young one. I merely seek to illuminate a different—darker—path now open to thee."

Alan didn't hesitate. "No... I am not Marik."

The voice exhaled, sounding almost disappointed. But beneath that, there was something else—acceptance.

"Very well... I understand that this time in thy life is difficult, and embracing my offer could jeopardize the relationships thee have so carefully cultivated with thine loved ones... However, as thou may have already realized, Alan Elwyn, I see all. I know a great many things... I have watched thee for so long, I consider thee a friend of sorts."

"And because of this... I will grant thee three questions. Akin to a tale from thy world—the genie in a bottle, I believe it is called. So ask, Alan. Whatever thou desires to know, I shall answer."

Alan hesitated. "How do I know you'll answer truthfully?"

The voice chuckled, amused.

"I have no reason to lie to thee, Alan. And fret not—I shall not count that among thy three questions."

Alan thought carefully before voicing his first question. "Where are Shadow-Lord, Abigail, Mei, and Tadashi?"

A brief pause, then the voice responded.

"Thine sister, friends, and antagonist travel through ruins within the mountains, parallel to the river thee now sails upon."

"And because I favor thee, I shall grant extra knowledge, freely given and not counted against thy remaining questions... When last thee spoke, Marik Ambrose told thee that thine sister is wholly under his influence. This is both true and false. There is a creature within Abigail's brain—a ctotles—a parasite manipulating her thoughts, making her more inclined to believe his lies. It feeds upon her reliance on her so-called 'gut feelings.'"

"An example: when she saw thy companions in a dream, Marik poisoned her mind with falsehoods. She now believes Cynthiana Kral to be a dangerous criminal who burned down an orphanage—a rather unimaginative and cliché deception, I must say..."

"Yet still effective, for she believes it. I find thine friends amusing at times—especially Tadashi. Such a pure soul... so much so, I find it remarkable that Marik has concealed his true nature from him for so long. But then, Marik is a masterful manipulator..."

"Take comfort in this—Mei and Tadashi bear no such parasite. They remain fully in control of their own thoughts. The reason? Marik was barely strong enough to summon a single ctotles—and he would not waste it on anyone but thee or Abigail. But worry not, for thy sister is not beyond salvation. The parasite's power is not absolute."

"Now... ask thy next question."

Alan exhaled slowly. He believed this entity was telling the truth.

It was not aligned with Marik.

Shadow-Lord would never offer Alan hope that his friends could be saved. And Marik would never admit to weakness.

"Where is the Mist Monster that attacked me in the Bramble?"

The voice chuckled. "Ah, yes... I was hoping you'd ask that. First, understand this: the Mist Monster, as you call it, is nothing more than an extension of Marik's will, a personification of his innermost darkness. As for its location, it has been closer than you think—it keeps its distance behind you. Marik plans to have it destroy you if you reach him, in front of your sister. Then, he will use an illusion to make it appear as though it is an extension of Avery. I suggest that once you've dealt with the perils of the river, you warn everyone about the Mist Monster and set a trap for it. Perhaps it will survive. Perhaps it won't. Now... one last question, Alan."

Alan thought for a long moment, the weight of his final question settling over him. One last chance to know anything.

"Why is Whenua actually dying?"

The voice hummed thoughtfully. "Hmmm, recall the story Avery told you about how he and his mother fought Materall beneath Ancient Arkarnia. He violated the very framework of nature itself. The corruption that ravaged that land is like a disease, or rather, a rash—one that manifested in several spots across the world. It gives off the illusion of death and decay, but in truth, it's a new form of life. As you saw in the Shadow-Lands when you returned to this world... It is possible to stop the spread of this transformation with the Orbs, but there is no restoring what has already been changed. The world, as it is, is not suitable for the Ak'spir to live. It was Marik's grandfather who promised them a new master and a new world to live in if they agreed to serve him and help him subjugate the masses. Mind you, not all of Whenua would be transformed. Primarily, it would be the western continent—Materall desired the east as his kingdom."

Alan stood still, breathless for a moment, struggling to grasp the enormity of what he had just heard. "Can I ask one last thing? Who are you?"

The voice came from behind him now, deep and resonant. "I am known by many names. To the Ak'spir, I am Kreshka the Hated Master. To the Arkarnians, I am G'thul the Keeper of Forbidden Knowledge. To the Pargellians, I am Daghlesh the Lord of Secrets. To the humans of this world, I am Apoktolis the Dark God. And to the humans of the world you were raised in... well, they call me many things. Too many to list in a single breath. But out of all of them, I find that I most identify with Daghlesh. The title of Lord of Secrets carries less animosity toward me..."

Alan's gut twisted as he realized he was speaking to something ancient and malevolent. He had a sinking feeling he knew some of the names humans on Earth had given this being, but something inside him told him that, even if he was an evil entity, the being was telling the truth about everything: his sister, the Mist Monster's true nature, and the extent of the corruption Materall had caused. Maybe not because it wanted Alan to succeed for its own sake—but to gain Alan's trust for some purpose that was still unclear.

"I do hope we speak again, Alan. It has been so long since I directly spoke to one such as yourself. I am rooting for you... I would rather the world of Whenua remain close to what it once was, for reasons I'd rather not divulge to thee..."

Alan turned toward Daghlesh's voice and saw a tall, enshrouded figure. The being's humanoid form was unsettling, and as Alan's gaze traveled up, he noticed the face—resembling that of a spider. The mandibles, however, were shaped like a beard, hiding the being's mouth. In its chitinous hands, it held a book. Daghlesh tapped his long, spider-like fingers on the book's cover, and Alan could feel the weight of his many black, pupilless eyes boring into him.

Alan stepped back, startled by Daghlesh's arachnid-like appearance, but this only seemed to amuse the Keeper of Knowledge.

"Some consider it a great honor to gaze upon my physical form," Daghlesh's voice was thick with a hint of amusement, "though those few are generally cultists who sacrifice their flesh, their loved ones, and strangers, just to hear secrets not meant for mortal minds. Forbidden knowledge that drives them mad as they try to unlearn what they've been shown. Then, they walk the path to death, where the suffering continues because they have already given themselves to me..."

Alan said nothing.

"Do not fret, Alan," Daghlesh continued, "I do not seek to trick you into becoming one of those lost souls. You are far too useful to me for such an unremarkable fate. I need you because if Marik wins, he will fulfill his grandfather's goals—and strip me of my kingdom and power. The Ak'spir will have no reason to remain my begrudging subjects. So, you will do as I ask. In return, I will not claim your soul."

Daghlesh moved closer, his long, bony fingers reaching out to rest on Alan's shoulder. The touch caused Alan to shudder, the bony hand stretching unnervingly across his back. "It's time for you to return to your luxurious river cruise, Mr. Elwyn. All humor aside... when you encounter the crustaceans ahead, their weak point is located on the roof of the middle mouth. There is a fluid sac there, shielded by a hard layer of chitin. I suggest you sever all the mandibles in your way first, then use your sword to finish it. Farewell, Alan. Don't be a stranger..."

With that, the darkness around Alan dispersed, and he was back on the boat, staring at the now-lifeless skull floating on the water.

Alan glanced over at Avery and approached, deciding it was best to keep quiet about Daghlesh for now. He wasn't sure how the others would react. Instead, he thought of a way to tell Avery about the Mist.

"Avery... I sensed something..." He reasoned with himself that hearing was a sense, so he wasn't technically lying—just withholding certain details. "The Mist creature... it's near us. Following, watching, waiting. I'm thinking it's Marik, or at least an extension of his will, if that's even possible."

Avery ran his fingers through his long beard. "That's possible, yes. But it's especially difficult to maintain a direct link to a familiar while on the move. If my nephew is anything like his grandfather, he won't risk losing progress just to check in with his familiar. Which means it may be more vulnerable. Whatever reason Marik has for sending it after us, we can't assume it's anything good. We must destroy it sooner rather than later."

Alan interrupted. "We could set a trap for it after we pass the river. Would one of those traps with a big hole covered by leaves work?"

Avery shrugged. "I've never encountered a familiar like this before. Usually, they take the form of animals. But there are no creatures like the Mist that I know of. For example, my familiar, Brokveer, rest his little soul, was a Northern Amphinarian Rovvit. Picture a regular rabbit, but with rock-like skin instead of fur, and not afraid to attack larger animals that venture too close to its den. If you ever encounter one, protect your neck—that's where they direct their main attack."

Alan nodded, though he hadn't paid much attention to the details. He was focused on the bigger picture. "I think it's a manifestation of Marik's inner darkness."

Avery gave him an odd look. "Hmm... yes."

"Alan, be honest with me... did someone—or something—tell you all this?"

Alan's gaze dropped as he felt sick for hiding the truth from Avery, especially after their recent conversation. But Avery didn't seem angry. He simply nodded and led Alan somewhere quiet, out of earshot of the others.

"It's okay, Alan," Avery said softly. "I understand why you didn't want to tell me. I don't think less of you for trying to deceive me. I understand the temptation to ask him for answers... He spoke to me long ago, helped me through some difficult situations. At first, he offered answers freely—said he wanted Materall to lose, never explained why. I didn't question it. But after Materall's defeat, the answers started coming with a cost I didn't understand..."

Avery paused, gathering his thoughts before continuing. "There's a part of Shadow-Lord's story he got right... and I hate to admit it. Marion did die because of me. When the Keeper of Forbidden Knowledge came to me and demanded I repay the debt I owed him, I reacted with arrogance. I thought that because I'd triumphed over so many great evils, he posed no threat to me. I told him I owed him nothing, and he couldn't harm me. He agreed. He left, and I thought that was the end of it... but the truth of Marion's death is this: Korvas killed her at the peace talks she and your mother had worked so hard to establish between the Rau-Trava and Wethen. But there's more to it..."

Avery paused again, before speaking in a more somber tone. "Korvas learned that the death of the previous leader of the Rau-Trava, his father, was caused by assassins from Wethen. He knew it had been one of the two diplomats at the meeting..."

Alan interrupted, his eyes wide with disbelief. "Wait... so Marion killed Korvas's father?"

Avery shook his head. "No. I said one of the diplomats from Wethen. But that... that's not my story to tell."

Alan's jaw dropped as he processed the weight of the revelation. "Are you sayin g...?"

The wizard raised his hand. "As I said, it's not my story. All I'll say is, I knew Daghlesh must have been the one who told Korvas. He kept the true identity of the assassin hidden, knowing Korvas would assume it wasn't Madeline, given her background with the Kalko. Daghlesh did this because I slighted him. And now you must understand... the answers he gives you are the truth, but the truth always comes with a price. Forbidden knowledge, learning the future, uncovering secrets through unnatural means—it's a dangerous thing. Promise me, Alan, that no matter how tempting, the next time he speaks to you offering answers, you'll refuse him. You have so much more to lose than I did... You have your father, your mother, Abigail, Mei, Tadashi... Cinder—"

Alan raised an eyebrow and cut Avery off, his voice strained. "Cin—Cinder? What? I don't know what you're talking about, Avery. I don't want to be tangled up in that relationship stuff..."

Despite Alan's best efforts, his words were hollow, and Avery's surprised expression didn't help.

Avery raised an eyebrow. "Alan, I never said anything about a relationship. I was listing your friends. You cut me off before I could even say Elis—Wait, hold up. Do you have... romantic feelings for Cinder?"

Alan looked around, avoiding eye contact. "I don't know... maybe. Look, that's not important right now. Let's get back to you warning me about Daghlesh."

Avery chuckled, giving Alan a moment of peace before returning to the serious nature of their conversation. He gave Alan a smile, then spoke urgently. "Just promise me, Alan, you'll resist the temptation. Now, tell me what else he said."

"I promise... I won't let him trick me. No matter how much we might need his help in the future... But, if he tries to interfere again, couldn't he speak to Cinder? Elis? My mother even?"

Avery shook his head. "No, he can't communicate with anyone who hasn't practiced dark magic. Now, continue. What more did he tell you?"

"Well, first I asked where Shadow-Lord and the others were, and he told me they're passing through the mountain east of us. After that, he started giving me information without it counting toward my two remaining questions. The biggest takeaway was that Abigail has some sort of dark magic creature inside of her, making her more susceptible to Marik's influence. Mei and Tadashi don't have one, though. You already know about the Mist Monster being Shadow-Lord's familiar. The final question I asked... was the most jarring. He told me the Forgotten Lands aren't dying. It's part of the transformation Materall started in Ancient Arkarnia. Materall was trying to change the western continent to accommodate the Ak'spir. He wanted to bring them here to help him subjugate the east. I imagine Whenua would have been only the beginning... Daghlesh said he wants us to defeat Marik because if Marik completes Materall's goals, Daghlesh will lose control of the Ak'spir."

Avery took it well at first, but then his face darkened, and his eyes widened. Alan could tell it took a moment for the full weight of the information to sink in, just as it had for him.

"That explains why he helped me defeat Materall... Perhaps that's for the best. According to legend, Daghlesh keeps the Ak'spir in line... As for Abigail, well... Let me think. The best way to remove the ctotles from Abigail is for you to talk to her. This sort of creature can be fought by the person it's within, and once they're aware of it, they can force it to leave. It may be difficult to get her to listen, but Abigail is strong and brave, just like you, Alan. She can overcome it. I'm sure of that. As for..."

Avery fell silent, his gaze drifting as he leaned against the canopy wall, sliding down to the ground. "With what we now know about the true fate of the world, the weight of this situation feels heavier than ever. Our mission remains unchanged—we must get Morimor's Orb. After that, we'll have to find where my mother took the other Orb."

Alan sat down beside him. "Don't worry. No matter how heavy this gets, we're all here to help hold it up. Me, Mom, Cinder, Elis..."

Then he smiled and added with a joke, "Mostly, Mom will carry the weight. It still amazes me that she used to be a mercenary. But it's undeniable when I see her fight. All those times when I was little and she said she'd protect me from the monster under my bed—I never imagined she could mop the floor with that monster. Speaking of which, she still needs to finish telling me the story of her past. You know, the one you implied earlier."

Avery smiled. "Now's probably a good time to talk. Go ahead and speak to her. But let's keep the gravity of this situation between us, for now."

Alan nodded. "Are you going to be okay?"

Avery patted him on the back. "I'll manage. I just need a few minutes to gather myself. Go on now."

With that, Alan stood up and walked away to find his mother, leaving Avery to silently curse his brother for his misdeeds.

***

As Alan approached Madeline, he felt conflicted about withholding the information he'd learned, but he agreed with Avery—there was no need to add more concern to her already heavy burden. Daghlesh's words would only worsen her worries, and keeping quiet seemed like the better choice for now.

"So, Mom, after you met Dad and Alfonse, what happened?" he asked, trying to steer the conversation into lighter territory.

Madeline smiled. "Well, we took an extremely awkward wagon ride. It was awkward because, as I mentioned, your father wasn't my biggest fan at the time, so it was mostly silent. We traveled to a human village near the Rau-Trava encampment. The people there were incredibly stubborn and had fiercely opposed moving away from their ancestral homeland for years. But with anti-human sentiment growing among the Rau-Trava, the younger villagers had become more open to leaving. That was when I first exercised my diplomacy skills—something I didn't even know I had back then. I assured most of them to do what was right for their families. Sadly, not all of them were convinced, but I've long since made my peace with it. There was no changing the minds of those who remained, and they eventually died when the Rau-Trava launched full-scale assaults on every unguarded human settlement they could find. After we sent the villagers away to Wethen, we headed for the Rau-Trava encampment."

Madeline paused for a moment, remembering. "Eshe had a plan to sneak in at night and kill the chief while he slept. But, as you might imagine from our recent river escapades, sneaking around Arkarnian warriors in the dark didn't go well. We ended up in an all-out fight. By the end of it, I had earned your father's respect, and no Arkarnian walked out of that camp alive. With no witnesses, no one knew the Rau-Trava Chief's death had been carried out by Wethen. Korvas must have figured it out because when he became chief, he focused most of the Rau-Trava's aggression on Wethen. But instead of targeting Wethen's leaders like his predecessor, he took it out on innocent people. In a way, avenging the Queen only made things more difficult, but with people like Marik walking around, it was probably only a matter of time before things went south."

Alan patted her on the shoulder. "Don't dwell on what could have been, Mom. It's not a good path to go down."

Madeline smiled and hugged him, then shifted to a lighter topic. "Trust me, I learned that lesson the hard way. Still, when a thought enters your mind, it's hard to control it—kind of like your father after he's had one too many drinks. He becomes even more stubborn than the vines we encountered. Eshe and I once had to coax him out of the castle kitchen after he locked himself inside to eat all the sweet rolls made for one of Alfonse's charity dinners."

Alan laughed. "How many did he end up eating?"

Madeline chuckled. "Well, let's just say the chefs worked overtime that day. Your father was banned from touching any of Alfonse's private wine reserves after that. He was also banned from buying alcohol from any inns or taverns in Wethen. Alfonse had been in a grumpy mood all week, so he made a new law just for your father. It only lasted a few months before Alfonse finally forgave him."

Madeline sighed happily. "I hope one day you can make memories like those here—ones that aren't weighed down by all this trouble."

Alan nodded. "Don't worry, Mom. I'm not so sure I'll be leaving Whenua when all is said and done. At first, I thought it'd be nice to go home once we got Abigail, Mei, and Tadashi back. But even with how tough it's been, I like it here. This world has its problems, sure, but so does Earth. And, well, I've got a lot of reasons to stay—like you, Dad, Avery, my grandparents who I haven't met yet—"

Madeline cut him off with a wink. "And don't forget Cinder."

Alan's left eye twitched. "Wh-what? What's with everyone? First Marik, then Avery, and now you—suggesting I've got a crush on Cinder just because we've had a few heartfelt conversations. I mean, come on, we haven't known each other that long."

Madeline smiled, finding it adorable how easily her son could get flustered. "I never said anything about a crush. Besides, your father and I started dating only a few days after our first quest together. But since we're on the topic, I take it you've reconciled your differences with Cinder, seeing how comfortable you've both been with each other lately?"

Alan reluctantly nodded. "Yeah, it wasn't that hard once I asked her what her issue with me was."

Madeline raised an eyebrow. "You know, Alan, I could give you some advice on what to look out for—subtle signs a girl might give when she's interested in you."

Alan struggled to think of something else to say, increasingly uncomfortable with where the conversation was going. But before he could find his words, the boat suddenly shook violently. Without warning, a massive crab claw burst through the hull, then retreated back into the water, leaving a hole the size of a watermelon.

Alan watched as Elis jumped down in front of the hole, pulled off one of his boots, and jammed it into the opening, trying to stop the water from flooding the ship.

The crew stood in silence as the shaking subsided. Alan unsheathed his sword and approached Elis. "I don't think your boot is a suitable plug," he said dryly.

Elis shrugged and smiled. "I don't know. I'm not exactly a shipwrite, you know?"

Suddenly, giant crabs began crawling over the side of the boat, snapping their claws at anyone within reach. Cinder shouted several colorful curses as she struck at the crabs with flames and her dagger. Alan rushed to her side and covered her back.

"Could be worse!" Alan yelled, slashing at the creatures. "Could be giant spiders! Avery's cell back near Darkspire had a bunch of spiders guarding it. I'd be losing it right now if monster spiders were swarming the deck."

Avery spoke up. "Ah yes, there are many giant spider species around the world, though none are naturally native to this continent. Most are found in the East, so Marik must have imported them to use in his prison."

Alan groaned, the unsettling images of the blind spiders flashing through his mind. "How common are they in the East?"

Elis kicked a crab onto its back and stabbed it in the soft belly. "I don't do too well around spiders, either, Alan. They creep me out!"

Cinder chuckled. "All bugs creep you out, Elis. I saw you freak out that one time when an airhopper landed on your shoulder—"

Elis stabbed another crab. "Oh yeah? What about when you got scared by a chair?"

Alan paused mid-swing, his confusion evident. "Wait! What?"

Cinder groaned. "It was one time! I thought a chair was a person because the cushion looked like one, and I jumped back thinking someone was about to ambush me!"

Alan killed another crab, slightly larger than the rest, in tandem with Elis. "I get it. I was in Avery's basement once and saw a chair that scared me."

Avery chuckled as he used wind magic to push a group of crabs overboard, clearing the area around one of the oarsmen. "The green one?"

"Yup!" Alan grinned, bringing his sword down into another crab. "Yikes! These things are annoying!"

"Agreed!" Sobek yelled as he and Okama picked up a large crab by its arms and hurled it overboard.

Alan was making his way toward Truvik when the largest of the crabs suddenly appeared, grabbing Truvik with its massive claw and snapping him in half. Blood splattered onto Alan as he quickly backed away, horrified. Truvik's screams were soon drowned by the loud, thunderous chittering of the giant beast. It turned and scuttled sideways toward the cloth-covered windows, then leapt through the next one, barreling through the ship. Alan reacted instinctively, positioning himself under the crab and stabbing upward into its belly. His blade tore through its chitin, causing the creature to shriek violently.

Cinder and Elis rushed toward the sounds of Truvik's screams and the crab's furious chittering. Cinder blasted the beast's mandibles with flames, while Elis grabbed a spare oar and threw it like a spear into the crab's open mouth. The oar lodged in its throat, leaving the creature's mouth wide open. Cinder sent more flames into its maw, burning the vital organs inside.

The crab smacked the canopy, forcing itself off the boat and back into the water. As it fell, the remaining crabs swarming the oarsmen and crew dove into the sea, sensing the weakness of the larger one. They knew there was a much larger, defense-less meal waiting for them.

Madeline and Avery exchanged a glance, both sighing with relief as the oarsmen hurriedly got the ship moving again, putting distance between them and the danger.

Alan retrieved a folded-up tarp from beneath the damaged canopy and moved toward Truvik's remains. Captain Yarba knelt beside the body, closing Truvik's eyes with a solemn sigh as Alan gently covered the blood-soaked remains. "He didn't deserve such a horrendous fate," the captain muttered.

Alan nodded in agreement. "Few people do... I'm so sorry. I should have been here to defend him."

The captain raised his hand. "Don't blame yourself. We had more warriors aboard than we did previously. You weren't expected to defend him. The blame is mine for not ensuring we were alert. I made the mistake of assuming the crabs would be dormant at this time, so I didn't have us ready."

Alan took the captain's words to heart. His guilt eased somewhat, but as he remembered Daghlesh's advice about the giant crabs, he couldn't help but feel bad for not mentioning it earlier. He pushed the thought aside, though, doubting it would have made much of a difference. Still, he was horrified by Truvik's gruesome end. Leaving the captain to mourn his lost crewman in solitude, Alan silently made his way to the bow, lost in thought.

Despite the harrowing experience, Alan felt a sense of ease as he sat on the edge of the boat, letting out a long, tired sigh. The burdens that had weighed on him seemed to slip away as the end of their river journey came into sight. However, that relief was short-lived, quickly replaced by the worries of what lay ahead. They would soon have to confront Marik's Mist Monster, and they were about to enter a hostile arctic environment.

Up until now, many of the biomes—aside from the Shadow-Lands—had been familiar to Alan, landscapes he'd seen and experienced on Earth. But now, they were headed toward a desolate expanse of snow and ice, inhabited by a group of arkarnians who thrived in brutal savagery, worshiping the very dark entity who had given Alan so much insight. He wished he had known about the connection between the Valthurg and Daghlesh before their encounter; if he had, perhaps he could have asked how to prevent the arkarnians from attacking.

However, those thoughts didn't linger long. Deep down, Alan knew that even the answers Daghlesh had given him came at a cost—the temptation to ask for more. He knew that if he spoke the eldritch being's preferred name, Daghlesh would appear and offer him solutions to any question he could ask. But that path, Alan realized, would be wrong. He couldn't take the easy way out. None of the heroes he admired—whether from history or the stories he cherished—had ever taken shortcuts. They had endured long, difficult journeys, and by the end, they had preserved their humanity, regardless of the sacrifices.

But that was the problem. Alan couldn't imagine sacrificing anyone he loved—his sister, Mei, Tadashi, his mother, or Cinder—for the greater good. He wasn't that type of hero. If being a hero meant losing those he cared about, instead of sacrificing himself first, then he didn't want to be one at all.

He buried his face in his hands, realizing he was overthinking again. Daghlesh had already told him there was a chance to get Abigail, Mei, and Tadashi back from Shadow-Lord, but that didn't stop the endless cycle of doubt and worry. He was tired of this mental loop, wishing he could break free from it.

As he sat there, reflecting, he realized that when he was with others, he could stay focused and confident. But alone, with no one to help ground him, his mind drifted to the subconscious guilt he carried—guilt for leaving his sister and friends with Shadow-Lord, for killing Okama's father with dark magic, and for allowing Shadow-Lord to enter his mind so freely.

Before he could contemplate further, Avery approached. "We're only a mile away from where we'll disembark and begin our walk to Kurlo Pass," he said, pausing for a moment before continuing. "Remember, we'll need to lay a trap for the Mist Monster before we reach the trading post in Kurlo Pass."

"I have a plan to draw it out," Alan replied. "Instead of focusing on all of us, it seems to be following you and your mother. At least, that's what Elis and Cinder told us from their brief encounter. Given how far Marik is from his familiar, I doubt even he could keep the creature focused on anything other than one or two people."

"Exactly," Avery said. "So you, Elis, Cinder, and your mother will continue on with Silvanus, Sobek, and Baldric, while I'll remain in hiding with Okama and her warriors. We'll wait for the Mist to come through, and then we'll attack."

Alan narrowed his eyes, his concern evident. "I want to be there to help fight that thing. No way am I leaving you to face it alone."

Avery chuckled and sat down next to him, throwing an arm around his shoulder. "Do you forget that I'm not just some college professor? I'm a very accomplished wizard. I'll be fine, Alan. Look, if you're worried because of how Marik captured me before our meeting in that damp old prison, I'll tell you this: the only reason he succeeded then was because he had the element of surprise. This time, I have the elements on my side. The shadow beast can't command anything but the power that gave it life."

Alan nodded. "I know you can handle it. I just don't want to feel left out. That thing nearly gave me a heart attack back in the Shadow-Lands—not once, but twice. It's personal now."

Avery smiled and got to his feet. "Then I'll be sure to let it know you're very cross with it before its destruction."

With that, Avery walked off to inform the others of the plan, leaving Alan alone with his thoughts. His mind briefly wandered to memories of Avery from back on Earth—when he was just a neighbor and occasional babysitter. Those simpler, happier times helped ease the tension in his mind, clearing away any lingering worries.

CHAPTER THIRTY-FIVE

Voices of Fear

As they walked through the old corridor, an eerie feeling began to settle over them—an inescapable, inexplicable dread. While the morgs and Marik seemed mostly unaffected, Abigail looked at everyone with a furrowed brow, Tadashi's eyes wide with panic, and Mei wore a face of concern as they descended deeper into the dark tunnel.

Marik walked up beside Tadashi but spoke for everyone to hear. "Steel yourselves. That feeling you all have... it won't improve by feeding it. There is a strong magical aura here. The residual effects of the rituals have had more of an impact than I feared. I can only imagine the horror gripping you at this moment. My armor shields me from the mind-altering magic, but you do not have that luxury. I'll need to do something else to protect your minds."

Tadashi turned to Marik, his voice tense. "Where did you get that armor, anyway?"

Marik chuckled. "The mask came from a very good friend of mine—one who guided me during a dark period of my life. As for the rest of the armor, it has a similar tale. It was gifted to me."

He continued, "When it became clear that my body was being ravaged by dark magic after my brief entanglement with it, I went to Skatchator, following the trail of an old folktale. Sure enough, it was true. There is a secretive group of shadow magic-wielders living there. They took me in and helped me hone my abilities. But my body was still suffering from the dark magic, so they led me to a blacksmith in a remote village within the Skatchator mountain ranges. He forged this armor from a special ore unique to that region. The rare properties of the metal shield me from anyone using dark magic against me and prevent my body from being disabled by the magic still within me. Now, it will allow me to use dark magic to protect your minds without harming me... I promised myself I'd never do it again..."

Marik smiled beneath his helmet, knowing they believed his words—his feigned oath of repentance, the idea of turning from dark magic. "But you are all too important to me to risk your minds being broken by this place. Worry not. This spell will not affect your bodies. It will only shield your minds."

They nodded in agreement, accepting Marik's decision. With a sigh, he raised his palms, hands open toward the ceiling. "Shlaka Denk Moika Denmi Sula!" he chanted. As he spoke the incantation, red rotating circles and glyphs appeared over their foreheads, fading as Marik lowered his hands.

"It is done. The protection spell should last for some time," he said, feigning weakness and stumbling, bracing himself against the wall. Abigail rushed to him, supporting his arm around her shoulder.

"Thank you, Abigail. I'll be fine. Let's continue on," Marik said, and the group pressed forward.

Just as Marik had promised, the suffocating dread lifted as they continued deeper into the complex.

Eventually, they arrived at a large intersection of hallways, where an altar adorned with sinister symbols and statues loomed. As they drew closer, they noticed faded patches of dried blood on the floor—red, green (arkarnian blood), and purple (myklin blood), the latter making Abigail's stomach churn.

The fact that these bloodstains remained visible after so long could either be a grim testament to the many lives lost there or a chilling warning that dark, ritualistic sacrifices were still being carried out deep within the cathedral. Distant voices echoed in the still air, but with so many adjacent hallways, it was impossible to tell from which direction the sounds came.

Marik gestured for them to follow quietly as he moved toward the northernmost hallway—a path whose floor was coated in the same dried blood that had once soaked the altar, alongside discarded bones of varying shapes and sizes.

Tadashi couldn't help but find a dark humor in the situation. If Marik hadn't cast that protection spell, they would likely be losing their minds with fear at this point, considering how unnerving the gruesome scene of ancient murder was.

The hallway led them to a wide stone walkway, suspended across a vast chasm on either side. Whatever purpose the builders had for leaving such an area of the deep underground cave system exposed—rather than walling it off—had been long forgotten.

Abigail stepped toward the edge and looked down. "Whoa... that's scary."

Mei grabbed her arm and yanked her back. "Careful!"

Abigail sighed. "Relax, Mei. I'm not trying to dive into the dark abyss."

Marik glanced back at them and grunted. "Mei's right to be concerned. There's no telling what might be staring up at a person when they gaze down into that vast sea of nothingness."

As if on cue with Marik's words, a cacophony of deafening sounds erupted from the depths below. "We should cross as quickly as possible. Stay to the center and be safe."

Once they reached the other side, the sounds abruptly stopped, as though it had been a warning they were trespassing.

Now that the group no longer feared the chasm below, they noticed ancient carvings on the walls. Marik studied the images, trying to decipher their meaning. "I believe what we're looking at is a diagram of the cult that lived here. This particular image is one I've seen before, back when I read some archaic texts on dark magic. If I'm correct, this pattern of lines and spheres depicts sacrifices. While this could be an educational glimpse into the past, we need to move faster or Avery will beat us to the Shrine of Morimor."

As they continued, the images on the walls became more visceral. The acts of violence portrayed grew harder to look at, and the explicit nature of it all made them increasingly uncomfortable.

"I don't like these pictures, Boss..." said Yerk, shielding his eyes to avoid the gruesome carvings.

Marik sighed. "Just do as I am. Keep your eyes ahead. Don't glance at the pictures."

Everyone followed Marik's advice—everyone except Abigail. She stopped walking, transfixed by one of the images. It wasn't the nearby depictions of people impaled on stone slabs that held her attention. It was the swirling coil carved into the wall above the bloody bodies. The coil was painted purple, speckled with black flecks, and at its center was an unusual skull embedded in the wall. It wasn't human nor animal.

Abigail turned to ask Marik what he thought of the skull, but when she looked around, she realized she was alone. The voices she had been hearing behind her weren't from the group; they were coming from the direction of the chasm. A feeling of isolation and vulnerability crept over her. She quickly abandoned her thoughts and hurried to catch up with the others.

Marik, who had been leading the group through the corridor, suddenly stopped and called out. "We have a decision to make. Should we go right, left, or continue straight ahead?"

The Morgs, not ones to make decisions for themselves, remained silent. Mei, who had been trying to track their position, spoke up. "We should go left."

Tadashi, eager to support his sister, chimed in, "Ditto."

Marik looked beyond the Morgs, Mei, and Tadashi, realizing Abigail was missing. "Where's Abigail? When did any of you last see her?"

Glum looked down, clearly guilty. "She was your responsibility."

Just as Marik's frustration began to show, Abigail walked up, calling out, "Sorry, everyone. I got caught up looking at something on a—"

Marik cut her off. "I thought I made myself clear. Avoid the images and stay together. This is no place to get lost. What if we'd gone past this intersection? You'd have had no idea where we were. Now, come up here and walk with me, so I can make sure you don't get distracted again."

Glum, feeling bad for not noticing, apologized to both Marik and Abigail. "Sorry. I not watch better."

Marik stared at him, but Abigail quickly reassured him. "It's not your fault. It's mine." Glum seemed comforted by her words.

The group followed Mei's suggestion and turned left. The path led them to the beginning of an aqueduct. Marik stopped and said, "We either turn back or walk through the remnants of water still flowing in this channel. We'll need to watch our footing so we don't slip."

Tadashi, looking at the shallow water and its flow, asked, "Why don't we just sit down and let the water do the work? It'd be like a really fun waterslide."

Marik shook his head. "If we let gravity take us, we could end up in a discharge pipe. And I, for one, don't want to get stuck in a pipe. By walking, we'll be sure to exit on the other end—if you all agree to continue this way."

The aqueduct stretched on for what seemed like forever. It wasn't a straight shot but filled with twists and turns. Thankfully, the water wasn't at full capacity; if it had been, they would never have made it across.

This time, Marik took up the rear, leaving Mei to lead the group through the water, with Gorb right behind her. When they first entered the aqueduct, the water was level with the ground, but now the earth below them had opened up into another chasm. The fear of being so high with little protection from the low walls on either side was chilling.

Mei paused for a moment before continuing, prompting another outburst from Marik. "DO NOT STOP! Shake off your fear, look straight ahead, and move!"

Gorb placed a hand on Mei's shoulder, offering support. "Boss being mean. He don't understand fear like we do."

Mei gave him an understanding smile. "Thank you, Gorb. Let's keep moving."

An hour later, they reached the end of the aqueduct. Mei realized why using it as a slide would have been a very bad idea—she had to grab onto an exit ladder or risk being swept into a pipe just two feet wide.

Once everyone had safely exited the aqueduct, Marik moved to lead the group. The aqueduct had brought them to a dark passage, and Marik used fire magic to light the way.

"Hey, Marik, you can use my light stone if you want," Tadashi called out.

Marik didn't even acknowledge him, his frustration mounting. He couldn't tell if they were ahead or behind Avery. He needed to get to a safe area within the Abyssal Cathedral so Abigail could rest and enter her brother's thoughts again.

The walkway stretched on for what seemed like forever. They could see other covered passages through cracks in the walls, dimly lit by what might have been torches. Marik's agitation grew as they moved forward. Abigail and Mei chalked it up to his fear of what might lie ahead, but Tadashi's anger began to build as well, especially after Marik's outbursts toward Mei.

Regret and contempt stirred in Tadashi's chest. He couldn't shake the feeling that he had been wrong to trust Marik, that Abigail had led them down the wrong path. "His name is the Shadow-Lord, for crying out loud!" he thought bitterly as they continued down the passage.

He felt sick to his stomach. Not long ago, he had regarded Abigail as one of his closest friends, but now, he could barely bring himself to look at her. He couldn't tolerate Marik's verbal abuse any longer—it wouldn't be long before he snapped. He began to question whether the Morgs were following Marik out of kindness or fear. Perhaps every act of kindness from Marik had been manipulation, a twisted game. He wanted to blame the voice in his head on the dark spirits of the Abyssal

Cathedral, trying to turn him against Marik. But deep down, he knew the voice was his own.

Meanwhile, Marik's frustration clouded his awareness, blinding him to Tadashi's growing ill will. Normally, when he sensed one of the three questioning their situation, he'd act quickly—speak with them, be kind, reassure them, and stop them from overthinking. But now, he was unaware that Tadashi had begun to see through the web of deception that Marik had so carefully woven around them. All that occupied Marik's thoughts at that moment was meditating to check on his Mist's progress in following Alan and Avery, to determine how far they were from the Polar Regions. After that, he planned to use Abigail to enter Alan's mind and slow them down.

Eventually, they reached an overlook, and from there, they could see a vast expanse of chasms, stone structures, aqueducts, and more tunnels.

Marik sank to his knees and pointed to a doorway. "You all go ahead and make camp. If you encounter a fork in the road, mark the path with an arrow. I need a moment to center myself... this place is... affecting me more than I'd care to admit. I just need to be alone right now..."

Tadashi narrowed his eyes at Marik, thinking, There he goes again. I bet Abigail is eating that excuse up...

But Tadashi kept his thoughts to himself. He didn't want to cause a rift between them—not while they were still down here. For now, Marik would still be useful to him, and Tadashi would try to play him the way the Shadow-Lord had been playing them.

Abigail placed a hand on Marik's shoulder. "Be careful... don't get too close to the edge. If you fall from here, it looks like you might fall for hours..."

Marik nodded. "Don't worry, but thank you for your concern. I'm sorry for my outbursts lately... the magic of this place is just... hard to deal with."

With that, they left Marik alone and continued onward to set up camp.

Marik remained still, his eyes lingering long after they had left. The feeling of being watched had returned, but this time, he refused to let it affect him. He closed his eyes and began to meditate, focusing as he established the spiritual link between himself and his familiar.

Chapter Thirty-Six

The Trap

Everyone watched as the remaining crew tied the boat to the wooden dock. The time to say farewell to Captain Yorba had come. Yorba smiled at them as they gathered near the wooden ramp the crew had laid out for disembarking.

"While the loss of Truvik is bitter, I wouldn't change the events of the past few days if I had the power to do so," he said. "I'm grateful to have met you all. Long ago, I saw things that made me lose faith in a future where Wethen might treat Arkarnians and other nonhumans with dignity and respect. But today, you've shown me that cooperation, understanding, and even brotherhood are always possible when we're faced with overwhelming odds that threaten not just one race, but all races. Every one of you is a capable warrior, and a pleasure to be around. I speak not only for myself but for my crew when I say we'll search for a new river to travel, one where we can offer supplies to humans displaced by the brutality of Korvas and the Rau-Trava. We'll offer our modest skills with weapons to help defend them, and contribute to easing the tension between our peoples. Farewell, and may the Four Spirits watch over you and guide you."

"Thank you all," Avery said, his voice steady. "Without this ship and crew, we couldn't have made it this far. When our quest is over and we return to Wethen, I'll ensure that word is spread of the heroic Captain Yorba and his fine sailors. My father and everyone else will see that the only way to stand against true evil is to remain united, not divided."

With that, Yorba approached Elis and placed his forehead against hers. "May the spirit of life watch over you."

Avery then led the others off the boat. Everyone, including the Boh-Rahl Warriors, sighed with relief as they felt solid ground beneath their feet. Cinder smiled as she helped Okama steady herself.

"I take it your tribe doesn't use boats often?" she asked.

Okama shook her head. "No... it took a great deal of willpower to stop myself from Ilklakee..."

Sobek chimed in, "She means vomiting."

Cinder chuckled. "Good job! I remember the first time I was on a boat. Avery was taking me to visit the home of the Mystic Masters, and I was sick for days, even after we got off the boat."

Avery smiled, reminiscing. "Yes, however, as you heaved, you sent out a powerful burst of air that hit one of the keep's resident monks so hard, he broke his oath of silence. It was this feat that helped me convince the council to allow me to take you on as my student."

Cinder's face turned a little red, hoping to leave that part out, but she brushed it off. It was a fond memory, albeit somewhat embarrassing.

As they reached the entrance to a forested area, Avery stopped. "This is where we must split up for a time," he said, walking toward Okama and her warriors. "If you don't wish to do this, continue onward with the others. I can handle it if you'd prefer not to endanger yourselves against this monster."

Okama and the other Arkarnians stood firm, hands resting on their weapons as they nodded. "We'll stay behind with you, Avery. Together, we'll silence this instrument of darkness."

Avery turned to Madeline and Silvyn. "We'll meet you at Kurlo Pass."

Madeline spoke in a lowered voice, so Alan and Cinder wouldn't hear. "And what if you don't?"

Avery gave her a warm smile. "Then you'll keep going. I'm not the glue that holds us together. What binds us all is our desire to protect this wondrous world. Should anything happen to me, I have no doubt you'll succeed."

Madeline, Alan, Cinder, and Elis all hugged Avery goodbye, each silently wondering if they would see him again. Baldric, Sobek, and Silvyn merely nodded at Avery before stepping back and walking away.

Alan and the others exchanged glances as they left Avery, Okama, and the Boh-Rahl warriors behind. There was little any of them could have said to convince Avery there was another way. They knew his plan was sound. Alan just hoped Avery was right about the Mist's abilities being watered down in comparison to its better half.

Avery watched as the others walked away. He knew how hard it was for Alan to listen to him at that moment, and he worried that denying Alan the chance to confront the avatar of the man responsible for so many of his hardships would make the inevitable confrontation between Alan and Marik all the more fierce.

They went over the plan while they waited. Okama suggested they hide in the treeline and wait for the Mist's approach. Avery agreed but told them to wait for his signal before revealing themselves. He had never faced a creature like the Mist before and didn't know what to expect. But based on what Alan, Cinder, and Elis had said about their previous encounters, he had a feeling that the best course of action would be to execute the first series of attacks alone, without the Boh-Rahl warriors. He needed to determine which of his spells could render it vulnerable to physical attacks. Given that the Mist was surrounded by a shroud of smoke-like shadow, he doubted any of their weapons would have any effect.

Once the plan was solidified, Avery and Okama perched in a tree, waiting for any sign of the Mist. Eventually, the air grew still, and an aura of dread filled the space around them.

"It nears us..." Avery said quietly.

He closed his eyes, listening for its steps. He had expected something thunderous and earth-shaking, but instead, it was a slow, quiet, almost imperceptible sound. Had it not been for the crunch of leaves and twigs beneath it, he would never have heard it approach.

Avery saw wispy shadows bleed off the evil entity as it passed beneath the tree he was perched in. He dropped behind it, slowing his descent with air magic.

"Go no further, you heartless spawn of darkness," Avery called out.

The Mist turned to face him, its bright red eyes narrowing as its piercing gaze intensified upon him. "Uncle... Where is the boy? Why is Alan Elwyn not with you?"

Avery took a step back, surprised it recognized him as "Uncle." He hadn't expected that. "Alan is far from here. By now, they've already reached the Shrine of Morimor... you and your master have failed." He knew it was risky to give the Shadow-Lord an edge, in case it could sense what his familiar saw or heard. It was better to make his nephew believe his defeat was inevitable. "I've been waiting for your arrival... I sensed your presence some time ago, before we left the Dinalo's gated community."

The Mist smiled. "You lie. I was watching your river escapades from a safe distance. There is no way the boy has made such progress... unless he's grown wings and learned to fly. This is truly desperate, even for such a tired old man..."

Avery felt Marik's hatred in the Mist's words. He needed to reach out to his nephew, to stop everything if he could only pierce through his hatred and find the light he believed still hid somewhere in his dark soul.

"Marik... if you can hear me... please don't do this. It's not too late. The Mystic Masters can help you. I can help you. I'm sorry I didn't learn of your existence sooner. I know you blame me for the abuse you and your mother suffered because of your father... but I refuse to give up on you."

The Mist snarled. "Fool! You only learned of my existence because I permitted it! You were nothing but a stepping stone in my plans. You dare say you won't give up on me, but I know who you really are. We both know that once your daughter and grandchildren hear you saved the world from the evil Shadow-Lord, they'll welcome you back with open arms, and you will abandon your nephew and your surrogate family. Abigail, Mei, and Tadashi are better off with me... It's such a shame Alan is too stubborn to relinquish his trust in you. By the end of this, I will become what my grandfather intended—and so much more. But enough of that. Now that you've derailed my plans, I'll take more drastic measures to secure Abigail, Mei, and Tadashi's allegiance. Instead of letting the Mist kill Alan and fade into your body, I'll have it fade into Madeline... I only hope the emotional impact of her believing she killed Alan doesn't break poor Abigail. Now, it's time for you to die, Uncle Avery... and fade into the annals of history."

Avery shook his head. "We all fade in time, Marik. I predict an era will come when the events of this age are nothing but legends and myths. And considering how poorly people remember Matteral, I doubt you'll even be a footnote. In this world, heroes will always be memorialized. If you won't turn to the light for family... maybe one day you'll choose it for your vanity."

Avery stepped forward and shot a beam of ice at the Mist from his staff. The creature moved aside, narrowly avoiding the cold blast as it sliced through the air.

The Mist moved toward Avery quickly, faster than a charging bull. Avery slammed his staff into the ground, conjuring a thick ramp of ice between them. The Mist couldn't move in time and was sent sliding into the air, leaving it vulnerable. Avery used air magic to slam the Mist back down onto the ice ramp, shattering the ice and creating a small crater. For a moment, Avery couldn't see the creature.

But then, the Mist leaped from the crater, charging straight for him. It lashed out with massive claws, ripping through his cloak and leaving four deep gashes across his chest. Avery cried out in agony as he was thrown backward by the force of the attack.

He lay motionless for a moment as the Mist circled him, like a vulture stalking the scent of death.

Slowly, Avery lifted his head and saw his staff nearby. If the Mist charged, he wouldn't be fast enough to grab it before it was on top of him again.

Instead, he waited, his mind racing as he considered his next move. The Mist's speed had prevented him from hitting it with a spell from a distance. He needed something quick, something he could conjure with his hands when the Mist was too close to dodge. The list of viable options was short—at least for the spells he thought could affect the creature.

The opposite of shadow magic was light magic, but that element was rare to master. Avery had failed to learn it in his youth, as neither his father nor mother could teach what they didn't know. The few wizards who specialized in light magic claimed it couldn't be taught—only learned by reflecting on one's soul.

Avery knew ice magic would have the greatest effect on the Mist, but without his staff, he couldn't conjure magic outside the four core elements. Then he had an idea. It was dangerous, but if it worked, it would stop the Mist in its tracks.

He placed his palms against the ground and willed the earth beneath him to rise. A pillar of dirt and stone shot up, lifting him high above the Mist. The pillar wobbled, unstable. As soon as Avery let go to stand, he felt it shake and begin to crumble. Quickly, he jumped off, using air magic to slow his descent as the pillar collapsed onto the Mist. Dirt and rock buried it for a few precious seconds, stunning it.

Avery grabbed his staff from the ground as the Mist roared in rage, bursting from the debris. It charged at him again, but this time, he remained patient. He waited for the perfect moment.

As the Mist leaped toward him, claws outstretched, Avery slammed the bottom of his staff into the ground to steady it. He conjured a beam of ice that struck the Mist in its torso, encasing it in a block of ice. The weight of the ice caused it to crash to the ground inches from Avery instead of landing on top of him.

Avery stepped back, watching as the Mist's eyes moved beneath the ice, still tracking him. But he waited, signaling to Okama and the warriors.

Just then, the ice began to crack. As the Mist struggled to break free, Avery walked backward, into the treeline where the Arkarnians were waiting.

The ice shattered, and the Mist broke free, charging toward him. As it passed under the tree, Avery yelled, "NOW!"

The arkarnians dropped onto the Mist's back. Avery's gamble had paid off. The warriors thrust their weapons into the creature's back, thick, oily blood spilling down its sides and dripping to the ground as it thrashed about, trying to throw off its attackers. In a desperate attempt, the Mist hurled itself at a tree, killing two of the warriors with the force of the impact. Another warrior was thrown off and impaled on a branch, but he survived, quickly cutting himself free.

Okama and the remaining warriors clung for dear life as the Mist roared, leaping and bucking like a bull. Through the chaos, Okama drove her sword deep into the Mist's neck.

Pain from the neck wound drove the Mist into a frenzy. It rolled onto the ground, crushing three of the arkarnians under its massive weight. Okama and four other warriors were thrown off and fell to the ground.

The Mist stood again, shifting form as it took ragged breaths. It grew bipedal, its claws lengthening, and with a violent swing, it cleaved one of the last arkarnians into six pieces. At that moment, Avery moved between the Mist and Okama's remaining warriors, now that the creature was no longer burdened by its riders. He was free to act.

Avery fired a ball of flame at the Mist's face. It ignited, and the creature's skin bubbled and melted away like tar, revealing a jagged, ramshackle skull. Enraged, the Mist swung its claws at Avery, missing by mere inches. He quickly retaliated with a beam of ice, striking the arm that had come at him. One of the arkarnians swung a warhammer, shattering the Mist's arm entirely, its body now showing signs of the toll the battle had taken.

The Mist, severely wounded, retreated toward a patch of dark shade. But Avery wasn't about to let it escape. He forced the earth and stone between them to rise, collapsing the ground around the Mist. However, manipulating the terrain came at a cost. Avery knew Earth Magic was volatile, and he feared his desperation would backfire.

As he pushed the land to work against the Mist, the ground shook violently, creating sinkholes and rising stone pillars. Earth Magic had its limits, and in this case, the landscape fought back.

Avery, Okama, and the remaining arkarnians rushed forward as the earth cracked beneath them. Using Air Magic, Avery pushed the warriors ahead, but when the ground beneath him gave out, he barely managed to catch a ledge with both hands, losing his staff in the chasm below. Okama and another warrior reached down and pulled him up just as the ledge crumbled.

Once the shaking ceased, they turned to survey the destruction they had wrought. What was once a lush, fertile landscape—full of beautiful trees and flowers—was now a chaotic scene of jagged stone columns, deep chasms, craters, broken trees, and trampled flowers.

The Mist was gone, leaving behind only a deep crevice. Avery exhaled deeply, regret heavy in his chest. So many of Okama's warriors had fallen, and he doubted the Mist had been destroyed for good. Still, he knew that, given the creature's injuries, it wouldn't survive another battle for quite some time. Hopefully, by then, they would have finished what they started.

Turning to Okama and the remaining three warriors, Avery spoke, his voice heavy with guilt. "I am... so sorry for what happened to your brothers and sisters... for the damage done to this land... your home. I fear that what's been done here can never fully heal."

Okama shook her head, her voice steady despite the loss. "They died as warriors. It was a good battle. As for the land, it will serve as a reminder of those who fought and died here. Come, we must reunite with the others."

Chapter Thirty-Seven

Lies and Remembrance

Tadashi grew impatient as he sat by the fire Gorb had made to keep them warm. The temperature in the Abyssal Ruins had dropped uncharacteristically cold, a stark contrast to the warmth of the underground areas they had passed through earlier. They assumed this sudden change was a side effect of the rituals.

Mei and Abigail chuckled as they reminisced about some of their oddest school experiences, but Tadashi could barely focus. He stood up abruptly and said, "I'm going to go look for Marik."

Mei shook her head. "Tadashi, he said he'd be a while. Just leave him be..."

"I'll be fine, Mei. I just... want to check on him, that's all. Look, if he's still meditating, I'll leave him alone and come back without saying a word, okay?"

Mei sighed. "Okay, just be careful, Tadashi."

Tadashi laughed, "Me?! Since when do I not take care?"

Mei and Abigail exchanged a knowing glance, then smiled back at Tadashi.

He waved them off, stepping back toward the path they had taken, heading toward the overlook where they had left Marik.

As he approached, he heard Marik's voice. Tadashi took a few more cautious steps, making sure to be as quiet as possible.

Peering around the corner, he saw Marik kneeling, muttering as he meditated. "By the end of this, I will become what my grandfather intended, and so much more. But enough of that. Now that you've derailed my plans, I'll have to take more drastic measures to ensure Abigail, Mei, and Tadashi's allegiance. Instead of the Mist killing Alan and fading into your body, so that all would believe it was you behind it, I will have it fade into Madeline. I can only hope the emotional toll of thinking her mother killed Alan doesn't break poor Abigail. Now, it's time for you to die, Uncle Avery, and fade into the annals of history…"

Tadashi froze behind a fallen pillar, his heart racing. Alan had been right. He'd gone to find Marik because something felt off, but this wasn't what he had expected.

As his mind raced, Tadashi noticed Marik's body convulsing violently, then collapsing into unconsciousness. Tadashi stepped forward, heart heavy. He had only one choice left. If he went back and tried to tell the girls, there was a fifty-fifty chance they would believe him. But he knew he could protect them this way.

He pulled out his knife and stared at it for a moment before glancing back at Marik. "It's him or us… just like with that Arkarnian. I have to do it…"

Kneeling beside Marik, Tadashi searched for a gap in his armor near the neck. But just as he was about to act, he froze. Yerk's voice echoed from behind him.

"What you doing, Tadashi?"

Tadashi stood quickly and turned to face Yerk. "I overheard Marik. He wants to kill Alan at the Polar Regions and blame his mother. He wants to do horrible things to this world… Did you know about this?"

Yerk's eyes widened. "I… no. Master want hurt Tadashi?"

Tadashi nodded slowly, feeling a sense of relief that the Morgs didn't know about Marik's plans. But he was still uncertain how Yerk would react.

"Marik no more my Master… Marik bad man…"

Tadashi smiled, but before he could act, Marik suddenly stood, glaring at them both. "I told you to make camp! Why are you here? And where are Abigail and Mei?"

Thinking fast, Tadashi replied, "I got worried. Yerk and I came looking for you to make sure you were okay. The girls are with Gorb and Glum at camp."

Yerk nodded in agreement. "Yeah, I glad Marik okay."

For a moment, Marik seemed to accept their explanation, but then he saw the knife in Tadashi's hand. Coupled with Yerk addressing him by name instead of "boss," it became clear he'd been found out.

Tadashi gasped as Marik grabbed him by the neck and lifted him over the abyss, a low, sadistic laugh escaping from under his mask.

"You know," Marik mused, "between you, Alan, and Uncle Avery... people really, really can't stop messing with my plans..." He sighed. "I'll admit, I do care about the three of you. I meant what I said about the world needing more people like you. But I'm a very, very bad man, and I learned long ago that friends either betray you or you betray them. But I respect that you were going to try and kill me while I was down. I never expected you to have the guts to try something like that. Or even consider it."

He paused, then added, "So, even knowing what you were planning... I can't bring myself to kill you. That's why the fall will do what I cannot."

As Marik prepared to throw Tadashi over the edge, Tadashi lunged forward, stabbing his knife into Marik's arm. The blade pierced through the armor, and as Marik released him, Tadashi caught the edge of the overlook. But his grip was slipping.

In a flash, Yerk dove to the ledge and grabbed Tadashi, pulling him back up just as the ground beneath them crumbled.

Tadashi shouted at Marik as Yerk helped him to his feet. "Everything you told us back at the Grotto was a lie, wasn't it? Avery didn't cause the death of my parents. Are they even dead? Or did your grandfather kill them? I promise you, your plans are ruined. The others will believe me over you."

But Tadashi never got the chance to finish his outburst. Marik ripped the knife out of his arm and hurled it over the edge. At that moment, Tadashi knew there was only one thing left to do. Marik kicked Yerk in the back, sending both him and Tadashi plummeting into the abyss.

Marik paused for a moment, listening to their screams echo before using Earth Magic to collapse the overlook. The cavern walls shook violently. Marik quickly turned and ran down the path marked out for him, reaching the makeshift camp where the girls and Morgs were already panicking.

He panted heavily, clutching his bleeding arm. "Tadashi and Yerk got cut off from me... Tadashi was injured by a falling rock. Yerk is going to travel day and night to get him back to the Gnoglins for medical attention... we have to get out of this passage... it's all coming down around us!"

Mei and Abigail exchanged worried glances, their concern for Tadashi's injuries evident. They scrambled to gather their things and began moving forward down the collapsing corridor.

The five of them sprinted through the path ahead as the ground shook and the walls crumbled behind them. Soon, they reached another aqueduct, this one sloping downward. Mei and Abigail froze, stopping just short of falling in. But Gorb, Glum, and Marik, running closely behind, collided with them, sending all of them sliding down the aqueduct, screaming. All except Marik, who shouted to Abigail, "Abigail! Use the water to slow our descent!"

Abigail struggled with the magic, even under such extreme pressure. It had been difficult enough learning magic under less stressful circumstances. But maybe, she thought, a life-or-death situation would help her learn better than her previous attempts. And it did. With great strain, she managed to conjure a ball of water around them, slowly turning their fall into a floating descent. Her arms trembled as she struggled to maintain control, her concentration faltering.

Finally, with a cry of effort, she let the ball of water dissipate, lowering them gently in front of a large wooden door. She collapsed onto the ground, breathing heavily. Marik knelt beside her, gently resting her head on his knee. "Good job... you did well... rest now... the tremors seem to have stopped... and this spot seems relatively safe. We'll make camp here."

Mei looked back to where they had come from. Glum placed a hand on her shoulder. "No worry, Mei. Yerk real good at running and carrying things. Tadashi be healed up in no time."

Mei nodded but couldn't hide her concern. "I know... but it just feels weird without him here with us. Just like it feels weird without Alan..."

Glum gave her a sad look. "That mean you got two bad feelings now. I sorry to hear that." He pulled her into a comforting hug.

She smiled weakly. "Thanks, Glum."

Mei sat down next to Abigail, leaning against the wall near the wooden door. "So... you must be really exhausted after all that."

Abigail nodded, her voice breathless. "Yeah... I wish I'd just passed out like when I brought that wall down. I don't think I've ever been this exhausted..."

Mei patted her on the shoulder. "Nonsense. Remember when we used to run track? You'd always fall asleep on the ride home because, even after everyone else had left the field, you'd challenge me to race five laps."

Abigail sighed. "You know I didn't have to challenge you... Sometimes I wonder if it was my ego... if I subconsciously hated that you were faster than me, hated that you always beat me and didn't seem exhausted. I think I'm a bad friend... a bad sister... I led you and Tadashi down this path. I should've let Alan go on his own." She stopped Mei from cutting her off. "No, Mei... I know what you're going to say. You're going to say the same thing you told me last time I started thinking this way..."

Mei chuckled softly. "Well, it's true. You aren't a bad friend. And wherever Alan is, I bet deep down he regrets leaving. He's probably having self-loathing thoughts just like you. I know you and Alan struggled before we were brought here. You'd hide it from everyone, maybe even from each other, trying to ignore it... but I could see it. And it was hard seeing it, knowing I couldn't do anything to help except be what I've always been—your friend."

Tears welled in Abigail's eyes as she threw her arms around Mei. "I never wanted to admit to anyone... even when I'm happy, that feeling is always there, lurking in the corner. Waiting for me to overthink so it can take hold again. I'm so ashamed of myself... I never wanted anyone to pity me, so I just put on a smile, even when all I wanted to do was cry or scream..."

Mei shook her head and hugged her tighter. "Hey... plenty of people feel this way at certain points in their lives. It'll get better, I'm sure. Back home, everything was always right in our faces—the seemingly endless suffering of the world. It was suffocating, to be subjected to the things we were. But maybe... here it can be different. As much as I'm afraid to admit it... maybe staying here after everything's done would be good for us. Maybe we could all be happier here. Think about it... the four of us, finding nice plots of land in a village with good people, spending the rest of our lives together as friends, never too far from each other. Imagine Tadashi trying to learn how to be a pig farmer... assuming this world has pigs!"

Abigail's sobs subsided as she weakly laughed. "Yeah... that sounds like a good life. One worth letting go of Earth for... unless there aren't any pigs here. I'm not sure I can give up bacon."

They laughed together, embracing. Meanwhile, Marik stood off to the side, listening to their conversation. His mind wandered back to a time when his life had been more like the one Mei and Abigail had discussed—a time when he had felt true happiness. It was something he had lost when he became Shadow-Lord.

It was long ago, on the Eastern Continent, in the aristocracy of Meri'Duus, that Marik lived in the village of Viridas with his father, Viktor, whom he despised with a passion, and his mother, Eva, who did her best to protect him from Viktor's drunken rages.

Not all of Marik's life in Viridas was miserable. As he had told Abigail before, he had his two best friends—Wulf Traver and Luna Fèvre.

As they grew up, Marik once felt love for Luna. He admired the way her emerald-green eyes sparkled and how her pure white hair, devoid of pigment, became the source of her name. But eventually, his love faded the day he realized she would never return his feelings. Her heart belonged to Wulf, and Wulf's to hers.

Marik closed his eyes, allowing the memories to wash over him, each one as vivid as the day it happened.

He could still recall it clearly—the day Marik Weton ceased to exist and Marik Ambrose was born. It was a day marked by the revelation of his true identity, one that came from an old man who had approached him on the streets of Viridas.

He was fifteen years old when it happened. As Marik walked to Wulf's house to meet up with him and Luna, he was stopped by an old man wearing a large satchel over his shoulder. The man was waiting for Marik to approach.

"Come here, I want to talk to you…"

Marik had no reason to fear him. There were plenty of townspeople around, and he recognized the old man as a hermit who lived nearby, surviving by trading ore he mined for fish. So, he did as the man asked and went over.

"Who are you?" Marik asked, curious why the hermit had singled him out.

The man smiled kindly at Marik before responding, "Your humble servant… Milord…"

Marik's face twisted in confusion and concern. The hermit continued, "I once served your grandfather… the great Dark Lord Materall…"

Marik stepped back, preparing to run, convinced the old man had lost his mind.

"My grandfather? You mean my father's father? He never knew him. He abandoned him when he was a baby."

Marik could almost hear his father's voice repeating that fact, the harsh reminder delivered every time Viktor lashed out at him. "You're lucky to even have a father," he would say.

But the hermit stood his ground, speaking softly so only Marik could hear.

"Your grandfather died the same year the flesh bag of booze was born. I am one of the true followers of Lord Materall, and I've been waiting for you to come of age…"

Marik's confusion deepened, but his curiosity got the better of him. "Come of age for what?"

"Magic..." the old man replied, "We never approached your father because he has no magical potential. But you... you do. I can sense it within you... boiling and swelling, as hot as the hatred you hold for your father."

Marik just stared at him in disbelief. "Alright then... I'm going to... uh..."

But he didn't run. The old man raised his hands, signaling for him to wait. Marik's curiosity outweighed his caution.

"Please... I can prove to you that we are who I claim to be..."

The hermit reached into his satchel and pulled out a large piece of unfamiliar metal, adorned with a strange white symbol.

"In my hands, it is silent and still, just as it has been since Lord Materall's death," the old man said. "Take it, and you will see..."

Marik remembered the rush he felt as he took hold of it. The white symbol began to glow red, and the metal shifted, morphing from solid to liquid and back again. It formed into a closed-face helmet, sharp, crown-like spikes adorning the top. It was the very mask Marik would one day wear in the Abyssal Cathedral.

The hermit smiled, explaining the significance of what Marik now held. "It was your grandfather's helmet. After his death, we retrieved it from his body and used a spell to ensure that it would only reveal itself when the heir of Lord Materall came into contact with it. You are truly his grandson... the next Dark Lord..."

Marik's mind reeled as shock overtook him. The nameless evil his teacher had spoken of in history class was his grandfather? The realization crushed him—his destiny was to be evil, too.

The hermit seemed to sense Marik's fear and spoke with a calm, reassuring voice. "Fret not, young master. The destiny of the Dark Lord is one of beauty and true heroism. Lord Materall sought to change this world for the better, to transform it into his image. Think of it: no other child would have to suffer the same abuse that you have at the hands of that spineless dolt Viktor. Everyone would do as you will, and the world would be yours. You would be a god."

Marik's breathing remained steady, though the old man's words did nothing to settle his shock.

"What about my friends? My mother? I don't want to leave them... I just want to be a normal person..."

The hermit placed a hand on Marik's shoulder, his voice filled with a quiet compassion.

"There's no rush. The ones who killed your grandfather know nothing of your existence. You may live a normal life for as long as you wish. But first... there's something you must do."

The hermit reached into his satchel again and handed Marik a dark violet flower petal.

"These are petals from a subterranean flower known as Dyr'kleiss. It's highly poisonous. Just one petal is enough to kill a grown man..."

Marik's eyes widened, the weight of fear pressing down on him. "You... you want me to poison my father?"

The old man nodded and placed his hands firmly on Marik's shoulders. He looked into Marik's wide eyes with a gaze full of wisdom and, strangely, unconditional love—the kind Marik had always wished to see from his own father.

"You say you want a normal life," the hermit said softly. "Ask yourself this: can you have a normal life while enduring his harsh, thoughtless words, his vicious and needless beatings? He has no love for you. He is a horrible man... if he can even be called a man. He takes his frustrations out on you because of his own mistakes. He doesn't deserve to be the father of a boy destined for so much more."

"You are special, Marik. More special than anyone or anything in this world. You and your mother deserve peace... peace from the cruelty."

Marik recalled how uncertain he had been in that moment. "I... I don't know. I don't want to kill anyone... not even him..."

The old man closed Marik's hand over the petals.

"There is no better way to rid yourself of him. No one would believe you or your mother if you went to the authorities—not when he is one of them. Why should someone so cruel be allowed to live?"

Marik nodded slowly, fear and uncertainty still clinging to him. "O-okay..."

He slipped the petals into his pocket, his hand trembling slightly.

"I'm going to see my friends now…"

Marik left the old hermit standing alone and took the familiar dirt path to Wulf's house. Normally, the route was dry and dusty, but after the heavy rain the night before, Marik's feet sank slightly into the mud with each step. As he walked, the thought of murdering his own father gnawed at him. He feared it would swallow his humanity, just as he imagined the wet earth might swallow his feet.

He needed someone to talk to. Someone he could trust—his friends. Their guidance was all he needed to clear his head. Wulf and Luna were two of the only people in his life he could rely on during the darkest of times. His mother, unfortunately, was not capable of offering him advice. Her mental state had deteriorated under Viktor's abuse, and worse yet, she might even tell Viktor, hoping he would treat her better.

Marik loved his mother, and he never blamed her for their situation. She had once been loving and confident, but as Viktor's alcoholism worsened, she became fearful and meek. In the beginning, she had tried to leave Viktor and take Marik with her, but Viktor used his position as one of the town's most respected guards to keep her from speaking out. Only Wulf, Luna, and Wulf's mother knew the truth.

Finally, after what felt like hours, but in reality was only a few fleeting minutes, Marik reached Wulf's home. As he crossed the wet blades of grass toward the treehouse where the three of them often spent time together, he heard nothing—no laughter, no conversation. It was eerily quiet. Climbing the ladder, he caught the sound of whispering. Peering up into the treehouse, he saw Wulf and Luna cuddling, gazing at the stars, whispering softly to each other.

Marik's heart sank, twisted with a surge of jealousy. A burning feeling rose within him as he descended the ladder, unnoticed by Wulf and Luna. His mind spiraled with irrational thoughts. How could they do this to me? Wulf should know that Luna is my great love… Unless… he does know… Is he doing this to break me? To belittle me? Just like Father does for my mistakes?

He backed away slowly, turning his back on them, turning away from whatever help they could have offered at that moment. Marik knew that his irrational reaction to their embrace was part of the reason he had become the person he was. Without his closest friends acting as his moral compass, he had changed—forevermore.

As he sat in the Abyssal Cathedral, Marik remembered the rest clearly. He had run back home in a daze. When he entered the house, he found his father passed out on the couch. Knowing his mother wouldn't be home until later, Marik grabbed Viktor's favorite beer mug and headed out to the rickety old shed. Inside, the mortar and pestle sat on a moldy table. He wiped his hand over the surface to make sure it was dry. By luck, it was.

He took the Dyr'kleiss petals from his pocket, recalling the old man's words: "Just one petal is enough to kill a grown man…"

Marik grimaced. "Better to be safe than sorry." He dropped all the petals into the mortar and ground them into a fine dust.

As he held the mortar over the mug, a chill ran through him. Suddenly, the door to the shed slammed shut behind him.

"What are you doin' out here, boy?" Viktor's voice cut through the air.

Marik froze, his back still to his father. "Did you go deaf while I wasn't looking?! I asked you a damn question!" Viktor's voice grew louder.

Marik turned slowly, gulping, still holding the mug and mortar. His father's eyes darted from his wide eyes to the objects in his hands.

"What are you—… is that my mug?! What were you about to put in my mug?" Viktor took a step forward, his voice rising. "Were you going to try and poison me?!"

Marik yelped as his father's fist collided with his cheek. The mug and mortar fell to the floor, breaking with a loud crash, but it was nothing compared to the impact of Marik's head hitting the ground.

"That was my favorite mug, you little shite!" Viktor grabbed Marik by the collar and began throwing punch after punch.

Marik could feel blood flowing from his nose as Viktor broke it with a savage blow.

"Who do you think you are? Trying to poison your father! You're nothing, boy! NOTHING!" Viktor's rage was unstoppable.

Marik braced for another punch, but when he forced his eyes open, he saw someone holding Viktor's arm back.

"What the hell—"

Viktor was pulled away by the old hermit.

"He is not nothing," the hermit said, his voice calm but firm. "He is more than you could ever hope to be…"

Marik watched as Viktor attempted to punch the old man, only for him to counter with practiced precision, forcing a knife through Viktor's elbow. Viktor cried out in pain, but the hermit didn't stop there. He kicked Viktor in the ribs, and Marik heard a definitive crack as Viktor collapsed to the ground, gasping for air.

The old man pulled the knife from Viktor's arm and walked over to Marik, helping him to his feet.

"Are you alright, young master?"

Marik nodded in a daze. "I... I was going to poison him... but he—"

The old man hushed him, pulling Marik into a comforting embrace. "Say no more. It's alright... Upon reflection, I believe poisoning him would have left more questions than desired. We will simply change the plan."

He released Marik from the hug and slipped a large stone into his hand. "I believe he has tormented you long enough, don't you?"

Marik wiped blood from his face with his sleeve and walked toward Viktor, who was groaning on the ground.

"N-Now wait just a minute, boy... I-I'm your father... You don't want to do this... I-I love you..."

Marik winced at the sound of his father's pitiful words, but he raised his hand high, the stone gripped tightly in his fist.

"No, you don't. And you're wrong... I do want to do this."

With that, Marik brought the stone down onto Viktor's head—again, and again—until one final, blood-curdling crunch rang out.

As Marik stepped out of the shed, he dropped the stone, his hand shaking. The old man guided him toward a group of armored Arkarnians.

"The Rau-Trava..." the old man spoke cautiously, but soon regained his confidence as the group knelt before Marik.

The tallest and most muscular of the Rau-Trava rose from his kneeling position and spoke.

"We have long awaited the heir of the Dark Lord Materall. You will not be blamed for what happened to your father. By the time the sun rises, there will be no doubt in anyone's mind that it was we who ended his life. And worry not—your friends will not be harmed."

Marik watched as the Rau-Trava stood and began marching toward the village. That night became one of the bloodiest in the history of Viridas. Wulf's mother had organized the town and led them against the Rau-Trava, driving them away. The leader of the Arkarnians, a man Marik later learned to be named Korvas, proved his words true—no one doubted that Viktor's brutal murder had been carried out by the Rau-Trava.

Marik stayed in the village for two more years. He came to terms with the idea of Wulf and Luna being together. Life, though far from perfect, had become better than normal without Viktor. But one night, as Marik went to meet with the old man, Wulf followed him. He overheard Marik discussing his "destiny" and how the old man believed it was time for Marik to journey to Skatchator and begin learning what it meant to become the Dark Lord.

Wulf followed Marik back to his home, and as Marik began preparing to leave, with a bag of supplies slung over his shoulder, Wulf confronted him.

"What the hell, Marik?" Wulf's voice was sharp as he walked up behind Marik, standing a few feet away.

"Wulf... 'What the hell' what?" Panic laced Marik's voice, betraying the emotions he was struggling to hide.

"I can understand if you killed your father in self-defense... but to do it because you think your grandfather was some kind of messiah of darkness? And now you're going to abandon everyone? Your mother, your friends? Just so you can become some... Shadow Lord?"

Marik felt his heart race. "Just... just come back now. No one else has to know that the Arkarnian attack was because of you."

Marik recalled the coldness in his voice when he replied to Wulf, the fear and panic gone, replaced with something far more distant. The memory of that conversation, and his refusal to let Wulf stop him, caused a tear to slip down his cheek—a tear that had become rare since he left his home.

"I think we both know it's too late for that... Go home, Wulf. Finish growing up. Marry Luna, grow old together, have kids. Enjoy life for as long as you can. Because I cannot guarantee that you'll even recognize life when my destiny is complete."

Wulf balled his fists, lowering his lantern. "You think I'm just going to let you do these horrible things? NO... Whatever this 'destiny' of yours is... it ends here."

Marik scoffed.

"You don't have it in you to take a life... let alone that of your friend."

Wulf narrowed his eyes, his voice trembling. "I don't even know who you are anymore, Marik."

Marik set his bag down with a heavy sigh. "Alright... alright... I'll come back. You're right... This isn't me."

But as Marik set the bag down, he grabbed a stone and hurled it at Wulf's forehead, knocking him backward to the ground.

Marik rushed to him, his hands closing around Wulf's neck, cutting off his airflow.

"Shhh... just remember I gave you a chance to walk away." Wulf tried to speak. "G-g-g—"

Marik loosened his grip slightly. "What?"

Wulf grabbed the lantern next to him and spat out, "Go to hell!"

Wulf smashed the lantern into Marik's head. Hot oil sprayed onto Marik's face and dripped down onto Wulf's jacket.

Marik recoiled, rolling on the ground in pain, while Wulf stripped off his jacket to avoid the oil burning through his skin.

Marik dragged his burning face through the wet grass before standing again, groaning. He looked at Wulf, part of his face bleeding from the burns.

In response, Marik grabbed a hunting knife from his sheath and charged at Wulf, tackling him down the hill. The two fought fiercely for control of the blade.

They punched, bit, elbowed, and kneed each other, tumbling down the slope until they reached the bottom. The knife flew from Marik's hand, landing nearby. Marik scrambled to maneuver above Wulf, attempting to choke him again. But Wulf was relentless, grabbing Marik's burned face, causing him to scream in agony and release him.

In the heat of the struggle, Marik seized the knife inches from him, intent on stabbing Wulf. But Wulf quickly grabbed a rock and bashed Marik's hand, forcing him to drop the knife. Marik retaliated with a forceful kick to Wulf's groin, sending him crashing backward, dropping the rock in the process.

Wulf lay on the ground, gasping for breath, his body wracked with pain. He curled into the fetal position, vulnerable.

Marik grabbed the knife with his other hand and lunged at Wulf, slicing deep into his arm. Wulf rolled away, reaching for the rock again. He stood, exhaling sharply, forcing himself to stay on his feet despite the pain, and slammed the jagged edge of the rock into Marik's stomach just as Marik stabbed him in the shoulder. Both twisted their weapons, falling back from each other, gasping for air.

"Cheap shot..." Wulf muttered weakly.

Marik coughed up blood and managed a grim laugh. "Yeah... but it worked..."

"For what it's worth... I'm sorry. You and Luna mean more to me than anyone else in this world... just not enough to stop me from embracing what I'm meant to be."

Wulf's voice was filled with pain and regret. "And that's where you've gone wrong. The only person you're meant to be is who you choose to be. And what you're choosing is pretty damn horrible, Marik."

"I hope you live long enough to see the world I'll make," Marik spat, his voice cold.

"And I hope you live long enough to regret it." Wulf's words were barely audible before he passed out from the pain.

Marik, with great effort, carried Wulf back to the village, unwilling to let him die there despite the injuries he had inflicted. He missed Wulf and Luna, wishing he could see them again after completing his quest. But such feelings were weaknesses. As he remembered how he had saved Wulf instead of killing him, a pang of guilt surged through him, and his thoughts turned to Tadashi.

"Did he not deserve to live just as much as Wulf did?" The thought crossed Marik's mind, but he forced it away. He couldn't afford to feel that regret. He needed to focus on the present.

Turning, he saw Mei and Abigail fast asleep, while Morg and Glum sat to his right, waiting for orders.

"I think the girls have the right idea. Get some rest. We leave in a few hours," Marik said, his voice steady despite the toll the night had taken on him.

He needed to regain his strength. Controlling the mist had drained him, and it was likely why his guard had slipped, allowing old emotions to resurface. Once he was ready, they would leave this place—once and for all.

CHAPTER THIRTY-EIGHT

Reunions and Introductions

Alan, Cinder, and Elis had been sitting on a large rock together for hours as they waited for signs of the return of Avery and the arkarnians.

They had passed the time exchanging stories about Avery, "There was a time, back home, the whole neighborhood had gotten all riled up because no one could find me, finally Avery checked his shed, he had these models, different miniature castles and trees, now that I think about it, I wonder if they represent a place here somewhere, anyway, he was thinking about where I could have gone, and so he deduced that I must have been in the shed, which is where I was, along with a big wolf spider that was sitting at the entrance and refusing to move, instead of killing or moving the spider, he talked me through my fear, but that only seemed to work at that time... arachnophobia has a tendency to relapse when you come across giant blind spiders I suppose..."

Elis and Cinder chuckled, finally Cinder spoke, "Here's one even Elis hasn't heard yet. Back in Overgate, as part of my training, he took me along on an investigation into what was rumored to be the illicit trade of dark magic-related products. After some careful investigating of where

the rumors began circulating from, we were led to the house of a street merchant named Homer, where we found out pretty fast that the so-called 'dark magic', was the name of the coffee he was selling."

She continued, "That wasn't the end of it though, because there was still a problem, The guy's coffee business was being run out of his basement, which you need to have special permits for, It's stupid I know, but more scandalous for him, was that he wasn't paying any taxes as a result of the business being secret..."

"But Avery took pity on the merchant, you see he was a dwarg, and the only reason he didn't get a permit was because he was trying to save money to open a tavern."

Alan raised an eyebrow, "Does it cost less to open a tavern than it does to get a permit for a basement business?"

Elis frowned, "Not exactly... This is something that most people, including my father, aren't very happy about. You see, non-Wethen- born citizens don't pay the same income tax as Wethen-born citizens do."

Alan interjected, "Wait... so... was it because he wasn't human? Do the other humanoid people of the Forgotten Lands have the same issue the arkarnians have with people in Wethen being racist? Are all human kingdoms like this?"

Elis shook his head, "While it is discriminatory, the heavy taxations aren't directed at specific species, it's directed at all people who weren't born in Wethen. My great-grandmother, Queen Rylei III, passed a law enforcing these taxation rules. By increasing the tax load on people who came from places such as Kardica, and the now nonexistent Astursis, it made things easier for native citizens, with little regard for the people it would negatively impact. So, when it comes down to it, after taxes, I doubt Homer could've afforded the permits to have started a tavern, let alone an area to build one..."

Cinder nodded, "Exactly, so instead of hauling him off to Undergate like one the city watchmen would have, Avery helped him get the permits and pay off any owed taxes, eventually allowing him to open his tavern, which is called 'The Singing Jester", named for an old dwarg folktale about a jester who was cursed to only communicate in song, it is one of the most popular taverns in all of Overgate, being a business welcoming all species and people. I haven't seen Homer in a while though, he left his business to his brother Gomer to go start a restaurant in Kalnia. I heard he got tired of getting harassed and having to break up bar fights, his passion was always cooking food more than it was serving drinks."

Alan snickered, "So one's name is Homer and the other's name is Gomer? Is there a third brother named Omer?"

Cinder smiled, "Omer was their Uncle's brother-in-law's stepson who had grown up alongside them in ... believe me, anyone who would go to the Singing Jester on a Tuesday night is going to get an earful, those two loved to talk about their life stories to anyone who would listen... Though it hasn't been the same since Homer left, Gomer's a lot more withdrawn, you can tell he misses his brother..."

Alan could relate, as his thoughts briefly began to dwell on how much he missed Abigail.

Alan turned and looked back toward the path they had come from. The thoughts of his sister faded, replaced by an overwhelming surge of relief as he saw Avery and Okama approaching. However, his relief quickly gave way to a deeper concern as he noticed the cost their ambush on the Mist had taken on Okama's group—only three of her warriors had survived. Alan ran with Elis and Cinder over to join them.

"Are all of you okay?" Alan asked.

Avery nodded. "Yes, for the most part. Marik won't be able to use that monster against us for some time; we wounded it heavily. But... it did escape."

Alan sighed. "I'm just glad you're okay." He turned to Okama and the remaining Arkarnians. "I'm sorry about your warriors."

Okama raised a hand. "Please, as I've already explained, the Boh-Rahl are honored to die as warriors. If you wish to pay tribute to them, I suggest we get moving and stop the destruction of our world."

Avery clapped Alan on the back. "Gather your things, everyone. You've rested long enough. We've got a four-hour walk ahead of us, and I don't want to stop until we reach Grimsby. Once there, we'll find shelter and rest until the first light of day."

As the others began to gather their belongings, Avery called out to Madeline and Okama. "Walk with me," he said. "I have something to discuss."

"I believe we're being followed," Avery began. "I sensed a presence earlier while we were traveling along the river, but I dismissed it as a Boh-Rahl. After your group joined us, though, I still felt as if we were being watched from afar. I ignored it again when I learned the Mist Monster was following our scent, but while I fought the Mist, I caught a glimpse of something in the trees. It was brief, and I didn't have the time to confirm if what I saw was real. However, on our way back to you, I allowed my senses to reach out, and I'm certain now that we have a presence among us.

"Now, do not turn your heads or react to what I'm about to say. There's someone in the tree line to our right, about one hundred feet away. They haven't attacked, nor have they tried to approach, but I'm curious as to who they are. Did someone send them to track us, or are they just curious?

"Madeline, I think your mercenary training will come in handy here. I want you to head into the tree line to the left, run as if you're trying to catch up with the others, then double back and surprise our tracker. Okama and I will stay behind the group and be ready if you need us."

Madeline nodded and followed Avery's instructions. She stayed back, allowing enough distance between her and the stranger to remain undetected. After a while, she carefully crept forward, using all the tracking skills she had learned in her mercenary days. In about half an hour, she was in position. The stranger was crouched beneath a tree, watching the others.

Madeline took her chance. With a swift jump from the tree, she kicked out her leg, landing a solid blow to the stalker's shoulder. She landed gracefully, daggers ready at her sides. "Stay down," she said, her voice firm. "I just want to know who you are and why you've been following us."

The stranger slowly rolled into a sitting position, rubbing her shoulder. "I'm not a threat," she said, grinning despite the pain. "I'm a friend. Nice kick, by the way. Honestly, I didn't see you coming."

Madeline lowered her daggers and extended a hand to help the woman up. She was a little taken aback when she saw that the stranger looked to be about her daughter's age.

"My name's Madeline. What's yours?"

The woman smiled. "I know who you are, Madeline. The stories I've heard are true. My name's Luna Fèvre, and we share a common enemy. My friend Wulf and I have been tracking your kids and their friends since they entered the Forgotten Lands. We knew we couldn't take down Marik on our own, and at the time, we were still trying to figure out his full intentions. I've kept my distance, though, out of caution because of the Mist that was also tracking you. If Marik knew I was nearby, he'd realize Wulf was probably following him too."

Madeline's heart skipped a beat, both shocked and relieved. "You've been watching Abigail, Mei, and Tadashi?"

Luna nodded. "Yes. I think it's time you meet the others. Avery will want to hear the whole story."

Madeline cupped her hands around her mouth and yelled to Avery to stop. Then, she and Luna jogged to catch up.

Avery and the others were waiting as Madeline and Luna arrived.

"Everyone, I'd like you to meet Luna Fèvre," Madeline said. "She's an ally in our quest, and she brings good news."

Turning to Alan, Madeline added, "Luna has a friend named Wulf. While she's been following us, he's been tracking the others."

Alan smiled, looking to Luna for more answers. "So, my sister and friends are safe? How did you know where we were? And, more importantly, why follow us?"

Avery placed a calming hand on Alan's shoulder. "All in good time, Alan. It's best we keep moving to Grimsby. We can't stand here talking. As long as you don't ask too many questions, you can walk next to us. I'm sure Luna will fill us in as we go."

Luna nodded. "Yes, we must keep moving. When I last spoke with Wulf, we learned Marik was headed to the Polar Regions, and we figured his route would take him through New Arkarnia and into the Abyssal Cathedral. When Alan left, we were certain he'd end up in Wethan. I thought I'd lost him when he ran off into the woods, but after almost two days, I caught sight of you both. Avery, I was relieved to see you alive. Wulf and I thought you were dead.

"The Mist was always on your tail. As I told Madeline, I couldn't risk Marik knowing I was near you, or he'd figure out Wulf was probably tracking him too. You see, Wulf and I grew up with Marik. We were friends until he left our home in Meri'duus. Everything changed when Marik tried to kill Wulf after Wulf found out he had killed his father. Wulf tried to stop him from following some old man who wanted him to become a Dark Lord. Marik couldn't kill Wulf, though. Instead, he brought his bloodied body back home and left him to heal.

"Wulf told me of Marik's plan to remake this world in his image. That was three years ago. At the time, we were too young to do anything, but we swore we'd be ready to stop him one day. Over the years, we've trained and researched, determined to bring him down. While spying on Marik, we learned that he planned to use Alan and Abigail to obtain a powerful orb. That's why we've been tracking you—to protect them and find our opportunity to stop him."

Avery saw that Alan was about to interpret Luna's pause as a signal that she was finished speaking, but he had his own questions. He raised his flat palm toward Alan and spoke.

"This is troubling. I knew Marik had an abusive childhood, but I didn't realize he was the one who killed his father. I had believed there was still good in him... but now I'm not so sure."

Luna glanced at Avery. "Don't put yourself on such a high pedestal that you can't understand. Viktor's death was the only way the abuse would have ever ended for Marik and his mother. He was a member of the Meri'Duus guard—there was no other way for justice to be brought to him. The only thing Marik did wrong was using it to further his transformation into a Dark Lord, instead of doing it to protect himself and his mother."

"That's the point I'm trying to make," Avery replied, frustration creeping into his voice. "It took this old man to convince Marik to kill his father in order to achieve greatness. I could have accepted it if he had killed his father to end his needless suffering... but no one else in my family, none of my brother's descendants, should have that kind of corruption in their blood."

Luna scoffed and cut Avery off. "If that were true, he wouldn't have stayed in Meri'Duus after killing Viktor. He wouldn't have saved Wulf after he was hurt.

Marik may be evil now, but the evil inside him isn't because of his blood—it's because of that damned old man. Just because you're his granduncle doesn't make you an expert on Marik's mental state. That old man showed him fatherly compassion that he never knew. Just because Materall went off the deep end doesn't mean Marik did. He loved his mother, just like he loved Wulf and me. But the old man manipulated him into thinking he could only feel whole if he embraced darkness.

"I've heard many good things about you, Avery Ambrose. Don't muddy the high regard Wulf and I have for you by assuming you know more about our former friend than we do. Maybe Marik is too far gone. Maybe he isn't. Speculating about it gets us nowhere."

Avery nodded apologetically, but he sensed there was something more behind her words. It wasn't the harsh judgment of Marik that had offended her—there was a deeper emotion, something he didn't want to press and risk upsetting her further.

"I'm sorry," he said quietly. "This whole situation has been incredibly frustrating for me. It's hard to accept that his suffering could have ended if I hadn't been blind to the fact that my brother had a child. If I had known about Viktor, maybe I could have taken him away from whatever conditions turned him into such a terrible father."

Luna placed a hand on Avery's shoulder. "Don't lose sleep over it. Viktor's mother is a very sweet old lady. She disliked the drunkard he'd become and couldn't stand living near him. She lives on the outskirts of Meri'Duus with her second husband. Wulf, Marik, and I would visit her sometimes. She's still alive. After all this is over, you could probably go ask her about how she met Materall if you're curious."

Avery nodded, a faint sense of relief washing over him. "I agree. That's something for later. For now, let's focus on finding some durbos. It's the only way we'll be able to reach the Shrine in time."

As the group continued walking, the air grew cooler, turning increasingly frigid. Avery called out for them to stop so they could add extra layers under their armor. He offered Luna some garments, but she was already reaching into her knapsack, clearly prepared for the cold.

It didn't take long after they stopped for the group to spot a small herd of durbos grazing on a patch of grass poking through the white tundra.

Luna asked, "Do you have any experience with mounting a durbo? If not, I'd be happy to show you how. Wulf and I used to ride the southern variety back in Kalnia."

Avery smiled. "To be honest, I had a failed attempt back in my youth, so any suggestions you have would be much appreciated. Everyone gather around; Luna will be showing us how to obtain our rides."

Luna addressed the group. "It's not difficult, as long as you follow three important rules."

She moved toward one of the grazing durbos as she spoke. "First, you must approach them from the front. They need to see you directly. Don't approach from the sides or back—they don't have peripheral vision and can startle easily."

Luna continued moving closer, then paused when the durbo raised its head to look at her. She slowly raised her hand and held it out. "Second, you must walk slowly toward them, looking them in the eyes while holding one hand with the palm up."

She waited for the durbo to approach, sniffing and licking her hand, just as she predicted. "Allow them to come to you. The important thing is not to show fear—they can smell it," she explained, stroking the durbo's face. "Finally, once they've accepted your presence, rub the side of their face and keep your hand on them as you slowly move to their side. They'll bend their front legs, allowing you to climb onto their back."

Luna smiled as she climbed onto the durbo's back, enjoying the soft fur beneath her.

"The only other things you need to know are how to stop them and steer them. It's not much different from riding a horse. These are just much larger, so more force is needed with your feet at their sides. The best way to hold on is to hug their neck and lean forward. Oh, and if they get startled and you get thrown off, try to roll onto your side—the armor should take most of the impact. Any questions?"

The group exchanged glances before shaking their heads and following Luna's demonstration. For the most part, they had no issues, save for Alan, who had attempted to mount a particularly feisty and playful durbo. The animal decided to repeatedly headbutt Alan with just enough force to knock him onto his rear.

Avery, Madeline, Cinder, and Elis watched Alan's struggle with amusement. Everyone, except Alan, had successfully mounted their durbos. Madeline had initially been concerned, but Luna reassured her that if the durbo were trying to hurt Alan, there would have been more obvious signs of aggression, like Alan screaming in pain.

Alan's voice oozed sarcasm as he failed to dodge the durbo's headbutt for the seventh time. "Ha ha! I'm really glad you guys find this hysterical!"

Elis chuckled. "Ah, don't worry, Alan. When we tell this story to the historians at Overgate, we'll say you had to help tame all of our durbos, and we were the ones getting knocked on our asses!"

Avery laughed heartily. "Come now, Elis, we all had our difficulties with our mounts—none quite as entertaining as Alan's current predicament."

Alan sighed. "Can one of you please help me? I don't think we have time for this..."

Cinder dismounted and walked over to help Alan. Together, they managed to calm the particularly playful durbo, allowing Alan to finally mount its back.

With the matter of finding their mounts settled, the group continued on toward the trading outpost of Grimsby. The ride had been uneventful. Alan had been wanting to ask Luna some questions, the most pressing of which was about what Marik had been like as a person years ago. However, after hearing her conversation with Avery, it was clear that Marik was a sensitive subject, and one wrong word would likely upset her.

Instead, as Alan rode, he sorted through his thoughts. He felt conflicted about Luna and Wulf's situation—it mirrored the exact scenario he had privately, and irrationally, feared would happen with Abigail. Though Daghlesh's reassurances that Abigail wasn't corrupted by the Shadow-Lord had eased his worry somewhat, those words came from an evil entity, so the comfort they provided was fleeting and ultimately hollow.

The idea that Marik had friends was something Alan hadn't considered. Until then, he had thought of him as nothing more than a manipulative monster. He felt guilty learning that Marik had been abused by his father. Realizing that Marik, at his core, was as human as Alan was difficult to accept. Alan wondered if, when things came to a head at the Shrine of Morimor, Luna and Wulf's presence might soften Marik enough for them to talk him down—or exploit a moment of weakness long enough to strike first and prevent him from hurting anyone. He knew the latter was an unsavory option and that the others would never support it, but the thought lingered, even though the idea of actually carrying it out made him uneasy.

Avery, on the other hand, was content with the journey. Though he wasn't one to complain, the fight with the Mist had taken a toll on him. The others had taken breaks to let him recover, but instead of delaying any further, he decided to push on and wait until they reached Grimsby for sustenance. When he saw billows of smoke in the distance, he called out, "Look, everyone! Grimsby is in sight. We'll stop there for a bite to eat at their cantina so we don't have to use up our supplies. I just hope Yarba was right about them being welcoming to all."

Alan pulled up alongside Cinder and Elis. "Race you there!"

Cinder immediately took off after him, both of them heading for what appeared to be the most direct route. Elis, however, quickly realized that the path was lined with trees, rocks, and shrubs, which would slow them down. He decided to take a different route, avoiding the obstacles Alan and Cinder would have to face.

As he raced ahead, Elis couldn't help but think about how different Cinder seemed lately. Her attitude toward Alan had shifted, and that made him happy for her. He hadn't seen her open up to someone like this before. Though he was glad to see her growing as a person, part of him was surprised at how quickly her feelings for Alan seemed to have developed.

In a way, Elis was envious. Not because he had feelings for Cinder—he didn't—but because he couldn't help but feel sadness at the thought of someone finding their soulmate so easily. He thought of Madeline and James Elwyn, and even his own parents. Elis's experiences with matters of the heart had been discouraging. Being the Prince of Wethen came with certain expectations, and those expectations didn't leave much room for personal happiness.

As Elis rounded the bend and pulled ahead of Cinder and Alan, he thought about his former girlfriend, Moira. She had been studying to become a scholar, analyzing historical texts and seeking new ways to understand the histories of Wethen and the rest of Whenua. Eventually, Moira had ended their relationship when she realized the responsibility of becoming Queen would prevent her from pursuing her academic goals. Elis didn't blame her, though he still saw her from time to time as a friend. But deep down, he couldn't shake the feeling that she had been his soulmate. He often wondered if their relationship could have worked if he hadn't been the Prince. Ultimately, he came to the conclusion that the good he could do as King outweighed his personal happiness.

Elis smiled as he turned to face Alan and Cinder, who were both baffled by how he had gotten to Grimsby first.

"How did you do that?" Cinder exclaimed, sounding more like a statement than a question.

"You guys need to pay more attention to the world around you, even when you're just messing around," Elis replied. "The path you took was thick with vegetation and rocks. I took a different route with fewer obstacles."

Avery, overhearing their conversation, chuckled as he rode up. "And that's why we've been able to stay ahead of Marik on the way to the Polar Regions."

Luna nodded slightly. "Yes, however, Marik's path has been more about avoiding obstacles that apply specifically to him. He could have taken the same route you did, but doing so would have likely drawn attention from Wethen's armies. Though the Abyssal Cathedral is much more dangerous than the river was... I'm uneasy about Wulf being alone in there, especially with the stories that Arkarnian told us about it."

Madeline scoffed. "His path went through New Arkarnia. I'd imagine that the Rau-Trava would have posed more of a danger to his plans than if he tried to sneak through Wethen."

Luna sighed. "There's something you don't know... I don't have all the details, but when Wulf was following Marik's party, he saw Marik and Korvas meet. He seemed shaken up by it, but there wasn't time for him to tell me what he learned from their conversation..."

Avery and Madeline's expressions darkened at this news, but Avery quickly shifted the subject. With Wulf's information still unknown, there was no point in speculating. "Come, let's go inside."

The group moved their durbos into the large paddock outside the inn before heading inside. Avery approached the bar and began speaking with the Arkarnian innkeeper, while Alan, Cinder, Elis, and Baldric found a table large enough for everyone.

"So, Alan," Baldric began, "Have you been having fun on this quest?"

Alan was taken aback by the question. While he had enjoyed many moments in the Forgotten Lands, he wasn't sure if it was appropriate to call it "fun," especially with all the death they had witnessed in recent days. He stammered, "Well... I—I mean, perhaps—"

Before Alan could respond, he felt a tap on his shoulder, which made him stop speaking altogether. He turned to see who had been trying to get his attention, his eyes widening as he exclaimed, "Tadashi!?" Without hesitation, Alan threw his arms around Tadashi and hugged him, overjoyed to see his friend after so long.

Tadashi grunted, "Alan! You're suffocating me! Let me go!"

Alan quickly released him, still staring in disbelief. Madeline and Avery walked over. Madeline embraced Tadashi just as enthusiastically as Alan had, though, judging by Tadashi's expression, her hug was much tighter than necessary.

Avery smiled warmly. "Hello, Tadashi... I don't know if you remember meeting me years ago, but you were much smaller then. I'm Avery... the real Avery, not the one who dragged you here to Whenua. But if you're here... where are Mei and Abigail?"

Tadashi sighed deeply. "They're still with Shadow-Lord... they don't know it, but he tried to kill me and Yerk after I figured out what he was using us for. He threw us off a cliff in this underground church..." He pointed behind him at Yerk, who waved jovially at them.

"Hi, friends of Tadashi!"

Luna's expression softened, and she closed her eyes for a moment, realizing just how far Marik had fallen if he was willing to kill the young boy standing in front of her.

Avery rested a hand on Tadashi's shoulder. "I'm glad you're both alright, but how did you survive? From the stories I've heard, the chasms down there are nearly bottomless..."

Tadashi gestured to someone standing off to the side. Had he not known the person was there, Tadashi might have missed him too. Avery's gaze followed Tadashi's motion, and his eyes narrowed. "Why did you bring him here?"

Tadashi looked confused for a moment, then realized who Avery was thinking of. He chuckled, trying to calm Avery down. "I didn't bring him here. That's not Shadow-Lord."

Avery stared at the figure, clad in dark gray plated armor, the design not too different from Shadow-Lord's own, except for gold ribcage-like designs on the front of the chest and purple trim on the lower chest-plate and greaves. Despite the ominous appearance, Avery's fear subsided when he saw Luna's face brighten in recognition.

"Hello, Wulf," she said with a nod.

Wulf returned the gesture, his voice heavy, carrying a weight that shifted the atmosphere in the room.

"Mr. Ambrose, we need to talk..."

Once everyone had settled at a large round table, Wulf began to explain the meeting between Marik and Korvas that Luna had mentioned.

"Marik and Korvas are working together. Marik brokered an alliance between the Rau-Trava and Valthurg. They've been tunneling toward Overgate. There's an attack coming. It sounds like they've been planning this for over a year. That's why

Rau-Trava activity on the frontlines has been minimal, and why investigations into Valthurg activity reported by the Dinalo went cold. They've been preparing for war in tunnels running from the Polar Regions to Overgate. Marik also recruited a tribe of Myklins he encountered while traveling north. The plan is to enter through Undergate, free imprisoned Rau-Travans, and recruit human criminals to turn them against their own kind..."

Avery's frustration was clear. "How did we all miss this? This is troubling news. If he's recruited one tribe of Myklins, he's likely convinced others to join. We not only need to inform King Belmont, but we must also warn General Mikan. They need to pull their forces back to the capital and infiltrate these tunnels from there. Silvyn, it's also crucial you warn your father about this threat and reach out to ask him to join the fight."

Avery paused, strategizing their next steps. The silence was soon interrupted by a small argument between Tadashi and Alan. Avery glanced up at them, knowing Alan wouldn't cause a fuss unless there was a good reason. "Alan, do you have a plan for our situation?"

Alan didn't get a chance to reply before Tadashi spoke up, as Alan tried to stop him.

"Alan doesn't, but I do," Tadashi began. "I've spent my whole life believing my parents were dead. Then I was brought to this world, and Marik told me you were responsible for their deaths. After being thrown into a chasm, I realized he lied, and my parents may still be alive. Now, after hearing you mention General Mikan, Alan told me he's my father. So my plan is to take Yerk, find him, and warn him."

Avery took a deep breath, his voice stern but not unkind. "I understand you want to meet your father. This news must be overwhelming. But this is not the time for a family reunion. As harsh as it may sound, you need to think about what's most important right now."

Avery raised his hand, signaling for Tadashi to stop speaking. "Madeline, I want you, Luna, Silvyn, and Okama to head to the front lines along New Arkarnia. First, locate Hiroto. Then, you and Luna need to travel as quickly as possible to Wethan to inform James and Alfonse. Silvyn and Okama will head back to the Dinalo Reservation."

Madeline nodded in acknowledgment before turning to her son and Tadashi. "Alan... Tadashi... as a mother, it pains me to leave you both as you face Marik. I wanted to be there to help Abigail and Mei realize that Marik is evil, but I trust you both to take care of them. I know you've grown so much in the past month and faced impossible situations, but I have faith that we can all defeat Shadow-Lord."

Tadashi and Alan embraced Madeline, while Wulf wished Luna goodbye by gently placing his helmeted forehead against hers.

Okama called to her warriors and then turned to Avery. "I will miss being able to witness your great battle with Marik, but from seeing how well you've handled things so far, I believe you will be victorious. I will do my best to convince the Dinalo that peace can only be achieved through fighting for it."

Avery turned back to the remaining members of the group. "Alan, I'd like you to teach Tadashi and Yerk how to mount a durbos, then meet us back in the cantina for dinner. Once we're well-fed, we'll turn in for the night. The owner has agreed to let us camp in the paddock with the durbos. Tomorrow, we leave at first light. The race is on."

Chapter Thirty-Nine

Abyssal Exodus

Abigail looked around at her surroundings. A wooden structure stood before her—an inn, she realized—where a group of people sat huddled around a table. As she approached, recognition dawned on her: it was Alan's group. However, this time, two unfamiliar faces stood among them, along with two others who took her by surprise. Abigail became acutely aware that she was experiencing another vision.

Standing before her were Tadashi and Yerk, along with a person whose armor bore a striking resemblance to Marik's. Beside them stood a girl, only a few years older than Abigail, with stark white hair.

Something was wrong. Yerk was supposed to be taking Tadashi back to the Gnoglins to recover from his injuries. Yet, in this vision, Tadashi appeared unharmed.

At that moment, a voice echoed from all around her.

"And now... she ponders... 'what is the illusion'? Is it what she is told by Marik in her waking hours... or the visage that appears before her as she lies asleep?"

Abigail spun around, startled by the sudden voice in the otherwise silent dreamscape.

"Who... who's there?"

A middle-aged man appeared before her, arms folded. His dark hair was tied back in a ponytail, and a short beard framed his face.

"My name is Aiden... Aiden Ambrose. I have been trying to reach you for some time. Only those with a rare gift can hear the voices of the dead. Peculiar that you should have gained such an ability... No one in the Ambrose family has ever possessed it, nor the Elwyns, by extension. Perhaps it comes from your mother's lineage... Regardless of the reason, it is... nice to finally be heard."

Abigail's mind swirled with questions, but she settled on the most pressing.

"Aiden Ambrose? You speak as though you are a relative of mine, of Marik and Avery. Who exactly are you?"

Aiden nodded. "Yes. I am your distant cousin—the father of Avery and Materall. Listen to me, child: you must not trust Marik. He is walking the same path my fallen son once did. This vision you see is the truth. Your friends, Tadashi and Yerk, are truly in the company of Avery and Alan."

Abigail shook her head. "Materall was a hero, though. Avery murdered him in cold blood."

Aiden lowered his gaze. "No... he was the furthest thing from a hero, dear child. Let me show you where it all began."

The world around them shifted. They were now in an ornate library.

"Where are we?" Abigail asked.

Aiden approached a table where two young boys sat across from each other, reading books.

"This is Materall, and this is Avery, decades ago, when they were much younger than you are now."

Abigail glanced at the books. The one in Avery's hands appeared to be a fairy tale, while Materall's was a tome on magic—a silent confirmation of Aiden's words. She wasn't sure whether to believe any of this, but she remained silent, listening as he continued.

"I held Materall in high regard," Aiden admitted, his voice heavy with regret. "He took to magic effortlessly, while Avery struggled for much of his early life. Because of this, my wife and I showered Materall with praise and neglected to see what kind of person he was becoming. Meanwhile, I was harshly critical of Avery's shortcomings."

The world around them shifted again, flashing through scenes of Materall standing with Avery and another boy Abigail did not recognize.

"I was blinded by my love for Materall... so much so that I failed to notice his descent into darkness. He not only learned the most forbidden forms of magic but began teaching them to Avery to ensure his loyalty. The third boy, his closest friend, was Tannis. You have met him before—under a false identity, he helped Marik deceive you all."

As Aiden spoke, the unknown boy's face morphed into the old hermit they had encountered in the ruins of Astursis.

The dreamscape shifted again, molding into a ruined hilltop, where a large gathering of people stood. Arkarnians and humans alike.

"This," Aiden said, "is where Avery brought my wife and me when he warned us of Materall's intentions. You see, they had a falling out. Avery learned of Materall's plan to raise an army of followers, but what he didn't realize was that Materall had already succeeded. Those assembled here were Astursian rebels and members of the Valthurg—persecuted groups from their respective kingdoms."

Aiden's voice darkened. "I refused to believe Materall had fallen so far. Foolishly, I revealed myself, my wife, and Avery to confront him. I scolded him as though he were still a child... and for that, I paid with my life. Materall ordered Tannis to stab me in the back. I couldn't speak... I couldn't breathe... all I could do was look at Avery one last time and hope he saw my regret. I failed him. I failed him in life, and it is only in death that I have the sense to admire the man he has become."

Abigail stood frozen, her mind struggling to reconcile the story she had always known with the truth unfolding before her.

"After this moment," Aiden continued, "Avery and Morgana fled. They could not defeat Materall, not with his followers surrounding him. But had they stayed, they would have died."

The dreamscape shifted once more, revealing the Grotto of Life. All around them lay the bodies of the dead as Materall approached two glowing spheres held by statues.

Abigail felt the weight of Aiden's words settle over her. What was the truth? What was the illusion?

Abigail interjected, "Are those—?"

Aiden nodded. "The Orbs of Morimor and Livimor... relics of an ancient time. Materall came here, to the place where they had rested since the deaths of their creators. He killed those who guarded them and took them for himself."

Abigail watched as the vision played out before her, scenes of Materall's murderous mission flashing one after another. Her voice wavered. "Why—why did he do this?"

"To gain power," Aiden said grimly. "Just before he came for the orbs, he convinced his Astursian followers to incite civil war, while the Valthurg did the same in Arkarnia. At the height of the chaos, he killed those among his own ranks who knew too much and couldn't be trusted with the burden of his manipulations. Then, through carefully orchestrated border attacks, he provoked Arkarnia into invading Astursis. The arkarnians overran the land, dismantled its government, and scattered its people... but it came at a price. The unity of Arkarnia shattered, dividing into the Rau-Trava, the Dinalo, and the Boh-Rahl.

"Amid this turmoil, Materall ventured to Ancient Arkarnia, where he corrupted a great source of magic to empower himself. That act transformed the land into an inhospitable wasteland. It was there, in the ruins of what once was, that Morgana and Avery confronted him for the final time."

The dreamscape shifted again, showing a crumbling underground chamber.

"Morgana managed to seize one of the orbs and used its power to open a portal as the chamber collapsed around them. They emerged at the very place where I had been murdered. In a last-ditch effort, Materall tried to sway Morgana to his side... but she saw through him. She mortally wounded him, took both orbs, and hid them, sealing them away with enchantments."

Aiden's expression darkened. "The corruption he unleashed in Ancient Arkarnia is what you now see in the so-called Shadow-Lands. That is why people believe the Forgotten Lands are dying. But it isn't death—it's something worse. It is a new, twisted form of life. An invitation for creatures from the Abyssal Cathedral to manifest here."

Abigail felt lightheaded, which was disorienting considering she was already asleep. "Do... do Avery and Alan know?"

Aiden nodded. "Yes. Alan and Avery are aware. Few truly understand the extent of these events as you and I do now. The only reason I know is that, in death, I have communed with what remains of Livimor and Morimor."

"Then how do Alan and Avery know?"

Aiden's gaze shifted. "Your brother... he gave in to darkness—if only for a moment—to prevent your mother's murder. In doing so, he caught the attention of a dark entity. The arkarnians believe it to be the godkeeper of forbidden knowledge. This being sought to gain Alan's trust, offering him three questions—answers with no strings attached, along with extra information beyond that limit. One of the truths it revealed was the supposed death of Whenua... and Alan, in turn, told Avery.

"I trust Avery to do his best to shield Alan from the entity's influence, so do not burden yourself with worry."

Aiden placed a hand on Abigail's shoulder. "I know you trust Marik. I know you admire him. And I won't deny that he's spoken words of wisdom to you. He is a gifted teacher. I do not believe he is wholly evil—not like Materall was. But please understand... his goals, whatever noble reasons he may claim, are not what the world needs.

"And... I know I have no right to ask this of you. But if you see Avery, tell him..." Aiden's voice faltered. "Tell him I'm sorry. Sorry I wasn't a better father. That I did love him. That I did appreciate him. I just didn't realize it until I was already gone."

As Aiden faded from view, Abigail's vision shifted back to the scene of Alan and Tadashi. She studied Avery, her mind churning.

Logically, she knew what she had just experienced may have been real. Perhaps Aiden Ambrose had truly reached out to her from beyond. But her gut told her otherwise. Something about the entire encounter felt... contrived. A ploy, perhaps, to sway her allegiance toward Avery.

She closed her eyes and forced herself awake.

When she sat up, Mei was still asleep nearby, but Marik sat on the edge of the rocky outcrop where they had made camp. Abigail pulled herself to her feet and walked over to sit beside him.

Marik glanced over at her. "Can't sleep?"

Abigail shook her head. "I think Avery entered my dreams... I saw Tadashi and Yerk with Alan and Avery. There was also a man claiming to be your great-grandfather, Aiden Ambrose. He said this world isn't dying—that the changes we see are the result of Materall's plan to conquer it. And... that you were continuing his plot of world domination."

She hesitated, then shook her head firmly. "But I didn't believe it. Not one bit."

Marik nodded, keeping his composure, but internally, he felt a tangled mix of relief, surprise, and anger.

He was relieved that Tadashi and Yerk were still alive and that his influence over Abigail had kept her from believing the so-called spirit. But he was also shocked—shocked that she could commune with the dead in her dreams. And furious that his plans had nearly been derailed by someone who had been gone for years.

"I'm glad you resisted his attempt to manipulate you, Abigail. Without you and Mei, I can't stop Avery. It's already going to be difficult enough making the rest of this journey without Tadashi." He sighed. "When we see him again, you'd better not tell him I said that... okay?"

Abigail grinned and let out a quiet laugh. "Don't worry—my lips are sealed."

A few minutes later, Mei stirred awake, and the five of them continued their journey through the tunnels ahead.

As they walked, Abigail felt an oppressive presence growing stronger with each step. A chill ran down her spine. Marik felt it too. Then, from deeper within the tunnel, they heard it—chanting.

The words were repetitive, nonsensical.

"Marik... what is that?" Abigail whispered.

He didn't take his eyes off the darkness ahead. "I've encountered beings like these before. Once, they were practitioners of the most twisted forms of magic. But after years of altering their own bodies in pursuit of greater power, they lost their sentience. Now, they're nothing more than hollowed-out creatures of habit, endlessly performing the same rituals that ruined them—because they can't comprehend anything else."

Abigail swallowed hard. "So... if they aren't all there in the head, can we just sneak past them?"

Marik shook his head. "I should add that they're incredibly violent and territorial. Predatory animals can be reasoned with under the right circumstances. These creatures? They cannot."

His tone left no room for argument. "Stay close to me. There's no telling what kind of mutilations they've undergone."

Marik took the lead, and the others followed.

They entered a vast chamber, dimly lit by a flickering fire in its center. A group of robed figures gathered around the flames, their black, tattered cloaks pooling around them.

It was difficult to make out their faces, but as Mei and Abigail looked closer, a sickening realization settled in. Their skin was dry and cracked, deep fissures running along their pasty complexions. But worse than that—bones jutted through their cheeks, noses, and chins, piercing through flesh as if trying to escape. A black, watery liquid oozed from the cracks.

Marik whispered, carefully examining one of them. "I believe they've replaced their hearts and organs with... something else. Perhaps one of the creatures they used to summon in their rituals. Some of them were small, insectoid-like beings..."

Mei, Abigail, and the Morgs shuddered at the thought of some twisted parasite writhing inside these people, keeping them alive.

Marik motioned for them to follow as he spotted what looked like a tunnel entrance. As he stepped closer, he could see it led into a corridor—one that glowed with light at the far end.

Finally. The exit from this accursed place.

But there was a problem.

A heavy steel gate blocked their path, locked tight with no key in sight.

Before Marik could think of a way to force it open, a guttural, braying moan echoed from behind them.

One of the cultists had seen them. And now, it was moving toward them—fast.

Marik reacted instantly. With a flick of his wrist, he reached out to the fire in the center of the room, sending a wave of flames outward. The fire spread, consuming several of the cultists, including the one lunging toward them.

But then... the cultists kept coming.

They didn't stop.

They didn't scream.

They barely even reacted to the fire consuming them.

Marik's stomach twisted. They don't feel pain... or they don't experience it like normal beings do.

Their movements were eerily familiar, and Mei realized with horror what they reminded her of.

Zombies.

She immediately regretted watching that zombie movie marathon with Abigail the weekend before their road trip to Red Pine Forest.

Abigail, thinking the same thing, braced herself and focused on the stone rubble around them. She concentrated, trying once again to wield her earth magic. Stones lifted into the air, then launched forward, crashing into the cultists and crushing them beneath the weight.

Marik turned back to the gate and summoned a flame in his palm, directing its heat toward the lock. If he could just melt through the mechanism—

But more cultists appeared.

Abigail's patience wore thin. Marik was taking his good old time melting the lock, and the cultists weren't slowing down. She clenched her fists and shouted—

"MOVE, MARIK!"

Marik barely had time to react before he saw a massive chunk of stone hurtling toward the gate. He yelped and leapt out of the way just as the stone crashed into the lock, shattering it.

Gorb and Glum hauled Marik back to his feet, and without wasting another second, the group bolted into the tunnel.

The cultists pursued.

Abigail skidded to a stop, turning back toward the ceiling of the tunnel. She focused, envisioning the rock collapsing, burying their pursuers beneath tons of stone.

The ground rumbled.

Then, with a deafening crash, the tunnel caved in, sealing the cultists behind them.

Silence.

They all stood there for a moment, panting, catching their breath.

When it became clear the danger had passed, they slowed their pace.

The tunnel ahead stretched long and winding.

The journey to freedom would take time. Running was no longer necessary. Walking, at least for now, would be enough.

Chapter Forty

The Cold

Even though Grimsby had been much colder than where they had traveled from, it was still shielded from the extreme temperatures of the Polar Regions by the towering evergreens. But once they passed beyond the edge of the forest, the landscape changed drastically. Before them stretched an endless expanse of snow, with mountains rising in the distance to the west, north, and east. Yet immediately ahead, all they could see were snowy outcroppings, devoid of any noticeable life.

They had left Grimsby at first light, just as Avery had planned. The night before, he had spent hours discussing their next steps with Wulf, Tadashi, and Yerk, filling them in on what had transpired and laying out the game plan. In return, Tadashi gave a quick rundown of their journey since leaving Darksprire, including his encounter with the Myklins and Gnoglins.

Avery was already familiar with the Myklins, and his concern grew as Tadashi described how Marik had brokered a deal with them to leave the Gnoglins alone. There was nothing Avery could do about it now—Madeline and the others were already miles away. He would have to set those concerns aside until they returned.

As they mounted their durbos that morning, Avery instructed everyone to ride close together but stick with their designated partner. He and Cinder led the group, followed by Alan with Sobek, then Elis with Baldric. Tadashi brought up the rear, flanked by Yerk to his left and Wulf to his right.

Avery was confident that the Shrine of Morimor lay northeast of their position, but Baldric had warned of the many dangers along the way. The shortest route would have taken them directly into quick snow, a risk they couldn't afford. Instead, they would travel north for a few miles before making a sharp turn eastward, skirting the Northern Shore of Albastru Bay. According to Baldric's last expedition into the Polar Regions, this was also the route where they were least likely to encounter the Valthurg.

As they pressed on across the icy plains, the cold became even more biting, and a fierce wind began to pick up. Then, without warning, Baldric called out for them to stop.

"The drop in temperature and sudden rise in wind speed means a snow squall is coming," he warned. "Up here, these storms are deadly. The snow becomes blinding, and the wind can separate people from their group. I've lost friends to these storms—found them buried days later, frozen solid. We need to form a circle with our durbos and huddle in the center. The durbos will lie down once the wind picks up, shielding us from the worst of it."

Tadashi frowned. "What's stopping them from running off in a panic? I'd rather not just sit here freezing while our rides bolt."

Baldric shook his head. "They won't run. Durbos don't fear squalls. Watching them is how I learned to survive in these conditions. They'll stay firm where they rest, and once the storm passes, they'll rise and wait for us to remount. Even the strongest winds won't knock them over."

Minutes later, the squall hit. Visibility dropped to nothing, and they shut their eyes to protect them from the stinging ice. The wind howled with an eerie intensity, and as instinct took over, Alan and Cinder instinctively reached out and held onto one another.

The storm raged for about half an hour before finally beginning to subside. As soon as it did, Alan and Cinder quickly let go of each other, but not before Tadashi caught sight of them and started snickering.

Alan shot him a warning look, daring him not to say anything.

Of course, Tadashi being Tadashi, grinned and said, "Way to go, bro. She's hot, but I think my sister's gonna be mad at you."

Alan groaned, rubbing his face as Cinder glanced at him curiously. "We're just friends. Just like I'm only friends with your sister."

Tadashi kept snickering as he climbed back onto his durbo. Alan thought about saying something to Cinder, but she had already ridden ahead to rejoin Avery.

With the storm behind them, they pressed on toward the shrine.

A few hours later, they reached the coast of Albastru Bay. The water was flowing, but chunks of icy slush bobbed along the surface, drifting between small glaciers. To the north, the foothills of the Muunte Mountains loomed.

"Hey, Alan," Tadashi said, nodding toward the water. "Look at that slush. It looks like a blueberry slushie."

Alan grinned. "From a humid, desolate, greyscale forest with red bubbling acid water to frigid, desolate white plains with freezing blue water—we've literally found the polar opposite of where we started. Polar pun intended."

Tadashi chuckled. "So, who are your new pals? None of them are as funny as me, right?"

Alan laughed. "Don't worry, Tadashi, no one could ever bring the kind of laughter you do."

Then, he added, "Well, Elis is the Prince of Wethen. He's one of the few humans there who actually cares about the rights of non-humans."

He continued, "Elis's father, King Alfonse, tries to improve things, but he struggles because the noblemen don't share his vision. They don't want better conditions or lower taxes. So yeah... turns out you can't escape bureaucrats even in another world. But Elis? He's a good guy. When he's king, he won't let others push him around. He'll do what's right for all people—not just humans. I'm looking forward to working with him. I can help watch his back however I can."

Tadashi raised a brow. "So... you don't wanna go back home, then?"

Alan hesitated, glancing to the side. "I mean... home is where the heart is, right? And everything I care about is here. Abigail. My parents. You and Mei. I have Avery back. Elis and Cinder have become important to me too. And... I even have grandparents here I never got to meet."

Tadashi nodded. "Yeah... I feel the same way. Even before I found out my parents were alive, I just liked it better here. Maybe I haven't met the worst people yet, but at least so far, no one's teased me for how I look."

Alan's expression darkened at the memory of how cruel some of the kids back home had been to Tadashi and Mei. They had always defended themselves well and developed thick skin, but it had never been fair.

"Yeah," Alan agreed. "I don't think people here are like that—at least, except when it comes to non-humans. Wethen still has a lot of problems, but I hope we'll get to see the other kingdoms one day. No Marik. No Korvas. Just us, on an actual vacation."

Tadashi smiled. "That would be nice. I think I wanna get to know my parents for a while before we go off on another adventure. I just hope Sobo moves here from Earth... So, what about Cinder? Who is she—aside from just a friend?"

Alan caught the sarcastic tone in Tadashi's voice and sighed. "She's Avery's apprentice in the magical arts. She's really good at it too—you should've seen her fighting the giant crabs and living vines. Anyway, when we first met, she seemed to really dislike me, but after some conversations, things got better."

Tadashi smirked. He was curious about the giant crabs and living vines, but the opportunity to tease Alan was too good to pass up. "Turned on that old Alan Foster charm, huh?"

Alan groaned. "Tadashi, will you quit it with that? Besides, the name is Alan Elwyn now."

Tadashi shook his head. "Nope. Not till you admit it. And yeah, I guess I better get used to the fact that we both have different last names now. I like the sound of Tadashi Mikan—it has a nice ring to it."

Alan huffed. "Admit what? That you're annoying me right now? And yeah, it does have a nice ring. It fits you better. Just think, if you'd used your real name on Earth, no one would have compared you and Mei to fish."

Tadashi's grin widened. "No, no, no—not that. Admit that you like Cinder. I mean, did you even notice the look on her face when you said you're 'just friends'? She looked really sad..."

Alan panicked. "Wait, what? How sad did she look?"

Tadashi's smile stretched even further. "She didn't. But the way you just reacted proves it." He then grinned mischievously and sing-songed, "Alan's got a girlfriend."

Alan groaned again, but Tadashi continued, "Besides, when Abigail described her vision, she said she saw Cinder staring at you while you weren't looking."

Alan sighed. "Tadashi, this isn't funny..."

Tadashi raised his hands in mock innocence. "I'm not kidding. She really did. Then Marik told us her name and recited some story about how she burned down an orphanage... I wonder how many times he practiced that one in front of a bathroom mirror. Do you think he even has a bathroom mirror?"

Alan fell silent for a moment. "Was Abigail sure Cinder wasn't looking at something behind me?"

Tadashi just smiled. "Hey, you know Abigail. It's almost like she has a photographic memory sometimes..."

Alan stared ahead as they rode on.

"Hypothetically... if I did have... feelings for Cinder... do you think saying we're just friends might've hurt her feelings—if she hypothetically had feelings for me?"

Tadashi shrugged. "Nah, you're good. Remember that time Laura Plisken kept harassing you to take her to homecoming? Even after you told her no five times, she still wouldn't leave you alone."

Alan narrowed his eyes. "Tadashi... Laura Plisken got sent to a mental health facility about a week before we came here. She was caught stalking Jeffrey Tubelesky. Cinder does not have a borderline sociopathic obsession with me."

Tadashi raised an eyebrow. "She doesn't? How do you know? You haven't asked her, have you?"

Alan rolled his eyes. "I'm not dignifying that with a response. I don't even know why I'm discussing this with you."

Tadashi smirked. "Because you missed me. And because I'm right, even if you won't admit it. Anyway, wouldn't the best person to ask whether Cinder has feelings for you be... Cinder herself?"

Alan facepalmed. "Tadashi, you can't just bluntly ask someone if they like you. That's not how that kind of thing works."

Tadashi shrugged. "Maybe it should be. Things would be a lot simpler if it was."

Their conversation ended as those ahead of them began to slow. As Alan and Tadashi rode forward to join the others, they saw the reason why.

A massive crevice yawned before them, leading down into a dark, cavernous abyss.

"This is it, isn't it?" Tadashi asked. "This is where they'll exit the Abyssal Cathedral... if they haven't already?"

Avery nodded. "Yes."

Cinder stared into the gaping maw. "I feel cold... and not because of the weather. There's something evil down there—something just below the surface that we can't see... Is that Shadow-Lord's aura?"

Avery shook his head. "No... I do not know what that is. But whatever it is, it will likely obstruct Marik's path into these plains. I do not believe they have exited yet—not after sensing this..."

Alan shivered. The presence was unlike anything he had felt before. Worse than the combined aura of Marik and Daghlesh. Even the durbos were restless.

"Will Mei and Abigail be okay?" he asked.

Avery nodded. "Yes... He won't let any harm befall Abigail or Mei."

Elis frowned. "You mean like how he wouldn't let any harm befall Tadashi? No. I don't think we should trust Shadow-Lord to keep them safe. Maybe we can afford a slight detour—see what's causing that evil aura. Maybe even fight it."

Avery stroked his beard. "I am unsure... If we interfere, we risk encountering them much earlier than expected. If that happens, we would be forcing Marik's hand. Harm would almost certainly come to Mei. If revealed, he would need only Abigail. But if we do not intervene... I believe he will keep Mei safe. I suspect he only tried to kill Tadashi because he learned too much about his plans."

Alan turned to Tadashi. "You and Mei learned Japanese from your grandma, right?"

Tadashi nodded. "Yeah. Why?"

Alan glanced at the stone archway standing near the entrance to the Abyssal Cathedral. "It's a long shot, but maybe you could carve a message over there—one only Mei would understand. I know there's a chance she might not see it, but... it's worth trying."

Tadashi nodded. "I agree." He rode over to the archway and looked back at the others. "Does anyone have a chisel or something?"

Avery shook his head. "I have a better idea. Use this chalk to draw the letters you want, and I will use my Earth magic to carve the message."

Tadashi took the chalk and carefully wrote out—

影 悪い 信頼 アラン, 愛してる、メイメイ

—which roughly translated to:

"Shadow bad. Trust Alan. I love you, Meimei."

No one aside from Mei would understand it. Not even Abigail or Alan knew that "Meimei" was his personal nickname for her.

Avery placed his hand on the archway, and moments later, the letters were etched into the stone as if they had always been there.

"There," Avery said. "Now, we must press onward."

As they journeyed ahead, Alan had shifted to riding beside Wulf. After a moment of silence, Wulf struck up a conversation.

"So, while we were following you, Luna and I caught bits and pieces of what you and your friends talked about—seeing as you all have a habit of speaking rather loudly," he said with a smirk. "If I heard correctly, Marik invaded your dreams, and then when you entered some red forest, someone took the form of Avery Ambrose and brought you here?"

Alan nodded. "Yeah... that's how it started. I kept having nightmares where Marik was chasing me, and they got more vivid and lasted longer each time... until finally, he sent me a direct threat, warning me not to go to the forest our school trip was headed for—where the fake Avery was waiting."

Wulf was quiet for a moment, considering this. "Marik never does anything without a reason. Any chaos in his actions is carefully calculated. So why tell you not to enter the forest if it went against his plans? Why invade your dreams if you were going to meet the fake Avery Ambrose anyway?"

Alan froze at the question, trying to piece together an answer. "I-I... I have no idea. Maybe he just enjoys messing with my head? Someone like him would probably take pleasure in mentally tormenting others."

Wulf shook his head. "I don't think that's it. I believe he studied you and your friends as much as possible so he could predict your reactions to every move he made. His father made him feel worthless, and when he discovered his family's dark heritage, it gave him a purpose. Completing his grandfather's plan—becoming the heir of Materall—is something he wouldn't risk on pointless cruelty. So if anything seems unnecessary, it's because he saw it as vital to ensuring his plan went accordingly. Think back to all your interactions with him. Is there anything that stands out about his invasion of your dreams?"

Alan thought hard before shaking his head. "No... not really. I mean, it just made me distrust him. I couldn't agree with the others about keeping an open mind toward him."

Wulf nodded. "Exactly. He wanted you to distrust him because he needed Abigail to be emotionally vulnerable. That way, he could influence her more easily. Either through Avery or someone he planted in your world, he must have learned that you tend to think with your heart rather than your head."

Alan swallowed. The way Wulf analyzed the situation was unnerving, but then again, he had been friends with Shadow-Lord. He knew the enemy better than anyone. Alan didn't want to dwell on it any longer—there was nothing he could do at this moment to change things. He would have to wait until he confronted Shadow-Lord himself. Instead, he changed the topic.

"Hey, Wulf... can I ask you something? It's about your armor. It looks kinda like... Marik's."

Wulf chuckled dryly. "Yeah, I guess it does. Though I actually wear a helmet, not a mask. Early on while tracing Marik's steps, Luna and I ended up in Skatchator. We came across a few of the scattered kingdoms in the mountains and hills, and in one of them, we met an old blacksmith. He'd made a suit of armor for someone matching Marik's description."

Alan listened as Wulf continued.

"The armor and weapons he forges are unique to that region. They're made from a special ore found only on the highest summits. They call it Dark-Stone Tungsten. It has anti-dark magic properties, and it's as strong as regular tungsten but far less brittle when forged into armor plating or blades. Another bonus—it's lightweight. My armor weighs about fifteen kilograms, but since the weight is evenly distributed, it doesn't slow me down. I mean, it did at first, but over the years, it's become like a second skin."

Now that the ice was broken, Alan felt comfortable enough to ask the question that had been on his mind for a while.

"So... what was he like? Marik, I mean."

Wulf looked ahead, thinking carefully before responding.

"He was... well, he was Marik. But not the Marik you know—not Shadow-Lord. He was kind, caring... a really good friend. With how he and his mother acted, you'd never have guessed the kind of abuse Viktor put them through."

Wulf's voice hardened.

"Marik loved animals—especially his dog, Kyr. The day Kyr died… I won't go into detail. All I'll say is that it was Viktor's fault. That's when Luna and I realized what a sick bastard he truly was."

Alan swallowed, feeling a heavy weight settle in his chest.

"Marik deserved a lot better than he got," Wulf continued. "But there wasn't much we could do to help him and his mother. Viktor was one of the village guards, so he had their protection. Worse, he had blackmail—against my mother, who was a respected member of the town council. There was nothing she could do except try to console Marik's mom whenever things got especially bad."

Alan lowered his gaze. There was no more doubt in his mind about why Marik saw the world as broken—why he believed it needed control.

"I'm so sorry… that all sounds awful," Alan murmured.

Wulf nodded. "It was. But even in the middle of all that, we still had good times. After Viktor died… well, this might sound cold, but it was a blessing in disguise. It felt like things had finally fallen into place. We never questioned whether the Arkarnians were truly responsible. We never thought about the fact that there were so few casualties—and that somehow, we'd been lucky enough that Viktor was one of them. But even if we had questioned it… I doubt I would have suspected Marik. That the Arkarnians had spared most of the town just to cover it up. That my friend—the boy I grew up with—was the heir of a long-dead dark lord I never even believed existed. I always thought Materall was just a ghost story the Mystic Masters spread to scare people away from dark magic."

Wulf let out a heavy sigh.

"I want to believe there's still something left of him to save. That the fact he didn't just kill Tadashi and Yerk outright means there's still some humanity in him. The part that loved his friends, his mother, his dog. The part that stayed positive, even through all the horrors Viktor put him through."

Alan nodded. "For the first time since I've known him… I think I want to believe that too. As you said before, I've felt nothing but hatred for him ever since he dragged us here. I hated that my sister and Mei trusted him, despite everything he did in my mind with those dream invasions. But now… after hearing you and Luna… I realize that my hatred is exactly what he wanted me to feel. I can't see him as just a monster anymore—he's the byproduct of a real one. An alcohol-addled father who despised his only son."

Wulf turned his gaze toward a pile of snow as Alan finished speaking. Something in his demeanor shifted, though Alan wasn't sure why.

"The day he left... it cut deep," Wulf said, his voice quieter. "I caught him talking to an old man and overheard them discussing what had happened. It wasn't the Arkarnian who killed Viktor. The Arkarnian attacked the village under Korvas's command to cover it up. I heard Marik say he was going home to pack, then he'd rendezvous with the old man. They were headed for Skatchator."

Wulf took a slow breath before continuing. "I waited for him on the old east road that night. When he arrived, I confronted him, told him what I'd overheard. I said I'd help cover up what happened with his father, that I'd even help hide the Arkarnian attack, if only he would stay. Stay with his friends. Stay with his family."

He shook his head. "That's when he threatened me. Told me to stay put, to enjoy life with Luna, and to let him go. But I wouldn't back down. Eventually, he relented... then he attacked me. We fought. We both got hurt. I'd like to say I got the better end of it, but he messed me up pretty bad. I blacked out."

Wulf exhaled sharply, as if trying to shake off the memory. "When I came to, I was with the village healer. Marik didn't abandon me. He didn't finish me off like I thought he would. He saved my life." He looked over at Alan. "That's why I can't stop believing that Marik is still in there... even if it's buried beneath all that dark magic."

Alan nodded. "You've given me a lot to think about. And from my experience... I think you're right. Dark magic changes people. When I accidentally used it to kill that Boh-Rahl chieftain attacking my mother... it was like I was myself, but also... someone else entirely."

Wulf gave him a knowing glance. "Even so, it wouldn't hurt to learn the basics—just enough to control it without hurting yourself."

Then, almost as an afterthought, he added, "If you're anything like your sister, you'd probably pick it up quickly."

Alan scratched his head, seizing the opportunity to change the subject. "Speaking of Abigail... how is she? Is she learning anything dangerous from Marik?"

Wulf shook his head. "No, don't worry. He's only been teaching her water and earth magic. I think, deep down—despite the whole mind parasite situation—Marik is afraid of her. That's probably why he wants to control her. He can most likely sense some kind of powerful magic within her.

"As for how she's doing..." Wulf's voice turned somber. "I think she's barely holding it together. Her heart is telling her one thing, but the parasite is whispering another. And... well, it's clear that you not being there has been hard on her. Hard on all of them."

Alan lowered his head. "I feel bad for leaving them... I feel bad for a lot of things. But recently, my mind keeps going back to the Arkarnian chieftain I killed. I keep wondering... how much of that was Marik's plan, and how much of it was my own doing?"

Wulf shook his head. "I get it. But tell me this—when that chieftain was attacking your mother, was there any other way to stop him without her dying?"

Alan hesitated, then sighed. "No... I guess there really wasn't. I didn't have enough mass to tackle him. The only choice was to cut him down."

Wulf looked ahead. "Then when you close your eyes and see his face... don't pity yourself. Pity him—for making the choices that led to his death."

Alan gave Wulf a small, half-hearted smile. "Thanks. I'll think about it. I think... there's wisdom in what you're saying. Cinder tried to tell me something similar, but at the time, I just didn't want to hear it."

At the mention of Cinder, Wulf chuckled. "Hey, I overheard your conversation with Tadashi. If you ever need advice, well... Luna and I have been a couple for, what, three or four years now? I must know something."

Alan's face turned red. "I'll think about it."

Wulf laughed. "Don't worry, your secret's safe with me. Hopefully, Tadashi can say the same and won't run off to tell Cinder. Actually... if you squint, I think he might be riding next to her right now."

Alan's eyes widened. "Wait, what? I gotta go!"

With that, he spurred his mount forward, leaving Wulf snickering behind him.

As the group pressed onward, they reached an overlook where the path ahead was blocked by high ridges of rock and ice. Only one opening remained—further north, leading down into what appeared to be a canyon.

Alan sighed and turned to Baldric and Avery. "It's getting late. We could at least make it to the rock face and set up camp with our backs against it. I don't know about trying to push through the canyon tonight. We should wait until daybreak. Besides... I don't know how much longer the durbos can handle constant movement."

Avery stroked his beard. "I understand your concern for the durbos, Alan, but we have no idea how close behind Marik is. I say we keep moving until we hit the canyon, then find a place to camp inside."

Baldric eyed the distant passage warily. "I don't like the look of that canyon. It's prime territory for the Valthurg. I can't imagine every single one of them left to mine out that tunnel to Undergate. I agree with Alan—we should take the canyon at first light."

Avery frowned. He had hoped Baldric would back his plan. But when Wulf spoke up, Avery abandoned all hope of convincing the group to push forward.

"We can't beat Marik to the shrine if we get our throats slit in the night by the Valthurg," Wulf said. "I'm not even sure we should move as far as the rock face. I think we should stop and make camp here."

Avery sighed. "Very well, I see your points. We can make camp here or continue onward to the cliffside. There are pros and cons to both, so we should weigh our options carefully. Baldric suspects the Valthurg may be lurking in the canyon, and Wulf has implied that setting up camp near the ridge could put us in a danger zone. However, if we stay here, we'll be more exposed to the elements."

Cinder and Tadashi remained quiet, both deep in thought, trying to come up with a solution. Their concentration was broken when Sobek chuckled cynically.

"Possibly freezing to death in our sleep or possibly getting our throats slit by the Valthurg. What lovely options."

Wulf grunted at Sobek's pessimism. "If we stay here, the durbos can at least form a circle around us for protection. I understand this journey has been difficult, but try to control yourself. Complaining out loud like that will only lower morale."

Sobek nodded slowly. "I apologize. I didn't mean to come across that way. I'm just frustrated that there isn't a more direct path to our destination."

Yerk suddenly spoke up. "What if magic people make big flame to burn hole in ice? Then we no go through canyon with mean ice lizards."

Avery considered the idea and nodded. "It could work. Cinder can carve a tunnel, and I'll use earth and ice magic to reinforce it. However, my knowledge of ice magic is fairly basic. If anything seems off, someone speak up."

Cinder added, "At some point along the way, you could create an ice wall with breathing holes to block the entrance, in case we can't get through before we need to rest."

With their plan set, the group pressed onward to the ridge. As they moved closer, there were no signs of Valthurg activity. Some of them, sensing relief, let their guard down—until Baldric's voice cut through the silence.

"Just because we can't see them doesn't mean they can't see us. Tread carefully. Unlike most Arkarnians, the Valthurg thrive in the cold. Sometimes they bury themselves in the snow, awakening only when they sense prey above them. The best way to spot them is to look for areas where the snow is finer and looser rather than packed and dense. But if the snow has been windswept... we won't be able to tell at all."

A chill ran through the group, but they pressed on.

When they reached the wall of ice, Cinder conjured flames in both hands, tracing an opening large enough for the durbos to pass through.

They continued like this for hours, Cinder melting a path while Avery reinforced the tunnel's structure. The interior was slippery at first, but Avery countered this by raising stone from beneath the ice to create a stable path.

Suddenly, Cinder stopped. She took a step back, her expression shifting.

"Avery..." she said slowly. "There's something in the ice."

Avery frowned. "What do you mean?"

"Look for yourself." She pointed to a spot just ahead.

Avery followed her gaze—and saw it. A large, five-clawed hand, feathered and white, protruded from the ice.

Then it moved.

Avery's eyes widened. "What in the—"

Before he could finish, the hand retracted into the ice.

Cinder and Avery exchanged a look and slowly backed away toward Alan. Avery bumped into him, startling him.

"Whoa—!" Alan turned to face him. "What's wrong?"

Avery raised a hand, signaling him to be quiet. A deep, resonating crack echoed through the tunnel. The sound moved around them, shifting through the ice like a living thing.

For a moment, silence.

Then, all hell broke loose.

The ice shattered as eight feathered appendages with hooked claws burst through, slashing and grabbing wildly. One of the monstrous limbs seized Wulf, slamming him against the tunnel wall. The impact sent cracks spiderwebbing through the ice until, with a final shattering explosion, the wall gave way—revealing a massive open cave.

Alan barely had time to process what he was seeing. A creature lurked within the chamber, massive and grotesque. It had the body of a cephalopod, covered in thick white feathers, with countless beady black eyes spread across its form.

Wulf reacted fast, pulling his sword from its scabbard and cleaving through the tentacle that held him. He fell hard onto the cave floor, a sickening pop sounding as his shoulder struck a rock.

Elis, Avery, and Alan rushed in to help him while Yerk grabbed Tadashi, hauling him onto a durbo and riding away from the monster.

Baldric and Sobek hacked at the thrashing tentacles, shouting in alarm.

"It's a Ktoves!" Baldric yelled. "We have to get out of here!"

Avery and Elis hauled Wulf to his feet as Alan and Baldric continued fending off the creature's claws. Cinder conjured balls of fire and hurled them at the beast.

Then, in a blur of movement, one of the monstrous limbs lashed out and seized Alan.

It hurled him across the cave. He hit the far wall, but a pile of slush cushioned his impact—barely saving him from a fatal collision.

Elis and Cinder rushed to his side. Cinder ran her hand over the back of his head, checking for blood. Satisfied that there was none, she met his gaze, scanning for signs of a concussion.

"I'm fine," Alan assured her. "Thank you."

As they helped him up, the Ktoves let out a deafening shriek.

The durbos panicked. Their fight-or-flight instincts kicked in, and five of them bolted into the tunnel. But their sheer size prevented them from turning around—forcing them into a direct collision course with Alan, Elis, and Cinder.

The three reacted quickly, leaping onto the durbos' backs just as the stampeding creatures passed beneath them.

Avery shouted after them. "Keep going without us! We'll take the canyon path and go around! Be careful!"

With no choice, Avery and Baldric turned and sprinted back the way they had come, chasing after the remaining durbos.

Alan steadied himself atop his mount, glancing to either side. Cinder and Elis rode alongside him, both wearing the same expression of concern.

They all knew the truth—

It was up to them now.

If they didn't reach the Shrine of Morimor before the Shadow-Lord, all would be lost.

As the durbos thundered across the open snow, Alan's mind raced. Had they managed to stay ahead of Marik? Or had he already passed them?

Had he already reached the shrine?

Pushing those thoughts aside, Alan focused on the task at hand. He tightened his grip on the reins, guiding his durbo forward—toward whatever lay ahead.

Once they brought their durbos to a halt, they moved forward cautiously, eyes fixed on the frozen lake ahead. In the center of the shimmering ice stood a structure—there was no doubt in their minds. This had to be the Shrine of Morimor.

"So... we're almost there," Elis murmured. "Just one final push. It looks mostly clear, but... considering what Baldric said about the Valthurg possibly hiding under the snow, we should probably move slowly and stay cautious."

Alan shook his head. "If anything tries to stop us, we'll handle it. But I think we need to keep a steady, direct pace. We can't afford to waste time." He glanced at Elis. "But in the end, you're the Prince here, so it's your call."

Elis chuckled. "Oh no, no, no. Me being a Prince doesn't mean I'm in charge here. As much as I appreciate being offered the choice, I'm going to let you and Cinder decide. You two should probably start getting used to making decisions together anyway."

Cinder and Alan exchanged a glance before Cinder frowned. "What do you mean, we need to get used to making decisions together?"

Elis stammered, then quickly came up with an explanation. "Well, when we get back to Wethen—once all of this is over—I imagine Alan will want to help Avery with whatever jobs my father assigns him. And since you're Avery's apprentice, you'll be helping too. A lot of those tasks will probably require teamwork."

Cinder blinked, seemingly accepting that reasoning. "Huh... well, I agree with Alan. We have no proof that the Shadow-Lord is still behind us, so we should assume he's already ahead and keep moving like we're racing against him."

With that, the three pressed forward in a straight beeline for the Shrine of Morimor.

Chapter Forty-One

Following the Trail

It had been a few hours since they escaped the cultists, but finally, after what felt like an eternity, the five of them emerged from the tunnel. They found themselves in an icy cave, the air much colder than before. Gorb and Glum quickly began opening a large satchel, pulling out warm clothing for Abigail and Mei. Marik called back to them as he looked ahead.

"Just put it on over what you're already wearing," he said, "You'll need the layers for this frigid hellscape..."

Abigail and Mei realized there were no clothes for Marik, as Gorb and Glum donned heavy winter coats.

Mei glanced at him and asked, "Where are your clothes, Marik?"

He turned back to her with a smirk. "The cold doesn't bother me. Through dark magic, I've learned how to maintain my body heat, no matter the temperature. Another positive application of dark magic."

As they exited the cave, they saw a large stone archway in front of them, leading to an incline. Footprints and hoofprints were scattered across the snow, heading in two different directions. Mei stepped toward the archway and scanned the area, while Abigail and Marik examined the tracks.

"There's no doubt they've passed through here," Marik said. "We have to follow their trail."

Abigail studied the two sets of prints. "Which way, though? The Abyssal Cathedral has me all turned around..."

Marik pointed in one direction. "That way. I'm certain of it. Come on, we must move quickly. I had hoped we'd exit near some durbos so we could use mounts, but that's not the case. We're far more exposed to the elements here..."

Marik, Abigail, and the Morgs started following the trail. "Come on, Mei!" Marik called. "You heard me! No time for sightseeing!"

Mei paused, staring at the arch. "Alright... I'm coming..." She kept reading the strange markings on the stone, realizing they were Japanese characters, quickly and quietly deciphering the message.

影悪い 信頼 アラン, 愛してる、メイメイ

... It translated to: "Shadow bad, trust Alan, I love you, Meimei."

A sense of dread washed over her, and her mind raced. Alan had been right. Somehow, Tadashi was with Alan, which meant Marik had lied about his injuries. Mei wanted to call Abigail over to show her the message, but she knew Marik would follow. And with how strange Abigail had been whenever Mei raised doubts about Marik, she felt her words wouldn't be enough. All she could do now was try to slow their progress and buy Alan, Avery, and Tadashi some time.

As Mei rejoined the group, she walked next to Abigail, subtly scanning the white plains ahead of them for something to use as a distraction. But aside from the occasional ice spike, there was little to see. Finally, as they climbed a hill, Mei saw the perfect opportunity. She stumbled and rolled down the hill, shouting out for cover, "Craaaap!"

As she hit the bottom, she heard a crackling noise, but it wasn't her body she was concerned about. Before she could call out to Abigail, she realized the ice beneath them was giving way. But instead of falling into water, they dropped into what appeared to be an old, abandoned village.

As the two girls lay on the ground, groaning in pain, Mei sighed. "I bet Alan didn't have to deal with this many underground places... What is this? The fifth time we've ended up underground?"

Abigail grunted, pushing herself to her feet. "Seventh, if you count the cave we went through when we arrived in the Forgotten Lands... the one with the dead arkarnians, the Grotto of Life, the brambly area, the gnoglin mine, and of course, the cathedral."

Abigail reached out and helped Mei up.

Looking around, they saw bones scattered beneath the ice and protruding from the snow. "What do you think happened here?" Abigail asked.

At that moment, Marik dropped down behind them, with Gorb and Glum not far behind.

"Are you two alright?" he asked.

Abigail nodded. "Yeah, just some bruises."

Mei started to wander around the village. Against her better judgment, she knew she needed to delay Marik as much as possible. So, she continued walking, with Abigail following.

"Hold on, Mei," Abigail called. "I think we can climb out where we fell in."

Mei entered one of the old village homes. "Hang on, I'll be right there. I want to take a look. This is probably the only chance we'll ever have to see this place. If we do come back to the Forgotten Lands, I doubt we'll want to return to the Polar Regions after all this trouble."

Abigail hesitated. "Well, yes, but we are in a bit of a hurry now..."

Mei chuckled. "Relax, Abigail. There's no proof those tracks were theirs. It could've been the Valthurg Arkarnians."

Abigail raised a finger in protest. "But Marik said they aren't known to leave tracks, and if they do, they conceal them."

Mei glanced back at Abigail, who was rummaging through an old cabinet drawer. "But if the Valthurg haven't been seen in over, what—40 years? How would he know? Unless he's been here recently, which would make one wonder... why take such a long, arduous journey if he had a shortcut?"

Abigail narrowed her eyes. "Where are you going with this?"

Mei shrugged. "I'm just saying... either Marik knows what he's talking about, which means he's been lying, or he has no clue, which means he's been making things up. He can't be both, Abs. And I wish you'd stop getting so defensive every time I'm critical of him. Remember what we told Alan? We wouldn't fully trust Shadow-Lord. I'm getting real sick of feeling like you're relying on him more than on me."

Abigail scoffed. "What is that supposed to mean, Mei?"

Mei crossed her arms and scoffed in return. "You don't know? No, I think you do. Don't think I haven't overheard the things you talk about with him."

Abigail's face reddened with anger. "Those conversations were private, Mei."

Mei shook her head, staring into Abigail's enraged eyes for a long moment. Marik hadn't followed them yet, but Mei knew it was only a matter of time before he grew impatient with their lack of progress.

Finally, Mei broke the silence.

"For someone so smart and attentive, you can be blind and stupid," she said softly. "You don't think I'm trying to look out for you? We've always had each other's backs. I've been your best friend since we were kids. But ever since Marik started training you, it's felt like our friendship's become one-sided. I'm trying to be there for you, Abigail, but it's getting hard. It feels like you're pushing me away, and I really hate that..."

Mei's eyes welled up with tears, which froze as they streamed down her face.

Abigail's anger faded, and she walked up to Mei, enveloping her in a hug. She whispered softly into her ear, "I'm sorry... you're right. I've been trusting him more than I probably should have... but I have this gut feeling that Avery is the real evil here. Now, come on... let's get moving."

Mei didn't say anything. She simply hugged Abigail back. She knew Abigail's gut instinct had never led her astray back home, but Mei had concerns of her own. She began to wonder if Marik was manipulating her emotions, making her believe something that might not be true.

The two headed back to where Marik and the Morgs were waiting. The five of them climbed out and made their way to the top of the hill. From there, they could see a mountain ridge in the distance.

Marik pointed. "Beyond that ridge is where we must go. I can feel it. Come, let's follow their trail."

As they traveled, they noticed some animals walking in their direction.

"Hm... durbos," Marik murmured. "Probably from Avery's party. There are too few of them for us all to use, so let's not bother with them."

They continued onward, eventually reaching a hole in the ridge that looked manmade.

"Hmm..." Marik observed. "There's a trail leading into that passage, and another heading toward the pass."

Marik looked between the two paths. He knew that if they went to the pass, they'd be more likely to run into Tadashi and Yerk, so he decided to explore what had caused their enemies to flee the tunnel they had seemingly created.

Marik stepped forward, and the others followed.

As they moved deeper, they stumbled upon a horrific creature, asleep in a large open cave.

"Number 8..." Abigail muttered to Mei with a hint of humor.

Marik scanned the area, then whispered, "It seems to be sleeping. Let's try to move past it quietly. I think I see a pathway over there that might lead out of the cave."

The five of them carefully made their way over one of the creature's long, bleeding tentacles. It was scorched in some places, suggesting that it had been injured by Avery's party.

Just as Mei was about to step over it, she stomped down hard on the tentacle when no one was looking. The creature let out a high-pitched growl as it awoke. Mei jumped aside just as it tried to swipe at her. She glanced at the others and saw Gorb and Glum already running for the exit. Marik and Abigail turned to face the creature.

Marik pulled his sword and slashed at one of the tentacles as it lunged toward Mei, cutting it down to size. A black, mud-like blood sprayed from the wound, splattering across Mei's upper body and face.

"UGH! IT'S IN MY EYES!" she screamed.

Abigail rushed to Mei's side, guiding her toward the exit as the creature flailed in pain. Marik kept attacking it, but the beast countered his strikes. Frustrated, Marik switched to another method. He used magic to slam the tentacled terror up into the ceiling with such force that not only was the creature killed, but the entire cave began to shake. Huge chunks of rock came crashing down.

Marik quickly realized he was cut off from following them. Even with Abigail's and his combined strength, it was too dangerous to try lifting any of the boulders blocking the way. With deep resignation, Marik's booming voice echoed through the chaos. "Keep going! You should be able to see the temple where Morimor's Shrine is located! I'll take the long way and meet you there! Don't wait for me!"

Abigail didn't respond. She focused on getting Mei out of the cave and into the snow. She scooped up a handful of snow, pressing it gently against Mei's eyes to wash away the blood.

Once Mei could see again, they both stood up and looked ahead. The temple loomed in the distance, sitting at the center of a frozen lake.

Abigail waved for Mei, Gorb, and Glum to follow her. "Come on... we're almost there. Marik said not to wait for him."

Mei wasn't sure how to feel in that moment. She didn't know if she had just bought Alan and Avery some time, or if she had just given Marik the opportunity to attack them as violently as he wanted, without any witnesses. But the recent animal tracks leading toward the temple filled her with hope. Maybe Alan and Tadashi were ahead of them, and whatever tracks Marik had seen heading toward the pass didn't matter.

Chapter Forty-Two

The Valthurg

Baldric and Wulf carefully navigated through the pass, searching for any sign of Valthurg activity.

Wulf glanced up at the top of the ridge that lined the pass and nudged Baldric's arm. "Careful... those rocks up there look like they'd be deadly if they fell."

Baldric grunted in response. "Those rocks didn't naturally form there... Now I'm certain we're approaching a Valthurg encampment or village, somewhere beyond this pass. In my experience with the Valthurg, they're often skittish and set traps. These boulders are probably part of one—something they'd roll down at intruders if they spot anyone coming."

Wulf shot Baldric a look. "If it is a village, what's your assessment of our ability to get through it?"

Baldric scratched his cheek thoughtfully. "Well... we either turn back and face one big monster, or we press forward, sneak through, and risk dealing with a whole lot of monsters. It might be easier to avoid the big one, since I've seen warriors I thought were stronger than me get slaughtered by the Valthurg. However, the lack of boulders rolling toward us means there might be no one living in the village, if it even exists."

Wulf turned and started walking back toward the others. "Alright... Let's run it by Ambrose."

Baldric silently nodded and followed him. "So... got any interesting war stories, Baldric?"

Baldric sighed. "This isn't the time or place for swapping stories, kid."

Wulf shrugged. "It's a long walk back to the others. If the Valthurg didn't hear you choking on your saliva a few minutes ago, they won't hear us talking."

Baldric scoffed. "It wasn't saliva. It was one of my baby teeth."

Wulf stopped walking for a moment. "Kirith! How old are you?"

Baldric pondered the question. "Pushing fifty-something... I can't say for certain. I haven't celebrated my birthday in quite a while."

Wulf blinked. "You're in your fifties, and you still have baby teeth?"

Baldric replied skeptically, as if Wulf should've known. "Yeah? When do humans start losing theirs?"

Wulf chuckled. "I was about six or seven when my baby teeth started falling out."

Baldric smiled, letting Wulf know he was joking. "Guess humans just aren't designed to last as long as arkarnians, huh? In all seriousness, though, imagine if that's why the Rau-Trava are so anti-human—not because of Wethen's treatment of arkarnians, but because of how long your baby teeth last."

Wulf laughed. "Now that would be an interesting revelation."

After a while, they reached the spot where the others had been waiting, minus Tadashi, who was busy teaching Yerk how to make snowballs.

Baldric shook his head and approached Avery. "The way ahead is clear for a few meters. We stopped advancing after a while, but we're fairly sure there's a village somewhere in the pass."

Avery nodded slowly. "Then we press onward. While you were away, I sensed Marik's presence... I believe he's approaching our position."

Wulf narrowed his eyes. "If you can sense him, then he can sense you, right?"

Avery nodded. "Yes, and this pass is no place for a fight."

Tadashi interjected. "But what if Mei got my message? Shouldn't we try to get her and Abigail away from Shadow-Lord?"

Avery shook his head. "No... I don't think they're with him. I suspect they took the same path that separated us from Alan, Elis, and Cinder, and that Marik has been separated from the rest of his group."

Yerk looked down. "Aw... I want to tell Gorb and Glum that boss is bad man..."

Avery placed a hand on Yerk's shoulder. "Worry not, Yerk. You'll get that chance, I'm sure."

Avery's eyes widened as Yerk suddenly pulled him into a huge bear hug. "Aww, thank you, Abery! You're really nice to me! You don't yell at me or say bad things!"

Avery patted Yerk on the back, struggling to breathe. "Okay, okay! I get it! You're really happy to have been freed from Marik's service. I'll be happy to help you and all your fellow Morgs find new jobs once you're all free!"

Yerk's hug tightened, and Avery struggled for air.

Finally, after what felt like an hour to Avery, but was only a minute in reality, Yerk set him down and released him.

The group moved forward through the pass together.

As they reached the point where Wulf and Baldric had paused before returning, the air became noticeably warmer. Soon, they realized the cause of the change: an open stretch of land with several hot springs. The ground ahead of them was dry, devoid of ice and snow. Over one of the smaller springs, a construct held what appeared to be meat, cooking in the occasional spray of hot water from the geyser.

Beyond the warmth of the hot springs lay igloo-like structures made of ice, reinforced with stone and scraps of metal. The group quickly crouched down, looking for any signs of the village's inhabitants.

Avery searched for an alternative path that would avoid the village, but after a moment, he knew there was no choice. The only path forward led straight into danger.

The six of them cautiously entered the village, leaving the comforting warmth of the hot springs behind, knowing they had no time to stop and enjoy it.

For a while, it seemed as though there were no Valthurg around, as if they'd all gone out hunting. But as they rounded a corner, they saw a group of at least twenty Valthurg arkarnians gathered in the village center.

A distinct, foul smell seemed to emanate from the Valthurg, causing Tadashi to cringe.

"Ew... what is that stench?" he whispered.

Baldric winced. "I'm not sure... It could be their village or the food they're cooking. I don't recall them having a foul body odor."

Wulf eyed the arkarnians carefully. He could count at least four separate occasions where he had battled groups of ten Rau-Trava warriors by himself, but these were Valthurg, and they were foreign to him. As he looked them over, he noticed significant differences from the arkarnians he had encountered before.

Their scales were thicker, pale, and translucent. They stood much taller than Baldric, about seven and a half feet, which explained the tall doorways he had noticed earlier. Their bodies were muscular, and their eyes appeared to be unblinking. Wulf and Tadashi, the least familiar with this subspecies, couldn't help but wonder if they even had eyelids, and if not, how they slept.

As they approached cautiously, the six of them saw the Valthurg gathered around some sort of sacrificial structure.

Two bloody bodies lay on the structure, and nearby, the hide of other Valthurg arkarnians was being tanned. The gruesome sight reminded Tadashi of the tanning racks of human skin and buckets of gore he had seen in a Rau-Travan camp days earlier.

Though the sight of the skinned bodies didn't faze Tadashi, who had seen much worse, he had to cover his mouth and close his eyes at what happened next.

Four of the Valthurg began eating their dead like wild animals.

Even Avery, who usually appeared the most hardened of the group, audibly gagged. The group all made noises of disgust as their nerves betrayed them.

The Valthurg turned and looked in their direction.

Tadashi muttered something in Japanese, which Avery assumed was a word he didn't want anyone to hear.

Avery cast a large wall of fire and pushed it forward, aiming directly at the group of arkarnians. As the flames engulfed the Valthurg only to dissipate, Avery's heart sank with horror—he realized, too late, that the Valthurg were resistant to fire magic.

The Valthurg clan began picking up their weapons and advancing toward them. Baldric quickly whispered, "Follow my lead. If we rush them, we should catch them off guard and run past. They'll never expect us to be bold enough to attack with such a small group."

They exchanged glances for a moment, then sprinted toward the Valthurg. Yerk grabbed Tadashi and threw him over his back to shield him from any incoming weapons.

As they barreled through the group, Wulf, Baldric, and Sobek slashed at the Valthurg warriors, taking down at least four of them.

It didn't take long—just as Baldric had suspected—the Valthurg were slow to react, dazed by how quickly they'd pushed through them. But the confusion didn't last long. Soon, their enemies yelled out in Arkarnian, and the chase was on.

While fleeing, the group noticed that there were more Valthurg in the village than they had originally thought. Many exited their homes to join the pursuit.

Eventually, the six of them reached a chasm that stretched across to the exit of the pass. Suspended over the chasm were five metal catwalks, all appearing to be in good condition. Avery chose one and began running, and the others followed closely behind.

Baldric glanced back, slowing down. "Hold on! Why aren't they following?"

The group stopped and turned to look. Avery froze as he saw a familiar armored figure walking across one of the adjacent catwalks—Marik.

Marik slowed as he approached, first looking at Tadashi and Yerk. "For what it's worth... I didn't feel very good about myself after our last meeting."

Yerk grunted and shot back, "Old boss can stuff it."

Marik nodded slowly and then turned his attention to Wulf, completely ignoring Baldric and Sobek.

"Hm... I don't believe I know you... But you—you were following me. I take it Tadashi and Yerk's survival is thanks to your intervention?"

Wulf nodded slowly as Marik continued. "And just who are you?"

Wulf had thought for years about what he would say if he ever encountered his old friend again. It had been a long, vicious debate in the recesses of his mind, but he had never been able to decide on the right words. For now, he chose silence, ignoring Marik's question entirely.

Marik then turned his gaze to Avery. "You appear to be... a few heads short. Did your headstrong apprentice, the idealistic prince, Lady Elwyn, and her son perish on the way here?"

Avery crossed his arms. "Alan, Elis, and Cinder are most likely at the Shrine by now. As for Madeline, she's riding back to Wethen to warn the King of your alliance with the Rau-Trava and Valthurg."

For a moment, Marik seemed to lose his composure. "How did you learn of that?... No matter. Abigail will deal with your lackeys soon enough, and I'll be there to claim my prize. It would be so easy to kill you right now... but since I want our final meeting to be one where I personally crush the life out of you—and because I don't want Tadashi to die—I'll simply ensure you won't arrive until I've completed my goals."

Marik raised a hand and cast an ice spell, summoning thick walls of ice that formed ahead of them. With the Valthurg closing in from behind, their only choice was for Avery to use his fire magic to burn their way through—something Marik knew would take them quite some time.

Avery sighed as Marik began to run off, knowing that he didn't have the necessary spells to deal with the ice as Marik had.

Tadashi's frustration flared. "Avery, start melting the ice! We have to catch up to him!"

Avery snapped out of his stupor and immediately began to focus all his energy on melting the ice. He pushed himself harder than ever before, fully aware that this would likely deplete him to the point where he wouldn't be able to face Marik in a one-on-one fight afterward. He knew Marik was aware of this vulnerability, too.

CHAPTER FORTY-THREE

The Shrine of Morimor

It had taken quite a bit of time, but Alan, Elis, and Cinder had finally figured out how to cross the frozen lake without disturbing the ice.

The three of them entered the temple, walking through its vast halls in search of the Shrine. After an hour, they reached a dead end and began to backtrack.

"It's much warmer in here than it is outside... and how is there so much light?" Cinder marveled, looking around at the strange but wondrous halls of the isolated temple.

Alan glanced at her a few times, amused by this unknown side of Cinder's personality. Elis and Alan exchanged a look, and Elis shrugged.

As they rounded a corner, Cinder stopped and stared ahead. When Alan followed her line of sight, he grinned and shouted, "Abigail! Mei!"

Mei smiled, ran over, and gave Alan a big hug. Abigail, however, folded her arms and stared at Alan. As Mei released her friend, Alan stepped toward Abigail, but she immediately stepped back, raising a hand.

"No... you stay back, Alan. Mei... come back over here."

Mei ignored Abigail's concerned tone and instead looked around at Alan's group. "Where's Tadashi?"

Alan smiled. "So you did get the message. He's not with us right now. He's with Avery, Yerk, and the others in our group. We got separated by a giant bird-squid monster."

Mei chuckled. "We got separated from Marik by that thing after I stepped on it to wake it up."

Abigail shouted across the hall, "You did what?! And what message are you talking about?!"

Mei turned to her. "Tadashi left a message in Japanese. It said, 'Shadow Bad, Trust Alan...' I don't know how, but Marik lied about what happened... just like he's been lying about everything else. But it's okay now, Abs. We can get the gang back together and stop him."

Abigail waved her hand dismissively. "Mei, Avery left that message to trick you. Think about it. If you'd just told me, we could've cleared up your confusion. Avery's trying to turn you against me, just like he's corrupted Alan..."

Mei shook her head. "No, Abigail, there's no way it was Avery. In the message, Tadashi used his nickname for me—neither you nor Alan ever knew it. Not even Sobo did. No way Avery knew it. Stop trusting Marik. We're your friends, not him!"

Alan sighed. "Mei... it's not her fault. We learned from a... reliable source that there's a parasite inside her. It's making her instinctively believe everything Marik tells her." He then turned to address his sister. "It's going to be okay, Abigail. Avery... he can help you. Please, don't listen to your gut feeling. Trust me, try to fight it."

Abigail's mind began to race. Alan's tone wasn't threatening, but suddenly, she felt threatened. "A dark magic parasite? Just like... those cultists in the Abyssal Cathedral... Oh no... no... stay away... I can't... I can't fight... oh my God... Mei, Alan, I'm so sorry... I can't—GAH!"

Abigail screamed in frustration as she realized she couldn't control her own body. The parasite, sensing danger, began to puppeteer her, forcing her to rip a chunk of marble from the ground with her earth magic.

She hurled the marble across the hallway at Alan and Mei, but before it could hit them, Cinder reacted swiftly, pushing the marble into the wall with a burst of air magic.

The two girls exchanged blows, casting and countering magical attacks, while Alan and Mei screamed for Abigail to fight back against the parasite.

Abigail's head felt like it was going to split in two as she battled the creature inside her. Slowly, her love for Alan and Mei overpowered the parasite's control.

After a fierce mental struggle, Abigail finally stopped attacking Cinder and fell to her knees, screaming in agony. Alan and Mei rushed to her side, helpless, watching as she thrashed, the bone-chilling sounds of her suffering echoing through the temple.

Then, with one final scream, Abigail's convulsions stopped, and there was silence. Mei's eyes filled with tears, fearing that Abigail had died.

But soon, Abigail's mouth opened, and a dark, chitinous creature—shadow bleeding off of it like smoke—crawled out of her body. It made a slow, sinister move for a crack in the floor. Mei stepped on it repeatedly until it stopped screeching and moving.

Alan could only stare at Abigail, stunned. Mei fell to her side, sobbing, her tear-soaked face buried in her seemingly lifeless best friend's chest.

Finally, Alan fell to his knees and screamed in anguish. Cinder could only watch, feeling a deep sadness at seeing Alan in so much pain.

Then, suddenly, Abigail took a sharp breath and opened her eyes. Alan and Mei's pain lifted as they helped her sit up and embraced her.

Abigail began crying. "I would've killed both of you..."

Mei hushed her gently, and Alan sighed in relief, comforting his sister. "It's okay... we're all okay. It wasn't your fault... everything will be okay now."

Gorb and Glum wiped tears from their eyes. "Gorb give me hug, my eyes all leaky!"

The Morgs embraced, their hearts touched by the scene in front of them.

Cinder smiled, but an urgent thought gripped her. "I don't want to spoil this moment... but I doubt Shadow-Lord is going to be far behind us. Abigail, if you can stand, we should get moving."

Abigail nodded, standing with Mei and Alan's help. "Yeah... I can stand on my own two feet, Cynthia. Any idea where the Orb is?"

Cinder's eyes twitched.

"My name is Cinder. No one calls me by my birth name, let alone any derivatives of it."

Elis whispered teasingly, "Well, nobody *except* Alan, right?" Cinder punched Elis in the arm, and he yelped in pain.

Cinder took charge, walking down the corridor with purpose. Everyone hurried after her.

As they moved through the temple, Abigail froze.

"I think... I think I can hear it... the Orb."

Cinder, Alan, and Mei exchanged looks before Alan asked, "You can hear it?"

Abigail nodded. "While I was sleeping one night, I was approached in my dreams by Avery's father. The parasite in my head told me it was just Avery trying to trick me, but now I know better. I know he was telling the truth. He explained everything about Matteral and what he did... but more importantly, he told me that I have a rare ability to hear and commune with the dead."

Mei blinked. "If you can hear the dead, why couldn't you talk to those skeletons we encountered when we first came here? Or any of the other dead things we've seen since?"

Abigail paused, thinking. "I'm not entirely sure... it might be limited to the spirits of highly magically adept people, like Avery's father... and Morimor himself..."

Alan nodded.

"Well, according to the story, Livimor and Morimor died after they ripped their souls out of their bodies and into each other's orb... Let's follow those voices."

Abigail led the group down a warm corridor. As they progressed, the temperature rose, growing warmer with each step. Eventually, they reached a large chamber, reminiscent of the Grotto of Life. Trees, grass, and a bright, sun-like light shone down from above. A massive crystal, larger than the ones Abigail and Mei had seen in the Gnoglins' mines, hung from the ceiling.

In the center of the room stood a large evergreen with ice-like bark and thick, heavy branches adorned with sapphire-blue needles that shimmered in the light.

"This is it... isn't it?" Elis said, his voice echoing across the chamber. "This is where our quest ends."

A voice answered from somewhere else in the room. "Yes... it is..."

They all looked around, desperately trying to locate the source of the voice. Then, Alan glanced at Abigail. She nodded, signaling that they were on the same page.

Abigail feigned calm, pretending to still be under Marik's influence. "Marik, where are you? Let's hurry up and find the Orb and get out of here."

Shadow-Lord stepped out from behind a tree, smiling beneath his helmet. Abigail's ruse had worked—he still believed she was under his control.

"Go on ahead, Abs... We'll accompany you shortly. I need to have some words with Alan and the others now."

Abigail nodded and began walking ahead, glancing back. She knew Alan and the others were in grave danger, but she also understood the importance of getting the Orb while Marik was distracted.

The others understood the unspoken message between Alan and Abigail, so they kept up the act and didn't betray her.

As Abigail disappeared down a path of bushes, all eyes turned toward Marik.

Mei frowned. "Nobody calls Abigail that except for her friends..."

Marik chuckled darkly. "Oh, yes, I know that. But you see, I'm her only friend now. She obeys me without question. By now, there's no thought in her little mind that wasn't preordained by me. You've lost Alan. You've lost your sister. You've lost the Orb. And soon, once the Rau-Trava and Valthurg armies reach Wethen, you'll lose your dear father. I predict James's final thoughts will be of how you failed him, how you screwed up."

Alan stood still, trying to center himself. He remembered his conversations with Wulf about Marik and refused to let Marik bait him.

Marik frowned, sensing a lack of anger in Alan. He needed Alan to lash out, to be blinded by rage. "Of course, I'll be sure to have your mother captured, so you can watch her scream as the life leaves her eyes."

That did it. Alan drew his sword and yelled, "Enough!"

With that, Alan surged forward, swinging his sword with the same fury he'd felt when he killed the Bohl-Rahl Chief on the river. But Marik was no ordinary opponent. He parried each of Alan's strikes with effortless precision. Alan realized Marik was toying with him, only letting him land blows to provoke him. Marik could have ended the fight before Alan even made his first move.

As Alan tried to regain his composure, Marik's words about his mother lingered in his mind.

The others watched anxiously, unsure how to help without getting in Alan's way. The Valthurg arkarnians emerged from hiding, engaging in battle with Cinder, Mei, Elis, and the Morgs.

Abigail, hearing the sounds of swords clashing, quickened her pace. She ran up a hill, leading her to a stone gazebo. Inside, she saw the orange orb glowing brightly on a pedestal. There was no doubt in her mind—it was the Orb of Morimor.

She winced as she heard the maddened howls coming from the Orb. It was likely Morimor's spirit, twisted by the millennia of imprisonment.

Abigail approached the pedestal and laid her hands on the Orb. The intense pain shot up through her forearms as her touch began to lift the enchantment binding it.

Her screams grew louder as the pain intensified, and she found herself unable to release the Orb.

Her cries carried through the chamber where the battle between Alan and Marik raged. Cinder, Elis, and Mei had just struck down the last of the Valthurg arkarnians when Cinder turned and took an offensive stance, hurling balls of fire at Shadow-Lord. Alan broke off his attack, allowing her to take control. But Marik let out a bone-chilling laugh, letting the attacks hit him. Then, with a swift use of air magic, he was upon her. He punched Cinder in the stomach, grabbed her by the throat, and threw her into a wall.

Alan moved quickly behind Marik, attempting to thrust his blade through his opponent's armor, but Marik sensed him and dodged at the last moment, head-butting Alan and breaking his nose.

Elis and Mei moved to strike Marik simultaneously, but he dodged their attacks with ease. When their flurry ended, he retaliated, landing brutal punches and kicks that slammed Elis to the ground. As his attention shifted to Elis, Mei swung her bok-raht across Marik's face, knocking him to the floor. But Marik quickly recovered, forcing Mei back and slamming her to the ground.

Marik stood, his gaze sweeping over the chamber. More Valthurg arkarnians entered, dragging away their fallen comrades. Marik put his hands behind his back, walking slowly around the injured teens, intent on breaking their spirits.

He looked down at Cinder. "You're just a street rat with no talent. You're here only because Avery felt pity. You were too weak to stop those men from killing your mother... you'll never be strong enough to protect yourself or anyone you care about. Your fire won't burn hot enough to hurt me..."

He turned to Elis, a mocking tone creeping into his voice. "The great Prince of Wethen. A petty idealist, far too weak to be king. Your father doesn't take you seriously. He respects strength, not heart."

Marik's gaze flicked to Mei. "You're just like your father—too slow to see the danger right in front of you. Oh, and yes, I lied about that. Your parents are alive. Your father is one of Wethen's generals. And in his time as commander, he's gotten countless civilians and soldiers killed because he didn't take Korvas's threat seriously. So don't blame yourself for your failures. It's in your blood to mess everything up."

Finally, Marik turned his attention to Alan, laughing coldly as he saw Alan struggling to rise. He kicked Alan in the stomach, then forced him onto his back.

"You and Cinder are perfect for each other," Marik sneered, "because, like her, you will always be weak."

Marik knelt on Alan's chest, pinning him to the ground, making it difficult for him to draw breath. As he continued to speak, a layer of fire formed in his hand.

"I want you to remember this moment," Marik said, his voice low and venomous. "The moment I held you by your throat. You'll always remember your weakness. Had you embraced your inner darkness fully, instead of resisting it, you could've protected yourself... you could've saved your sister from me..."

Marik grabbed Alan's neck with the flaming hand, and Alan screamed hoarsely as the burning mark of Marik's touch was seared into his skin.

Content with the mark, Shadow-Lord stood up and turned to see Abigail returning, the Orb in hand.

"Good," he said, his voice dripping with satisfaction. "I can always count on you, Abigail. You will be a tremendous asset in my quest to retrieve the second Orb and the new world order I will create once I have both. Now, please, be a dear and hand over the Orb. I need it to conjure a portal, so we can watch Wethen's destruction unfold from the front row."

Abigail looked at Alan and Mei, both lying on the ground, struggling with pain. She clenched her jaw but nodded. "Okay... I'll give it to you..."

She held the Orb with both hands, her eyes burning with determination as she shouted in anger. Focusing all her energy, she unleashed an orange beam of magic aimed directly at Marik, hoping to do to him what the Orb had done to Morimor's soul.

As the beam struck him, Marik used dark magic to create a barrier of black mist, trying to shield himself from the magic's draining effect. Fear began to rise in him. His strength was waning. The spell he'd used to block the pain of his dark magic use was dissolving under the Orb's influence.

"I see I was wrong," he muttered. "Alan did free you from my influence... and deprived me of my student. It's time for one final lesson, Abigail... a lesson in pain..."

Abigail screamed in anger as she used the Orb to hurl rocks of various sizes at Marik, breaking through the mist and striking him. Marik retaliated with flames and energy bolts, but Abigail's resolve only strengthened. She was overtaking him, despite his vast knowledge. Through sheer willpower, she used the Orb as a weapon. A sharp stone pierced Marik's chest, cracking his ribs and causing him to spit blood.

Desperate to regain control, Marik ducked behind the evergreen tree, realizing that if the fight didn't end soon, he would lose.

Emerging from cover, Marik screamed in pain as he blasted Abigail with raw dark magic. Purple strands of energy shot from his palms, lashing at her with unbearable force. The intensity of the pain brought her to the ground, but Marik could feel his own exhaustion.

Suddenly, Avery's voice rang out. "Get away from them!"

Marik turned just in time to see a massive ice spear, conjured by Avery, strike him in the shoulder. The spear pierced his already weakened armor, and he staggered back. Drawing his sword, he prepared to face Avery and Wulf, who were closing in on him. Avery blasted him with a gust of wind, not giving him a chance to recover. The force sent Marik crashing into the base of the evergreen tree.

Wulf moved toward Marik, nodding at Avery to hold back for now.

As Wulf approached, Marik's eyes widened in recognition of the familiar gait and stance. When Wulf spoke, the realization hit him like a blow.

"Look at you..." Wulf said, his voice laced with sadness. "So full of hate... so cruel... just like him... just like...—"

Wulf paused for a moment, gathering his thoughts.

"Just like... our father..."

Marik's eyes widened as his mind raced. The words sank in slowly, and for a moment, he felt as if the world had tilted beneath him. Fury flared in him, but he was stunned by the revelation about Wulf's parentage. He had always wondered about the identity of Wulf's father. Marik had assumed he was a mercenary or adventurer who had died long ago.

"Wulf... you're saying... that you're my..." Marik's voice faltered.

Wulf closed the distance between them, his sword sheathed as he spoke with a mixture of pain and hope.

"After you left, my mother told me about a brief relationship she had with Viktor. It ended in heartbreak. Just before your mother moved into the village... Viktor was... my father. We're half-brothers, Marik. I've been following your trail for a while, not to hurt you, but to save you. Please, stop this. It's not too late. You can get help... come back home. Your mom... our gramma, they miss you."

Marik removed his helmet, staring into Wulf's eyes. For a moment, his expression softened, a flicker of doubt crossing his face. But Wulf knew, as Marik stood and gripped his sword's hilt, that the darkness had already claimed him.

"I'm sorry, Wulf..." Marik said coldly. "I didn't take your offer back then... I can't take it now. It's too late for me. My destiny is clear... but yours isn't. Step aside. I'm going to kill Avery. And if you get in my way... well, I know what I'll do to you. But I don't know what I'll do to Luna once I find her..."

Wulf immediately drew his sword. "You should have kept your big mouth shut and not mentioned Luna."

Wulf stepped back, giving Avery the opening to use earth magic and fling a chunk of stone at Marik. He raised a pillar of rock to block the incoming projectile, but the distraction allowed Wulf to close the distance. He struck Marik with quick, precise swings, intending to overwhelm and disarm him.

As their duel raged on, Cinder, still struggling with pain, crawled over to Alan. Her eyes blazed with fury when she saw his neck, and despite Avery's attempts to get her to rest, she forced herself to stand. Her body burned with an intense, fiery rage, the snow around her beginning to melt. Marik felt the heat rising as he ducked under one of Wulf's strikes. He rose quickly, delivering a powerful uppercut to Wulf, knocking him onto his back. But Marik's victory was short-lived. Cinder's fiery rage had reached its peak.

"Didn't I already tell you your fire doesn't burn hot enough to—" Marik's mocking tone faltered as he was hit with a blast of bright blue flame from Cinder, mixed with her air magic. Avery joined in, blasting him with fire. The combined beams warped his armor, and the metal began to melt under the intense heat.

Marik, desperate, used dark magic and air magic to force everyone away, knocking them all to the ground. The pain from the burns and his dark magic use sent him to his knees. Using his sword to prop himself up, he attempted to heal himself. But before he could fully recover, Wulf sprang to his feet and closed in.

With a swift motion, Wulf slashed down into Marik's forearm, cutting deep into the bone. Marik cried out in agony, dropping his sword. With his rage mounting, he released a wave of dark magic, sending Cinder, Wulf, and Avery flying. The dark magic seeped into their bloodstreams, weakening them.

As Marik stood, his injuries barely holding him upright, he lashed out again, blasting the three with dark energy. His voice, ragged with pain, echoed in the chamber.

"This is over... I wanted to gloat more when I killed you, Uncle, but with how much pain I'm in... I'm a bit pressed for time..."

Suddenly, Yerk body-slammed Marik, breaking his concentration. Yerk began pummeling his former master's face, cracking his helmet and mask. Then, with a fierce roar, Yerk lifted Marik and threw him over a ravine that cut through the chamber.

"Yerk! You great green idiot! Release me!" Marik screamed.

"That's my plan, boss, but first—you don't hurt my friends! And you don't insult me! You're not the boss of Morgs anymore!"

With that, Yerk sent a screaming Marik plummeting down into the ravine, just as Baldric and Sobek battled the Valthurg, with Gorb and Glum at their side.

Cinder, Avery, and Wulf recovered from Marik's attack and helped the injured to their feet as the Valthurg closed in around them.

Gorb groaned in pain as an arrow struck him in the leg. Abigail winced, holding the Orb out to Avery.

"Avery... Marik mentioned using the Orb to make a portal to Wethen. Can you do that and get us out of here?"

Avery took the Orb. "I can try." He focused his energies, visualizing a portal to Overgate's central plaza.

Moments later, a gateway of pure light opened, revealing a bustling street.

"Hurry! Into the tunnel, now!" Avery urged, his voice urgent. "Marik won't stay down long."

Wulf grabbed Abigail, Baldric took Cinder, Sobek took Elis, Yerk and Tadashi took Mei, and Glum helped Gorb.

The eleven of them began walking through the tunnel, with Avery helping Alan along behind them.

Alan could hear the Valthurg and Arkarnians closing in.

Halfway to Overgate, a beam of dark magic hit Avery in the back, sending him crashing to the ground and dropping both Alan and the Orb.

Alan strained to look back and saw Marik, with the Valthurg in tow. Their eyes locked. Marik waved, signaling the Valthurg to halt.

With Avery unconscious and the Valthurg backing off, it was just Alan and Marik.

Marik scrambled toward the Orb, but Alan mustered all his strength and tackled him. He tried to pry Marik's broken helmet off, but before he could, Marik punched him across the face with a gauntlet.

Marik then crawled toward Alan, his movements sluggish from blood loss. "It's just you and me now. No one else!"

Marik lunged for Alan's neck, his hand engulfed in flames. Alan caught Marik's wrist, then rammed his knee into Marik's groin, repeatedly. Alan flipped Marik over, pried his helmet off, and, despite Marik's struggles, forced the burning hand onto Marik's own face, leaving a searing handprint on the right side of Marik's scarred skin.

Alan pummeled Marik as much as he could, their blood mingling. But Marik pushed him off, conjuring the last of his strength into a blade of mist. He stabbed Alan in the abdomen, sending him sprawling to the ground.

Marik stood, his injured arm cradling the damaged mask of Materall, the blade raised high in his good hand.

"You're so weak… If I wasn't so drained from your sister's attack, I'd have killed you much sooner. Once I have the Orb, I'll kill everyone you love."

Before Marik could strike, Alan kicked one of Marik's knees, exposed by significant armor damage. Marik dropped the mist-blade to clutch his knee, allowing Alan to seize it and drive it into Marik's side, piercing the armor.

Alan collapsed back, grabbed the Orb, and aimed it at Marik.

Marik's eyes widened as Alan yelled defiantly, "You want the Orb so badly!? TAKE IT!"

Instead of channeling his anger, Alan poured his love for his friends and family into the Orb. Memories of his mother, father, sister, Mei, Tadashi, and the new bonds he'd formed with Cinder and Elis filled his mind. Those memories fueled the magic, and a beam of energy shot out from the Orb, striking Marik square in the chest.

For a moment, Marik tried to resist, staggering forward despite the raw energy blasting him. But his strength faltered, and he was hurled into the wall of the portal tunnel, screaming as he disappeared somewhere along its path.

The beam hit the tunnel wall, causing glowing cracks to form just as the Valthurg started to regroup.

Alan struggled to his feet, moving to help Avery, who had regained enough consciousness to walk. Together, they reached the end of the tunnel and emerged into Overgate's plaza, where the others waited, their eyes filled with concern.

The tunnel collapsed violently onto the Valthurg, leaving their fates unknown. But for now, Alan knew they were safe.

Abigail rushed to Alan's side. "Alan! Are you okay? We tried to go back when we saw Marik attack, but the portal only opened one way!"

Wulf gently took Avery from Alan and set him down, while Cinder and Abigail helped Alan lie down. Wethen Medics ran to tend to the injured.

Alan closed his eyes, the weight of exhaustion pulling him under as everything went black.

CHAPTER FORTY-FOUR

The Quest Ends... for now

Alan lay in bed, recovering from the stab wound Marik had inflicted. As he opened his eyes, he found Abigail, Cinder, Mei, Elis, and Tadashi sitting beside him. He smiled at each of them, but when his gaze met Cinder's, it felt as though they were both peering into each other's souls, trying to understand what the other was thinking. Before either of them could make sense of it, a commotion from the medical wing of Overgate's palace drew their attention.

The sounds grew louder, and it became clear that Madeline and James were hurriedly pushing through the crowd, trying to reach their children. In their rush, they knocked over a cart of medical supplies, spilling everything onto the floor. Shouting apologies, they finally burst into the room and rushed to pull Abigail into a tight embrace.

"Abigail... I'm so sorry we didn't tell you about all this... I should've protected you from Shadow-Lord. Your father and I... we feel like we failed you..." Madeline's voice trembled.

Abigail cut her off, shaking her head. "It's okay, Mom. I was mad at first, but you and Dad didn't fail us. I'm sure you've had a conversation like this with Alan already, but I think I speak for both of us when I say that we're alright because you prepared us. All the HEMA training, the camping trips, the exercising since we were kids... we got the Orb and survived because of you two. You never failed us. But I... I failed you. I let Marik—Shadow-Lord—get into my head. He manipulated me into thinking things about my own family that I hate myself for now. If anyone should apologize, it's me."

Madeline's eyes welled with tears as she hugged Abigail tighter. "I'm so proud of you, Abigail... and proud of Alan too. You're both here now... that's all that matters."

Madeline and James then turned to Alan, hugging him more gently than they had Abigail, careful not to aggravate his still-healing wounds.

"Alan..." James began, his voice shaky. "When you and Abigail came into this world... I knew something like this might happen, no matter how much your mom and I tried to protect you. I was afraid we'd lose one—or worse, both—of you."

James continued, his voice thick with emotion, "I was angry when you and your mother left Overgate without telling me. I thought I'd already lost Abigail, and I thought I was about to lose you both. But you two... you've proven me wrong. I know now you can take care of yourselves. I'm so proud of both of you."

Abigail walked over to Alan's bedside, and the reunited family huddled together, sharing tears of joy.

But Alan's thoughts quickly darkened with worry. "Wait... what about the invasion of Wethen? Were you able to stop them from reaching Undergate?"

Madeline nodded, her face serious. "Well, Marik was able to send a message to call off the attack. General Mikan's forces searched the tunnels, but they found them empty. The Valthurg and Rau-Trava did emerge from the tunnels in another part of Wethen, and they've quickly taken control. It's an all-out war in Northern Wethen. For now, our lines are holding—they can't advance. But we can't move in to retake the territory yet. We're planning a summit with the Dinalo and the leaders of Kardica to discuss a military alliance. With Okama's Boh-Rahl on our side, along with Silvyn, Sobek, and Baldric, I think we can convince Chief Pyramus to lend his support."

Madeline's attention then shifted to Mei and Tadashi. "Speaking of General Mikan... while he couldn't be here today, there are others who would like to see you both very much..."

"Sobo?!" Tadashi exclaimed excitedly. "Is she here?!"

Madeline smiled and chuckled. "Let me rephrase that: *two* people would like to see you both very much."

At that moment, Sobo and Nori appeared, walking toward Mei and Tadashi. Nori's voice trembled as she spoke softly, "Hello... I don't know if you recognize me, or if you even want to speak to me... but I'm—"

Before she could finish, Tadashi and Mei ran to her, throwing their arms around her. "Mama!" they cried.

Nori's eyes welled up as tears of joy streamed down her face. After all these years, she had finally been reunited with her children.

Elis, watching the joyful reunions around him, smiled. But his expression quickly shifted to one of fear when he heard his parents' voices calling his full legal name.

He turned to face them as they approached briskly through the infirmary. "Oh, uh… Mom, Dad, before you start yelling or lecturing me, I can explain—"

He was cut off as Alfonse and Eshe enveloped him in a hug.

"Elis… there's nothing to explain," Alfonse said, his voice thick with emotion. "Listen… I know I'm not the best King I could be. I've made many mistakes… let my personal feelings get in the way. But despite my failings as Wethen's King, I can rest easy knowing I did something right as a father. You're a wonderful, heroic, charming, and brave son… I'm proud of you, Elis."

Elis choked up, surprised by his father's words. He could only silently let the tears fall.

Just then, Avery rolled into the room in a wheelchair. Alan looked over and called out, "Avery… are you okay?"

"Don't worry about me, Alan," Avery replied with a smile. "I'll be fine. My strength will come back soon. We can talk strategy in a few days. But for now… let's just… what's the phrase… veg out?"

Everyone laughed, nodding in agreement.

A few hours later, everyone gathered for a small celebratory party to mark their victory in securing the Orb.

Alan decided to approach Wulf and Luna, who were standing on a balcony.

"So… were you ever going to tell us that Marik is your brother?"

Wulf smiled. "I told you when I told him. Besides, I didn't want to spoil the shock for any of you. I thought maybe knowing I'm his half-brother would sway him. But… the Marik Luna and I knew is gone. There was a flicker of the boy from Meri'Duus, but it faded as soon as I saw it. For a while, I thought if it came down to it, I'd be the one to finish him off."

Alan nodded. "Yeah… no way to know if he's alive or dead now. Part of me wants to think he's gone, but something tells me he's still out there. So… is that it for you and Luna? Are you heading back to Meri'Duus?"

Luna shrugged. "We haven't decided yet. We want to see if we can be of help with the war effort. But if you or Avery ask, we'd love to help you find the Orb of Livimor.

Wulf and I may only be a few years older, but I think we have a few tricks to teach you and the others when it comes to sword techniques."

As Alan turned to walk back to the party, he called over his shoulder, "Well, I appreciate everything you both did for us. Things wouldn't have gone as smoothly without you. I'll definitely take you up on that offer to learn from you. But for now, I should go. I think some of the Morgs have gotten into the... 'adult' drinks. That's bound to be a spectacle."

Wulf and Luna chuckled as Alan walked toward Gorb and Glum, who were standing on a table, drunkenly singing—quite beautifully, in fact.

"And so we sing today upon today! Words that sound nice when sang songingly! We thank our new friends Ab-i-ga-il, Mei, and Ta-da-shi! For helping us see the light of the new daaaay! And most import-anty, A-very!!!! He is new boss man!!!"

Mei, sitting with Abigail, looked around. "Well... I guess we're not going home just yet. But maybe... this is home now. I mean, everyone we love is here. Well, minus a few less important people we know back on Earth."

Abigail nodded. "When we first talked about this, I was reluctant to consider it. But... I think this is home now. Back home... I don't know... it felt like I was choking sometimes, the way things were. Anyway, who knew Gorb and Glum had such beautiful singing voices?"

Yerk raised his hand. "Oooo me! I did! They sing real nice since I can remember."

Alan looked around. Everything felt right, but he couldn't shake the worry gnawing at him—the war, and whether Marik had truly survived.

Mei noticed Alan lost in thought and walked over to him, sensing something was wrong.

"Hey," she said gently, "We haven't really talked yet. How have you been?"

"Well, aside from encountering giant spiders, crossing a river full of living vines that tried to strangle me, angry Arkarnians, giant killer crabs, and a few other things, I'm good... better now that everyone is back together. I was worried about all of you every day after I left. I know it was probably one of the worst things I could have done in retrospect, but... I wouldn't have found Avery if I hadn't. Shadow-Lord was keeping him in a prison cell in an old mine shaft near his castle. That's how I met Elis and Cinder—they were looking for Avery too. When I say that out loud, I realize I could've stayed with you all because Avery would've been okay..."

Mei shook her head. "Whatever that thing was that Marik put in Abigail's head, I'm sure you were susceptible to it too. I'm glad you did what you did, even if I was upset at the time... things turned out okay, as you said. We're all together again. But your face is all scrunched up like it was the day we went to Red Pine, which means something's up. So spill it—give me the deets."

"Marik..." Alan's voice dropped, "I'm worried he's still alive. I think we got lucky this time. If he's alive, we need to be ready for anything. But for now, I'm just glad we'll be able to find the Orb of Livimor together. No more splitting up, no more spats. I'm not sure if Elis can come along this time, though. I'll have to ask him. I figure Cinder is in, but I need to ask her too."

Mei raised an eyebrow at the mention of Cinder. "You know I still need to talk with her—properly introduce myself. I'm going to go do that real quick." She patted Alan on the shoulder before heading over to the corner of the room where Cinder was standing alone.

"Hi, Cinder," Mei said, approaching her. "I don't think we've made a proper introduction yet. I'm Mei." She extended her hand to shake, and after a moment's hesitation, Cinder shook it.

After they let go of each other's hands, Mei took a sip of water. Cinder spoke up first.

"I've been wanting to have a conversation with you, Mei, about something your brother said to Alan. Do you have feelings for him?"

Mei choked on her water for a moment before spitting it out. "Tadashi told Alan I have feelings for him? That little—! It was one time, years ago, when I was like, nine. I told Tadashi that when we grew up, I'd marry Alan. But that's changed. I'm just protective of Alan because he's one of my best friends, which is why I wanted to talk to you. So, you know how Abigail could see visions of Alan while she was sleeping, right?"

Cinder nodded. "Yes, please continue."

"Well, Abigail said she saw you ogling Alan. Can I ask what your intentions are with him?" Mei folded her arms defensively.

Cinder was taken aback by Mei's bluntness. "Well, I—listen, I've come to care about Alan. At first, I didn't like him much. I didn't understand why he was here. But... we had a lot of personal talks. I've felt safe enough with him to share things I've never shared with anyone else. We've trained together... held hands... I think we have mutual feelings for each other. But I also think we're discovering those feelings at a complicated time, in the middle of all this unfolding history. Our quest needs to come first. If we happen to find time to discuss things, well... I wouldn't complain."

Mei nodded, her expression softening. "Okay, you don't seem like a bad person. But if you hurt Alan, I think I speak for Abigail as well when I say we will kick your ass. Got it?"

Cinder laughed, thinking Mei was joking, and nodded. "Sure..."

As the night wore on, Abigail and Avery sat down to discuss her magical training.

"So, could you take me on as a student?" Abigail asked. "Or can you only teach one student at a time?"

Avery scratched his beard. "There are no rules against having multiple students. We'll first work on whichever element you find to be your weakest."

Abigail nodded. "I've never tried using fire or wind magic, but I'd say I'm still a novice with water and earth magic too. You can be the judge of that. Also, I can hear and commune with the dead—at least, with magically adept ones. Your father spoke with me, and tried to tell me the truth about Marik. I didn't believe it at the time, because of the parasite, but he wanted me to tell you something..."

She paused, giving Avery a moment to prepare himself emotionally before continuing.

"He wanted you to know he's sorry he wasn't a better father. He did love and appreciate you. He just didn't realize how important you were to him until the moment of his death."

Avery closed his eyes, absorbing the weight of her words. For the first time in decades, the anguish he'd carried began to lift, a piece of him finally feeling whole again.

"Thank you, Abigail," he said quietly. "Thank you... so much."

Abigail nodded. "You're welcome." With that, she left Avery to enjoy his peace.

A few hours later, as the festivities wound down, everyone—except for the Morgs and Arkarnians—gathered in a circle around the Orb of Morimor.

Avery stood and addressed the group. "The Orb will stay here for now, until the Mystic Masters can assemble a group to retrieve it and take it far from the reach of those who would misuse it. As for the war between Wethen and the Arkarnians, we cannot burden ourselves with Wethen's defense. That is not our primary focus.

Instead, we must first focus on our own recovery. Many of you will need to learn about this world and undergo training, which will be necessary for our journey to find the Orb of Livimor. For now, time is on our side. If Marik survived, he'll need time to recover from his injuries. As for tonight, rest. Tomorrow, do as you will. Spend time reconnecting with your families and friends—both old and new. You may want to familiarize yourselves with the city of Overgate. It has many shops and locations I believe you'll all find extraordinary."

"Once you're all ready, training will begin. While Shadow-Lord, if alive, was gravely injured, it was only thanks to Abigail's quick thinking that we managed to make it out. But, as you all know, we can't simply take the Orb with us and risk losing it in a fight against Marik again. If he's still alive, there will be no games this time. The mask of kindness he wore will have been firmly stripped from his face... So we must be ready. He will use everything he has against us. Any questions?"

When Avery was met with silence, James stood and addressed the group. "Everyone will be assigned 'apartments' within the castle. This will give each of you your own space, while still keeping you close enough in case anything goes wrong. While I am confident in the men and women defending this city and castle, there have been too many times when hostile forces infiltrated our walls unseen."

As they were escorted to their rooms, they exchanged goodnights. Soon, only Alan and Abigail remained, the servant leaving them at their doors. Once alone, Abigail turned to Alan.

"Alan... I just... I need to know... Do you think of me differently now? I mean, even before the parasite, I was leaning more toward trusting Marik than your instincts. I need to know if... if you think I'm weak."

Alan pulled his sister into a hug. "No way. You're one of the strongest people I know. You willed that thing out of your head. And that parasite isn't the reason you made it to the polar regions. You have Mom's perseverance and willpower, and Dad's ambition and gall. Avery put it best earlier—if it weren't for your quick thinking, we'd have never gotten out of there with the Orb."

Abigail smiled. "And you've got Mom's ability to make people feel better about themselves. Thanks, Alan..."

Alan let go of her. "Tomorrow will be a new day, a new beginning, a new life. Not like the one we're leaving behind, but it's the world we were born in. We've got family here we still need to meet. Goodnight, Abs."

Abigail nodded. "Goodnight, Alan."

They parted ways and entered their rooms. Alan walked over to the wardrobe, changed into his sleepwear, and then lay down in bed, letting out a sigh of content-ment. At long last, it was time to rest. For the first time in a long time, Alan closed his eyes—and had no nightmares.

Epilogue: The Shadow-Lord

The walls of the boat's lower deck creaked as it sailed across the churning waters. Marik stood alone in the quarters assigned to him by the Rau-Travan captain. He had been flung from the portal tunnel and onto a rocky island off the coast of New Arkarnia. Lucky for him, the Rau-Travan ship had been passing at that very moment, and his body had fallen onto its deck.

Marik approached the mirror in his quarters and studied his reflection. Most of his injuries had healed to the point where they were no longer life-threatening, all thanks to the Rau-Travans. He gazed at his face, noting the scar left from when Alan had forced Marik's own flaming hand upon it. It was the same curse Marik had used to burn Alan's neck, which meant the scar would never fade—at least not without great, excruciating pain.

His gaze in the mirror deepened, his eyes narrowing with bitter intensity. By the time he returned to Darkspire Keep, it would likely be empty. Losing control over the morgs was an insult, a wound that cut deeper than any physical injury. It haunted him, more than he was willing to admit.

The Rau-Travan and Valthurg soldiers accompanying him on the boat would soon replace the morgs' role, but Marik knew he would miss the morgs' honest simplicity. The arkarnians followed him because they believed he would grant them power and revenge, but the morgs had followed him because they simply wanted to. That pure, unwavering loyalty had once meant something to him.

But Marik shoved aside the nostalgia. What was done could never be undone. The morgs, Abigail, Wulf, Luna, his mother, and his grandmother—they were all chains, holding him back, tethering him to a humanity he no longer desired. A humanity that made him feel weak. And whenever he looked into the mirror, that scarred face was a constant reminder of his failures.

Marik reached for a knife on the counter in front of the mirror.

The boat shifted, creaking as it continued through the turbulent waters. Below deck, an arkarnian crewman patrolling the halls heard a strange, disconcerting squelching sound coming from Marik's quarters. He paused, unsure, then cracked the door slightly to peer inside. His eyes widened at the sight before him—his commander was mutilating his own face.

But as the crewman continued to watch, he realized Marik was using magic to force his skin to regenerate quickly. This time, as the flesh reformed, it was free of the accumulated scars he had carried for years—even the ones from the brutal beatings he had endured at the hands of his father.

In that moment, Marik believed he was finally free of his past. Free of his humanity. And he was reborn.

"A new beginning... all for me," he whispered, his voice low and venomous. "No more sentiment, no more weakness. No more Marik... just me now..."

A sinister smile crept across his face as he admired his renewed reflection.

"The Shadow-Lord..."

The End.

www.ingramcontent.com/pod-product-compliance
Lightning Source LLC
Chambersburg PA
CBHW060815120726
47909CB00006B/1940